The DARK LEGACY *of* SHANNARA

WARDS *of* FAERIE

TERRY BROOKS

BALLANTINE BOOKS • NEW YORK

2013 Del Rey Mass Market Edition

Copyright © 2012 by Terry Brooks
Front matter map copyright © 2012 by Russ Charpentier
Interior maps copyright © 2012 by David A. Cherry
Excerpt from *Bloodfire Quest* by Terry Brooks copyright © 2013 by Terry Brooks

Published in the United States of America by Del Rey, an imprint of the Random House Publishing Group, a division of Random House, Inc., New York.

DEL REY and the Del Rey colophon are registered trademarks of Random House, Inc.

Originally published in hardcover in the United States by Del Rey, an imprint of The Random House Publishing Group, a division of Random House, Inc., in 2012.

This book contains an excerpt from the forthcoming book *Bloodfire Quest* by Terry Brooks. This excerpt has been set for this edition only and may not reflect the final content of the forthcoming edition.

ISBN 978-0-345-52348-8
eBook ISBN 978-0-345-52349-5

Printed in the United States of America

www.delreybooks.com

9 8 7 6 5 4 3

Del Rey mass market edition: March 2013

WARDS *of* FAERIE

For Judine
forever in my heart

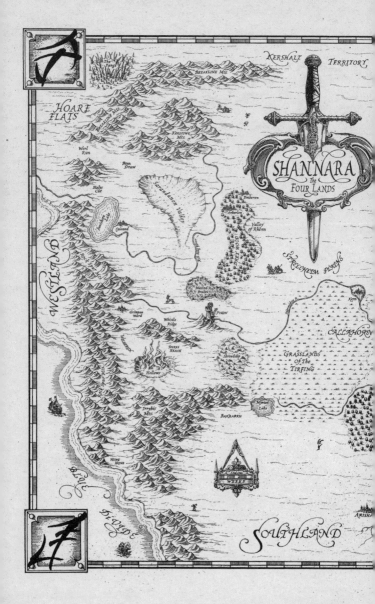

WARDS *of* FAERIE

I

◆

It was almost one year to the day after she began her search of the Elven histories that Aphenglow Elessedil found the diary.

She was deep in the underground levels of the palace, sitting alone at the same table she occupied each day, surrounded by candles to combat the darkness and wrapped in her heavy cloak to ward off the chill. Carefully she read each document, letter, or memoir in what had taken on the attributes of a never-ending slog. It was late and her eyes were burning with fatigue and dust, her concentration beginning to wane, and her longing for bed to grow. She had been reading each day, all day, for so long that she was beginning to think she might never see Paranor and her fellow Druids again.

It was dark each day when she began her work and dark when she ended it, and aside from an occasional visit from her sister or her uncle, she saw almost no one. She had read through the entirety of the histories, including their appendices, and had moved on to the boxes and boxes of other writings donated by prominent families over the years. These papers were intended to supplement, embellish, or correct what was considered the official record of a history that stretched back thousands of years. She had found little that she didn't already know or was in any way useful, yet she had persevered because that was how she was. Once she started something she did not give up until the job was finished.

And now, perhaps, it was. A diary, written by a young girl, a Princess of the realm living in the age of Faerie, had caught her eye just as she was on the verge of putting everything aside and going off to bed. It was buried at the bottom of a box she had finished emptying, small and worn and stiff with age, and she had glanced at the first couple of pages, noted the girlish writing and the nature of the entries, and been prepared to dismiss it. But then something had stopped her—curiosity, a premonition, a quirk in the way it was written, and she had paged ahead to the final entries to find something unexpected.

23, month 5

Something both terrible and wonderful has happened to me, and I can tell no one.

Today I met a boy. He is not of our people and not of our moral and ethical persuasion. He is a Darkling child of the Void, but he is the most beautiful boy I have ever seen. I am hopelessly in love with him, and even knowing that it is wrong of me to be so and that nothing good can come of it, I want to believe that it might be otherwise.

I was down by the Silver Thread, deep in the woods seeking bunch lilies and ardweed seeds for the shelter, when he appeared to me. He came out of the trees as if born of them, a lovely mirage given substance and form. So striking was he, so perfect. Blue skin (I have never seen such a depthless blue), golden eyes, hair of midnight black and stars, his voice as soft as the ending of a summer rain when he greeted me. I loved him at once, in that first moment. I could not help myself.

Even when I knew what he was and that he was forbidden to me, I could not turn away from him. I like to believe that there was something more than physical attraction that drew me to him. I had enough presence of mind to be able to warn myself against what I was doing. But after we talked and I heard what he had to say about himself and his people, I knew I could not change things. It is said that the most ancient of our race frequently found love at first sight and seldom through lengthy consideration. Perhaps I am a throwback, for that is what happened with this boy and me.

We sat in a quiet glade and talked for hours; I cannot say for how long. By the time our encounter ended, twilight was approaching. I left him with a promise to meet again. No plans, no details, but I know it will happen.

I want it to happen.

26, month 5

Today, unable to help myself, I returned to the forest to try to find him again. I was not back in the glade for more than the half split of an hour before he reappeared. Again, we sat and talked of our lives and our hopes for the future. I feel so free with him, so able to be open about my life. He is the same with me, and I am reassured that the love I feel for him is not built on a foundation of false expectations but on real possibilities. While the prohibitions cannot be changed, I see no reason why they might not be ignored for a time. So I tell myself. So I am persuaded.

28, month 5

We met again today. Our conversations were of ourselves, but also of the strife between our peoples and the terrible toll it was taking on all our lives. He told me he did not see all of his people as bad or all of ours as good. It was not so simple in his eyes, and I was quick to agree with him. The war is ongoing, centuries old, a struggle that has its roots in the beginnings of all our Races and of the world itself, and it will not end in our lives. We are its children, but we feel so apart from the war when together and alone. If only we could keep it that way. If only we could shelter what we feel for each other so that no one could ever destroy it.

Before we parted, he told me how he had come to find me. He was delegated by his elders to spy upon the city from the particular vantage point into which I had ventured. He was not to interfere, only to observe and report. He hated what he was doing, but it was his duty and his parents would be shamed if he failed. Yet when he saw me, he found he no longer cared about anything else. He had to reveal himself. He had to talk to me.

By now I am no longer thinking of anything but how to hold on to him, how to make him mine forever.

2, мопτн 6

When he came to me on this day, our first day of meeting in the new month, I gave myself to him. I did so freely and with great joy. We did not speak while it was happening, did not even pause to consider. We simply did what we had wanted to do from the first time we had met. It was so wonderful, and the feelings I experienced while in his arms are with me still and will be so forever. It was my first time, and he is my first real love. I could not ask for anything more wonderful. I have been made happy beyond my wildest expectations. Now that I have taken this final, irrevocable step, there is no going back, nothing more to consider.

I am his.

3, month 6

We met again today. I couldn't help myself. Nor, I think, could he. We are so in love. We are so happy.

5, month 6

Again. Another sweet time.

12, month 6

Such agony! Mother kept me busy all this week with studies and housework, and I could not go to him even once. Today was our first time together again in an entire week. He says he understands, although it is hard for him, too. I will not suffer such separation again!

15, month 6

Even three days is too long. I was in such despair, and he was so wild with worry and so in need when we met. Oh, how I love him!

17, month 6

Just when I think matters have returned to normal and we will be left to our regular meetings, something else has intruded. I must go to visit my grandparents in the city of Parsoprey across the Dragon's Teeth and down onto the plains of the Sarain and so will be gone for two entire weeks. I cannot go to him to let him know—we are to leave at once! I think I shall die!

2, month 7

Home again at last. I went straight to the glade and took him to our home and into my bed. It feels so right to have him there. I told him everything of where I had been and what I had been forced to endure and he, sweet boy, told me he understood and forgave me. He worried that I had forsaken him and would not return.

But I would never do that. He must know this, I told him. I will love him until the day I die.

22, month 7

I take him to my bed at every opportunity, no longer content with our time in the forest glade. I want him close to me. I want him with me always and constantly, but I must settle for what I can have. I choose times when I know the house will be empty. I live for those times. I am consumed by my need for them. I want them to go on forever.

10, month 8

Today I did something that may have been foolish. I spoke of the magic that keeps the Elves safe. I revealed too much of what I knew in an effort to impress— though only after he had done so first, speaking of the magic that keeps his own people safe. We spoke in general terms and not of specifics, but I am troubled nevertheless. We spoke of magic in the course of our frequent discussions on how the war between our peoples might be brought to an end. If there were no magic, there might be less cause for fighting, we reason. He sees it as I do, and so we speak of it openly. It is only talk, and nothing much could come of it. When we are together, what does talk of magic and conjuring and endless conflict matter anyway? Nothing matters, save that we are together.

But now I wonder. Because even though we spoke mostly in generalities, I did once speak in specifics.

I told him about the Elfstones.

"Aphen, are you still down there?"

She looked up quickly from the diary. Her uncle. "Still here," she answered.

She shoved the diary under a pile of papers and took

up something else as if she had been looking at that instead. She did so out of habit and instinct, aware not only that was she forbidden to remove anything from the archives but also that she was constantly watched in her comings and goings and never certain who it was that might be doing the watching. Mostly, it was Home Guards stationed at the top of the basement stairs, but it could be anyone. She liked her uncle and was close to him, but to the larger Elven community she had been a pariah for so long that she never took anything for granted.

A candle's dim light wavered its way down the steps from the level above, and her uncle appeared out of the darkness. "The hours you keep, dear young lady, are ridiculous."

Ellich Elessedil was the younger of the two brothers who had been in line for the throne many years ago and, to her mind, the one best suited to the task. But his older brother, her grandfather, was the one who had become ruler of the Elves on the death of their parents. Now her grandfather's son, Phaedon, was the designated heir apparent and, as her grandfather continued to weaken from his chronic heart and lung problems, increasingly likely to be King soon. Aphenglow's mother was Phaedon's much younger sister, and her refusal to become involved in the business of the court allowed Aphenglow to remain comfortably clear of family and state politics.

Not as far clear as she would have liked, however. Her choice to become a member of the Druid order had put an end to that.

Her uncle took a seat on a stool she was using for stacking notes, moving the papers aside without comment. Though he was actually her great-uncle, Aphen found the designation awkward and called him simply Uncle, mostly as a term of endearment because they were so close. He was tall and lean and as blond as she was, although his hair was beginning to go gray. "It's getting on toward midnight, you know. Whatever's keeping you here could wait until morning."

She smiled and nodded. "Nothing's really keeping me. I just lost track of time. Thank you for rescuing me."

He smiled back. "Find anything of interest today?"

"Nothing." The lie came smoothly. "Same as always. Every morning I think that this will be the day I discover some great secret about the magic, some clue about a lost talisman or a forgotten conjuring. But each night I return to my bed disappointed."

He looked around the room, taking in the shelves of books and boxes, the reams of papers stacked in their metal holders, the clutter and the scraps of documents and notes. "Perhaps there is nothing to find. Perhaps all you are doing is sorting documents that no one but you will ever read." He glanced back at her. "I'm not trying to discourage you, not after all the work you've put in. I am only wondering if this is a fool's errand."

"A fool's errand?" she repeated. Her blue eyes flashed. "You think I may have spent the last three hundred and sixty-four days on a fool's errand?"

He held up his hands in a placating gesture. "That was a poor choice of words. Please forget that I spoke them. I don't know enough about what you are doing to be able to question it with any authority. I only ask because I care about you."

"You know why I am here, Uncle," she said quietly. "You know the importance of what I am doing."

"I know that you *believe* it to be important. But if there is nothing to find, if there is no magic to be found, no talismans to be recovered, then what have you accomplished?"

"I will have made certain of what you clearly suspect," she answered. "I will have eliminated the possibility that something has been missed. A lot of time has passed and a lot of history been forgotten or lost. We are an old people, after all."

He shrugged, leaning back on the stool. "Old enough that we are no longer the people we once were and probably never will be again. We have evolved since the Faerie Age. We do not rely on magic as we once did—or certainly not the same kinds of magic. We share the world now with other, different species. The Faerie that served the Void are locked away behind the Forbidding. Now we have humans to deal with instead, a less imaginative people, and the need we once had for protective magic no longer exists."

She gave him a look. "Some might question that. Grianne Ohmsford, for one, if she were still alive."

"Yes, she probably would. After all, she was the Ilse Witch."

"She was also Ard Rhys of our order after that, and she saved us all from the very humans you seem to think we no longer need protection from." She sighed. "Listen to me, engaging in a meaningless argument with my favorite uncle. To what end? Let's not quarrel. I have a job to do, and I intend to do it. Maybe I won't find anything. But I will make certain of that before I return to Paranor."

Her uncle rose, nodding. "I wouldn't expect less of you. Will you take dinner with us tomorrow night? You might enjoy a real meal for a change. Besides, Jera and I miss you."

Her aunt and uncle lived in a cottage just outside the palace grounds, preferring to distance their personal lives from his work as a member of the Elven High Council and adviser to his brother. For as long as she could remember, they had chosen to forgo the benefits they could have enjoyed as members of the royal family.

She gave him a warm smile, standing with him. "Of course I'll come. I miss you, too. And I promise not to forget this time, either."

He reached out and took her hands in his. "Whatever anyone else tells you, I am proud of the work you are doing with the Druid order. I don't think you betrayed anyone by accepting their offer to study with them. The betrayal would have been to your own sense of right and wrong had you refused. I will say, however, that when this task is done, perhaps you will think about staying in Arborlon for good."

He squeezed her hands once, and then turned and started back for the stairs, candle in hand. "Good night, Aphen. Get some sleep."

She watched until the candle had flickered out of sight and sat down again quickly. Digging under the papers where she had hidden it, she retrieved the diary.

She opened it and began to read anew.

14, mоптн 8

Something terrible has happened, something that changes everything. He has told me he has been ordered to return to his home in Rajancroft by week's end. His term of service as a watcher is complete. He wants me to go with him. He said it was necessary if we were to be together. My people might not accept him, but his would accept me. His Darkling clan is less disposed toward the exclusion of other Races, and I would become his bride and his people would embrace me. As I listened to him, I felt such a deep, abiding panic at the thought of leaving Arborlon and the Elves that I could barely breathe. I asked him not to speak of it again; I told him we must find another way.

17, month 8

It seems I know him less well than I believed. He is proud and insistent, and he has refused to change his mind. I must go with him, he tells me. It is our only chance for happiness, our only way to make a life. We could not keep meeting secretly forever even if he were allowed to stay on. Someone would find us out eventually. His recall merely requires that we act sooner rather than later. I must delay no longer. I must go with him.

To my surprise and consternation, I found I could not agree to this. I want to be with him, but I cannot leave my home and my people. I told him so. I begged him to reconsider. I pleaded. If we could not be together as often, we would simply be together when we could. But even as I spoke the words, I could detect in his expression his refusal to accept this and I knew he would never be satisfied until he took me away.

What am I to do? I know I am going to lose him and cannot bear it. Please, let him see reason! Please, let him stay!

18, month 8

I am ruined. I am the most wretched and miserable creature alive. I have betrayed everyone by my foolish, selfish behavior, and I cannot begin to imagine the price that others will pay because of it.

My boy is gone. My beautiful, wonderful lover and friend has abandoned me and perhaps worse. I do not know what I should do. I am reduced to writing down what has happened in an effort to understand. But perhaps I only delay the inevitable recognition that in the end nothing can be done.

Earlier today, we met for the last time. I took him to my room and to my bed and spoke the words I thought I would never speak. I told him I could never leave my people and we must end our assignations and our hopes for a future life. What he wanted, I had already refused him. What I wanted, he would never accept. What point in continuing what was clearly doomed?

I did this in a misguided effort to change his mind, hoping that the prospect of losing me would be as painful for him as it would for me to lose him. I did so out of desperation but also with an understanding that when I told him I could not leave my home and my people, I was telling him the truth.

Amid tears of despair and hurt so deep I thought I would never be well again, we coupled a final time, and then he left me in my bed, sated and sleeping and thinking that perhaps I had won my victory and he would stay.

I was wrong. I had won nothing. He did not leave the house when he left my bed. What he did instead is the cause of my humiliation and despair. Because he was a Darkling, I knew he had use of magic. Because I loved him, I never asked its nature. It seemed irrelevant to our relationship and to our love. I knew it was there; I did not care that it was.

But when I woke later that afternoon, I found a note lying next to me. It read thus:

> *I cannot give you up.*
> *You must come to me.*
> *Use these Elfstones to find me*
> *And to reclaim the other stones*
> *Which I hold hostage.*
> *I love you that much.*

Lying beneath the note were the three blue Elfstones, the seeking-Stones of the five precious sets.

I rushed at once to where my father kept the Elfstones hidden and secured, dreading what I might find. Releasing the locks embedded in the stronghold by using the words of magic with which they were imbued, I discovered to my horror that my Darkling boy had not lied. The Elfstones were gone—all but those three he had left me.

At first, I did not understand. That he was gone and asking me to come after him was clear enough, the rest less so. The implications of his wording were dark and dangerous; I was unsure of what conclusion to reach. Had he taken the Elfstones only for the purpose of persuading me to follow him, or had he stolen them for a different reason entirely—to aid his people, to give them the magic they lacked as servants of the Void? The first bespoke a rash and desperate act. The second was purposefully evil. I could not believe that of him. But if I were wrong, what then? What did he know of the Elfstones? Did he know that he could not use them—that none of his Darkling kind could? Did he realize that it required a true Elf to make the magic come alive? Did he know that the Elfstones must be freely given if they are to serve the holder?

What was the true reason he had taken them?

I had told him nothing of where they could be found or how to get to them. Of that much, I was certain. Yet somehow he had known. How much more did he know of which I was unaware? How much that I thought I knew about him was false?

I am made very nearly hysterical by my uncertainty. I cannot see how to resolve the matter in any way that is satisfactory. I cannot go to him not knowing the truth about his intentions. How can I be certain of what he has planned? Has he betrayed me or does he honestly think that this theft will bring me to him?

If he is the boy I think he is—the one I fell in love with—it is the latter. But why hasn't he trusted me if what he wants is for us to be together? Why has he resorted to this desperate act? Surely he realizes the posi-

tion in which he has put me? Does he think I can escape the blame that will attach for his theft or do I no longer matter to him?

What am I to do?

25, month 8

Days have passed since I have written here, my thoughts too poisonous to be recorded. I have told no one of what has happened. Those who need to know will find out the truth soon enough. But not yet, it seems, for I have heard nothing of the theft. I know where he has taken the Elfstones, but I cannot think how I should go about getting them back.

So I wait. I sit for hours thinking on what I must do. The longer I deliberate, the less clear my course of action becomes. In spite of what I feel for him, I cannot trust my emotions to guide me. I must find a way to set things right, and to do that I need to make certain that my failures of judgment will not bring harm to my people. It is bad enough that my parents should suffer for my transgression; it is unbearable to think that the Elven people should pay for my foolishness, as well.

Perhaps even with their lives.

I could not bear that.

28, month 8

I know now what I must do. I have considered long enough. I must risk all and use the blue Elfstones to go in search of the others and of my Darkling boy. I must know the truth about him, and I must set right what he has made wrong. I leave in the morning with a small contingent of Elven Hunters, having given my father a false story of what I intend—a fresh transgression added to the others. But what is one more by now?

24, ΠΟΠΤΗ 9

*I have returned empty-handed. In the course of my
search, I found neither the Elfstones nor the boy. No
amount of effort or use of magic could help me recover
my treasures. It is as if they have vanished off the face
of the earth. Inquiries yielded nothing. Someone may
know what has become of them, but no one is saying. I
have given the blue Stones back and admitted all. I am
disgraced and undone.*

*Yet events conspire to make possible a chance for re-
demption, and I will take the chance offered. Perhaps
history will remember me for doing what was right and
so provide me with a measure of grace.*

*I beg your forgiveness, my dearest Mother and Fa-
ther. Let no one accuse Meresch and Pathke Omarosian of not sufficiently loving and embracing their
wayward daughter. Let it be known here, in these
pages, that I will treasure forever the life I have shared
with you. If you should read this, as one day I hope you
will, be not sad for me. Be happy that I have found
peace. I have found my second chance and I go now
happily to embrace it.*

All Honor, Your Daughter Aleia

2

APHENGLOW DEPARTED THE PALACE, NODDING amiably to the guard who stood just outside the door to the archives as she passed, and crossed the palace grounds to the divergent paths that led into the city proper, covering the ground in long, smooth strides. She had trained once upon a time to be a Tracker, back when she was still a girl. But her real skills lay with her enhanced instincts and her unusual connection to the magic of the elements found in earth, air, water, and fire—and so she had been invited to join the Druids at Paranor. She had accepted almost without thinking about it, excited at the prospect of exploring magic's limits and of finding fresh ways to bring healing and the chance for a better life to the Races and their homelands.

In retrospect, she had acted without sufficient forethought, ignorant of how the decision would impact her life. The Druids were held in low regard by the Elves, and those who chose to join them were seen as lacking in both common sense and moral balance. Once you chose to side with the Druids, you were automatically considered to have sided against the Elves. This was the common thinking of her times, and Aphen's assumption that as a granddaughter of the King she would somehow be treated differently proved optimistic. If anything, it infuriated the Elves even more.

Now, six years later, she was back in Arborlon and thoroughly disappointed to discover that nothing much had changed when it came to how her people viewed her. Slow to anger, they were even slower to forgive, and her return had not generated much in the way of good feelings. Even her family—her sister and uncle aside— had seemed less than pleased to see her. But she had come for a purpose, and she intended to see it through. It was an effort supported by her fellow Druids, who instantly saw the value in it, but was regarded by everyone else as a waste of time. The King, her grandfather, had granted her the permission she requested, but only after making it clear that the same search had been conducted repeatedly by others over the years and that even if she found something useful her discoveries would belong solely to the Elves and not to anyone else—especially not to the Druid order.

She understood the reason for the prohibition. Hard feelings endured from the time when Grianne Ohmsford had served as Ard Rhys and the Elven nation had been threatened by the Southland and its Federation armies. Though it was Grianne who had put an end to that threat, various members of her order had allied with Federation Prime Minister Sen Dunsidan, and both she and the order had been tarnished by the perceived treachery. Queen Arling Elessedil, already harboring a deep dislike and distrust of the Druids, had cut all ties to the order.

It didn't matter that Grianne Ohmsford had been gone for more than a hundred years, or even that her successor as Ard Rhys was herself a member of the Elessedil family. The old King, Arling's son, held fast to his mother's beliefs where the Druids were concerned, and it was only because Aphenglow was an Elf and his granddaughter that she was allowed to conduct her study.

Many others thought she should take her studies and her practices elsewhere if she could not remember where her loyalties should lie.

Head up, eyes sweeping the landscape watchfully, she left the palace grounds behind and moved down the pathway that led to the cottage she shared with her younger sister. Wherever she went in Arborlon, she paid close attention to what was happening around her. The city might have been her home once and it might be so again one day, but for now she was no better than a visitor from a foreign country. There were enough Elves who mistrusted her presence that she could not afford to take her safety for granted.

Especially not tonight, when she was carrying that which she was expressly forbidden from having. One of the agreements she had made was that she would take nothing from the storerooms. Not at any time. Not for any reason. Yet buried amid the collection of notes and papers contained in her pack was the diary.

And if she were caught with it . . .

She shrugged the matter away. She had done what she needed to do. The diary was important—perhaps the most important piece of information that had been un-covered since the First Council of Druids convened.

Everyone knew about the existence of the missing Elf-stones, of course. But only in the abstract and not in the specific. They knew primarily because the blue Stones, the seeking-Stones, had survived whatever had become of the other sets. There were three stones in each set—one each to reflect the strength of the heart, mind, and body of the user. No one knew what had become of the other sets. No one knew their colors or their functions. No written record of their history had ever been found, save vague references to a time in ancient Faerie when all the Elfstones had been crafted—just enough to indicate that there had been five sets altogether and that by their absence it could be concluded that four had been lost. It was the great mystery of all Elven magic.

Yet after virtually everyone had decided the missing Elfstones were gone and would never be recovered, now there was this—a diary written by a girl named Aleia that might at last solve the mystery.

She could hardly believe her good luck in finding it. Imagine, if they could recover the Stones! She smiled at the thought. Everyone knew about the power of the blue Stones. But no one knew the first thing about the other four sets; no one even knew their colors. No records existed that described them. Or at least, none that had been uncovered. It was all so long ago, so far back in time. It was as Ellich had said. The Elves were a different people then. The world was different. The other Races hadn't been born. Only the Faerie people were alive, imbued with various forms of magic—some of which they shared with creatures now consigned either to mythology or by powerful magic to the dark world of the Forbidding.

It gave her pause. All those who had followed or sworn to the Void were imprisoned in the Forbidding— Darklings, Furies, Harpies, dragons, Goblins, and others. Yet the author of this diary had fallen in love with one of them. She had found him beautiful and enchanting, had given herself to him freely and had envisioned a life with him.

With a creature of the Void.

It didn't seem possible, but sometimes Aphen wondered if those viewed as evil were in fact only those who had lost the war and were tarnished by the victors. She understood that reality wasn't as simple as everyone wanted to believe, not as straightforward or as easily explained. Not black and white, but mostly gray.

She reached the cottage, dark now and apparently empty. Perhaps her sister was in bed or perhaps she was not home yet. Her work as a Chosen of the Ellcrys was difficult and demanding, and sometimes her days were eighteen hours long. Aphenglow didn't think she could ever do what that job demanded. But she guessed there were those who didn't think anyone could do her job, either, or even be what she was.

She opened the door and went inside, pausing for a moment to let her eyes adjust to the darkness. The silence enfolded her, and she gave herself over to it, using her senses to detect her sister's presence. She found the signs quickly enough—a gentle breathing, a stirring beneath sheets, a rustle of bedclothes—just up the stairs in the bedroom they shared whenever she was home, which was not often these days. Aphen sighed and sat down, her mind still mulling the entries in the diary and the questions they raised about the fate of the missing Elfstones.

She wondered first and foremost how the Stones had disappeared. Apparently, Aleia had tried and failed to find either them or her Darkling boy. That seemed odd, given that she had the use of the blue Elfstones to seek them. But of course, if she wasn't trained in their use—which was likely—then she might have lacked the sophistication to detect them.

Still, hadn't others tried to find the missing Elfstones since? Hadn't the Elves themselves used the blue Stones to attempt it? She couldn't imagine that efforts hadn't been made. And yet in all those years, no one had found a thing.

She put her deliberations on that subject aside and gave consideration to what had become of Aleia after her return to Arborlon. She had indicated in her diary entry that she had been given another chance at making things right, one that she hoped might give her a measure of redemption. But what sort of chance? The diary didn't say.

And what was the truth about the Darkling boy? Had he taken the Elfstones solely as a means of forcing her to come in search of him? Was he motivated entirely by his love for her, as she so desperately wanted to believe? Or had he intended all along to steal the Elfstones or whatever other magic he could lay his hands on? Was he the dark creature she feared he might be, his seduction of her purposeful and lacking in any real feeling or passion? Had he been pretending the whole time? There were arguments both ways. She had a feeling this was something no one would ever know.

Which was perhaps for the best. It would be sad to discover that Aleia had been deceived, that she had given herself to a liar and a thief.

Aphen leaned back in her chair and stared out the window. There were so many questions—and so many needing answers when answers were in short supply. Tomorrow she would look into the records of the Kings and Queens of Faerie, at the carefully recorded lineages of royal parents and children. Most were still intact. Aleia and her parents would be listed somewhere. There would be little information beyond the names, but it was a start to the search she now knew she had to undertake.

Her hand strayed to her pack where it rested by her side, her fingers finding the flat surface of the diary where it nestled inside.

"Coming to bed anytime soon?"

Arlingfant stepped into the room, small and delicate and wreathed in silk. She came over to her sister and knelt in front of her as if in supplication. Her perfect face—oval in shape, and dominated by her dark eyes and pronounced Elven features—canted upward, a smile appearing like a crescent moon come out from behind a cloud's shadow.

"I heard you come in. My senses are every bit as good as yours, Aph."

"Everything about you is as good. Were you sleeping or just lying awake waiting for me?"

"Lying awake. I was thinking." She brushed away loose strands of her dark hair absently. "The tree is so mysterious to me, even after almost eight months of caring for her. She almost never communicates, even in the smallest of ways. She relies on us to do what is needed, and we are expected to anticipate what those needs might be. It seems impossible that anyone could do this. Even though there are twelve of us serving her, we might miss something. We might interpret what we see the wrong way. We might do any number of things to cause her harm. Yet somehow we don't. But that doesn't mean we don't spend every waking minute worrying about it."

She looked away. "Today, while I was cleaning her bark, working at the things that might sicken or mar its surfaces, I had the oddest feeling. I thought I heard the tree say something. The voice just came out of nowhere, like a whisper in my ear. I knew it wasn't one of the other Chosen because I know their voices and this wasn't one I knew. I looked around, but I didn't see anyone near and didn't hear the voice again. But later, I mentioned to Freershan that I thought one of the tree branches had touched me. The tip of a branch, reaching down to touch my shoulder. But when I turned to look, there wasn't anything there."

Aphenglow reached out and touched her sister's face. "The tree is magic, Arling. It doesn't seem too odd that magical things might happen in its presence. Even ones of the sort you describe. Is the tree all right?"

Arlingfant nodded. "She seems fine. No one mentioned anything at the end of the day. It was just these . . . things."

Aphenglow stood up. "Do you want a glass of milk?"

Her sister nodded, and Aphenglow walked into the kitchen, opened the cold box, took out the milk pitcher, and poured a little of its contents into two glasses. She put the milk away again and carried the glasses back into the living room.

"It will help you sleep," she said, handing Arlingfant the glass.

They drank the milk in silence, sitting in the darkness, the quarter moon's soft light spilling down through the trees and filtering in through the cottage windows. Her mind drifted back to the diary, and for a moment she toyed with the idea of telling her sister what she had found. It would be good to have another opinion, to share her thoughts with someone who might bring a fresh perspective. But she resisted the impulse. She didn't want to put her sister in the position of having to cover for her if someone found out. Shared thoughts and fresh opinions could wait until she knew something more.

"Find anything interesting today?" Arlingfant asked suddenly, as if reading her mind.

"Nothing," Aphen lied. Lying was getting easier. It was starting to feel natural. "I'm getting to the end of my search, though. Not too many more boxes of letters and notes to go. I finished the last of the history appendices a week ago. It's exhausting work."

"Translating must be hard. So much of it is archaic. Ancient Elfish. Different dialects. It's good that you're trained to read those."

Aphenglow nodded. She had studied ancient Elven languages starting at the age of ten. She had a knack for it, a real sense of meanings and purposes in the use of words, and when she'd returned a year ago to undertake this task, she had come prepared with more than fifteen years of experience in deciphering what Elves thousands of years gone had written down.

"I might have to return to Paranor for a bit," she said suddenly. "For a week or so, perhaps."

The idea had just occurred to her, although in truth she must have known from the moment she had read the first few entries in the diary. She needed to consult the other Druids. A decision had to be made about what to do with this information, and where to take the search from here. She had promised her grandfather she would not take anything away, but the promise had been falsely given. She had always intended to take whatever she found. She was an Elf and loyal to her people, but not at the expense of the other Races. In that regard, she was a Druid first. Magic was meant to be shared, and it was safest in the hands of the Druids, who would make sure that happened.

"Aphen." Her sister moved close to her, placing her hands on Aphen's shoulders. "Take me away. I want to leave here. I want to go with you."

Aphenglow shook her head. "You know I can't do that."

"I know you've *said* you can't. But there's nothing you can't do, if you want to. A Druid has immense power, and you are the best of them all. If you tell them you want me there, they will have to let me stay."

They had covered this before, many times. Arlingfant had it in her head that she was meant to be not a Chosen, but a Druid like her sister. She didn't care about the inevitable repercussions. She was prepared to give up everything if Aphen would just take her to Paranor.

"You can't leave your friends to tend the Ellcrys without you," Aphenglow said pointedly. "They need you. If I am the best of the Druids, you are ten times the best of the Chosen. You are the one who always knows what to do. How many times have you ferreted out sickness or blight that no one else even noticed? You can't walk away from that. Later, maybe, when your year of service is finished. But not now."

"I know, I know. You've said this often enough. But I want to study magic with you!"

"Which leads to something else you keep ignoring. I don't make the choice of who becomes a Druid by myself. All in service must agree, and the Ard Rhys must be awake when that happens. At present, she rests in the Druid Sleep and is not to be woken for another two years unless an emergency requires it. Taking in another Druid—even you, Arling—does not qualify as an emergency.

"Besides," she added, "there is a reluctance to accept members of the same family into the order. You know this. There are genuine concerns about how blood ties would affect their performance as Druids."

She embraced her sister. "Nevertheless, when your service is over I will put your name before the others and make every effort to gain you a place. Don't you think I would like to have you with me? Don't you know I miss you?"

Arlingfant hugged her back. "I do know, Aphen. I don't mean to be unreasonable. But it's hard sometimes to have to wait so long."

Aphen laughed. "I know what you mean. Go on to bed, now. I will be up shortly. I just need to go through my notes one more time to be sure I've written everything down."

Her sister kissed her on the cheek, got to her feet, and left the room. Aphenglow listened to the soft pad of her feet on the stairs, the squeak of the bed ropes, and silence.

Then she took out the diary and sat looking at the last entry. Pathke, Meresch, and their Aleia. Very likely a

King, his wife, and his daughter. She must find their place in the Elven histories and determine if that might in some way help with her search for the missing Elfstones. Certainly it had happened a long time ago; the Elfstones had been missing since the last war between the Word and Void, in the time of Faerie.

And the city of Rajancroft where the Darkling boy had lived—where was that?

She must find all this out and begin fitting the pieces together. She must ferret out—

A shadow passed by the window on her right, and the thought was left unfinished as her attention shifted immediately. She did not react to the movement—she was trained to do otherwise—but instead closed the diary and slipped it down between the cushions on her left, effectively hiding it from view in a smooth natural movement that wouldn't be noticed by watching eyes.

She waited a moment, giving herself time to think and her watcher time to reappear at the window.

When nothing happened, she stood up, looking as if she might be ready to retire, but using the act as a way to glance from window to window.

Nothing.

And then a silken cord, its threads strong and tightly wound, slipped about her neck and cut off her air.

Her attacker's moves were so practiced and smooth that she was certain he had killed this way before. It would have meant the death of many others, and she had only a moment to ensure it would not be hers. She slammed her head backward into his, stomped down on his right ankle, and thrust her elbow back into his rib cage. She had been trained in hand-to-hand combat by no less an authority than the formidable Bombax, and she knew exactly what to do.

The problem was that it seemed to make no difference

to her attacker, who barely responded to what would have crippled others.

Pressed close against him as he continued to twist and tighten the cord, she tried to throw him and failed. He was too heavy, too well balanced. Even as tall and strong as she was, she was no match for him. She tried to use his weight against him, to trip him and topple him to the floor. That, too, failed. They were careening about the room like wild things, slamming into the walls, furnishings flying about, tipping over, breaking. Aphenglow possessed defensive skills that made her the equal of anyone, but she was losing this fight. She could feel her strength seeping away and could see spots before her eyes.

Then Arlingfant came tearing down the stairs, screaming like a banshee, a cudgel gripped in both hands. Without slowing, she whacked at her sister's attacker, catching him on the side of the head with a blow that rocked him just enough for Aphenglow to tear herself free of the killing cord.

But when she turned to engage her attacker, he was already out the door and had vanished into the night. Arling started to give pursuit, but Aphenglow pulled her back, shaking her head.

It took her a moment before she could speak. "Let him go," she said, gasping for breath. "We don't want to give him the advantage he seeks by bungling out into the darkness."

Her attacker was male. Of that she was certain—of his sex if not his Race. She had seen his wrists when he broke away—just a glimpse, but enough to be able to tell by the size and the amount of hair.

She moved over to a bench next to the dining table and lowered herself gingerly. The cord had burned her neck, and her breathing was still ragged. "You saved me, Arling. He was too strong for me. I couldn't fight him off."

Her sister bent close, examining her neck. "I hope I bashed his head in," she muttered. "Sit still. I'll bring cold cloths and ointment for the burn."

She moved into the kitchen, and Aphenglow quickly stepped over to the chair, retrieved the diary, and slipped it into her blouse. She was furious with herself for allowing someone to get that close. It shouldn't have been possible for an attacker to creep up on her like that; her normally dependable instincts should have warned her. That they hadn't was troubling.

Arlingfant was back, carrying a small, lighted lantern, which she placed on the table next to her sister. Then she proceeded to clean the burns with cold cloths and to apply a pain-relieving ointment. She worked quickly and efficiently, her small fingers smooth and clever.

"Who would do this?" she asked, the anger in her voice undiminished. "Why would anyone attack you in your own home?"

"I don't know," Aphenglow lied, already suspecting why, if not who.

"Did they take anything?"

"No. What is there to take? It was probably just someone who doesn't care for young women leaving their Elven family to join a Druid order. Perhaps someone with a grudge or a perceived hurt."

"Well, whoever it was will have a sore head in the morning." Her sister finished with the cleaning and ointments. "He tried to kill you, Aphen!"

"Or scare me. Wanting to send a message of some sort, maybe. We can't be certain."

But she was certain. Whoever had attacked her was experienced and skilled. It wasn't some common person, someone with resentments or a misguided sense of duty. And the nature of the attack suggested her assailant had been trying very hard to injure her badly, not merely scare her.

But who would want to hurt her? Who would benefit from that? She didn't know. She didn't have any identifiable enemies and couldn't think of anyone who carried a grudge of this magnitude. She couldn't help thinking she had been attacked because of the diary. But who would even know she had it? Who had come close enough to find out?

Only her uncle, Ellich. But her uncle loved her and would never do something like this. So was there someone who would benefit by having her dead and the diary in hand? Someone who had been watching her and saw her take the diary from the archives?

But if she had been seen taking the diary, why not just demand it back? Why try to injure her? Or why not just steal it from her, or try to frighten her into giving it up? Harming her seemed extreme, if getting possession of the diary was the principal goal.

Whatever the case, she was determined to press on. The attack had only strengthened her resolve. She would begin her search of the lineage charts first thing in the morning, just as she had planned.

But she would be keeping careful watch when she did.

3

When Aphenglow Elessedil woke the following morning, she ached everywhere. Moving slowly and stiffly, she went to the basin, dropped her sleeping shift, and washed herself gingerly. She was a mass of bruises and scratches, and the marks from the cord that had been wound about her neck burned at the slightest touch. She took time to reapply the ointment Arling had used the night before. Then she stretched to relieve the tightness in her body, dressed, and went down to breakfast. She ate standing up at the kitchen counter, staring out the window as the night's shadows receded and sunrise brightened the eastern sky.

Her sister had already gone. She would be down in the Gardens of Life with the other Chosen, gathered to welcome the Ellcrys to a new day and anxious to begin their assigned tasks. Her sister might say she didn't want to do the work of her order, but Aphenglow knew she took great pride in what she did. She was particularly suited to the position of Chosen, and was looked up to by the others for her skills and instincts as a Healer and caregiver. Yes, she wanted to be a Druid, and there were reasons to think that she would be a good one; she had talents that would lend themselves to the complicated and demanding work of the Druid order. But as impatient as her sister was to join her, Aphenglow knew she was better off where she was. Arling was still young, nine years Aphen's junior, and she was not yet fully cognizant of what it would do to her life if she followed in her sister's footsteps.

Aphen finished her fruit and bread, but stayed at the window and continued to watch the day brighten. Something was troubling her, though she couldn't put her finger on exactly what it was.

After five minutes or so of staring at nothing much, she left the kitchen, walked to the front door, and stepped outside. No one in the nearby residences was in evidence, so she couldn't ask if they had seen or heard anything last night. Instead she began walking around the little cottage, picking her way toward the window where she had seen the shadow pass. Her tracking skills were good enough that she soon found footprints—a man's, by the size of them. She followed them a short distance. They stopped, backtracked a bit, and then, with an obvious change in the length of the stride, signaled that the man had begun running. She followed the prints to the end of the yard, where they disappeared out onto the pathway that led from her tiny neighborhood into the city.

She stood looking at the footprints, perplexed by what she was seeing.

And then she realized, all at once, what was troubling her.

How had her attacker passed by the window one moment and gotten behind her the next? The time frame was too short for that to have happened. Which meant there had to have been more than one—the first man, whose shadow had drawn her attention, and a second who had come in through the kitchen door and attacked her.

She stood looking down the pathway for a moment

and then walked back to the window and around the house to the rear door. Sure enough, the clear depressions of a second set of prints, larger than the first, were outlined in the bare earth by the flower beds Arlingfant so carefully tended. The second man had lingered here, and then come through the door to attack her.

Or had he been inside already, waiting?

She felt a sudden chill. Her assailants had known what they were doing. One to distract her so that she wouldn't sense the other—a way of making sure her normally reliable Druid senses did not warn her of the danger. Her instincts were good, but not infallible, and she was not always able to pick up on everything happening around her.

The other thing she realized was that her attacker had made it impossible to defend herself with magic. She hadn't thought of that last night, still shaken by the attack, but she saw it clearly now. By cutting off her air he had throttled her voice and paralyzed her hands, preventing her from summoning any sort of magic. Her reaction had been instinctual—use physical force to get free. Perhaps subconsciously she had known that without her voice and hands she couldn't conjure any sort of magic anyway.

Everyone knew she was a Druid and had the use of magic. Not everyone knew how that magic worked: that voice or hands or both were needed to evoke it. Her attackers must have, though. The first man, the one at the window, would have been the leader, the one who thought it all through. The second, her attacker, was a skilled fighter and likely a trained assassin.

So now she had two mysteries. Who knew all this and would want to hurt her, and who knew about the diary and wanted to steal it?

She opened the back door and walked into the kitchen again. In truth she had more than two mysteries that needed solving, if you considered all the questions surrounding the diary's entries and the unknown history of their author. But only two that mattered regarding the attack.

A course of action that might help resolve all this eluded her at the moment, so she returned to her plan regarding the lineage charts of the Elven Kings and Queens. Picking up her backpack with its notes and stuffing the diary into a deep pocket in the trousers she was wearing, she departed the cottage and headed off to the palace for more research.

The walk was short and uneventful, but she found herself on edge the entire way. The attack had left her shaken, even if she wouldn't admit it to Arlingfant, and she knew that for a while, at least, she would be looking over her shoulder everywhere she went.

Deep in the lower levels of the palace, alone once more, she pulled out the lineage charts and went to work. The charts went much farther back than the Elven histories, although nothing had survived that went all the way back to the beginning of things. She started at the place where the recordings of lineages began and worked her way forward, hoping that any reference to Pathke and Meresch would not be so long ago as to have escaped all mention.

It was tedious work. The charts were old and handwritten, and all sorts of smudges and discolorations marred the information. In addition, she had to translate the ancient Elfish language that was being used at that time in order to comprehend what she was reading. But most troubling of all was a tendency of the early Elven scribes to leave things out, not believing them important enough to mention—a deficiency that over time had become apparent to later chroniclers who had discovered such absences while reading other writings. If that had happened here, she might miss what she was looking for without even realizing it.

In any event, it was slow going, and she had been at work almost the entire morning before she found the entries for which she had been searching.

She was still far back in the early years of Elven history, back before the advent of Men and the other Races—back when the Elves and their allies were still at war with the Darklings and theirs—when she discovered a Pathke Omarosian who had been King with a Meresch his wife and Queen. Their reign had lasted for over forty years, and they had been together for eight or nine before that. Their daughter, Aleia, had been born after Pathke had been King for seven years, and she had died when she was only eighteen.

Aphenglow stopped reading. Only eighteen. That would have been about the time she met and lost the Darkling boy. Her voice in the diary and the impetuousness of her acts would be appropriate for that age.

So had her death been linked to that event?

Aphen couldn't tell. There was nothing written anywhere on that page or any of the dozen that followed to reveal what had happened. Pathke had ruled for another seventeen years and then Meresch had succeeded him and ruled for twelve more. Aleia had been their only child.

Aphenglow set down the records and stared off into the shadows. It was too big a coincidence to think that Aleia's death was not in some way connected with her affair, but it didn't look as if there were any way to determine the connection. Still, she wasn't ready to let go of the matter just yet.

Picking up the records anew, she began working her way forward through the lineages once more. She pressed on for the remainder of the afternoon and found multiple instances of other members of the Omarosian line who had become Kings and Queens. But oddly, all of them seemed to serve sporadically, with great intervals of time falling between periods of rule. Given that they were not in the direct line of succession, it was odd to see them appear so frequently—almost as if they were brought in as caretaker monarchs. It also appeared that they married and split off into other families; many of the lineages were interrelated.

It was nearing twilight, and she had worked uninterrupted all day. She had eaten nothing for lunch and was beginning to feel hunger's impatient tug when she remembered that she had promised to dine with Ellich and Jera. She had reached the place in the records where the Old World had destroyed itself, and the survivors of Men and Elves and their descendants had endured a one thousand-year journey to the coming together of the First Council of Druids, with no mention of the Omarosians for centuries. She was about to put down the charts and go off to dinner when a notation made shortly after the convening of the First Druid Council caught her eye.

She translated it twice, wanting to make certain what she was reading. But there it was: a clear reference to a marriage that linked the Omarosians of the past to at least one branch of the family that had survived to the present.

The Omarosians had merged with the Elessedils.

Which meant that, improbable though it seemed, she was related to Aleia Omarosian.

Dinner with her aunt and uncle that evening was a decidedly quiet affair. Jera answered Aphenglow's questions with brief comments, and Ellich didn't speak at all. Long silences were punctuated only by the sounds of eating utensils against plates and the big willow outside scraping the roof. It was the longest meal that

Aphenglow could remember, and she could not seem to do anything to improve on it. Her uncle and aunt were pleasant enough, but non-conversant in spite of her efforts to elicit more than half a dozen words at a time. For all their warm friendship and family ties, it felt to her as if they were strangers.

She couldn't account for it and decided not to try. Sometimes you were better off just letting things go.

When dinner was finished, Ellich asked if she would take a walk with him. Jera began to clean up and refused Aphenglow's offer to help, insisting that she accompany her uncle. It wasn't hard to figure out that this was something they had talked about before she arrived and been thinking about all through the meal. Aphen knew she wasn't going to like whatever it was her uncle wanted to talk about, if he and Jera were this nervous about bringing it up, but didn't see any reasonable way to avoid it.

Ellich took her outside into the clear, cool night air. The sky was filled with stars and the city was wrapped in silence. Side by side they walked down the lane that bordered the surrounding cottages, neither of them speaking. Aphenglow was conscious of how alike they would appear to anyone passing—both of them tall and lean, fair-haired and blue-eyed, and both possessed of a long, swinging gait and a confident presence. This wasn't entirely an accident or even the result of genetics. Aphenglow had been raised as much by Ellich and Jera as by her own parents, and as a little girl she had tried very hard to emulate everything her uncle said or did, following him around for hours like a devoted puppy.

That had been a long time ago, but some of what she had taken from him she had kept as her own, from the way she walked to her slow, careful approach to solving problems and uncovering mysteries.

"I'm worried about you," her uncle said finally, apparently deciding it was time to address whatever was bothering him.

"You needn't be," she answered at once. "I'm fine."

"Which would explain the burn marks around your neck, I'm sure."

She had worn a scarf to conceal those, but somehow he had caught a glimpse of them anyway. "All right, I'm not entirely fine. Someone attacked me, but I drove him off. No harm."

Her uncle glanced over. "No harm this time. But what about the next? You've attracted enemies with your decision to serve the Druids, Aphen. You can't pretend otherwise. I've heard the talk, and people are usually careful about what they say around me. But they don't like what you are doing, and as a consequence they don't much like you."

"I'm aware."

"Well, then. What I want to ask is whether you've given any thought to withdrawing from the order and coming back here to live permanently."

She sighed. "I haven't given it one moment's thought, Ellich. I like what I am doing and I like the people I am doing it with. I can't help it that certain Elves are angry with this. I would have thought Elves, of all people, would be less inclined to discriminate. But maybe I'm not seeing this as clearly as I should."

He glanced over. "Don't get your back up just yet. I'm not one of those who think you made a mistake. I'm just wondering how much more of your life you ought to give over to this choice. While you're spending days down in dusty storerooms searching for something that very likely doesn't exist, more pressing problems go unresolved."

"What are you talking about?"

He stopped walking and turned to face her. "The world isn't what it was, Aphen. We came out of a world that was dominated by science, not magic. Magic was the old way, and we left it behind with the fall of Faerie and the coming of Men. But with the destruction of the world that science and Men built, we turned once more to magic for ways to sustain and improve what was left to us of the Old World. We were mostly successful for more than three thousand years. But now that's changing."

She stared at him. "How is it changing? Magic still governs our people. It still dictates the balance of power among the Races."

"At the moment, but not for much longer. The Federation works hard to recover the lost technologies. Men distrust magic; they believe there is more reliability in science. This is especially so for those governed by the Federation and even more so by those doing the governing. They have a clear and possibly unalterable worldview. They seek domination over the other Races and they intend that science give them the power that will allow for that. They fought for it during the wars on the Prekkendorran, and even after they were defeated they harbored a desire to pursue it. They outnumber the other Races two to one, and they are working hard at increasing those odds through alliances and treaties. All they need is a way to negate the magic of the Elves and the Druids."

"That won't happen." She met his gaze squarely. "The Druids won't allow it."

He nodded. "So you think. But the Druid order is tiny and isolated. How many of you are left? Six? Eight? And your Ard Rhys hasn't been seen in how many years? Even the Elves want nothing to do with you. How much can you accomplish with so few?" He paused. "This is not to say we are any better off. We aren't. We have some use of magic, but nothing of real consequence beyond the blue Elfstones. We study the use of magic, and a few of us possess talismans handed down over the centuries, but by and large we are bereft. Once, the use of magic defined us. Now it seems an oddity, a remnant of another time.

He sighed. "It is a worrisome state of affairs, Aphenglow. Without magic, we are vulnerable on many fronts. Our army is well trained, but dwarfed by that of the Federation. We disdain the help of the Druids; our only meaningful alliance is with the Dwarves. If that should fail, we would be susceptible to an all-out attack."

"The Federation wouldn't dare. The other Races wouldn't stand for it."

"I think they would. I think the other Races would stay clear of the whole mess, very much the way they have in other times. If the Dwarves were persuaded to stay out of it, the Gnomes and Trolls would do the same. The Federation would have the match they seek."

She leaned back and studied him. "Why are you telling me all this? What does my status as a Druid have to do with anything?"

"Just this. As the King's granddaughter and an Elf and Druid both, you occupy a unique position in the Elven hierarchy. Even disliked as you are by some, you still command respect. I wish you would consider using it. Come back to us and be the leader we need."

"My grandfather is King and his son Phaedon after him. Since Phaedon has no children, you would be next in line. And after that, there are others who would be favored over me."

Ellich shook his head, eyebrows arching high on his forehead. "My brother is failing. My nephew would be a dangerous and foolish choice, and I would be a worse one. All of the others lack your skills and training. You are the right person to lead the Elves."

"This is dangerous talk, Ellich. You might not want to repeat it to anyone else."

"I am not suggesting that you should claim the throne, Aphen. But as a member of the Elessedil family, you can help by sharing the magic that is rightfully ours."

For just a second she thought he had uncovered her secret and was speaking of the missing Elfstones. She hesitated, uncertain of what to say. But then she realized he was speaking in more general terms.

"The Elven magic is lost, Uncle. What there is of it is being sought out by the Druids. The Elves do nothing to help. They might have created the magic in the time of Faerie, but they let it slip away. They put it aside and forgot it."

He nodded slowly. "But it is theirs by right of prior ownership, Aphen. It doesn't belong only to the Druids."

"No. Nor do they claim it does. It belongs to everyone. The Druids seek only to keep it available to all."

"That might be so, but the goal is unattainable. Not everyone can have use of it. Much of it, like the blue Elfstones, can be used only by Elves. It is specific to us; it *belongs* to us. I don't suggest that the Druids shouldn't have a say in its use. But in practical terms, the Druids must come to an understanding with the Elves on what that use should be. You are the one who can make that understanding possible. You need only change your thinking sufficiently to allow that to happen."

She paused, realizing now what he was asking. "You want me to act as an intermediary between the Druids and the Elves on the subject of using magic?"

"I do. I want you to remember that you have one foot solidly planted in both camps. You know this. Don't try to take sides. Don't think you must make a choice. Serve both. It won't be easy, but it will be necessary."

She shook her head. "I don't know. I can't even think of how to approach such a task."

Her uncle took her hands and squeezed them gently.

"Begin by promising me this. If you uncover magic in your search, either here or later, tell me about it first. Don't go to the King or the High Council. Come to me. Together we can form a strategy for making the necessary alliance between Druids and Elves. We can find a way to form an agreement that will unify the two camps so that they may stand against the Federation."

She thought about the missing Elfstones—the only real lead she had come across in a year's hard work. Was there a way to share that magic if it were to be recovered? She knew the danger posed by the Federation. Her uncle did not exaggerate. But she could not speak for the other Druids and knew that her mandate was to gather and place control of all magic in her order—not to allow any other claim to it. Grianne Ohmsford herself had declared that this was the only way to keep power among the Races in balance.

But she also knew that advancements in the development of new science were threatening that balance. And the Druids were poorly equipped to do anything to change that.

"I will give it some thought," she told him, "but I can't promise anything more. I have to think on it. I respect what you are saying, Ellich. I just don't know if there is a way to bring about what you would like to see happen."

He smiled. "Nor do I. But if you are willing to try, if you will trust me enough to talk to me about it when there is need, I think we might find that way. Come, now. Enough talk. Let's walk back and see if Jera might have something sweet prepared to complete our dinner."

No more was said that evening about their discussion. Conversation returned to something more or less approaching normal, and when Aphenglow departed for home and bed it was with a sense of renewed warmth toward her uncle and aunt. She was not done thinking about what she had been asked to do or even close to any sort of decision, but she cared enough for her uncle that she would give his suggestion careful consideration. There was no question in her mind that she would rather take him into her confidence than anyone else at Arborlon.

Except perhaps for her mother, but confiding in her mother was no longer possible.

Ellich offered to accompany her home, but she dismissed the idea out of hand. She was a Druid trained in the use of magic; she needed no other protection. She walked with her backpack slung over one shoulder, inhaling the cool night air, enjoying the sweep of the starlit sky and thinking of Afrengill, wishing things could be different between them, knowing they might never be. How could they? Her mother didn't speak to her anymore. They had been close once, but Aphenglow's decision to become a Druid had brought an end to that.

Her father had died years earlier in a hunting accident, when Arlingfant was still very little, so Aphen and her mother had become the foundation and heart of the family unit. When she had decided to leave for Paranor, her mother had begged her not to go. She had insisted she could not manage on her own. Arlingfant was ten by then and old enough to give what help was needed, but it made no difference to their mother. Afrengill was no longer being rational, would not even try to be so, and they had parted ways screaming at each other while Arlingfant hid in her bedroom and cried.

On her first visit back, Aphenglow had gone to see her mother, intent on patching things up. She had walked up to the door and knocked. Afrengill had opened the door, stared at her wordlessly as she attempted to say how sorry she was, and closed the door again without a word. Arlingfant had been forced to sneak away to come see her, forbidden by their mother to have anything to do with her sister.

Each time on her return, Aphenglow went to her home and knocked on the door. By now, her mother rarely bothered to answer. Arlingfant said she wouldn't even allow Aphenglow's name to be spoken. Her daughter was dead to her, she declared. She was dead to all of them.

It hurt so much that even thinking of it brought a quick sob that caused her to catch her breath. Her mother, whom she loved, would have nothing to do with her, and even though Arlingfant insisted she would come around in time, Aphenglow was no longer sure.

In light of this, her uncle's plea that she consider departing the Druid order to return to Arborlon had merit. Everything that was wrong with her life, that made her unhappy, could be traced to her decision to join the order. Was it time for her to leave? Was she not seeing things as clearly as she thought? She loved her work, her Druid companions, and the cause for which she labored so hard.

But maybe that wasn't enough.

Maybe . . .

She was aware of the possibility of danger after the other night's attack, her senses alert and her wards spread wide, so she sensed as much as heard the almost inaudible whisper of fabric as the black-clad figure hurtled out of the darkness behind her, and she threw herself aside in plenty of time to avoid his blade. She knew at once it was the same man who had attacked her last night. But last night he had caught her by surprise, and she had already made up her mind that he would not do so again. Ever since she had set out from the palace to have dinner with Ellich and Jera she had been watching and listening, anticipating that he might try again.

Even so, he had almost gotten to her.

She rolled and came back to her feet in a single fluid movement, dropping the backpack in the grass and bracing herself as he flew out of the darkness once more. Whoever he was, he did not give up easily. Instead of waiting for him, she counterattacked. She dropped sharply as they came together, rolled and swept her legs into his ankles, and took him off his feet. He lost his balance and went down, but was up again instantly. He came at her again, and she sidestepped another lunge with the blade. He was quick and practiced, and given enough time he would find his target. But she had her magic in place by then, flaring at her fingertips, and when he attacked once more, she used it. White light exploded out of her hands, picked him up, and flung him away like a rag doll. She used more force than she had intended, but there was no time to modulate or adjust. He catapulted backward as if yanked by a rope, slamming into a tree, his arms flailing wildly as he tried to cushion the blow and failed.

Down he went in a crumpled heap and lay there.

She approached him cautiously. There was no movement. She toed him gingerly, ready for him to spring up and attack anew. But he failed to respond. Still using her boot, she rolled him over. His head was bent awkwardly to one side, loose and unhinged.

His neck was broken.

Shades, she thought, appalled at what she had done.

She picked up the knife he had been carrying, which was lying to one side. It was a Southland weapon, forged in one of the Borderland Cities, probably in Varfleet where they did such skilled work with blades. She knelt next to him, still watchful, ready to respond if he moved. But when she pulled back the black hood that concealed his features, his eyes were fixed and staring. She studied his features, trying to place him.

She had never seen him before.

A search of his clothing turned up nothing that revealed who he was or where he had come from. He was a Man, not an Elf, and she felt a small ripple of gratitude for that. She did not want to think that there were Elves this anxious to see her dead.

Was killing her the dead man's idea, or did he serve another?

She remembered there had been two of them last night . . .

She turned to look for the backpack, scanning the ground where she had dropped it, but it was gone. So, she thought: one man to attack her and one to steal the bag. A small variation on last night's attack, and this time they'd had better success.

She glanced out into the darkness and down the pathway, but there was nothing to see. The second attacker would be far away by now. He would not stop until he was safe and could examine the contents of her bag at his leisure. She wished she could be there to see his face when he opened it and found it stuffed with old maps and a couple of books on the care and feeding of hogs.

She smiled in spite of herself. She knew a trick or two. She had been expecting the attack and had left nothing to chance. The diary was back at the palace, down in one of the storerooms, safely tucked away where only she could find it. After last night's assault, she wasn't about to take foolish chances.

What she could not decide was how her attackers knew about the diary in the first place. How could anyone have found out about it in so short a time?

Whatever the answer to her question, it was clear that someone wanted it as badly as she did and would kill to get it. Using an assassin as skilled as the dead man was a clear indication of their determination. It changed her thinking measurably. She was no longer equivocating about what she must do.

She went back to the assassin, knelt beside him, and spoke a Druid grace to give him peace and forgiveness. Even the worst of the dead deserved that much.

Then she rose and went to find her sister to say good-bye.

It was time to return to Paranor.

4

WITHIN THE JAGGED RING OF THE DRAGON'S Teeth, fading daylight turned scarlet splashed across the canopy of the Forbidden Forest all the way to the spires of Paranor. The Druid's Keep rose stark and solitary out of an ocean of trees, its ancient stones blackened by time and weather—a vast sprawling complex in the midst of a wilderness. At the helm of the *Wend-A-Way*, Aphenglow eased off the thrusters, bringing the craft almost to a halt, creeping forward so that she could consider what she had left behind. It had been a long time since she had been home to Paranor, and she felt the need to prepare herself for her return.

She had left at sunrise, awake before Arlingfant so that they could say their good-byes. Her sister had asked again to come with her, to join her as a Druid and leave her life as a Chosen behind. She had cried, which had caused Aphenglow to cry, as well. But in the end Aphenglow only kissed her sister, hugged her close, and promised she would be back to see her again soon. "Take care of Mother," she whispered before breaking away.

It all seemed very long ago now that she was coming up on Paranor and the life she had chosen for herself. She felt excited as she watched the details of the towers

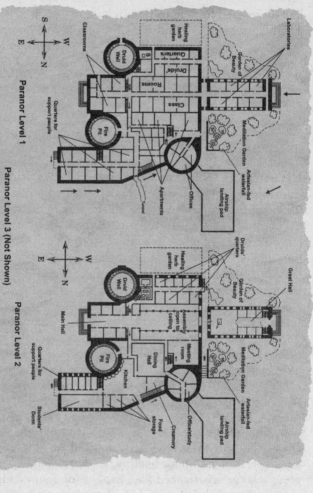

Paranor Level 1

Druid History archives, library, cold room, Ard Rhys's quarters, Druid Scribe's office

Paranor Level 3 (Not Shown)

Paranor Level 2

and walls come into focus, the places she had always favored revealing themselves one by one, the secrets she had discovered finding fresh purchase in her memories. The history of the Druids was intriguing and compelling, but it was the structure of the Keep itself that left her breathless. Sometimes she thought back to the days of Galaphile and the first Druids and wondered how they had managed to construct such a massive and complex edifice in a time when so little in the way of machinery and skill had been available.

As she neared, she saw the dim shapes of the Trolls who served as the Druid Guard at watch on the walls. Dark-clad and imposing, they were the protectors of the order. They were walking the battlements, lighting the torches with nightfall's approach. Garroneck, Captain of the Guard, disdained the use of the flameless lamps present throughout the Keep's interior. Fire was more dramatic and forbidding, and it was his task to keep those who were not invited away. Aphenglow could picture his blunt features and fierce expression as he explained the reason for this. The Keep had been assaulted only a handful of times since its construction, and it had fallen only once, when it had been betrayed. The big Troll did not intend to see it happen a second time, not while he was in command of the guard.

She closed off all but the parse tubes aft, and then walked forward and drew down the jib and mainsails on her skimmer and stowed them away. She would coast in and use the wing sails to steer the little ship. Measuring less than sixty feet, it could be flown by a single person, assuming one knew what to do. Aphenglow was an experienced flier, capable of commanding even a ship-of-the-line, and she had done so with the *Walker Boh* on several occasions. The only Druid who was her equal when it came to flying was Bombax, but then he was her equal in almost everything.

Readied for landing, she worked the thrusters in tandem and allowed the skimmer to settle slowly within the interior walls of the Keep, down into the courtyard that had been converted in Grianne Ohmsford's time to a landing platform where the ships could be anchored just off the ground or docked for servicing. All the other ships were visible save *Arrow,* so it was likely all but one of the other Druids were in residence.

She brought *Wend-A-Way* down carefully, the landing platform blazing to life with hastily lit torches; the Troll guard had seen her approach and recognized her vessel. Garroneck was already waiting, standing off to one side, huge arms crossed over his chest until he raised one in a casual gesture of greeting. Very like him. Never any show of impatience or excitement, everything measured and steady. In all the time she had known him—which covered the entire period of her Druid tenure—she had never seen him make a rash or foolish decision or lose his temper with anyone who did.

She lowered the skimmer anchor, which Garroneck came forward to secure, dropped the rope ladder over the side, shouldered her backpack, and climbed down to greet him.

"It's been a long time, Aphenglow," he rumbled, his great hands swallowing hers. "Are you well?"

"Well enough," she answered. "How are things here?"

"Steady sailing, favorable winds. We do what's needed and then some. The Ard Rhys still sleeps. Is that about to change?"

Perceptive, as always. "Perhaps. I'll need to speak with the others first. Who's missing?"

A short growl that might have been laughter. "Who else but that impetuous Borderman. He comes and goes like the weather, never entirely predictable. I think he's gone to Arishaig to test the political winds."

Bombax. He would. "Has something happened?" She started for the doorway, taking Garroneck's arm to keep him close.

The big shoulders dropped slightly and his head inclined until it was close. She was tall enough that it didn't take much. "Rumor has it the Federation is getting a new Prime Minister."

"Nothing unusual about that. They have a new Prime Minister almost weekly."

"Very unstable government. You would think with so much territory to govern and so much responsibility to bear it would be otherwise. But that's not the way they do things in the city-states."

They passed into the tower and started down the stairs, still keeping side by side.

"So what does this matter to us?" she asked.

"We might be at risk."

"That's old news. We are already at risk."

"We might be at greater risk." He shrugged. "Let the others explain. They are better able than a simple Captain of the Druid Guard."

She smiled in spite of herself. They both knew he was astute enough to appreciate the political situation in any corner of the Four Lands. But he was also deferential toward the members of the Druid order and would never have presumed to tell them what to think.

Garroneck left her at the door to her chambers and walked off to advise the others that she had returned. But she hadn't gotten much farther than throwing her backpack on the bed and washing her face and hands when Seersha appeared in the door.

"The despised and disinherited Elven girl returns," she greeted, a welcoming smile spreading over her broad features. "Are you forgiven yet for your poor choice in occupation and friends?"

"Not yet, I'm afraid. I remain a pariah." She reached

out and hugged the other woman, kissed her cheeks, and backed her off for a closer look. "What's this? You look tired."

Seersha shrugged. "Working late on elementals. There's magic waiting to be unlocked if I could just decipher the language."

She was a big woman, wide rather than tall and solid in the way of Dwarves, but average in height and weight. Her hair was cut short against her head, and her neck and arms were tattooed with Dwarf symbols. She wore traditional black robes, but they were striped with crimson and gold about the shoulders and down the back. One eye was gone, the result of a childhood accident, and she wore a patch over the socket that adhered to the skin and bone without need for a cord. Seersha was not like anyone Aphenglow had ever known, and it was those differences that drew the Elven woman to her.

"Are you here because you've finished with your search of the records?" her friend asked, arching an inquisitive eyebrow.

"I'm not finished, but I may have found something important. Let me change out of my clothes and gather my things and I will meet you and the others in the south Council chamber in an hour."

Seersha nodded and, without pursuing the matter, went back out the door. As she disappeared, she gave a wave and said, "You-know-who has gone off alone again but is expected back soon. Still your heart, if you can."

Bombax again. Aphenglow laughed and closed the door behind her.

It was way too late to do anything about her heart.

When she had washed and dressed in clean clothes, she walked through the corridors of the Keep toward the south Council chamber, taking her time, drinking in the smells, tastes, and sounds she had been missing during the year she was away. It was a ritual for her, a reconnecting with the place she called home. That she could feel such pleasure in a structure built of stone and iron would have surprised the Elves of Arborlon. But she saw so much more than simply the cold surfaces of the materials. The Keep was a living thing, a presence that could be felt and on occasion heard. It was protective of its children and incredibly dangerous to those who threatened them. Down in the Well, in the heart of the Keep, there was a magic that warded everything and could not be dislodged or destroyed. Time and again, when the Druid order had disappeared, died out, or simply stayed away for a long time, the magic of the Keep had come awake to keep watch until those who belonged returned.

Sometimes, when she was alone, walking down cavernous halls and through rooms layered with tapestries and shadows, she would sense the magic keeping her company, a silent, undemanding presence that wished only to share her space. It was little enough to request, and she gladly gave back what it asked.

Interestingly, no one else seemed to share her experience. In the early days after her arrival, she mentioned the unseen presence of the magic to the others. But while they nodded and smiled agreeably, she could tell they had no idea what she was talking about, that her experience was completely foreign to them.

"May I walk with you, Aphenglow?" Garroneck asked, appearing next to her out of nowhere.

She nodded wordlessly, forcing her heart to drop back down out of her throat. How did a creature so huge and ponderous appear like that without a sound? He could be a wraith when he chose, as silent as death's shadows.

"Is your family well?" he asked conversationally.

"My sister is fine. My mother doesn't speak to me."

"One day she will."

He said it with such conviction she was instantly persuaded he was right. "I would like that."

They walked on without speaking until they reached the Council chamber entry. Light spilled through the open doors into the hallway, and she could hear the sound of voices coming from inside.

"I will be standing watch," Garroneck advised. "No one will be allowed in while you give your report. Close the doors behind you."

"Do you think we might be disturbed?" she asked.

He gave her a small shrug. "Not now I don't."

She smiled, turned, and entered the chamber, pausing to seal the doors behind her as he had asked.

The others, all but Bombax, were gathered about the long Council table. Long-limbed, loose-jointed, and rail-thin Carrick, the other member of the Race of Man, lounged in a chair at the far end, draped over the arms and seat like the scarecrow he resembled. He was bald and clean-shaven, and his pale skin seemed to radiate in the light, giving his startling blue eyes an especially vibrant look. He sat up at her appearance and clapped his hands enthusiastically.

"There she is, the woman of the hour! Welcome home, Aphenglow Elessedil. We have missed you greatly."

"Not that greatly," Seersha said quickly, giving her a wink. "But enough so that we have agreed to hear whatever it is you wish to say. Assuming it doesn't go on all that long."

Aphen crossed the room and took a seat about halfway down the table, close by Seersha and across from Pleysia Ariana. Pleysia gave her a nod and a desultory wave of one hand. Pleysia, an older and more accomplished user of magic than Aphenglow, was also Elven, but the women shared little else and did not much like each other.

"Did they throw you out?" Pleysia asked, trying for humor.

"If you mean the Elves, no." Aphenglow smiled as if she thought the attempt at a joke funny. "I came back all on my own." She glanced at Seersha. "Which is not to say anyone was unhappy to see me go."

Carrick leaned forward. "Their loss is our gain. But tell us. Have you found something useful? Seersha suggested that maybe you had."

Aphenglow hesitated. "I'm not yet certain. That is why I came back. I need you to listen to what I am about to read and then tell me your thoughts. I believed my discovery important enough to bring it now rather than wait. And there is reason to think I might be right. But leave that until I have finished."

She reached into her pocket and produced the diary. "This book contains the writings of a young Elven girl named Aleia Omarosian, who lived and died centuries ago. I stumbled on it quite by accident. It isn't a part of the official histories or even something that would be considered important, absent a thorough reading, to anyone looking to add to or embellish the information contained in those histories. That, I think, is why it has been overlooked for so long. It was kept because the writer was the child of a King and Queen of the Elves in the time of Faerie. But mostly, it was forgotten."

She opened the diary. "I won't read you all of this, only those parts that are pertinent to what seems important. Listen."

For the next fifteen minutes or so, she read from the diary, taking each entry in turn, reading it through in its entirety and without comment moving on to read the next. Her three listeners did not interrupt, but sat quietly, paying close attention.

When she was done, Pleysia said. "I don't know. Is this story even real? It sounds like something Aleia Omarosian might be making up. Young girls do that. They create an imaginary existence hoping that some of the angst and excitement might relieve the ennui of their real lives."

"Maybe," Carrick mused, rubbing his chin. "But it doesn't sound made up to me."

"I thought as Pleysia does," Aphenglow said. "I wondered if the reason the diary had lain undiscovered so long was that somewhere along the way—maybe as far back as when she was still alive or right after her death—it was determined to be only a young girl's musings. But on the same night I took the diary back to my cottage, I was attacked."

She proceeded to fill them in on the details of the first night, then went on to relate how the attacker had returned on the second night and she had been forced to kill him. "Until then, I wondered. But the attacker's persistence and knowledge of the book suggest it might have value. The attackers, at least, must have thought so."

"But they don't even know what's in it, do they?" Pleysia pressed, leaning forward, brow furrowed. "Why would they bother with something they know nothing about? And if they did know what it contained and thought it dangerous for some reason, why wouldn't they have tried to steal it or destroy it long before this?"

"I don't know what they were thinking. The one is dead and the other's identity is a mystery. But he did take my backpack in the clear anticipation that the diary was in there."

"Or he took it because he knew *something* was in there that you believed had value," Seersha offered. "He might not have known it was the diary, only that it was a document that you had found valuable. So it might still be true, as Pleysia thinks, that the diary is only a young girl's imaginings."

Carrick nodded. "That's true, Aphen. Who knew you had found the diary and taken it out of the archives?"

She shook her head. "No one, so far as I know. I was alone in the storerooms the entire day, except for my uncle Ellich. But I hid the diary before he got close enough to see what I was doing, and I didn't take it out again until after he had left. There was no one else down there."

"So this girl, Aleia, takes this Darkling boy as her lover, changes her mind about the relationship when he insists she must leave Arborlon and come to live with his people, and then after refusing him discovers too late that he has stolen all but the seeking-Stones, leaving them behind so she will have a way to track him down." Seersha grimaced. "Then she tries to do so, but can't—even with the seeking-Stones to aid her—returns empty-handed and lives out the rest of her life. And you've no idea what happened to her?"

Aphenglow shook her head. "She wrote she had found a way to help set things right, but didn't say what it was. She died shortly after, according to the genealogy charts of the Elven Kings and Queens. The Elfstones were gone for good after that. If there was any record of the specifics of their disappearance, it has been lost. The records as a whole are incomplete, of course, going that far back. All we know for certain is that the Elfstones disappeared during the age of Faerie, and it now appears it might have happened in the way the diary relates."

Pleysia frowned. "What exactly are we supposed to do with this?"

"That is what we are here to discuss," Carrick declared. "What do you think, Aphenglow?"

"I'm not sure. I suppose we need to decide if there is a

way we can track the missing Stones that hasn't been tried before. Does the diary offer any clues that might help us with a fresh search? If it does, I haven't found them. But I would like us to consider any possibilities. For instance, do we know if anyone other than Aleia has tried using the blue Stones to track the others? I can't believe someone hasn't, but the Elven histories don't say."

"If no one else has been able to find them in all this time," Pleysia pointed out, "why do you think we can?"

Carrick stood up and started walking around the table. "The point is, Pleysia, that even if others have tried, we haven't. And Aphen is right. We have to. Think what's at stake! The Four Lands stand at a crossroads. Science and magic are pressing up against each other, both seeking dominance and the welcoming embrace of all the Races. We have been a long time with only magic to empower and fuel civilization's advancement. Now science has begun to reemerge as a force to be reckoned with. It surfaces everywhere, and where once it was reviled and disdained as the instrument of humanity's near destruction during the Great Wars, now it gains increasing favor—and it is magic that is mistrusted."

"It is not our duty or obligation to sort out whether magic or science will empower future development in the Four Lands," Pleysia snapped. "Our job is to employ magic in the present and to see that it is used wisely and to the benefit of all equally. The future will take care of itself."

"Then you would resist any search for the missing Stones?" Carrick pressed.

"Talk of a search is premature. We have other work to occupy our time—equally important work." Pleysia shook her head. "This feels like an exercise in futility. There was nothing in Aphenglow's reading that offered even the smallest clue about where or how the Elfstones could be found. Are we to set aside everything and just go off blindly hunting? I don't think so. Not without something more to convince us that a search will actually yield something."

"We have nothing 'to occupy our time,' as you put it, that is even remotely as important as finding the Elfstones," Seersha declared. "If there is a chance they might be recovered, we have to take it."

"We are the caretakers of magic in this world, are we not?" Carrick leaned forward across the table toward Pleysia. "As such, we have a responsibility to find, retrieve, and safeguard any magic that might impact the people we serve. They may not appreciate our efforts, but that has never been the measuring stick of our commitment as Druids. I think we have here the sort of challenge we cannot refuse to accept. I think we have been given a responsibility of proportions impossible to measure. Finding the missing Elfstones might initiate changes that would dictate an entirely new future for the Four Lands. To pretend otherwise is foolish."

"Yes, think what it would mean if we found them," Seersha added quickly. "Power of the sort that five sets of Elfstones would bestow could offer solutions to so many problems. I am not yet ready to toss aside magic in favor of new science. All I have seen so far from what's been recovered are killing machines and weapons. I've seen the chronicles compiled on the new forms of destruction introduced during the war on the Prekkendorran. I've seen the Races grow increasingly hostile toward one another, all of them ready to do battle at the first challenge thrown."

"That might well have come about even without the advent of the new science," Pleysia pointed out. "It might have come about in the presence of magic alone. You are conjecturing."

"But what if the missing Elfstones are out there waiting to be found, and we have a chance to do so," Carrick pressed. "Why not try?"

Pleysia gave him a look. "Because that is how people get killed, Carrick—by trying foolish things and taking needless risks. Druids are not exempt from such fates." She paused. "Or so our histories tell us."

There was an uneasy silence as the three glared at one another across the table. Aphenglow thought she should say something, but she was at a loss as to what that might be. The lines were drawn, and everyone knew what she wanted just by the fact of her having returned with the diary in hand. But in truth she wondered if Pleysia might not be right about the slimness of their chances of finding the Elfstones after so long.

Carrick walked back to the head of the table and sat down again, his fingers steepled in front of his face. "We must wake the Ard Rhys."

The others stared at him. "We are not to wake her unless an emergency requires her presence," Pleysia reminded him. "Where is the emergency here?"

"You might argue that there isn't one, and I might be inclined to agree with you under other circumstances. But the twin attacks on Aphenglow indicate a clear determination on the part of someone to find out what she knows." Carrick leaned back. "I think that makes this an emergency."

"Well said, Carrick!" a familiar voice boomed out from behind them. "We must wake the Ard Rhys at once!"

All heads turned. The four Druids already in the room had been so deeply involved in their discussion that they had failed either to hear or see the entry doors open to admit the fifth. Bombax stood in the opening, Garroneck looming just behind him.

"I've been standing outside the door for some time,

listening. I didn't want to interrupt Aphenglow's report." He grinned broadly—that devastating smile that left her undone every time she saw it. "But now I think I must. Aphenglow might not want to say so openly, but I expect she brought the diary back with every intention of seeing the Ard Rhys awakened. Because a decision on a matter of this sort requires that she be consulted and directly involved. Am I wrong, Elfling?"

Aphenglow hated it when he called her that, but she could not seem to stop him from doing so, even after expressing her dismay to him in private countless times. "You are not wrong. I did think it necessary."

"Well, there you are." Bombax came all the way into the room and stood looking from face to face. He was a big man, much taller and stronger than she was and almost as tall as Garroneck, though more limber and rangy. His thick mop of black hair fell to his shoulders in a tangle, and his travel-worn cloak was dusty and weathered. He had the look of a man who had journeyed hard and fast.

"Nice of you to drop in on our discussion," Pleysia purred. "But you might want to learn all the facts before you offer an ill-advised opinion. Though I realize that is not your way."

"No, it really isn't," the other readily agreed, giving her a quick sideways glance. "But then I know something about this that you don't. So I might say the same about you."

She glared at him. "What are you talking about?"

He moved over and sat down beside Aphenglow, taking a deep, slow breath as he faced her, as if trying to breathe in her scent. "Just this. We have a new Federation Prime Minister as of midnight yesterday, and it isn't good news for us."

"Drustan Chazhul," Seersha guessed, leaning forward to look past Aphenglow and meet his gaze. "Isn't it?"

"Chosen last night after only one ballot. No opposition besides the few who have always opposed him— And their number steadily dwindles. Unfortunate things keep happening to them. So we are left with the worst possible choice. He has sworn he will see the order disbanded and Paranor razed. I fully expect him to try to carry out that threat."

Carrick shrugged the threat away. "What happened to the old Prime Minister?"

"One of those unfortunate accidents I mentioned. He poisoned himself. Perhaps with help."

Even Pleysia laughed at that, all of them aware of how desperately Chazhul wanted to be Prime Minister and how blind his predecessor had been to the duplicity of those around him. It was difficult to overestimate the machinations engaged in by the Ministers of the Federation High Council in their efforts to advance their positions. And Drustan Chazhul was the worst of the lot.

"He is a dangerous man," Seersha said quietly, and gave each of them a look.

"Well, we can't do anything about the Federation's choice of a new Prime Minister," Carrick said. "But beyond the obvious, how does this impact the business at hand?"

"Drust Chazhul's reach is long and sure. He will have at least one spy in the Elven camp. Which suggests in turn the possibility he might have had something to do with the attacks on Aphenglow."

Everyone went silent, thinking. "That's a stretch, isn't it?" Pleysia said finally. "How would he have found out about the diary quickly enough to order an attack? Besides, he has no interest in magic. He mistrusts and dislikes it. He wants it eliminated."

"A good reason for seeing to it that no new discoveries come to light, don't you think? As for the attacks, he might have planned for that a long time ago, thinking the day might come when they would be needed and needed quickly. Don't underestimate him. He intends to rule us all. And now he has the means to find a way to do so."

"He's ambitious, but not flawless." Seersha made a dismissive gesture. "He will have trouble finding allies."

"We're not here to discuss the Federation or the boundless ambitions of its Ministers," Pleysia snapped. "We are here to decide whether or not to awaken the Ard Rhys from the Druid Sleep. Again, I do not think we have an emergency that requires it. How do the rest of you vote?"

The five Druids stared at one another, waiting to see who would speak first. Finally, Carrick came to his feet. "You are outnumbered four to one, Pleysia. I will wake the Ard Rhys."

"No, I will," Aphenglow said at once. "This is mostly my doing. I will take the responsibility."

Without waiting for a response, she pushed back her chair, rose, and went out the chamber door, feeling the weight of their eyes against her back.

5

◆

HER SLEEP WAS DEEP AND ENDLESS, A LONG SLOW
*unwinding of time and space. She floated on the air currents of the
world, riding the back of the wind, gliding like a bird across the sky
from light to dark, day to night. Her journey was smooth and undisturbed, and she drifted in her dreams from the real to the imagined and back again. At times, she dwelled in the past amid
memories of what had once been and now was forever gone, as if she
were paging through a book in which pictures captured perfectly the
years of her life. At times, she was cocooned by blackness with no
pictures, no memories, and no sense of what had been or might be;
only a warm, comforting sense of well-being.*

*But at other times, she could hear and see and smell and taste the
world about her, the one that was real and present and active even
though she lay dormant. She could see the faces of those she knew
and hear their words as they lived their daily lives while she slept.
The voices whispered and buzzed and told her of the fears and hopes
and joys and promises of the people she monitored in her subconscious, tracking their movements and reading their thoughts in a
slow, languid unraveling that was able to penetrate even the deepest
layers of her sleep. The effort came unbidden and as a consequence
of the magic that shaped her half-life sleep, so it was always there,
weaving its way through the stretches of darkness and sudden
bursts of dreaming and small moments of remembering. It was
there in the way that her breathing was there, a function of her*

body, a necessary reaction to her need to stay alive and informed within the confines of her strange and special sleep.

She drifted and spun, waiting for the time when she would be awakened. She flew unfettered, knowing that one day, when it was time, waking would come, brought about by a hand on her shoulder or a voice in her ear.

Or come instead when her own monitoring of the world told her that it was time . . .

Time . . .

Time . . .

Her eyes blinked open, and Khyber Elessedil, Ard Rhys of the Fourth Druid Order, came awake.

She lay wrapped within coverings in a chamber whose walls were layered with tapestries and whose windows were covered and sealed with heavy drapes. There were no lamps or candles in the room, and the light that seeped through past the edges of the drapes was pale and gray. It was either early morning or evening. She did not move at first, but lay collecting her thoughts and recovering her memories from where she had shelved them when she first entered the Druid Sleep. Years ago now, she guessed, but it was impossible to tell without talking to someone who had been awake and monitored time's passing while she slept.

How much had changed? How different was the world into which she had awoken from the one in which she had slept?

Something had summoned her from her sleep, a thought or a dream, a voice or an act, but a thing of such power and immediacy that it commanded her attention and demanded that she be present. No one had come to her; no one had disturbed her sleep. This was something else. This was raw instinct telling her it was time to come awake.

And so she had obeyed.

She sat up slowly, taking her time, lifting the covers away so she could sit on the edge of her bed and determine that her sense of balance and the strength of limbs and body were sufficient to allow her to function. When she was satisfied, she stood up and walked to the closest window and looked out. She was facing west and could see the sun just slipping behind the horizon as the shadows of the forest trees stretched toward Paranor's walls and towers with inky fingers.

She turned away and stood looking into the darkness of her chamber. She must discover why was she awake, what it was that in her dreams or subconscious musings had been so compelling.

She closed her eyes, centered herself, and waited.

Elfstones.

The word came unbidden, but she couldn't know its portent.

She walked to the dressing table, shedding her sleepwear as she went, soaked the washcloth that was always waiting next to the basin of water that was always kept fresh, and began to wash herself. When she was finished, she dried and dressed in fresh clothing chosen from her closet. Her Druid Sleep was ended. She was back in the real world to deal with whatever real problem was waiting.

She walked to the mirror and began to brush her long, once-dark hair, streaked now with gray, the years having caught up to her in spite of the temporary reprieves granted her by the Druid Sleep. She had used it five times since becoming Ard Rhys, each period chosen carefully and with consideration for how matters fared both within and without the walls of the Keep. She had been alive for almost 110 years, yet she looked 50. She glanced at the reflection of her mostly unlined face. Possibly even younger, she corrected herself. But she did not take the sleep out of vanity or a desire to prolong her life; it was out of need and worry. Before she could give herself over to the death that awaited them all, Druid Sleep or no, she needed to find the next Ard Rhys. Among the members of the order, among those who had come late into her service but had stayed true to their vows, she must find a new leader.

She wondered suddenly how many remained of those she had left behind.

She would know soon. She hoped all had stayed. Bombax, Aphenglow, Pleysia, Carrick, Rendellin, and Seersha—they were among the best of those who had served. All of those with whom she had begun the new order in the time of Grianne Ohmsford were gone. Age and circumstance had caught up to them. None slept the Druid Sleep save the Ard Rhys, so it was inevitable that at some point she would find herself alone.

But others had traveled this path before her, and so she did not complain. She had made the choice all those years ago. It was pointless to harbor regrets now.

She finished with her brushing and stood looking at her face: Elven to the core with all of the defining, distinctive features. An Elessedil, like Aphenglow, and it had made her think now and again that the young woman was the best choice to lead those who remained. But Aphenglow was conflicted and troubled by what she had done in choosing a life in the Druid order over one in the Elven community. The resentment and disappointment of the Elves shrouded and haunted her. She was not at peace, and Khyber did not think she could lead until she was.

The others were a mix of raw talent and dangerous flaws. But she did not care to consider the matter just now and so pushed it aside.

She was wrapped in her Druid robes and standing just inside the door, preparing to go out, when she heard the latch release and quickly stepped back.

Aphenglow appeared in the doorway and on seeing her was so startled she gave a small cry. "Mistress! I didn't . . . I thought . . ."

Khyber extended her arms in greeting. "It's all right, Aphen. I came awake on my own. Is that why you are here? To wake me?"

The young woman nodded. "My return from Arborlon is the reason for needing to do so, and I thought it should be me."

"Is it something about the Elfstones?"

Aphenglow looked shocked. "How did you know? I only just found the diary three days ago! But you already know?"

Khyber smiled. "I know only a little. You can tell me the rest. Are the others waiting on you? Good, then let's not keep them waiting any longer." She hesitated. "Tell me. How long have I been sleeping?"

"Five years, Mistress."

That long. She sighed, took the young Elf's arm in her own, and side by side they walked from the sleeping chamber into the waking world.

She was hungry, even though the sleep kept her sufficiently nourished, hydrated, and muscle-toned. But she put aside thoughts of food and drink and followed Aphenglow straight to the chamber where the others were gathered.

"Rendellin disappeared two years ago," Aphen was telling her as they neared the chamber doors, responding to her question about who still served the order. She saw Garroneck standing watch, face expressionless, only his eyes revealing a hint of surprise. "We looked," Aphen finished, "but we never found out what happened to him."

Bad things happened, Khyber thought. So, another gone. Now there were only five besides herself. The order was still too small and too weak. She needed to find a way to strengthen it.

She greeted Garroneck with a smile and a touch on his broad shoulder as he opened the door for her. Inside, the others were gathered about the table talking. They turned to look and went instantly silent before coming to their feet.

"She shouldn't have woken you, Mistress," Pleysia said at once.

"I woke without help." Khyber motioned for them to sit. "We have business to discuss, and we should do it now."

For the next hour, she listened to a reading of Aleia Omarosian's diary followed by a heated discussion about its validity and intent. She let the others argue until she felt everything new or interesting had been said, and then brought the discussion to a halt.

"What are your thoughts, Mistress?" Carrick asked her.

"My thoughts?" She smiled. "In the main, I don't think you want to know. As for the diary, it is possible we have discovered what happened to the missing Elf-stones. More important, there is at least a remote chance we might be able to track them down. Aphen was right in bringing the diary to Paranor, and I am proud that she took the risk. If she had been caught, there is every chance we would not have seen her again. I am also proud of her for defending herself and protecting the diary twice when she was attacked."

Aphenglow blushed deeply. "Thank you, Mistress."

"I regret that you were forced to kill a man. But it is clear evidence of the determination of those involved. I would not expect that these attacks were undertaken solely for the purpose of harming you, although we cannot dismiss the possibility out of hand. But I think it more likely it was the diary they were after—that even without knowing exactly what you had found, they suspected it had value. Did you sense that you were being watched at any time during your research, Aphen?"

The young woman shook her head. "My guard was up; my wards were always in place. I made certain to secure the rooms in which I worked, and I checked my preparations each day. I was always alone save when either my sister or my uncle came to see how I was, which was infrequently. I did not sense another's presence the entire time I was working. I could not have been spied upon without knowing it."

"You were there for almost a year. Someone might have found a way."

Aphenglow shook her head. "I would have sensed it. Anyway, who would go to such trouble?"

"Someone who was afraid you might find something useful regarding the old magic and either not give it to them or give it to the wrong people."

Aphenglow shook her head, troubled and uncertain. The idea was appalling, even now.

"Do you think the Elves themselves might have done this?" Seersha asked quickly. "Attack the King's granddaughter?"

"Or someone who hates the Druids," Bombax broke in. "Someone who would like to see the order disbanded and their magic confiscated and destroyed."

He explained what had happened the previous day in Arishaig with the death of the old Prime Minister and the election of Drustan Chazhul. Khyber listened and nodded. "Perhaps. Anything is possible. What matters is that someone thinks what Aphen has brought us has value."

"Or might have value," Pleysia corrected. "The attempt to steal the diary might have been a protective measure to assure that nothing gets taken out of those storerooms, no matter the value."

"A preventive act?" Khyber rose and walked over to the chamber doors and opened them. "Would you find something for me to eat and drink?" she asked Garroneck as he stepped forward to see what she required. "Bring it here."

When he was gone, she dismissed the others, all save Aphenglow, whom she asked to remain behind. With the young Elven woman sitting across from her, she read through the entirety of the diary, pausing only to eat and drink when Garroneck brought her hot food and cold ale.

"Where is Woostra?" she asked her Troll Captain as he was leaving. "He is still with us, isn't he?"

Garroneck nodded. "Very much so. He is probably down in the library, poring through his books. Do you wish to see him?"

She nodded, and the big Troll departed to find him. Woostra was her personal secretary and the keeper of the Druid records. When she wanted to know something about the history of the Four Lands, she went first to him. She finished her meal while waiting, feeling a measure of strength and contentment return as a result. She had nearly finished reading through the rest of the diary when Woostra finally rushed in, somewhat in a state of dishevelment.

"Mistress, I didn't realize you were awake." Rail-thin and bent, he might have weighed a little more than a wool travel cloak soaked through. Hair stuck out of his large ears and tunneled down his neck. His chin hooked up and his nose hooked down. *Odd looking* didn't begin to cover it, but his memory was astounding and his work ethic faultless. "Are you well? You look perplexed. Do you need help with something? You must tell me at once!"

That was Woostra, somewhat overbearing but always anxious to help. "I want to know if you have ever come across the name Aleia Omarosian in our books and papers."

Woostra assumed a thoughtful pose, gaze directed outward through the nearest window in a thousand-yard stare. He shook his head. "I don't think so."

"Will you have a fresh look to see if there might be a mention somewhere? Look, as well, for references to the Elfstones. Any of the Elfstones, not just the blue ones. Take your time. Do a thorough search."

"Mistress!" He straightened to his full height, which just about brought him up to Aphenglow's shoulder. "I am not aware that I have ever performed any other kind!"

Looking misunderstood and put upon, he wheeled about and left the room without glancing back.

"Awfully thin-skinned, isn't he?" Khyber said, mostly to herself.

She went back to reading the diary, finished a short time later, and leaned back in her chair. "I think this is real, Aphen."

Aphenglow allowed herself a relieved smile. "I'm pleased. But what are we to do with it? Pleysia is right. It doesn't give us any clue as to where the missing Elfstones might be found. The Darkling boy might have taken them to his home city, but he could just as easily have taken them somewhere else. If Woostra doesn't find a mention in our records of a sighting of the Elfstones at a later time, we have nowhere to start a search. Perhaps I should go back and search the Elven histories again, this time looking for a mention of Aleia."

"Perhaps." Khyber thought a moment. "But I don't want to risk you being attacked again."

"I'm not afraid."

Khyber smiled in spite of herself. "I know that. You are braver even than Bombax and twice as brave as me."

Aphenglow blushed. "I doubt that. You must be thinking of Pleysia."

"Pleysia?" She kept to herself the first words that came to mind. Better that her thoughts remained hidden. "Sit here a moment while I move about a bit, Aphen. The Druid Sleep has left me stiff and achy."

She rose and walked to the far end of the chamber, looking out the window at the coming night. It was almost fully dark now, the sky gone deep blue, the first stars coming out to the north, shadows overlapping across the parapets and towers of the Keep. Torchlight blazed in tiny pockets atop the walls, and in the distance the horizon was a blood-red band of light fighting off the night's descending blackness. She could hear the sound of the night birds and the soft tinkle of wind chimes.

What should she do?

To ignore the diary was unthinkable. She had to discover if the lost Elfstones still existed and, if they did, where they might be found. She had to gain possession of them for the Druid order before they fell into hands that would not use them well. Elfstones were a powerful magic, and while she had given back the seeking-Stones long ago, believing when she did so that the Elves would keep them safe and use them wisely, she had kept the Black Elfstone—the most powerful of them all and the only other Stone that had ever been recovered—believing its magic better off in the hands of the Druids.

Which was what she believed about all magic.

It wasn't that the other Races were incapable of good judgment and clear thinking. It wasn't that the Druids possessed special insight or better reasoning, though she believed they did. The difference lay in the depth and breadth of commitment to a way of life that respected what magic could do and how it should be managed. Only the Druids had given their lives to this cause. Only the Druids understood and respected the power that magic offered, both good and bad. Only the Druids studied endlessly what history had to teach about the mistakes and misuses that had doomed so many before them.

To abdicate magic of any sort to a political entity or even to any one of the Races that populated the Four Lands, no matter the promises offered or the feelings expressed, was a failing of monumental proportions, and she would not be part of it.

Everyone who knew of the missing Elfstones, Races and individuals alike, had been seeking them since their disappearance in the time of Faerie. But no one had found them. No one had found even a trace. Not a word written. Not the briefest glimpse. Nothing.

What made her think it would be any different this time?

She walked back to where Aphenglow sat watching her and stopped in front of her.

"Do you know what to do?" Aphen asked softly.

Khyber Elessedil shook her head. "But I know who to ask."

6

KHYBER SLEPT LITTLE THAT NIGHT, HER MIND roiling with possibilities and the plans for bringing them to fruition. She walked the halls of the Keep alone, thinking of the missing Elfstones and how finding them might help the Druids in their efforts to bring the Races together in a peaceful alliance. They had been at war for so long—struggles like the war on the Prekkendorran, which had lasted for more than fifty years. If the magic of the Elfstones could in some way serve to contain such wars or even keep the Races from instigating such conflicts, she would have accomplished something that no Ard Rhys ever had.

She basked in the warmth of the idea one minute and went cold with her doubts about the reliability of the diary in the next.

Once, she came across Pleysia sitting alone in a nook writing at a small table, but Pleysia failed to see her and she turned another way to protect her solitude. This was not a night when she wanted to visit with others. This was a night to consider what she would do on the morrow.

At daybreak, after advising Garroneck what that was and asking him to make the necessary preparations, she washed, dressed, ate her breakfast alone, and then summoned the Druids to the courtyard that housed the airships. Woostra was there as well, restless and ill at ease as he waited to see what she intended. Garroneck had refitted the *Wend-A-Way* with supplies and a fresh store of diapson crystals, and was working with two of his guardsmen to fasten the radian draws to the light sheaths from their links on the railing to the parse tubes. The ship was already straining at its anchor ropes in response to the power running through the lines and filling out the sheaths.

"Young ones," she said to her followers, her friends and fellow Druids, after drawing them close. "After thinking it through, I have decided I need to seek advice from those who know more than I, from those who have access to secrets kept from me. I go to the Hadeshorn to speak with the spirits of the dead. Perhaps one of the Elder Druids will know something more than we do and consent to speak to me."

"That form of contact is dangerous, Mistress," Seersha said at once. "You have never done this, and there is no one to teach you how."

Khyber smiled at the young Dwarf's concern. "All true, Seersha. And yet there is no need for you to worry. An Ard Rhys knows instinctively what is required to summon the dead. The spirits of the dead cannot physically harm the living. Nor can their words. I will be fine."

"Which of us will go with you?" the other pressed. "You will need at least one or two."

"Thank you, Seersha, but I will need no one save Garroneck and his guards for this journey. I want the rest of you to stay here and continue your discussions about the diary. Try to think of ways we might make use of its contents. Look for anything we might have missed. I will be back within two days' time."

"I don't like the idea of you going alone," Seersha insisted.

"Neither do I," Aphenglow agreed.

"But I have to." Khyber gave them each a hard look. "It is required of me. Garroneck will be enough. Now, go on about your work. Woostra!"

She dismissed them by turning away and joining her personal secretary at the fringes of the little gathering. He bowed deeply, waiting.

She pulled him upright. "Don't forget. I want you to find out something about this girl, this Aleia Omarosian. I want information about who she was and what became of her. Am I understood?"

He nodded quickly. "Yes, Mistress."

"Then do as I ask before I return. Find something. Anything."

Then she turned from him, and because she didn't want to prolong her leaving she walked over to where Garroneck stood waiting. The big Troll's rough, impassive face revealed nothing of what he was thinking, and he was quick to offer her the rope ladder to climb. She went up it swiftly, still strong and nimble in spite of her years. She climbed through the slot in the railing and waited for Garroneck to join her.

"Are we ready?"

"On your signal."

"Then lift us away. I'll take the helm. I feel like doing something. Maybe I can still do this."

"This, and a great deal more, unless I am mistaken."

His deadpan voice made her smile. "Let's hope so."

She gave a quick wave to the members of her Druid order as she walked to the cluster of thruster levers and steering gears, but she did not stop to look closely at them. She didn't trust herself with what she might see on their faces. Instead, she set herself in place at the controls. As the anchor ropes were freed, she eased the skimmer out of its berth and into the air, wheeling south toward Kennon Pass and the far side of the Dragon's Teeth. The *Wend-A-Way* responded smoothly, flying over Paranor's walls and battlements, her towers and spires, her courtyards and ramps, and finally the deep woods surrounding them all. Sunshine beamed down out of a cloudless sky, and the wind was soft and cool on her skin.

She glanced back once to see the other Druids disbanding and moving indoors until only a couple of the Troll guards remained.

She sighed, watching it happen. It was as if her leaving made no difference to anything, and yet she could not quite shrug away the feeling that she was about to begin a journey that in the end would be life changing.

They flew on through the remainder of the day, traveling south through the Kennon before turning east, then tracking the wall of the Dragon's Teeth, brief glimmerings of the Rainbow Lake visible to the south through mist and haze, the land spreading away in a patchwork carpet. By midafternoon, they had crossed over the Mermidon River where it angled south through the valley formed by the Runne Mountains and could see the land ahead turn stark and bare as the mountains broadened and the woods disappeared.

Such a beautiful, wild place, Khyber thought as she surveyed the passing landscape in the winding down of the day. Ahead, the mountain peaks rose in jagged spikes, their slopes layered as far north as the eye could see. Night was sliding out of the east in a dark wave, swallowing everything as it advanced. Behind her, the sun was edging below a horizon dominated by the broad sweep of the plains of Callahorn and Streleheim south and north respectively of the Mermidon, the whole of it green and flat and still bright with sunshine.

She found herself thinking of other times, long since

past, and other trips taken to faraway places on undertakings similar to this one. She could remember the details in spite of her age and time's passing—especially those in which Grianne Ohmsford, who had been Ard Rhys before her, had been involved. If not for Grianne, her brother Bek, and his son Penderrin, Khyber would still be living in the Westland, gone home to Arborlon and her family, and not be Ard Rhys of the Fourth Druid Order. But the events surrounding the disappearance of Grianne into the Forbidding and the ill-fated efforts of the Druid Shadea A'Ru to take control of the order had changed everything for Khyber and all those who had stood with Grianne against Shadea and her allies.

In the end, Grianne had prevailed over Shadea, but the Druids had been decimated, and in the aftermath of Grianne's disappearance Khyber had become Ard Rhys and leader of the Fourth Order. It was not a position she had sought, but one she had accepted out of a sense of obligation for the Druid future and toward those who had fought so hard to see it secured. She was more accomplished in the use of magic than any of the others by then, and she knew she was the most likely candidate. So it came down to whether she would accept the responsibility she was being asked to assume or turn away and leave it for another to shoulder.

She knew right away what her decision would be. Her friendships and her personal interest in and commitment to the study of magic persuaded her that she needed to do whatever she could to preserve the Druid Order. To have come so far and paid so heavy a price only to see it all have been for nothing was not something she could live with.

So she did what she had to do, what she was expected to do, and what she felt she owed to all those who had fought beside Grianne.

She smiled sadly, thinking of it. It seemed so long ago. All those she had known in that time, all who had been so influential in shaping her life, were gone—dead, save for Grianne, who had been transformed and was now something else entirely. She wondered about her sometimes, and how she had felt when she had given up her human form. She wondered if Grianne regretted it, if she felt her life now had fresh meaning, and if she still believed she had done the right thing in changing. Khyber couldn't say, and it didn't seem likely that she would ever know. But she would have liked it if she could.

She would have liked seeing Grianne one more time.

She would have liked seeing any of them.

Garroneck appeared beside her, caught her eye, and pointed ahead through the deepening gloom to where the mountains split apart. There a long, steep trail wound upward from the foothills to the summit of a distant ridge, where it formed an entry into the Valley of Shale and the Hadeshorn. She nodded her understanding and shifted the bow of the *Wend-A-Way* left toward the ascending slope. Pulling back on the thrusters, she brought the skimmer to a crawl and eased her skyward toward the split in the mountain rock. The other members of the Druid Guard were at the radian draws, ready to detach their ends and haul them in for stowing.

Garroneck gestured, indicating the helm. "Shall I, Mistress?"

She stepped away, giving him control, and walked forward to the bow where she could watch the high end of the pass appear. She searched the landscape for movement, but the terrain was barren and empty everywhere, nothing but boulders and scrub grass and rutted earth. It was miserable, blasted ground, forbidding enough that nothing that breathed or moved would give much thought to doing more than passing through quickly. Ahead, far beyond the entry, an odd glow rose from within the mountains, a strange greenish light that grew in intensity as the darkness deepened.

The Hadeshorn.

The entry to the world of the spirits of the dead.

Garroneck and his Trolls anchored *Wend-A-Way* just below the narrow defile that led into the mountains, dropped a rope ladder, and helped Khyber climb through the railing. She didn't need their help, but didn't want to refuse it, either. When she was down, she walked forward several yards to stand alone with Garroneck.

"Wait here for me. Keep watch. You are exposed on these slopes to anyone passing by, especially someone in an airship—at least until it gets darker than it is now."

"I will keep watch, Mistress." The big Troll cast a quick glance about the empty skies. "I think we will be safe enough."

He handed her the black staff she preferred, and she took it from him with a nod. "I won't be back before morning. Don't worry for me."

He blinked. "Should I stop breathing, as well?"

She put a hand on his arm, squeezed gently, and turned away. "I'll be careful."

She went up the steep slope using the staff for balance, picking her way over the loose rocks, taking her time so as not to slip and fall. She had discarded her Druid robes and was wearing pants and a tunic, a brace of long knives strapped to her waist. She commanded sufficient magic that she could protect herself if she was threatened in any way, although she doubted she would need to. The Valley of Shale was never visited by anyone but stray travelers eager to find a way out and Druids like herself who were intent on speaking with the dead. She believed she would encounter neither this night.

Within the hour she arrived at the head of the pass

and began working her way through the long, twisting defile that led to the valley. The night was dark and still, and while there were stars visible in the ribbon of sky above the cliff walls, the moon was down. She stopped frequently to drink from her waterskin and took time when she did to listen to the absence of night sounds. Her senses sought the presence of other life, but each time they assured her she was alone. She created, organized, and reviewed the questions she intended to ask whatever spirits came to her, and then she revised them. She considered what it was she wanted to learn and how she could be assured she would get the answers she needed, knowing that phrasing was so important.

But in the end she let it all drift away, aware that it came down to the willingness of the spirits of the dead to speak directly. She knew they seldom gave clear answers—if they answered at all—because clarity for the dead was different than it was for the living. The dead knew more of life, for they had lived it and passed beyond it and could look back on it at their leisure. But their ability to speak of what they saw was limited. They often responded in riddles and asked questions in turn, and they almost never gave a clear and precise answer.

So she would have to work hard to find out what she needed to know about Aleia Omarosian and the missing Elfstones.

She would have to work very hard indeed.

The air was colder this high up, and she wished she had thought to bring a travel cloak to ward off the chill. She hunched her shoulders and clutched the black staff close against her body, but nothing helped much. She glanced up at the clear, bright sky, the cold so sharp-edged and penetrating that she could almost see it. When she exhaled, her breath frosted the air in front of her.

Too cold for her to continue for long, she decided. She had to do something to warm herself.

She held out her staff, used her magic to coat one end with pitch, and then set the pitch afire. It would reveal her to anyone looking, but she had already decided that chance encounters were unlikely. She trudged on, the flaming end of the staff held out before her, working her way down the defile, her path blocked repeatedly by boulders and landslides she was forced to either go around or climb over. It had been a long time since anyone had passed this way. Certainly no Druid had come through in the years that she had been Ard Rhys unless they had done so in secret.

Finally, midnight having come and gone, she reached the end of the defile and found herself looking down into the Valley of Shale. It was a broad, shallow depression perhaps a quarter mile wide, its walls littered with pieces of obsidian that shone like black glass beneath the light of the stars. At its center was the lake they called the Hadeshorn, its waters flat and still and vaguely greenish from light emanating far down within their depths. The light pulsed sluggishly, but the waters never moved.

She took a seat at the edge of the bowl, just beyond the beginnings of the field of obsidian, choosing a flat shelf of rock and wedging the black staff into a crevice off to one side, there to await the hour just before dawn when the shades of Druids dead and gone would be most likely to respond to a summons from the living. She watched the still waters of the lake and the glimmerings of the rock and the flat black of the sky and its stars until she fell asleep sitting up. She slept without dreaming, waking often to shift positions, trying to gain a small measure of warmth from the dying fire of the staff. Her mind felt sluggish and weary, and the muscles and joints of her body ached. A couple of times she drank from the waterskin, but never too much and only when she needed the hydration. She didn't know how long she would be here or to what extent the water would sustain her, so conservation of her only source of fluids was important.

Drinking from the waters of the Hadeshorn was not an option. A single swallow was instant death.

When she sensed the night coming to a close, long hours and repeated wakings later, when the pitch had burned away and the staff had gone dark and the stars had shifted in the sky and signaled the morning's approach, she climbed to her feet and began to walk down to the Hadeshorn. The slopes were made treacherous by the loose rock and the uncertain footing, so she took her time, leaning heavily on the staff. Her head had cleared and she felt oddly renewed even though she had gotten so little real rest. She was ready for this, she told herself. She was strong and determined, and she would find a way to achieve her goals.

At the base of the valley, close enough to see the waters of the Hadeshorn clearly, she stopped for a final survey of her surroundings. She was still alone, the valley empty of life, the air crisp and cool and very still. Satisfied that she was safe from interruptions, she continued on until she was standing at the very edge of the lake.

She looked out across a glistening expanse that was as still as stone.

I am here. Speak to me.

The waters sensed her presence and stirred ever so slightly.

She conjured a form of magic she had mastered long ago and sent it flowing through the black staff. When the staff was ablaze with light, she dipped one end into the Hadeshorn. Instantly the waters began to churn, the movement increasing, growing in power until there were waves crashing and spray flying everywhere. She held her ground when the waters came at her as if to attack. She ignored the spray that coated her face and the pulsing of the greenish light, which had grown in force.

But when she heard the voices lift out of the ether in wails and cries that chilled her to the bone, she began to shiver violently. It felt as if her skin were being scraped from her body, and she knew what it meant. The dead were coming to see who had disturbed them, and they were not happy. The cacophony of sound grew until it filled the valley and threatened to bury her. She could pick out individual voices, ones she thought she knew, even though she could not put names to them. The connection of living and dead was there, and the past was brought back into the present as memories were torn from the places in her mind where she kept them hidden.

Then the waters heaved wildly, and the dead surfaced. They burst from the waters in droves, thousands of them, rising into the still dark night, white and ethereal, drained of life and substance, re-formed as diaphanous shades, their voices joined in an endless scream.

She was close to breaking at that point, all her preparations and the steeling of her resolve shattered and vanished, and she felt naked and exposed. Everything about her was revealed in an instant and nothing left hidden. The dead knew her. The dead could see all she was and all she ever would be, and it was terrifying.

"Someone speak to me!" she screamed, trying to hold on, wanting this to be over.

Her words had reached compliant ears, and the spirits of the dead scattered like moths caught in a sudden wind, their wails following after them, switching like lizard tails. In the wake of their passing, the waters of the Hadeshorn thrashed with new fury, and a black form heaved upward from their center, a giant rising from the depths, growing in size until it dwarfed Khyber ten times over.

Silence returned, undisturbed save for traces of the wailings and the hissing of spray. The black figure, huge and forbidding, stood upon the waters as if their surface somehow provided it with solid footing.

–Do you know me–

She did. Instinctively, immediately, and unquestionably.

"You are Allanon," she said.

7

♦

THE SHADE OF ALLANON GLIDED CLOSER ACROSS the hissing, roiling waters, black robes pulled close, hood covering everything but his terrible face. In life Allanon was said to have been frightening, a man with a dark temper and a darker history who had no hesitation about using either to intimidate. That he could reinforce his reputation with a command of magic unequaled in the annals of the Druid Histories cloaked him with the trappings of legend.

To Khyber Elessedil he seemed no less intimidating in death than the stories reported he had been in life.

–Speak to me, Ard Rhys–

So he knew her. Khyber felt exposed and vulnerable before him, helpless to protect herself even though there was no reason to believe she needed to. The spirits of the dead were said to reflect the substance of their lives, and no one had been more of a presence in life than this man. Strong features shaded by a short black beard and eyes that seemed to look right through you—there was nothing of weakness apparent in Allanon, nothing to suggest that he would ever equivocate or doubt himself. Even now, when she compared him with the other more transparent and ephemeral spirits, he seemed whole and unchanged.

"I would speak with you about the missing Elfstones, Allanon," she managed finally.

–Speak to me then–

"Do you know, from there in the dark world into which you have passed, where in this world of light the Elfstones may be found?"

–Where they have been for countless centuries–

"But where exactly?"

–Hidden. Shrouded from all eyes. Ask me something else–

"There is a diary, found by one of our order, that tells of a theft of all the Elfstones but the seeking-Stones, back in the time of Faerie. A girl wrote it. It was her Darkling lover who stole the talismans from the Elves. What do you know of this?"

–Nothing–

He had gone motionless now, hanging there in the darkness, illuminated by the strange light that emanated from the depths of the Hadeshorn. When he spoke, his voice did not reflect the weakness of those spirits who wailed and bemoaned their fate. Instead it was strong and hard-edged.

"We would go in search of these Elfstones for the Druid order so they could be used in our efforts to secure a lasting peace in the Four Lands. They would be used to protect the Races from the creatures of the Void, from the demons that escaped the initial creation of the Forbidding."

The shade's hiss seemed to reflect the sounds of the waters over which it hovered, its breath exhaling in a cloud of steam.

–Foolish talk, Ard Rhys. There is no lasting peace. There is no protection you can offer to those who will not help themselves. All our struggles do is hold back a tide that will finally and inevitably sweep us away–

She felt her heart sink. Allanon's dark worldview did

not allow for hope. He saw the end as inevitable and the battle of good and evil as nothing but a holding action. He might not even accept that the struggle was worth the effort. Yet even so, even though his words were flat and empty of emotion, she could sense something more behind them.

"That may be," she said finally. "But does that mean we should quit trying? Should we give in?"

—Answer your own question, Ard Rhys. Should you?—

"I don't think so."

—But you are not certain—

"I am certain. I won't quit. The members of my Druid order will not quit. Have you, in death, decided we should? Do you tell us we must follow your lead?"

—I tell you nothing. The dead can only question or suggest—

"Then I say again we do not quit. Nor should you, if that is what you intend. Instead, you should help us."

—You must help yourself, Ard Rhys. You are more able than I—

There was a challenge in his words, a veiled threat. But she sensed that he was still waiting, hoping for something more. Her mind raced, trying to discover what it was.

"I am willing to do that," she answered. "To do whatever is necessary. I would begin my search, but I don't know where to start. I have a story and the name of a girl and nothing more. I don't even know if any of what is written is real. The tone suggests it is, but there are questions anyway. There cannot help but be questions." She paused. "Do you know of this girl? Aleia Omarosian—that is her name. She is the one who wrote the diary. Do you know her?"

For the first time, the shade of Allanon did not answer right away.

—I know something of her—

She waited. "What is it you know?"

The shade did not answer. She contained her exasperation as the delay lengthened. "Did she write the diary? Is the diary true? Is there more that she can tell us of the Darkling boy who stole the Elfstones? Is there anything at all?"

Still the shade was silent, perhaps contemplating, perhaps weighing what answering might cost, perhaps doing something else entirely. She kept her peace, not wanting to disturb whatever debate was taking place, not wanting to do anything that would cost her a chance to learn even one new thing that could be useful.

When he spoke again, he surprised her.

–Have you considered the cost of your questions? To yourself? To others you care about? To the people you hope to save?–

She had no idea what he was talking about, and she hesitated before answering. "The Druids are prepared to give up their lives if it will help advance the efforts of the order. You know this. As for those we seek to help, I think that doing nothing might cause them more grief still."

–What if your efforts in this undertaking are for nothing? What if you are doomed to fail?–

"Then at least we will have tried and not let fate and chance dictate the outcome."

–Fate and chance may do so anyway–

"I know that. To some extent, I am sure they will. But there will be some things we can influence, that we can change or make better or illuminate in ways that teach and guide us."

–Brave words–

"Would you have us do nothing, Allanon? I'll ask it again."

It was a bold, almost accusatory question, but she could not help herself. She wanted a better response from him, a more positive and encouraging one. She would not leave here burdened with doubt and guilt. She would not leave it so. If that were all he had to offer, she would have been better off not coming.

"Speak to me!" she demanded.

But the shade said nothing. The seconds slipped past, and she wondered if she had lost her chance, if she had angered him sufficiently that he would refuse to help at all. There was nothing to make him do so. He was of the dead, and the dead cared little for the living, resentful and jealous that the living still possessed what had been taken forever from them.

Finally, Allanon moved, his black cloak shimmering. Slowly, he began to withdraw from her, sliding back across the Hadeshorn.

"Don't, Allanon!" she called after him. "Don't go!"

His voice hissed softly.

–For now, I must. Wait for me to come again–

Then his black form sank from sight and was gone, leaving her to stare at the empty lake as the first tinges of sunlight crested the jagged rims of the distant mountains and stained the waters brilliant gold.

In Paranor, Aphenglow rose, dressed, and left Bombax sleeping in her bed. She had missed him terribly in the time she had been away in Arborlon, but not so much, it appeared, as he had missed her. At some point, they would be wed and she would bear his children. But that was in the distant future, for the Druids were not allowed to partner formally. Partnering for Aphenglow, as for most Elves, was just a word. The Elven kind bonded with hearts and a sense of commitment far stronger than what could be written or spoken. It was enough if you knew that your choice was for life. She and Bombax had promised themselves to each other long ago, shortly after meeting, knowing even then that they were meant to be together. Their union was as strong now as it would be when officially recorded or celebrated in public, and they were pledged never to belong to anyone but each other.

So she slept with him as a wife would with her husband, and she would be true to him until death.

She thought this as she left him and walked the empty halls of the Keep, searching for a place to begin her day. She carried with her the diary, intending to read it through once again, to think carefully on Aleia Omarosian's words, to consider all possible ramifications. The Ard Rhys had asked them to look once again at everything, and she would do that now.

Or shortly after brewing tea and eating toasted bread for her morning meal, anyway.

After rereading the contents of the diary, she spent the better part of the day conversing with the others about possible interpretations of the phrasing and ideas for starting points in their search. But all of them had the same read on the diary's entries and no fresh ideas for where to begin a search. Aphenglow kept thinking she was missing something, but try as she might she could not decide what that something was.

The day was nearly done when she trudged up the long stairways to the rooms that housed the Druid histories and provided Woostra with his working space. The hallway leading to these rooms was already dappled with twilight shadows when she reached them, the sunlight gone so far west that it cast almost no light. Soon, triggered by the descending darkness, the smokeless lamps would begin to burn, giving a warmer glow to spaces that now already seemed cold and abandoned.

She was almost to the library doors before she glimpsed the soft glow of lamps Woostra must have already lit. She knocked and waited.

"Come," Woostra called from somewhere inside.

He was deep in a warren of rooms that housed the Druid papers, poring through sheaves of writings and clusters of files. It looked chaotic to Aphenglow, but Woostra seemed untroubled by the clutter. His head buried in an ancient tome, shoulders hunched as he bent over his worktable, he didn't even bother to look up at her as she entered.

"What is it?"

She sat down on the end of a bench that was otherwise stacked with books and papers and files. "I just wondered if you had found anything."

"No, I haven't. Anyway, I don't report to you. I report to the Ard Rhys."

He was so abrupt about it she was taken aback. "I was just asking."

She got up and started to walk out, and she was almost to the door when he called after her. "Aphenglow, wait." She turned around. His head had lifted out of the book he had been absorbed in and there was a hint of contrition on his lean features. "I didn't mean that. I'm sorry."

"That's all right. I know you're busy. You don't need me bothering you while you are trying to do your work."

"It's not you who's causing me trouble. It's someone else. Close the door. Come back in and take a seat. I've something to tell you."

Intrigued, she did as he asked and resumed her position on the bench. "Is something wrong?"

The narrow, bladed features wrinkled in distaste. "Something is always wrong. That's the trouble with this order. Or maybe all Druid orders. Something is always wrong. And usually we cannot do anything about it. We just nudge it aside and hope for the best."

He seemed genuinely distressed, but she had no idea

what he was talking about. "Is there something in particular that needs fixing?"

He shook his head dismissively. "No, no. I'm just rambling. I get discouraged sometimes. I expect you do, too. We are faced with such obstacles, and we have so little support for our work. The Ard Rhys has given her entire life to helping the Races and they barely acknowledge her efforts. Mostly, they just want her—all of us, for that matter—gone. I might be only a scribe, not a Druid like the rest of you, but I have adopted your commitment and effort as my own. I have become one of you in all the ways that matter."

She smiled gently. "You have, Woostra. No one would argue that. You have done more for us than anyone, and I cannot imagine how we would manage without you."

Her words seemed to perk him up a bit, and he mumbled a few self-effacing phrases as a way of putting the matter to rest.

"We're all tired and discouraged sometimes," she added. "You are not alone in feeling that way."

"Well, that might be so, but it still isn't any reason for snapping at people." He backed away from his worktable and swung his chair around so he was facing her. "I let personal feelings intrude on common sense. I was distressed over something that happened earlier and took it out on you. And I shouldn't have."

"It's all right," she repeated.

He shook his head dismissively. "Enough. On to other matters. I have something important to tell you, as I said. I have been searching our own histories and papers, and in the course of doing so I found something unexpected about Aleia Omarosian."

He leaned forward. "I had thought that what I would find would have something to do with her parents, who were King and Queen of the Elven people at different points in their lives, the one right after the other. I also thought it was odd Aleia died so young and there was no explanation as to what had become of her. It seemed to me that if anything were to be found, it would be in the chronicles of those times, in the records of the families. What we have is incomplete and rather scant, but I thought there was a chance. But do you know what, Aphen?"

She shook her head. "What?"

He paused. "Now you must promise me first. I have a duty to report my findings to the Ard Rhys, and technically I shouldn't tell anyone else before I tell her—not even one of her Druid followers. But I like you and trust you, and you were the one who brought the diary here in the first place. So that gives you special dispensation, in my opinion. Still, I need your word. Until I speak of this to the Ard Rhys, you must keep it to yourself. Tell no one, not even Bombax. Can you do that?"

"I can," she said at once. "I promise I will not tell anyone." She gave him a wry smile. "Especially not Bombax."

"That's good enough for me." Woostra rubbed his bony chin. "So it turns out I was looking in the wrong place. What I wanted wasn't to be found in the records of the Elven Kings and Queens. It was right here."

He took the ancient tome he had been studying when she entered and handed it to her, pointing at an entry.

The lettering at the top of the page spelled out a single word.

Ellcrys

Aphenglow bent close and began to read.

Khyber Elessedil slept most of the day, curled up close by the shoreline of the Hadeshorn while the sun crept out of the eastern horizon and slowly worked its way across the sky toward twilight. She fell asleep not long after the departure of the shade of Allanon, exhausted from the previous day. Facing Allanon's ghost had been stressful, and she still wasn't certain when she woke at sunset if he intended to help her.

She could assume that his promise to return indicated he would at least consider answering some of her questions, but the extent of his willingness remained in doubt. He'd told her almost nothing of value when they talked before, and his recalcitrant attitude toward and outright disdain of her commitment to the tenets of the Fourth Druid Order suggested he was less than enthusiastic about what she was attempting. Dismissive, in point of fact. She knew he was a hard, secretive man; she had read the chronicles of his time and knew he had been the only Druid alive when the Sword of Shannara was recovered and brought to bear against the Warlock Lord. She had read how he led the Elven struggle to withstand the collapse of the Forbidding and repel the invasion of the escaping demons. Finally, she had read how he'd died in his quest to destroy the Ildatch, killed by a terrible creature called a Jachyra. His death had marked the end of any Druid presence for three hundred years.

She had read it all, and she could tell from those readings that Allanon had been a powerful influence on the Races during his life. He had fought for their survival and died doing so. Nothing of what she had discovered suggested that he would be any different in death than he had been in life.

But she had hoped he might be more sympathetic to her struggle and consider trying to do something to help her.

When sunset approached and she was awake again and at least marginally rested, she rose and ate and drank from her small supply of provisions. She had come prepared to spend more than a single day in her efforts to summon one among the dead who would help her. That it was Allanon who had appeared had given her hope and raised her expectations that her needs were recognized and embraced. It was only in the unsettling aftermath of their talk that she wondered if she had been mistaken.

But she resumed her place at the water's edge and waited as he had commanded, hopeful that this time she might gain more from their meeting. If he reappeared at all, she added, her doubts nudging at her like a rock in her boot pressing into her sole. The sun slipped below the horizon and a scattering of stars came out. Khyber settled herself to wait, recounting over and over what she knew about Aleia Omarosian and the theft of the Stones.

Doubts plagued her, and for the first time a sense of inadequacy took root. She was Ard Rhys and a proven leader with years of life experience in the study and use of magic. She had survived much during those years and had guided the Druid order with a steady hand. But her followers were few and mostly untested. They were brave and they were committed, but they were also young. Pleysia, at thirty-six, was the oldest, and that was not old at all. Even if Khyber found a way to go and was given a map to follow, how dangerous would it be to make the journey, and how prepared were her Druids to undertake it? She did not feel easy in her heart at the thought of it; she did not think them much prepared at all.

But then others before her had undertaken equally dangerous challenges and completed them. Others had faced terrible risks and overcome them—many much younger even than Aphenglow. She shouldn't assume it would be different this time. She shouldn't be too quick to think that her followers were unequal to what might be demanded of them. They couldn't know what they were capable of until they were actually tested. None of them.

One day soon, they would find out, and she wasn't particularly eager for that day to come.

As the twilight deepened and night set in, she prepared herself for the long wait until the hour just before sunrise, when she assumed the Shade of Allanon would come—if it were coming at all. So she was surprised when in the first hour of true night, the waters of the Hadeshorn abruptly began to boil and steam, and the familiar sluggish swirling began its slow, clockwise motion. The voices of the dead lifted and intensified, filling the air and blanketing the valley in a harsh cacophony. The waters heaved in response, and hundreds of white forms rose through the surface and into the air, circling like birds.

She sat up quickly and clambered to her feet, shocked by the unexpectedness of it, wondering why Allanon was coming so soon.

Then his shade was there, a knife blade skimming the waters in a smooth, clean motion, a two-dimensional form that quickly broadened into something more substantial. Soon he dwarfed her once more, grown into a giant, gliding to a halt before her, hanging just above the waters, his black-cloaked form motionless. She could see his dark face and the strange glimmer of his eyes as they fixed on her, and she felt her heart go cold. The eyes held her pinned against the valley's obsidian floor, and even if she had tried she could not have moved away.

–Ard Rhys. I have spoken with Aleia Omarosian. She hides much from me and what she tells me cannot be entirely trusted. But I will tell it to you anyway. You will judge for yourself and do what you feel you must–

She waited, breathless. The shade seemed to be considering what it would say.

—What was written in the diary is true. It happened as she wrote it. She left the diary for her parents to find, after she was gone. She would not say where she had gone or why. But her early death suggests she knew her life was almost over. She was leaving, and she did not want to leave without telling her parents what she had done—

So it was real. Khyber was strangely exhilarated. "Did she know anything of where the Elfstones were? Or what happened to them after the Darkling boy took them?"

—She said they were lost to people like herself—

"To the dead?"

The shade seemed to hesitate, as if uncertain.

—No. She meant something else—

"Are they destroyed?" She found herself pressing for an answer. "What did she mean by 'lost'? Lost in what way?"

The waters hissed as if echoing the dark emotions of the shade, and she could see anger and impatience reflected in its face.

—I am telling you what I know, Ard Rhys. It is for you to discover the rest. I will not put words in your mouth or thoughts in your mind that you have not conjured up yourself—

She felt her heart sink. "Then there is nothing more you can tell me? She said nothing that would help our order in its search?"

She knew she sounded every bit as desperate as she felt, but she could not accept that there was nothing more to be learned.

—One thing—

She felt an abrupt surge of hope. "One thing?"

—Aleia Omarosian was a Chosen—

A Chosen? Khyber stared at Allanon's ghost in confusion. The writer of the diary was a Chosen? Why was there no mention of this anywhere in her writings? For there had not been a single reference to either the Chosen or the Ellcrys in the diary. A young girl in service to the tree would almost certainly have made some mention of it, wouldn't she?

A fresh hissing filled the night air like a long, slow sigh, and Khyber found the eyes of Allanon's shade fixed on her anew.

—Listen to me, Ard Rhys. I do not always know things, but I often sense them. It is so here. This quest must happen, and you must lead it. The search will take you to what you seek. I feel this the way I once felt my own future on the currents of the wind and the changes in the season. It was my gift then and is so now—

The shade shifted slightly, black robes billowing. Behind and safely away, lesser ghosts floated on the air, gone strangely silent, as if listening to his words.

—You will need help. Help of a sort that cannot be easily obtained. Your order is too small for what will be required. And it is too inexperienced. Even with the aid and protection of the Druid Guard, you will need others. Trackers and survivalists and hunters—men and women who can live off the land—you will need those. You will need wielders of magic with powers even stronger than those of your Druids. Perhaps even stronger than your own. Find these among the Races and persuade them to your cause. And heed me. You must find an Ohmsford to go with you. The presence of an Ohmsford is crucial. The whisper of that truth is everywhere about me and so strong that it cannot be ignored. Do not be deterred by those who question your choices. Do not be dissuaded by those who dismiss your efforts and denigrate your character—

It was so much for a shade to say, all at one time, that

she stood silent in the aftermath, wondering that he should give her so much of himself. She had changed her mind about him. He had not abandoned her as one doomed to failure. He had embraced her cause and her spirit, and he was giving her what he could to help. But he was fearful for her.

"Thank you," she said to him. "Thank you for everything."

—You will not thank me later. Later, you will see me differently. But that is as it must be and not within my control. So heed me one last time. If you choose to undertake this quest, many of those who go with you will die. Many will be lost. This, too, I hear in the wind's whisper and feel in the air's currents. This quest will be hard, and its toll on lives and souls will be high. No one will come back the same. No one will emerge unscathed. Perhaps, in the end, no one will think it was worth it. Not even you—

"No," she said, "I will never think that."

—You will think that and much worse. You will curse me. You will hate what has happened. And you will trace its beginnings to this moment—

He seemed so certain, yet he did not know the particulars of anything he was predicting and was giving voice to words he heard whispered in the air. She could not decide how much of what he was saying was substantive and how much guesswork.

"I hope you are wrong," she said finally.

—I am Allanon—

He said it as if it were an answer to everything, as if he were possessed of abilities and knowledge denied to others, herself included. She almost replied that who he was did not necessarily dictate what he knew. But she could not quite bring herself to do so.

—We are finished—

His shade was already backing away over the surface

of the water, receding toward its distant center, black and forbidding in the light of the stars and a quarter moon just risen to the east. The voices of the dead had begun to wail anew, the white moths of their spirits to circle the giant form of the Druid shade, and the waters to hiss and boil with fresh intensity.

–You will not see me again in this life, Ard Rhys. May you not see me too soon in the next–

The words were a cold spike in her heart, but she held her ground as the winds rose to a howl and whipped about her violently, stirring spray and grit in equal measure from the lake and the surrounding rocks. She ducked her head against their sting, flinching in spite of herself, eyes closed.

When she opened them again, only seconds later, the shades were gone, the waters were quieting, and the voices had gone still.

She was alone, and she was frightened.

8

THE FOLLOWING MORNING APHENGLOW WOKE BEfore sunrise and slipped out of her sleeping chamber on cat's paws, pondering anew Woostra's discovery that Aleia Omarosian was one of the Chosen. She went down the empty, silent corridors to the Druid's Keep and took a seat just outside Woostra's offices in the Druid Library. She was waiting for him to appear at the start of his workday, intending to question him further about what that odd listing meant, when a shadow passed across her face and caused her to look up.

The Ard Rhys stood before her, clothes rumpled and dusty, graying hair disheveled, face drawn and haggard, brow wrinkled.

She stood at once. "I didn't know you were back, Mistress."

Khyber Elessedil nodded. "I just returned. I've spoken to no one yet. I came to find Woostra, but here you are, instead. Tell me. Has he found anything in my absence? Have you?"

Aphenglow considered equivocating, but decided it was unwise to do so with the Ard Rhys. "Woostra did. I promised to say nothing until he reported his finding to you, but I will tell you anyway. The Druid records say that Aleia Omarosian was a Chosen."

Khyber Elessedil nodded calmly and took a seat beside her. "Is there anything else recorded? Anything regarding the circumstances of her choosing or of her service?"

Aphenglow shook her head. "No, nothing." She paused, considering the other's reaction. "You knew this already, didn't you? You're not surprised at all."

"I knew. The spirits of the dead told me. But what does it mean, Aphen? How could she be a Chosen in service to the Ellcrys and make no mention of it in her writings?"

"I've thought of that. I think there is only one explanation. She did not become a Chosen until after she stopped making entries in her diary. Until after the Elfstones were stolen by the Darkling boy. The time of her choosing didn't happen until later." Aphen shrugged. "Nothing else makes sense."

"Do you think it was *because* of what happened with the Darkling boy and his theft of the Elfstones?" the Ard Rhys asked.

"I think so, although I don't understand the connection. But I would like to try to find out. Mistress, I want to go back to Arborlon and look again through the Chosen histories. I wasn't searching for anything about the Chosen before, only for mentions of Elven magic. The Chosen keep records that are different from the Elven histories. There might be something there that would help us understand."

The Ard Rhys shook her head. "I don't like sending you back just now. Not after two attempts have been made on your life already. It might be better to send Pleysia, instead."

Aphenglow tried to conceal her alarm. This was her discovery, and she did not want to turn it over to someone else, especially Pleysia. "I can ask my uncle to assign an Elven Hunter to keep watch over me, if you wish. But I should do this, Mistress. I have the King's permission already and have been given access to the records. Pleysia would have to start all over, and there is nothing to say that my grandfather would be favorably disposed toward anyone who is not a member of the royal family."

The two women faced each other in silence for a moment, each knowing that the other understood perfectly the implications not only of what had just been said, but of what hadn't, as well.

"I am not happy with the idea," Khyber Elessedil said at last, "though I recognize the need for it. But you will secure protection, and you will make certain whoever you choose can protect you adequately. Agreed?"

Aphenglow nodded quickly. "I promise. I won't stay any longer than it takes to complete my search of the Chosen histories. But they suffer from the same deficiencies as the others. There are gaps and omissions throughout, particularly from the early years when record keeping was less meticulous. Some of what was known then was recovered from personal journals and stories passed down from the families who lived in those times. But not all."

"Do what you can." The Ard Rhys took Aphenglow's hands in her own. "I wish I had been awake and able to spend more time with you, Aphen," she said suddenly. "You have great potential, great promise. You are skilled, and your mind is sharp. But I am troubled by the weight you bear in your heart. Choosing to come here, to leave your people and your city to serve us, left you little better than an exile in the eyes of many. Worse than that, in the eyes of a few. I know this causes you great pain."

Aphenglow blushed at the unexpected praise. "It does. But I have made my choice and learned to live with it. I would not take it back now."

"Even so, it is a burden, and it might never be lifted from your shoulders. No one should have to bear such a stigma, especially when it is so undeserved. I worry for you, Aphen."

Aphenglow stared in surprise, unable to respond to such deep concern with anything remotely appropriate. Should she thank the Ard Rhys for her solicitude? Should she declare it unnecessary?

Khyber Elessedil saved her the trouble by releasing her hands and standing. "Woostra comes. I will hear his report now and pretend that I have heard nothing of it before." She smiled. "I think I can do that well enough. So say nothing."

Aphen rose with her, turning to watch the scribe's approach, a stiff-legged shuffle that suggested not all of his parts were functioning. Woostra gave them a nod.

"Go find the others," the Ard Rhys said quickly to Aphen. "Tell them to gather in the main Council chamber at midday. We will discuss this further at that time."

Then Woostra was next to her and she was guiding him by the elbow into his offices, closing the doors behind them. Aphenglow stood looking after them for a moment longer, almost expecting the Ard Rhys to reappear. But she didn't, and the young woman finally turned away.

Midday brought a change in the weather, which at sunrise had seemed bright and clear but had now turned gray and chilly. The winds had picked up, clouds scudded across the sky in waves, and it was clear that a storm was on the way. The Druids were seated around the huge table that dominated the main Council chamber. Khyber Elessedil had just finished her report on meeting with the Shade of Allanon, confirming what Woostra had discovered in his search about Aleia Omarosian's ties to the Chosen, and in the silence that ensued she was now looking from face to face. She wasn't entirely sure what she was looking for. Maybe some hint of inner strength and determination to see through what must inevitably happen next. Maybe some sense of how strong each could be when their metal was placed in the fire. She didn't know, but she searched anyway.

"What are we to do?" Carrick asked finally, his lean figure draped in his chair like a straw man's.

It was *the* question, of course. But she had already thought it through after leaving Aphenglow. She had returned to her chambers, bathed and dressed in clean clothes, had Woostra bring her food and drink, and then sat by her window and considered her options. It wasn't so much what she should do as what she should do *first*. They needed to undertake a search for the Elfstones, but before doing so they needed to be better prepared. She had listened carefully to Allanon's shade. She might have dismissed such advice coming from anyone else, but not from him. Even dead, he knew people and their vicissitudes better than most. That he could sense things hidden from others came as no surprise to anyone who had studied his life, and she had studied it thoroughly.

In particular, if he said they needed help from others more talented and better trained in areas where they were not, she knew to pay attention to his advice.

"If we are to find the Elfstones, we will need the help of others," she said when the silence following Carrick's question had lengthened sufficiently. "Allanon's shade made it clear that we could not do this alone. No reason was given, nor was any argument encouraged. I felt strongly that the matter was not open to discussion or equivocation. So we will do as we have been advised. We will seek out others who will accompany us on our search."

Pleysia shook her head. "I don't like involving other people. People who are not Druids."

"Others have always been there to aid us." Khyber met her dark gaze and held it. "Any number of times. Have you forgotten your history?"

"Members of the Ohmsford family," Seersha interjected, "helped Allanon three times, Walker Boh twice, and Grianne Ohmsford twice. Other families have aided us, too. The Leahs. The Elessedils, as well."

"But it was the living who made that decision, not the dead." Pleysia would not back down. "And in each case the decision was made because those who went possessed magic that was necessary to the success of the quests undertaken. This isn't the same."

"You are splitting hairs, Pleysia," Bombax observed quietly.

"Am I? Then perhaps they need splitting."

"And perhaps you need to consider your words more carefully before you speak them."

Pleysia was on her feet, furious. "Why don't you consider what it meant to rely on Allanon's word in those earlier times? He was duplicitous and manipulative in life; why would he be any different in death? Some essential part of any truth he knew was always hidden from those who relied on his words! Why do you think it would be any different here?"

She wheeled on Khyber. "You might trust this shade. You might believe the advice it gives you is valuable and should be heeded. But I suggest you forget more of history than I do. How many of us will be sacrificed in this effort because of that?"

Khyber Elessedil shook her head slowly. "None, I hope. Some of what you say is right. But that doesn't mean everything I was told is a lie or duplicitous. If that were so, I would sense it. My mind is made up on this, Pleysia. I have accepted Allanon's warning as valid. I accept that we must heed it. We must seek help to complete this quest. Starting right away."

She paused, making sure they were done arguing the point. Pleysia shrugged and looked away. "Allanon's shade warned me that there must be at least one Ohmsford who comes with us," Khyber continued. "It will be my responsibility to find that one. An Ohmsford has been involved with the Druids on every quest since the return of the Warlock Lord. Grianne Ohmsford was Ard Rhys before me. The history is there, and I don't intend to ignore it."

"Perhaps the history you rely on is not applicable to this situation," Pleysia muttered. "Perhaps we should consider another approach."

"Do you have one in mind?" Bombax pressed. "Because if not, perhaps we should let the Ard Rhys finish."

Pleysia glared at him but stayed silent. Khyber gave her a moment, waiting to see if she wanted to pursue her argument, and then she continued.

"I think we need a Seer. I think we need a skilled Tracker and a warrior stronger in arms and more experienced in fighting skills than any of us—perhaps even than Garroneck or his Trolls. We need all of these before we even think about setting out. I would like each of you to help in securing their services. Men or women, either will do. But we need balance in our expedition, a cross section of skills and abilities."

There was an extended silence. "I will go to Varfleet," Bombax declared. "Better Callahorn than a return to the Federation cities. Men and women possessing such skills as those you describe, Mistress, can be found in the Borderlands."

"I will go home to the Dwarves," Seersha added quickly.

"Aphenglow returns to the Elves to search further through the Elven writings in case there is something more on Aleia Omarosian's time with the Chosen. Carrick, will you travel down into the Federation and look there?"

"Better you send me than Carrick," Pleysia interrupted suddenly. "He is not skilled enough to avoid being identified, Southlander or no. I am more familiar with travel in the Federation than he is."

Khyber was surprised. "I gathered from your disagreement with my intentions you would prefer to stay here."

Pleysia shrugged, her smooth features wrinkling. "I might not agree with your decision to include others in our efforts to find the Elfstones, but that doesn't mean I don't intend to take part in the search. I don't trust Allanon, but I do support you. I am disagreeing, Mistress, not withdrawing."

She said it calmly, without rancor or disgruntlement. Khyber was impressed. "Your point is taken. I will send you both. Carrick can go into the Eastland with Seersha. Where will you go, Pleysia?"

"Not where anyone else is going. Not to the Elves especially. I leave that to Aphen. Somewhere else. But I would prefer to keep it to myself for now. Will you trust me?"

Khyber nodded. With Pleysia, you never knew what to expect anyway. "Of course I will. Do what you think is necessary."

She turned back to the others. "We will leave in the morning, all of us. Take skimmers and go alone. Avoid being noticed. There may be some who would attempt to interfere if they learned what we are doing. One man for certain. If Drustan Chazhul learns what we are about, he will almost certainly act on it."

"What can he do?" Carrick was dismissive. "Send a fleet of ships to intercept us? Try to take over the search himself? He is only one man, even if he is an unpleasant one."

"A very dangerous man," Bombax said at once. "I should know. I've spent enough time around him over the past year, watching him manipulate and deceive everyone from Ministers to his mother. What he will do if he finds out about this is hard to imagine. But I wouldn't be too quick to assume that anything is beyond him."

"We'll take no chances," Khyber agreed. "While you are looking, you will not discuss the specifics of what we are about. This is an expedition that requires men and women who possess certain skills. The pay will be high and the work dangerous. That is all anyone needs to know. The rest can be revealed later. There is to be no mention of magic.

"And," she added, drawing out the word, "there will be no communication among us until we are returned to Paranor. Attempts at communication are too dangerous. The danger of giving something away is too great. We will allow one week for this effort. Then we will return. Remember. One week only."

Heads nodded and a chorus of mumbled agreement was voiced. Khyber asked each in turn, wanting a solid commitment. No one, not even Pleysia, spoke a word of objection.

Moments later, when they had adjourned the meeting and were filing out the door, Khyber felt a hand touch her arm lightly.

"Mistress." Aphenglow was standing very close, clearly not wanting any of the others to hear. "Can I speak to you in private?"

Khyber led the young Elven woman down the hall and into her personal study. She gestured for Aphenglow to take a seat and then set about making tea. Only after the tea was ready and both were sipping from the steaming mugs did she ask what Aphen wanted.

"Two things, in fact." Aphenglow seemed to gather her thoughts. "Let me start with a request. I would like permission to seek an audience with the King when I reach Arborlon. I intend to ask him to lend us use of the Elfstones."

Khyber nodded, keeping her face expressionless. "Why would you do that, Aphen? In all the centuries the other Elfstones have been missing, no one has ever been successful in using the blue Elfstones to find them. Why would it be any different now?"

"I don't know that it would." Aphen brushed back strands of her long blond hair and tightened the ribbon that held the thick mane back from her face. "But if it were to turn out that the blue Elfstones could help, wouldn't we want to have them in our possession?"

"We would. Do you know of my agreement with Arling Elessedil?"

"When you returned the Elfstones almost a century ago, you extracted a promise from her that if you asked to borrow them, she would allow it. That was the condition for their return."

"So you would rely on that in making your argument to the King?"

"He is bound by his mother's word."

"I wouldn't count on that, Aphen. Your grandfather is of a different mind and temperament than your great-grandmother, but he is still her son."

"Nevertheless, we are family, and even if he doesn't agree with my choice to come here and study with you, he respects my decision. I think he might agree because of that."

"But all of this is pointless if the Elfstones won't help. Why do you suddenly think they would?"

Aphenglow shook her head. "I don't think anything.

I am just considering possibilities. It would support my request if it came through you, so I am requesting permission to approach the King on the matter if I deem it useful."

Khyber studied her quietly. Wheels within wheels. Aphenglow had something specific in mind—something she wasn't revealing. "Very well. I give you permission. But don't abuse it by taking unnecessary risks. And you are not to tell your grandfather or anyone else in your family what it is we are seeking. Not a hint of it. What is the second matter you wish to discuss? Another request?"

Aphenglow shook her head. "In all the excitement of finding the diary and coming back to find you awake, I forgot to tell you something else I discovered while searching through the Elven records. Not through the histories themselves, but through the ancillary records— the genealogy charts of the Elven Kings and Queens, in particular."

"You found something else?"

"I did, although I haven't decided what to make of it. I found that before the Omarosian line died out, it merged with the Elessedils. So the Elessedils are related to the Omarosians in a very distant way. I have kept this private because it only has to do with us. With the Elessedil family."

Khyber was instantly certain Aphenglow was wrong about this, but she couldn't say why. It was an instinctual reaction but one so strong that she could not ignore it. The connection between Elessedils and Omarosians was much more important than Aphenglow realized.

"We can keep this private," she agreed. "At least until we understand more fully what it means. When you return to Arborlon, expand your search to look for something about the connection between the two families.

There must be something on this. The Elessedil records are very thorough. Speak to your mother about it."

She saw Aphenglow blanch, and she knew that her relationship with her mother had not improved. "Do what you can, Aphen," she finished.

The young woman made a face. "I will try, Mistress."

"And be careful. Be wary of everyone. I don't want anything happening to you while you are back there."

Aphenglow gave a quick smile, rose, and left the room. Khyber Elessedil watched her go, resisting the urge to call her back. She did not want to lose Aphen. But she had to let her go.

Be careful, she repeated silently.

All of us.

9

THERE WAS NO DOUBT ABOUT IT. THOSE SPRINTS were one wicked pair of machines.

They sat side by side in the metal-clad storage shed, resting on wheeled trailers that allowed them to be pulled out into the open where they could be readied for use. Painted black from mast to keel, light sheaths black as well to better absorb the power of the sun, they had long, narrow hulls stripped of everything that might slow them down. The parse tubes were embedded in the hull behind hatches that facilitated easy replacement of the diapson crystals. The controls were set to either side of a shallow depression that served as a cockpit, all within easy reach of the pilot. The pilot lay on his back with his head slightly elevated, facing forward down the length of his body toward the bow. A thin padding lined the cockpit floor and walls, providing a modicum of comfort and a small amount of protection. A leather harness strapped the pilot in place, and a windshield constructed of metal, wood, and mesh allowed him to peer ahead over the rim of the hull's curved surface without an undue amount of risk of being blinded by flying debris.

Inside the cockpit, the thrusters and steering levers were manipulated by a combination of hands and feet, the cords that ran from the levers to the sheaths, rudder, and fins drawn so tightly that even the smallest amount of pressure would produce a response in the vessel's handling. The twins had built the Sprints this way on purpose. These slender black monsters weren't designed as transports; they were built to race.

What the Sprints were, when you came right down to it, were modified flits, their superstructures pared down to the bare minimum of weight and material. They were a work in progress, of course, but it appeared that they were now as close as possible to what their builders intended.

Today's test would determine whether or not this was so.

"They certainly look ready," Redden Ohmsford offered, contemplating the sleek craft with satisfaction. "I don't know what else we could do to make them go any faster."

His brother nodded. "Are we going to take them into the Shredder?"

Railing Ohmsford smiled as he said it, knowing full well that this was exactly what they were going to do, having already decided as much while they were testing the Sprints over the broad expanse of the Rainbow Lake. But testing a craft over open water wasn't as challenging as taking it through an obstacle course of dead trees and jagged rocks. Their mother had made them promise not to race the Sprints anywhere but over the lake, but like most boys verging on manhood and testing the limits of parental authority, they didn't always listen.

Besides, they had rationalized, talking it over to convince themselves that it was all right to breach this agreement, they had flown everything from flits to skimmers to sleeks, so surely they could handle this. They might not have flown warships yet, the great ships-of-the-line that required entire crews to sail them, but they would get around to it eventually.

Their unwritten rule regarding airships was that if they could build it, they could fly it. Anywhere they wished.

"Well, it's a good day to try it out," Redden replied, grinning back at his mirror image—small, lean, and fit, with mischievous blue eyes, wild red hair, and only a hint in his ears, brows, and cheekbones of the Elven blood they had inherited from their mother. It was a wonder, he thought for the umpteenth time, that anyone could tell them apart.

It was scary fun, really. Frequently, they pretended to be each other, just because they could get away with it. Sometimes twins weren't really all that much alike, in either looks or behavior. Sometimes they looked a lot alike, but you could still always tell them apart. But not Redden and Railing Ohmsford. Right down to their Elven features, they looked exactly the same. A human father and an Elven mother had produced Halfling twins in a family that had never had twins before. What were the odds that an anomaly would produce exact duplicates? Even their mother had trouble, and she saw them practically every day and knew everything there was to know about them.

Well, practically everything. No boy ever told his mother everything.

In any event, only one person—Mirai Leah—could tell the difference. The brothers thought they knew why, but it wasn't something they ever discussed.

Railing looked over at Redden. "What are we waiting for?"

They hauled the trailers out of the storage shed using ropes attached to the trailer hitches. Each chose the one he would fly, Redden going first as Redden usually did, and then they climbed aboard to ready their vessels. It took them longer than usual because they made certain to check everything twice, knowing that the element of danger in today's exercise was much greater than anything they had encountered before. They put up the raked-back masts, attached the cut-down light sheaths to the radian draws, and ran the draws to the parse tubes. The diapson crystals were already in place, but they kept the parse tubes hooded so that the crystals wouldn't start to power up too quickly.

They had built the Sprints themselves, working together, skilled enough in the construction of small vessels that they could almost do so blindfolded. There were adjustments and changes required for a vessel intended to be this fast and maneuverable, one designed solely for racing. It took a bit of trial and error to get it right, and they had reconfigured and reconstructed both Sprints any number of times while they were testing them out over the open waters of Rainbow Lake. But they lived in Patch Run, as had their parents, their grandparents, and their great-grandparents before them, so they had ready access to the perfect testing ground and a raft of seasoned shipbuilders located all around them who were ready and able to teach them whatever it was they needed to know to improve their skills.

Beyond what help was available close at hand, they also had access to the considerable experience and skills of their Rover kin, the Alt Mers, who lived in the Westland in the country surrounding Bakrabru on the shores of the Myrian. Their great-grandmother had been Rue Meridian, who had married Bek Ohmsford, and Redden was named for her brother, Redden Alt Mer. Railing was given the name of a favorite uncle. Both Rue Meridian and Redden Alt Mer were famous for having flown with the Druid Walker Boh aboard the *Jerle Shannara* in search of Parkasia, and Rue had later fought with the Druid Ard Rhys Grianne Ohmsford against the Federation and the rebel Druids under Shadea a'Ru. Both brother and sister had been skilled fliers in their time; those skills had been passed down through both families and were now firmly a part of Redden and Railing's own talents.

But they had another advantage, as well. Both brothers had inherited the magic of the wishsong, a part of the genetic makeup of the Ohmsford family since the days of Wil Ohmsford that had manifested itself in various members of their family over the years. Wish for it, sing for it, make it come alive—that was what the wishsong could do for you. You could change and reshape anything. You could create something new out of something old. You could affect the way animate objects reacted. You could influence life and death.

It was an awesome, terrifying gift—or curse, if you believed some of the Ohmsford family history. Both their great-grandfather and their grandfather had possessed the magic, and it had saved them and many others during the course of their lives but also maimed and killed. It was a dangerous and not altogether predictable power. It had skipped their father, for which their mother was eternally grateful, but had surfaced anew in the twins, for which she was not.

They didn't use it much or even talk about it. Especially not in front of their mother, who mistrusted the magic and those who used it, particularly the Druids. She knew it was a part of her sons' makeup—it was impossible to disguise its presence completely—but had no idea of the extent to which they had employed it. They were very careful not to let her discover the truth because their mother, like so many others, had ways of knowing things she wasn't told.

If they were very good at hiding which of them was

which, they were masters at hiding their involvement with the wishsong.

Thinking of it now, Railing stopped what he was doing and looked over at his brother. "Are we going to use the wishsong this morning?" he asked quietly. "Or do we wait for another time?"

Redden paused midway through securing a line. They had experimented only a little with using the magic to enhance the power emitted by the diapson crystals, which in turn would make the Sprints go faster. "I don't know. What do you think we should do?"

Railing grinned. "You know what I think. One pass without using it, one pass using it. Wasn't that what you wanted me to say?"

His brother shrugged, his lean face expressionless. "Maybe."

They went back to work, finishing up with their preparations, making both Sprints ready to fly. When they were done, they leaned over the sides of the vessels and released the stays securing them to the trailers. A last check on the controls, making sure they were loose and ready to respond, and they were ready.

"This should be fun," Redden offered drily.

"If we survive," Railing replied.

They lay flat in the cockpits facing forward toward Rainbow Lake, secured their safety belts, and gave each other a final glance.

"A quick swing out onto the lake and back first?" Railing asked.

"Out and back and right into the Shredder."

With a final nod to each other, they unhooded the parse tubes and let the light sheaths billow out. The radian draws began to glow immediately, and they felt the hum of the diapson crystals as they came alive with the sun's raw power. The brothers engaged the controls, and the Sprints lurched sharply, lifted off their cradles, and wheeled toward the lake.

"Let's fly!" Redden shouted.

Railing flipped the thruster levers all the way forward, and his Sprint leapt away with the quickness and power of a moor cat lunging, smooth hull cleaving the air like a knife, mast vibrating with the force of the acceleration, and light sheath whipping sideways, the boom barely missing the top of his head. Out across the surrounding woods flew the Sprint, whipping so close to the treetops that Railing could hear branches scraping the underside of the hull. Reacting quickly, he eased the craft upward, away from the danger, following the sleek black hull of his brother's Sprint. Wind whipped across his eyes, causing them to tear, and he wiped his face quickly against his shoulder.

Together the Ohmsford brothers skimmed across the canopy of the woods bordering Rainbow Lake, gained the shoreline, and burst into the clear, leveling out about twenty yards above the water's surface. They flew north out into the open water, the lake spreading away before them in a brilliant blue that mirrored sunlight and sky. The waters were still this day, free of waves, untroubled by wind. The sun was high overhead, the sky empty of clouds. Everything was bright and sharp and clear, and as they raced out into the emptiness they could smell the lake and feel its coldness.

Only minutes had passed before Railing caught Redden gesturing in a circular motion, indicating he was getting ready to swing back around toward the Shredder. Railing signaled back that he was ready, too, and tightened his hands on the controls. Even in the few short days he had not flown while working on the Sprints, he had forgotten how free and wonderful it felt to fly them. There just wasn't anything else like it, nothing even close. Flying the bigger skimmers and transports and scout craft was fun, but they were slow and cumbersome and predictable compared with the Sprints. Speed made all the difference. When he was flying like this—fast and unencumbered and barely under control—it felt as if he could escape everything, rise right on up into the stars and leave it all behind. Sometimes he wanted to do that. He would feel his life pressing down on him, the constraints and obligations, the demands and expectations, and all he could think about was breaking free and flying away.

It was a selfish way of thinking, but he knew Redden felt the same. They had talked about what they would do when they were old enough to leave home to explore the larger world and discover what was out there waiting for them. They could have left by now if they'd wanted; certainly they had skills and ambition enough to make their way. But they weren't adults yet, and their mother had already made it clear she didn't want them going until they were. Their father was a dozen years gone, dead in an airship crash—an accident that had left their mother shattered and bitter and determined to protect her children. As if that were possible, Railing thought. As if you could ever protect your children from what life might bring their way. Or even from themselves and their impulses.

But the illusion of it was all their mother had to cling to, so they had promised her long ago they would stay until they were grown. It was only now they were beginning to regret that promise. Life in Patch Run was safe and predictable, and the brothers were ready for something else. They had always been wild, a condition Railing attributed to their genetic makeup. If there was a risk to be taken, a dare to be accepted, or a boundary that shouldn't be crossed, they were willing to defy the odds. He couldn't explain it. But he knew how they were, and he knew it was unlikely they would ever change.

Like now, as their Sprints whipped across the surface of Rainbow Lake and closed on the wicked maze of rocks and dead trees that formed the Shredder. They had made this run several times before with much slower craft, with hybrids and modifieds and junk they had cobbled together and tested in ways that the poor things weren't meant to be tested, just to see what they would do. When it came to airships, they never troubled themselves with measuring risk. It was the experience that mattered, and that wasn't likely to change as long as their mother didn't find out what they were doing.

So far she hadn't.

Well, mostly.

They couldn't keep everything from her. She had caught them a few times. But the things she'd found out were so insignificant she wasn't overly troubled. Like the time they stole Arch Ehlwar's skip and rode it across the lake and up the Runne to Varfleet to watch the Sprint races two summers ago. Or the time they flew down into the Mist Marsh and stayed the night. But she hadn't found out how they had acquired the diapson crystals that powered their various vessels, including the ones they were flying now. She hadn't found out how they had manipulated the black market for these and other materials they needed to construct their experimental craft.

The memories flashed through Railing's mind as the shoreline neared and the jagged edges of the Shredder came into sharper focus. He flattened himself further against the padding, gently testing the controls, making sure everything was responding. Redden had moved into position ahead of him, leading the way. In the Shredder, there wasn't room to fly side by side, only in line. Even then, it was extremely tight. Going as fast as they were, it was suicide.

Which made it all the more irresistible.

"Hang on!" Redden yelled sharply.

Then they were whipping through the twists and turns of the Shredder, skimming past jagged cliffs and over the tips of rugged boulders, sliding between tree trunks and through dead branches, all the while pushing the thrusters harder, making the Sprints go faster. They were flying mostly on instinct, relying on quickness of response. They knew the course they were following, had memorized it thoroughly over the past few months. But the margin for error was so tiny that all it would take was one mistake and they would be a part of the landscape.

They didn't think that way, though. They were young, and they believed nothing could really hurt them. They were convinced their flying skills would protect them. They believed a crash was out of the question.

Except that Railing recognized that some tiny part of him wanted to know what a crash would feel like and how much punishment his Sprint could take. Stupid to think that way, but there it was.

They raced through the obstacle course, hearing the scrape of branches against their hulls, the thrumming of the radian draws, and the rush of the wind in their ears. Everything was quick and fast, everything a blur, there and gone again in an instant. It was insanity, Railing thought suddenly. And it was such fun!

His brother increased his speed as they neared the return to the shoreline, then changed course abruptly and shot between a series of trunks at no more than six feet off the ground, mast raked all the way back. Railing hadn't been expecting it and couldn't make the adjustment fast enough. He was forced to settle for keeping to the old way, a less risky, more reliable side turn around a massive old cedar's broad canopy before racing into the open once more.

Then they were back out over the waters of Rainbow Lake, flying side by side again, paired up in perfect formation. Railing saw his brother grinning at him, aware that he had done something Railing hadn't. A challenge. Railing gave him a thumbs-up, an acknowledgment. But he would lead next when they went into the Shredder, and it would be his chance to respond. He was already thinking of how he would do that, what sort of trick he might try that would leave Redden eating his parse tube exhaust.

Only this time they would be using the wishsong to enhance the experience, and neither of them knew what that would mean. Flying faster, they hoped. But maybe something more, as well. The magic was unpredictable, and the user could never be entirely certain how it would respond. There were stories about this, some of them very dark indeed. The brothers had heard more than a few. Not from their mother, of course, who wouldn't even speak of the magic, but from the Alt Mers and others who had known Bek and Penderrin and especially Grianne. The magic, they said, could do anything. It could even kill.

But the brothers weren't planning on using it that extremely, so Railing pushed aside his concerns and focused on his intent for the next pass into the Shredder. He glanced over at Redden, made a quick sign that he was ready, saw his brother motion in response, and brought his Sprint around in a wide sweep so that he was again facing toward the shoreline.

Then howling like a wild man he jammed the thruster levers all the way forward.

The Sprint bucked and lurched in response, the entire vessel shaking with the sudden influx of power fed down into the parse tubes. The racer catapulted forward like a great cat, whipping across the flat, broad surface of the lake, tearing toward the opening of the obstacle course. Railing risked a quick glance over one shoulder. Redden was right behind him, tracking in his wake.

Ahead, the Shredder's rocks and trees came into sharp focus, the opening easily discernible. Exhilarated, Railing flattened himself further in the cockpit of his craft, flexed his hands on the thruster levers, and summoned the wishsong's magic. It began as a humming changed to words, a small flux within his throat that ran down into his body, warming his lungs and belly, then was carried through his bloodstream and into his limbs. He felt a sharp tingling, and then the rush of the magic as it exploded to life, hard and certain. He fought to keep it under control, reining it in when it tried to break free, channeling it into his hands and from there into the controls and down into the diapson crystals, feeding and enhancing their power.

Abruptly, the crystals responded, and the little Sprint shot ahead as if a pebble from a sling. The force of the acceleration was so powerful that Railing was almost thrown from the cockpit. Only the restraining straps kept him from being tossed out. The wind whipped into his eyes with renewed force, bringing fresh tears to his eyes, nearly blinding him. Spray from the surface of the lake waters, which this sudden surge had disturbed, whipped across his face, cold and sharp.

Too much power!

He tried to hold it back, to slow the Sprint's forward momentum, but he had lost control. He was tearing into the maze of rocks and trees so fast that he could barely make out where he was going. But somehow he managed to keep the vessel righted and on course, though barely able to track the terrain ahead. He felt a rush of adrenaline sweep through him as he maneuvered the craft through its twists and turns, this way and that, bank and slide, raise and lower—look out!—everything suddenly becoming a part of what he could feel more than what he could see.

He screamed with joy, unable to contain his excitement.

Then, just for a second, he lost his focus, momentarily distracted by a shadow's movement to one side, and his attention wavered just enough that he lost control. The Sprint yawed wildly, sideslipped through a maze of rocks, skidded into a nest of branches, and flipped upside down in midair. Railing hauled back on the thruster levers and dropped the power to almost nothing, fighting to stay airborne. In the split second that was left to him, he wrapped himself in a cocoon of the wishsong's magic and waited for the inevitable.

It was just enough.

The Sprint went down in a tearing of radian draws and a shrieking of ripped hull boards, its mast snapping clean off. He felt the steering come loose completely and the light sheaths collapse. The Sprint slid wildly across the ground, bouncing off trunks and boulders, spinning and rolling. Railing lost all track of where he was, tossed first one way and then the other against the safety harness, fighting to maintain the wishsong's flow. He kept his head down and his limbs tucked into the cockpit, teeth clenched against his expectation of pain and maybe death.

But when the Sprint finally came to rest, he was still alive. He could scarcely believe it. He lay motionless inside the cockpit, tipped sideways and turned backward, clouds of dust and debris billowing all around him, the sudden silence unexpected and deafening.

He was still trying to decide if he was hurt when Redden appeared next to him, frantically working at the buckles and straps of the safety harness, trying to help him get free. "You idiot!" he was screaming. "What were you thinking? Are you all right? Shades, that was a monster crash!"

Railing nodded. "Oh . . . I don't know. It wasn't so much."

Then he passed out.

When he regained consciousness, he was out of the cockpit and lying on the ground nearby. Redden was kneeling beside him, holding him up so that he could drink from the aleskin.

"Am I alive?"

"Alive?" Redden snorted. "You aren't even hurt! How did you manage that? I thought you were . . ." He trailed off, looking exasperated. "You better not try something like that again!"

Railing drank from the skin, long deep swallows. He could feel the burn of the ale going down, restoring his heart rate and giving him fresh life. He moved his arms and legs experimentally. No damage. "Help me up."

Redden lifted him to a sitting position and then to his feet. He was achy and battered, but no bones were broken and there were no external signs of any injuries. Railing took a deep breath, exhaled, twisted his shoulders, and stretched.

"I think I'm all right." He said it incredulously, not sure why it was so. "It was the wishsong, Red. That's what saved me. I was feeding the magic into the crystals, but when I lost control of the Sprint, I used it to protect myself. Sort of wrapped it around me like a cushion. It worked!"

"All of which means that you can overlook the fact that you wrecked your Sprint and gave me heart failure, I suppose," his brother snapped.

Railing glanced at the remains of his flying ship and shook his head. They would have to rebuild it entirely.

Or maybe he would. Redden might make him do it alone since he was responsible for wrecking it.

"No, it was my fault," he said. "I caused it, so I have to fix it."

Redden put his arm around Railing's shoulders. "Not likely. Not while I'm your brother. You couldn't do it without me anyway. Come on, let's take out the crystals and fly my Sprint back to the shed."

They removed the diapson crystals from the parse tubes of the wrecked Sprint and stuffed them in the back of the second Sprint's cockpit. They could not afford to leave the crystals. Anyone finding the remains of the Sprint would steal them at once and sell them on the black market. Everything else could be replaced from their stores. With a final glance back at the wreckage, the brothers climbed aboard the remaining Sprint, sitting up in the cockpit now, Railing in back, his brother in front. Redden engaged the thruster levers, and the Sprint lifted out of the Shredder, turned east, and headed for home.

"We'll have to try that again," Redden said over his shoulder. "Using the wishsong, I mean. But next time I get to be in the lead."

Railing nodded vaguely, recalling momentarily the terror he had experienced during the crash and then just as quickly dismissing it. Still, he wondered that neither one of them could seem to learn to leave well enough alone.

They flew back along the shoreline until they neared Patch Run, and then angled inland to where the storage shed was situated deep in the woods. It took them only a little while to settle the Sprint back in place on its trailer and then to release the radian draws, take down the mast, remove the diapson crystals to be stored in the hidden compartment under the floor beneath their workbench, and cover the cockpit with a piece of fitted canvas. Then they wheeled the trailer into the shed, secured the wheels with wood chocks, and closed and locked the broad entry doors. They did it all quickly and efficiently and without saying much of anything.

When they were finished, they looked at each other and broke out laughing.

"I can't believe you did that!" Redden repeated.

Railing threw up his hands and howled. "I can't believe I might actually do it again!"

They set out for their home, trading jokes and wry comments, the Sprint crash already a thing of the past. The momentary shock had faded, and neither was thinking about what might have happened but only about what had. Railing was alive and well, no harm suffered, no damage done. And hadn't it been fun!

The house was some distance off, down closer to the shoreline and well away from the shed and its experiments. They lived on twenty acres, but the house and docks occupied only a fraction of that space, and while their mother knew about the airships—though not how they were experimenting with them—she had not as yet come down for a look at the shed or showed more than the normal amount of motherly concern for what they might be doing. To her credit, she seemed to understand she couldn't do anything to change how they were, and while she might not like it the better choice was to accept it for what it was.

They made their way along the lake until the docks used by past generations of Ohmsfords for paid expeditions came into view. Then they caught their first glimpse of the armed transport. It was anchored at the far side of the storage buildings, occupying one of the larger slips, its light sheaths down, radian draws detached. Big and weathered, its paint job was a mottled black and brown and green, colors designed to make it blend into the landscape when viewed from above. Its hull was broad and pregnant with the space allotted for its contents, and its decks and railings were fitted with empty cradles clearly meant for heavy weaponry. The main and forward masts were raked slightly, denoting a ship that had been built for both speed and power.

All of which indicated she was a ship expecting to be attacked and prepared for when it happened.

The brothers exchanged a quick glance. They knew the ship. The *Quickening*. Only one family flew it and only one member of that family would have brought her here.

Mirai Leah.

10

"SHE'S UP HERE!" THEIR MOTHER SHOUTED, CATCH-
ing them both off guard. "Where have you two been?
You were supposed to be back by midday!"

Sarys Ohmsford stood squarely in the open door of
their home, staring down at them with a look on her
face that reflected both suspicion and irritation. She was
tall and slim, her Elven features all sharp planes and
angles, her red hair worn long and loose about her
shoulders. At times she had the look of a cat caught out
in a windstorm. Today was one of those times. She
looked wild and frazzled and out of patience.

Redden was quick to recognize the cause. "Sorry,
Mother. We lost track of time. We were helping an old
man down by the lake bring in his nets. It took longer
than we thought."

His mother gave him a look that clearly indicated she
had doubts about his story. "Which old man would this
be?"

They were walking toward the house now, Redden in
the lead and Railing content to let him be so. "We don't
know his name. Never saw him before. He said he lived
over by Shady Vale. He even knew our family name,
from the old days. He came east in a lake skiff."

Sarys shook her head. "I'm sure he did. Come say

hello to your visitor. She's beginning to wonder if you still live here." She turned away as if dismissing them. "She's in the kitchen eating lunch, but I wouldn't test her patience any further if I were you."

They hurried the rest of the way up the path, edging around spools of wire, barrels of nails, bundles of staves tied up with cord, and stacks of lumber under canvas. Building materials new and reclaimed were scattered everywhere, the source of what livelihood the family managed to produce. It was a bare-bones existence, but with their father gone it had been up to the boys from the time they were small to help their mother keep food on the table. Trade and barter with neighbors and the small towns that dotted the shoreline supplemented their efforts at self-sufficiency. It was a combination that provided a way of life for most of those who lived along the lake.

They passed the pens with the animals, the small forge and the cold storage, and were coming up on the house when they smelled the fresh-baked pies and suddenly found Mirai Leah standing in the door beside their mother.

"Your mother is right," she said. "I was beginning to wonder if you were coming back at all."

"No, no, we were coming, we just . . ."

"Just found things a little confusing . . ."

"More than we . . . what, Red?"

"Confusing, 'cause of the nets . . ."

Mirai Leah wasn't just pretty; she was beautiful. Not in the way of delicate things like flowers or rainbows, but in the way of stone carved into bold, suggestive images. When you first saw her face with its wide smile and fine, chiseled features, you might have thought her delicate. Her long blond hair and startling green eyes might have attracted you initially; you might have taken note of her perfect skin. But after you looked more

closely, shifting your eyes from her face to other regions, you would have noticed the broad shoulders and
strong hands. You would have seen the confident way
she held herself, the cat-like, fluid way she moved, and
the strength evident in her arms and legs. If you came
much closer, you would have noticed the penetrating
gaze and the glimmer of humor that was almost, but
not quite, hidden behind it.

Redden and Railing noticed all this every time they
saw her, and every time they saw her all the strength
went out of their legs. Their otherwise abundant confidence evaporated, and they suddenly felt flushed and
more than a little out of their depth.

It was embarrassing, but they couldn't seem to do
anything about it.

Mirai came down off the steps of the veranda and
walked up to Redden. "Hey there, Red. Happy to see
me?"

She leaned in and kissed him on the cheek, and he felt
the iron in her hands as she gripped his shoulders. No
hesitation, not even a pause as she approached and
decided—rightly—which twin he was.

"Railing," she greeted his brother, moving over to
kiss him, as well. She touched his cheek and wiped
something away. "Busy morning?" she asked, eyes
laughing, smiling widely. "Helping that old man must
have been hard work."

Railing started to say something in reply, but she put
a finger on his lips to silence him and shook her head.
"Why don't you just come inside and eat something before it's time to leave?"

Without further explanation she took his hand, then
Redden's, and tugged them both after her up the steps
and through the door. She was the same age as they
were, but it always felt to them as if she were much older
and much more in control of things. The brothers went

docilely, smiling at their mother who was watching it all with narrowed eyes, feeling like little boys caught out.

Mirai did that to them. She was the one thing they didn't share. Couldn't share. They were both in love with her and had been for as long as they could remember, and they both realized that in the end only one of them could have her.

They sat down together at the kitchen table and exchanged small talk while they ate. Their mother refrained from asking more about the old man, so Redden was not called upon to embellish his lie. Because both twins had washed up before coming to the table, Railing had been able to wipe off a few other telltale stains and scrapes that might have invited additional questions. But Sarys seemed content to sit and listen to her sons and Mirai visit, enjoying their conversation, even smiling now and then at what was said.

It was one of the oddities of their lives that the twins were allowed to spend so much time with the blond-haired girl from Leah. Sarys was cautious about almost everyone with whom her boys came in contact, even other members of their extended family—maybe especially other members of their extended family when it came to the Rover clans—yet seemed to harbor no doubts at all when it came to Mirai Leah. Which was exceedingly odd. Of all the people she should have been worried about, Mirai belonged at the top of the list. Not because she was a bad person. Not because they were both in love with her and this sometimes caused friction. Not even because her family had once been rulers of the Highlands of Leah, but had since abdicated and become just another family working for a living like everyone else.

Not for any of these reasons, but because when you stripped away what was on the surface—her looks and her manners and her ability to charm—she was just a female version of the twins, warts and all.

"You said something about leaving?" Redden asked after they had finished eating and were sipping from glasses of ale. Their mother had started clearing the dishes and momentarily left the room. "You just got here. Where are you going?"

"Not me. We. The three of us. To the Westland, if you want to make the trip with me." She gave him a look. "But only if you want to come. I wouldn't dream of taking you away from anything important. Like helping out old men with their fishing nets."

Redden shrugged. "We're done with that. Why are we going to the Westland?"

"Hauling transport," Railing guessed. She nodded. "What sort of cargo is it? Weapons?"

She shook her head. "Radian draws salvaged from downed airships. I've been scavenging them for months. Papa says it's time to sell. So I found a buyer." There was a twinkle in her green eyes. "Guess who?"

The twins hesitated. "Rovers?" Railing guessed.

She nodded. "But not just any Rovers. Family. Farshaun Req, as a matter of fact."

"Bakrabru!" Railing gasped, and almost let out a whoop as he started to leap up. Farshaun Req had taught all of them the most complex and useful tricks for flying airships, back when they were just beginning their education. Without his encouragement and patience, they might not be flying now—and this included Mirai. But in the process of helping them, he had run afoul of Sarys, who had since forbidden the twins to have anything to do with him.

"Mother won't let us go," Redden said, grabbing his brother and pulling him back down. "Not in a million years."

Mirai gave him a look of incredulity. "Since when do you tell your mother everything you plan to do?"

Redden stared at her. "What does that mean? Are we supposed to lie to her?"

She made a rude noise. "Of course not. I wouldn't expect you to know how to do it properly. So I took care of it for you. I told her we were going to make a delivery on behalf of my father to people he trades with regularly in Bakrabru. You could tell her the same thing. Say you're taking some of those skill masts you spend so much time fashioning." She shrugged. "Don't mention Farshaun."

"But she must have already guessed just from what you told her," Redden pressed. "Even she isn't that gullible."

Mirai shrugged. "Well, I might have mentioned that Farshaun was away for several weeks in the Sarandanon so she wouldn't have to worry about us seeing him."

"And she agreed to let us go?"

Mirai winked. "What do you think?"

When Sarys returned a moment later, Mirai was finishing clearing away the dishes and her sons were grinning at each other like mad fools. She shook her head in despair. Love was a terrible thing.

A little more than two hours later, Redden and Railing were flying west over the Duln, the last glimpse of Patch Run behind them. Working the radian draws and light sheaths, they bounded here and there across the deck of the big airship while Mirai stood at the helm. *Quickening* was the Highland girl's ship, given to her two years earlier when she entered into the family transport business, a measure of her parents' confidence in her abilities. *Quickening* was named for a fairy creature said to have been the child of the King of the Silver River, a young woman who possessed great magic. If the legends could be believed, she was created to aid one of the Ohmsfords in becoming successor to the Druid Allanon and in recovering a talisman called the Black Elfstone. A member of Mirai's own family, Morgan Leah, had gone with them on their quest and fallen in love with Quickening. He had lost her in the end, but their love story had been passed down from generation to generation and Mirai liked it enough to name her transport for the girl.

Quickening was a fine ship. Big and sturdy, she could be nimble and dexterous, as well. She was armor-clad from bow to stern and equipped with rail slings and winch-fired crossbows. The empty cradles positioned at all four corners had been built to hold and utilize fire launchers. Illegal everywhere in the Four Lands by Druid Edict since Federation Prime Minister Sen Dunsidan had built one secretly and then tried to use it against the Elves, fire launchers were nevertheless available if you knew the right people. Thus, every transport making a regular run from one quarter of the Four Lands to another tried to have at least one hidden on board.

Quickening was blessed with a full complement thanks to the efforts of Redden and Railing, who had secured them through their contacts on the black market and delivered them unbidden in an effort to win Mirai's admiration and favor. She had bestowed both on each twin, although neither was fully aware of just how much she had lavished on the other.

This was because they didn't talk about their feelings for Mirai—at least not in the way they might have if they weren't in competition for her. It was the only matter on which they did not share opinions and feelings. Each of them was fiercely protective of his relationship with her, even without entirely understanding its nature.

Certainly, Mirai never gave them much to work with.

She treated them both the same and never gave one the benefit over the other. She acted as if all three were close friends and nothing more. Except that now and then she did things that suggested maybe there was something more with one or the other. A moonlight walk with Redden. A swim down by the lake with Railing. A special word here, a meaningful look there, a private smile, a sexy laugh, all of it suggesting she felt something more than what they believed or understood.

Redden was thinking about the unfairness of all this when Mirai called down to him from the pilot box and asked him to come up and take over the controls.

"I want to speak with Railing a moment," she announced casually, as if to confirm his worst fears.

She went down the deck to where Railing was tightening the draws on the forward light sheath and spoke to him for a very long time. Redden watched with a mix of suspicion and envy, and when she returned and took back the controls it was all he could do to keep from rushing down to ask his brother what was so important.

Instead he said to her, "Why did you ask us to come? Didn't your father offer to send some of the sailors who work for him?"

She glanced over and held his gaze. The wind was whipping her blond hair all about her face, forming a kind of shifting veil. She looked so ravishing it was all he could do to keep his thoughts together.

"Maybe I didn't want my father's sailors with me as much as I wanted you. Maybe I don't want him to know everything I do on this trip." Her laugh was slow and rolling. "Or maybe it was a whim and nothing more. What do you think?"

He grimaced. "I think maybe I shouldn't have asked."

"No, no, you can always ask, Redden. But you can't always expect to get the answer you'd like." She was working hard to make herself heard over gusts of wind that nearly knocked him backward from his perch. Only his handhold on the cockpit railing prevented him from being toppled. Mirai, on the other hand, barely moved. "Windy, isn't it? Don't you love days like this?"

In truth, he did. Wild and windy, no clouds, all sunshine and blue skies—perfect flying weather. He loved them as much as he loved cold ale in summer and his mother's warm bread in winter. He grinned in spite of himself.

"There, you see?" She laughed and gave him a playful shove. "I like it so much better when you smile!"

He felt himself blushing and turned away, pretending to study something down by the ship's railing. "I smile enough."

She shoved him again. "Get out of my cockpit, Troll boy! Go talk to your brother. Ask him to tell you what I told him. That should give you something to think about."

He hesitated a moment to see if she was serious, but when she pushed him again he did as she said and headed downship toward Railing, who was still at the bow. Before him and to either side, the vast green canopy of the Duln spread away in a rippling blanket of leaves and tiny branches, giving the landscape the look of a vast emerald ocean. To the north, Rainbow Lake shimmered in clips of silvery light, and beyond its bright reflective surface you could just see the dark smudge of the Dragon's Teeth through a haze of mountain brume.

"Mirai told me to ask you what she said when she spoke to you," he said grudgingly, positioning himself next to his brother, both of them leaning on the worn surface of the ship's railing.

"Did she?" Railing gave him a surprised look.

"Yes, actually, she did. But you keep it to yourself if you want. It doesn't matter to me."

"Glad to hear it. I'd tell you if it was important to you that I did, but not otherwise. It isn't important, is it?"

Redden clenched his teeth. "Not in the least."

"Good. Because it was kind of private. Personal, really."

Redden's fingers tightened their grip. "You are pressing your luck. You know that, don't you?"

Railing grinned. "She told me she wanted us to come with her to Bakrabru because she's expecting trouble along the way. Raiders. Gnome pirates using flits. Apparently they've drifted down out of the Northland, tracking vessels in our shipping lanes. There have been reports of them along the eastern shores of the Myrian. Her father hasn't heard the reports yet or he wouldn't have agreed to let her go. Obviously, Mother hasn't heard or she wouldn't have agreed, either. Mirai has been busy covering up some stuff, it seems."

"Nothing new there. She's always covering up something." Redden relaxed his grip on the railing. "But that's okay. I'm glad she decided to take us with her. I think we need to get away for a few days. See something new. Have an adventure."

"Maybe get in a fight?" Railing glanced over.

"Maybe."

"Almost as much fun as crashing a Sprint."

"Almost."

"So Mirai thinks we might get attacked?"

"She thinks it's certain."

Railing gave him a solemn nod. "I hope she's right."

They left it there, staring out at the world below, lost in their separate thoughts. A few minutes later, Redden moved away.

They spent the night anchored just east of the Duln Forests, not quite into the Tirfing, but safely onto a stretch of flats where they could keep watch. The night was clear and bright with moonlight, so it was easy to see anything approaching from some distance away. They took turns at the watch post, much of the time all three of them awake and talking about everything from airships to Federation politics.

By dawn they had eaten and raised anchor and were flying west again toward their destination.

Three hours later they were under attack.

It happened all at once, just as they were entering the airspace over a rugged clutch of lowlands dotted with heavy woods and riven with deep ravines and twisting rock formations. The lowlands stretched far enough north and south that trying to fly around would have taken them well out of their way, so Mirai simply pointed *Quickening*'s bow toward what she believed to be the narrowest part of the unfriendly lowlands and increased speed, intending to be over and past before they could be challenged.

But the Gnome raiders were waiting, hidden in the ravines under cover of trees and scrub, and their flits were airborne and winging toward the transport in minutes. Redden, standing forward on the port bow, spotted them first. Yelling a warning to his brother and Mirai, he leapt to man the forward port rail sling. Railing, standing on the starboard side, was quick to seize control of the rail sling opposite his brother, and Mirai accelerated the *Quickening* further.

But outrunning the lighter, faster flits was virtually impossible, so the raiders were on them almost immediately. Zipping about like angry hornets, the flits swarmed over them, the raiders wielding poles with blades attached to rip at the light sheaths and cut at the ship's rigging. Enough damage and the ship would go down or the crew would surrender. Because the flits were one-man airboats, they were quick and maneuverable, and even the wide scattershot of metal pieces fired by the rail slings seldom found their targets.

But the Ohmsfords had practiced extensively with rail slings and fought off Gnome raiders before, and they took down three of the flits in minutes. Even so, there were dozens to replace them. The Gnomes relied on superior numbers to overcome defenders, and frequently that was enough. Railing took a dart in his shoulder early on, the bolt fired with such force that it penetrated the heavy padding he wore for protection. Redden heard his brother grunt, yet when he turned to help found him still at his post.

But the light sheaths were being shredded, causing the flow of power from the radian draws to diminish and the airship to slow. The Gnomes, sensing victory, shifted their efforts from disabling the ship to disabling her pilot, launching an attack on Mirai in the cockpit.

During all of this, the Ohmsfords had failed to make use of the fire launchers. They had carried two of the weapons topside from their hiding places early that morning and placed them in the forward cradles before setting out. But the brothers were not extensively practiced with fire launchers, and on talking over how they would function in the event of an attack they realized for the first time a number of problems with trying to use them to fight off flits. First off, the launchers were not easily maneuvered and would have trouble tracking the tiny craft. Second, if they swung them even a little too far one way or the other, they would set fire to their own vessel. Third, it took time for diapson crystals to charge sufficiently to maintain the intensity of the fire stream necessary to burn attackers out of the sky, and once their power charge was exhausted the launchers were useless.

So the brothers had turned at once, on sighting the flits, to the more reliable rail slings for defense.

But seeing the raider attack shift toward Mirai, Redden had a flash of inspiration. He abandoned his rail sling and rushed to the port fire launcher, swinging the big weapon's barrel about so that it was facing toward the speedy attackers just off the port side of *Quickening*.

This better work, he thought, *because otherwise we are in serious trouble.* And he cursed Railing for his impetuous wish of the night before.

Railing was screaming at him from the other side of the bow, presumably because he had abandoned his station, but Redden ignored his brother. He opened the barrel cap, released the trigger safety, and with the launcher ready for use summoned the wishsong's magic.

Worked for Railing with the Sprint. Should work for me here.

He channeled the magic out of his body and down through his hands into the fire launcher. The weapon bucked in response, a lurching that very nearly unseated it from its cradle.

Redden hauled back on the trigger.

The magic-enhanced fire exploded from the barrel in a sharp burst of light and heat, the backwash of which very nearly flattened Redden. But he held on to the weapon's handles, maintaining control of the wishsong through his grip, directing its path. Normally, the launcher's fire would have assumed a tight, narrow beam with sufficient intensity to burn right through iron. But Redden used his magic instead to create a swath wide enough to impact a whole raft of Gnome raiders, mustering less force than a more concentrated beam would have, but enough to knock dozens of them all over the sky. Caught by surprise, the flits spun this way and that and toppled out of sight.

As quick as that, the attack was broken up. With half

their force either downed or disabled, the rest of the raiders broke off and flew back the way they had come.

Redden glanced toward the stern and the pilot box. Dozens of darts and javelins sprouted from the wooden cockpit walls like quills from a porcupine; dozens more littered the decking. Mirai was still at the controls, disheveled and streaked with sweat and dirt but miraculously unharmed. She gave him a reassuring wave and began brushing splinters from her clothing.

He released his grip on the fire launcher and stepped back—right into Railing, who had appeared at his elbow.

"Good to see I can still teach you something," his brother quipped. He had pulled the dart from his shoulder and was holding a makeshift compress to the wound. "That was pretty impressive, using the wishsong like that. I should have thought of it."

Redden gave him a weak grin. Maybe so. But he hadn't, and so he didn't know that invoking the wishsong to control the power of diapson crystals in a fire launcher was debilitating and scary. Even now, Redden was shaking. The power of the wishsong had been drained by that single use, that momentary effort. He was left light-headed and dizzy, and there was something happening inside of him that he couldn't quite define.

Whatever it was, he didn't much like how it made him feel.

II

◆

KHYBER ELESSEDIL STOOD AT THE BOW OF HER
personal vessel, the *Ard Rhys,* and watched as the docks
of the Ohmsford home at Patch Run came into view.
She had traveled down from Paranor with the new day,
wending her way over the peaks of the Dragon's Teeth
until she reached the Mermidon, then traveling down
the length of the Runne Mountains to Rainbow Lake
and from there across to her destination. She was making the journey with Garroneck and a crew of four, but
only out of deference to the wishes of her Captain of the
Druid Guard who believed that an Ard Rhys should always travel with an escort.

Otherwise, she would have come alone.

She glanced around momentarily to watch as the
Trolls prepared the airship for landing. Garroneck
stood at the helm, and while she was certain he was
watching her, he showed no signs of doing so.

Vigilance without interference.

She turned back to watch the shoreline. She could see
the walls and roof of the Ohmsford house emerge from
between the trees of the surrounding forest. The docks
were mostly empty of craft; only a couple of skiffs and
a barge were in moorage. A large boathouse was situated off to one side, the kind that could be used for

dry-docking and repairs. Seabirds circled the shoreline, hundreds strong. Stacks of materials and assorted equipment sat in neatly stacked piles at the ends of the docks and in scattered clumps throughout the grassy rise leading up to the house. A typical workingman's home if you ignored the absence of any men or work.

Nor was there any sign of the home's inhabitants.

She thought about Sarys Ohmsford, with whom she would have to deal, and was immediately sad. Sarys Starleigh of the Elves—a woman of strong will and stronger emotions, a mother who loved her sons more than anything and would fight to the death to protect them. Born of a people who had embraced magic for centuries, she had been less entranced than most right from the first. Shy and skittish, she had avoided things that frightened her. Magic was one of them. But when she fell in love with Kierst Ohmsford and discovered the Ohmsford legacy, she was forced to reassess her thinking. Unable to give him up, she had persuaded herself that her children would be among the generations skipped by the magic of the wishsong. The odds were excellent, after all. Her future husband's father, Penderrin Ohmsford, and his father and his father's sister, Bek and Grianne Ohmsford, had all possessed it. It was time for the legacy to skip her children as it had their father. If it did not, that would mean three out of four consecutive generations would inherit the magic. That had never happened dating all the way back to the siblings Brin and Jair Ohmsford, who had been the first to have use of it.

Her terror and dismay when she discovered her twin boys had been born with the wishsong had driven a schism between herself and the rest of those in the Ohmsford family who were magic wielders—a schism that even Kierst's efforts had failed to bridge. Once it was determined that the magic was there, Sarys had undertaken a campaign to make certain that it was never employed. From the time they were small, Redden and Railing Ohmsford had been forbidden to use it or even to acknowledge publicly that the potential for doing so existed.

The death of her husband put a finish to the Ohmsford line save for her boys, unless there were distant relatives out there in the world that no one knew about. So she was immediately confronted with the problem of how to deal with her sons' growing desire, in the wake of their father's death, to embrace their unique legacy and explore their magic's potential. Beyond distraught, she had done her best to stop this. She knew she could not prevent it entirely; she understood their need to satisfy their curiosity. She resorted to negotiation, conceding one use while forbidding another, always doing her best to keep them in check. Part of her strategy was to allow the boys greater freedom in exploring other areas of interest—such as building and flying airships—to keep them distracted. Some freedoms were mandated in any case by the inescapable need for the family to find ways to survive, and her sons proved adept when it came to making favorable trades on the open market. The black market, too, though she would never have admitted to anyone that she knew they were active there, as well.

Khyber considered how she would approach the business at hand. Sarys Ohmsford had not been speaking to her at the time Khyber had gone into the Druid Sleep. In large part it was because her husband had been killed while flying with the Druids, and she had decided for reasons best known to herself that a failure of their magic was the root of the cause. She had forbidden her sons to have contact with any of the Druids and especially Khyber. While she slept, it wasn't an issue. Now it most certainly would be. But there was no getting past what needed doing, and somehow she must persuade Sarys to allow her sons to aid the very people she distrusted most.

She might as well have been trying to persuade pigs they could fly.

The airship glided toward the docks and settled into the largest of the slips, rolling slightly with the motion of the disturbed waters before coming to rest. While the Troll guards set about securing the mooring lines, Khyber walked back to where Garroneck stood at the ship's helm.

"When we are secured, I want you and your men to wait here for me. Let me go up to the house alone."

He looked at her doubtfully. "Yes, Mistress."

She relented. "You can wait for me on the dock, if you wish. But Sarys Ohmsford is a difficult woman, and she won't like it if I trudge up to the front door of her house with Troll guards at my back."

"She won't like having you here under any circumstances." Garroneck's implacable face showed no hint of humor. "But that is as it may be. My men and I will wait."

She left him where he was, walked over to the railing door, slipped the latch, and climbed down the rope ladder ten rungs to the dock. By now, Sarys would know who had arrived. She would already be angry and worried. Something would have to be done quickly to diffuse both. Khyber was already thinking about what that something might be.

Redden and Railing Ohmsford had grown from boys to young men in the time she had slept the Druid Sleep. She had known them when they were little. She had visited them and spoken with them and taken them for airship rides with their father. But with their father's death, all that had stopped. Most of their growing up had taken place without her. She had no idea how they would see her now. She had made certain the family was watched over from afar, and so she knew something of how the boys had turned out. Wild, unpredictable, brash, and daring—that was the report on their involvement with airships, particularly Sprints. They were frequently in trouble, but always able to extricate themselves, although sometimes it required help from their Rover cousins. Their mother knew less than half of a half of what they did, but she had been successful, mostly, in keeping them from using the magic.

That, of course, would have to change.

How could she get Sarys to agree? Perhaps the boys would help her with this. If they were present, they might find her offer intriguing enough to take her side. But she didn't want to pit a mother against her sons in this matter, creating a breach that might never be repaired, so she had to be careful in her choice of words. Telling Sarys too much would be fatal to her chances; she would have to skirt the edges.

She climbed the trail from the docks to the house, her legs stiff-gaited with age and her breath shortened long before she completed the climb. She had aged and worn down while she slept, though not nearly as much as she might have had she been awake. The problem was that she was already aging when she went to sleep, though she might try to deny it. Elves lived longer than humans, but their longevity wasn't as pronounced as it had been in the time of Faerie.

Listen to me, she thought. *Indulging in self-pity and remorse. What next? Regret for lost youth and no child of my own?*

She said it to herself, in the privacy of her mind, where no one could hear. But she said it only half in jest, and her smile was bitter.

She had gotten to within a dozen feet of the porch when the door opened and Sarys stepped out to confront her, tall and slender and regal, eyes as hard as stones.

"You are not welcome here," she said, folding her arms across her chest, blocking the way.

Khyber stopped where she was and nodded. "I know that. But I am here because I have no other choice."

Sarys made a face. "The reason doesn't matter. You have been told not to come. You waste my time and yours. Go back to Paranor."

"I cannot do that until you hear what I have to say."

"Nothing you have to say is of any interest to me. Nothing ever will be. Get back aboard your ship and fly out of here. Do it right now."

Khyber held her ground, not moving, not speaking. She just stood there, her eyes locked on Sarys, waiting her out.

"I thought you were in the Druid Sleep," the other woman said finally.

"I was, but something happened that brought me awake. The Four Lands are in danger, Sarys— threatened by the very thing that you fear most. By magic. By magic so powerful that if it were to fall into the wrong hands, it would put us all at desperate risk."

"But those 'wrong hands' would not be your own, of course." Sarys shook her head. "No, never the clever hands of the Druids. You would use the magic wisely, wouldn't you?"

"We would at least use it in an informed way. Or perhaps not use it at all, but put it away where it could not be *misused*." She paused, holding the other woman's gaze. "May I please come inside so that we can sit down and talk? If you find what I have to say repellent, ask me to leave then. I will have had my say and be gone from here. But I must at least speak to you first."

Sarys shook her head, and suddenly there was a glint of tears at the corners of her eyes. "You took Kierst from me, and now you want to hurt my boys. Whatever you intend, that will be the unavoidable result." She wiped furiously at her face. "Look what you've done to me, just by coming here like this."

"I didn't come here to hurt your boys. You know better. I came because I am compelled. Please let me explain."

"Go away, Ard Rhys. Go away, and never come back."

"I can't do that. If I don't speak to you, I must at least speak to Redden and Railing."

"No!" She shrieked the word. Her face transformed into something terrifying, and she came halfway down the steps, her posture suddenly menacing. "You will not speak to my boys! Not ever! Do you hear me, witch? Not ever!"

"Then you must let me speak to you. Let me explain what has brought me and then you can decide how necessary this visit is."

Sarys was incensed, her hands clenched, her face contorted in fury. "Get out of here!"

"If I don't speak with you, I will have to speak with your sons."

"If you say one word to them—just one word—I will see you dead!"

Sarys's voice was low and quiet and hard. There was no mistaking her commitment to carrying out her threat if she were forced to do so. But Khyber had been threatened before, and she knew when threats were real and when they were simply born of desperation.

She came forward until she was standing at the bottom of the veranda stairs within arm's reach of Sarys Ohmsford. "I came to you out of respect. I could have avoided you entirely and gone straight to Redden and Railing. You wouldn't have known if I had. I could still do so. And I will, if you continue to refuse me. No,

Sarys." She held up one hand in warning as the other started to speak. "No more threats. Threats are beneath you. You are better than that. Stop arguing with me and listen to what I have to say or you will force me to do exactly what I have been trying to avoid. You will force me to go behind your back."

Sarys stood her ground. "You don't scare me, Khyber."

"Good. Then neither of us holds an advantage over the other. Let's go inside and sit down and talk. Please."

There was a long moment of indecision before the other woman finally nodded, turned around reluctantly, and led the way up the porch steps into the house. She took Khyber into the kitchen and without a word set about making them both tea. When she had completed the task, she brought the cups to the table at which Khyber was sitting and joined her.

"This changes nothing," she said pointedly.

Khyber nodded. It did, of course, but there was no reason to say so. "Are you well?" she asked instead.

Sarys smiled faintly. "Say what you've come to say. Don't waste my time. I want you gone as quickly as possible."

"Then listen well, Sarys." Khyber put down her tea. "The existence of a very powerful magic, an ancient Elven magic, has been discovered quite by chance. As yet, only the Druids know about it. But that may change. It is important that we find and secure it before certain others do—others less dedicated to protecting the Four Lands."

"By that, you mean the Federation, of course," Sarys sneered.

"I mean men and women throughout the Four Lands for whom power is an elixir and an addiction. I mean anyone who thinks that wielding magic is a way to enhance their own status and will use it at the expense of others. They are out there, and we both know it. Who they are affiliated with matters not in the least. Their intentions are what trouble me."

She sipped at her tea but didn't look away from the other woman. "I was uncertain what to do when I learned about this magic, and so I went to ask the advice of the shades of the dead. Often they know things hidden from the living, and I was hopeful that they would help me in my search for this magic. One of those shades, a very powerful Druid now long dead, came to me and told me something of what I needed to know. Among the things it told me was that my fears were justified—the danger of a misuse of the magic, should it fall into the wrong hands, was real. It also told me one thing more. It told me that when I went in search of this lost magic I must take with me both Redden and Railing—that they were crucial to my success in finding where the magic was hidden."

She was skirting the edges of the truth, trying to avoid anything that suggested the twins would be in any danger. Sarys was staring at her openmouthed. "Actually," she continued, "the shade told me that the quest to find the magic would fail without your sons to help me. It gave me no explanation of why that was so. But in all of the great quests and struggles that have defined the history of the Four Lands since the recovery of the Sword of Shannara and the defeat of the Warlock Lord, there have been Ohmsfords involved. I think it is their destiny, Sarys. I think it is the family's destiny. You and I, we might wish it otherwise, but we have nothing to say about it."

The other woman nodded slowly. "You have nothing to say about it, perhaps. But I most certainly do."

"But is the choice yours to make? Do you speak for your sons? Or will you let them speak for themselves?"

"In this instance, I will speak for them. They are not

going. Find someone else to help you with this nonsense."

"There is no one else." Khyber sipped delicately at her tea, watching the other carefully. "You have raised your boys to look after themselves and not to depend on you. They are boys in name only. They are almost men. How ready are they to make wise choices? How well have you taught them? Have you faith in their ability to reason things out?"

Sarys laughed softly. "What I have faith in is none of your business. What I know is that your ability to manipulate, like that of all Druids, is boundless. What I know is that trickery and deceit are the tools of your trade. When it comes to magic there is nothing you would not do to achieve your ends. If that is what compels you, so be it. I wish you well. But you will not entangle my sons in your schemes. I will not allow it."

"Even if the Four Lands are at risk? Even if we are all at risk? At what point does the danger become sufficient that you will set aside your prejudices and permit the needs of the many to override your fears and persuade you to do the right thing?"

"Not when you are the one who suggests I must!" Sarys snapped. "You have no right to tell me what I should do when it comes to my sons!"

Khyber took a deep breath and exhaled slowly. "This quest must be undertaken. The danger must be overcome before the threat grows too large to control. We are at a crucial juncture in our history, Sarys. Science has begun to resurface as a force that will determine the direction of our evolution as a culture. It was lost and shunned with the destruction of the Old World in the cataclysm of the Great Wars. And rightfully so. But now we find remnants of it being rediscovered and put to use in such terrible struggles as the war on the Prekkendorran. It competes with magic for dominance.

Each new discovery, each fresh revelation, shifts our perspective on whether it might be time to reintroduce science into the world. Now, all at once, a magic thought lost forever reemerges. If it is recovered, the struggle between magic and science will escalate. No matter where we stand on the issue, no matter how we feel about it, we cannot afford to pretend it doesn't matter. We cannot ignore its potential impact. History tells us what will happen if we fail to act. I know it and you know it, too, even if you refuse to acknowledge it."

She paused, shook her head. "I don't like having to come here. I would not be here at all if I were not convinced that your sons' help is necessary. I do not intend that they should be forced to do anything. But I do intend that they be given a chance to decide for themselves."

Sarys seemed to be thinking it over, and then she said, "Well, any decision will have to wait. They're not here. They've gone camping with a friend. I don't know when they will return. Come back when they have and ask them then."

It was such an obvious attempt at trying to avoid the inevitable that Khyber almost felt sorry for her. But feeling sorry for anyone in this business was something she could not afford.

"Where have they gone? They must have told you."

"They tell me little these days. They left yesterday with a friend. On an airship. They could be anywhere by now. I can't help you."

Khyber was silent a moment. "You are aware of the Ohmsford family history—especially that which is most recent and which has impacted you and your family most directly. Where would we all be now if Bek Ohmsford had not gone with Walker Boh to Parkasia on the *Jerle Shannara*? Where would we all be if he had not found his lost sister and helped her become Ard

Rhys before me? If he had not then fathered Penderrin and helped bring an end to the war on the Prekkendorran and closed the door into the Forbidding, would we be here at all? Not many know this part of our history; most never will. But you know it, Sarys. Your husband told you. Penderrin told you. In each case, a choice was made by a young man to do the right thing—not to refuse to participate because it was too dangerous but to accept what fate and circumstance had given them to do."

"What *Druids* had given them to do! Isn't that what you mean?" Sarys was stone-faced. "What *you* would now give my sons to do? Tell me what that is, why don't you! Tell me what you would ask of them!"

"I would ask them to make the same choice as their ancestors. I don't want to have to involve them. I don't even want to be here. But I cannot ignore what is staring me in the face. Magic is a part of our lives. It has been so since the time of the Great Wars. We can't pretend otherwise. Magic defines who we are, your family and mine. We ignore this at our peril. Magic is a gift and a curse. If we manage it in the right way, it can be of great benefit. If we don't, we risk destroying ourselves."

"You have *chosen* to make this your work, Khyber. My sons have not. I will not allow them to be dragged into your machinations. I refuse to help you. You had better go."

Khyber nodded. "You know that sooner or later I will find a way to speak with them, don't you?"

"I know nothing of what you will or won't do, and I care even less. Please leave."

Khyber rose and stood looking down at her. "Who is the friend they went camping with?"

Sarys shook her head stubbornly.

"Was it Mirai Leah?"

She saw the look of shock and anger that flashed across the other woman's face and knew she had guessed right. She felt a quick surge of satisfaction, but also an odd sense of shame.

"Do you spy on us, witch?" Sarys Ohmsford cried. "Are you so desperate that you must stoop to that? Get out of my house!"

Khyber did not move. "When I leave here, I will travel to Leah and ask the same questions of Mirai's father. He will tell me what you won't. Then I will fly to wherever Redden and Railing have gone and speak with them. Fate and circumstance have made it necessary, Sarys. You cannot avoid either any more than I can. Now tell me where to find them. Do the right thing."

Sarys rose slowly and faced her down. "My sons will never agree to go with you. I have made certain of that, Ard Rhys. I have taught them of the Druids' schemes and their destructive history. You are wasting your time."

"Then let me find that out for myself. Let me go to them and tell them of my need. Let them refuse me face-to-face." Khyber kept her voice calm and even. "Do not presume to speak for them. They will resent you for it. You raised them to think for themselves and to act as they determined best, didn't you? Prove it here."

There were fresh tears in Sarys Ohmsford's eyes as the women faced each other across the table. "I hate you," Sarys said softly. "I hate all of you. You Druids, who think you are so special and believe so deeply in your twisted causes. I hate you with every fiber of my being."

Khyber nodded. "You are entitled to that."

"If the earth opened and swallowed every last one of you, I would not shed a single tear. I would rejoice. Druids, with your magic and your black arts, twisting the lives of others, shaping events to your own purpose. I despise you."

Khyber said nothing, waiting.

Sarys looked away, suddenly defeated. "They are in Bakrabru," she said quietly.

"Thank you," Khyber said.

The other woman looked back again, a hint of disbelief in her dark eyes. "I don't know why I am helping you."

"Because it is the right thing. Because you trust your sons."

"But not you, witch. I don't trust you."

Khyber kept her anger carefully in check. "I will say nothing to them I do not know to be true. I will do nothing to force them to choose. I will leave it to them. Even if I could make the choice for them, I would not. Help of the sort that is required of Redden and Railing can only be useful if it is given freely."

Sarys smiled thinly. "If you say so."

Khyber hesitated a moment longer before nodding and turning away. She was at the door when the other woman called out to her.

"If anything happens to my sons," she said, her words sharp and bitter and coated in ice, "you had better make certain it happens to you first. Otherwise, I will kill you, Khyber Elessedil. Whatever it takes to do so, I will kill you."

The Ard Rhys of the Fourth Druid Order remained perfectly still, looking out toward the waters of Rainbow Lake and the dark sweep of storm clouds moving in from the west.

I believe you, she thought.

Then she went out the door and down the path that would take her back to her airship and her Troll guard and did not look back.

12

APHENGLOW ELESSEDIL HAD PROMISED THE ARD
Rhys she would do two things if she were given permission to return to Arborlon. First, she would find someone to protect her, and second, she would speak to her mother to discover what she knew of the relationship between the Elessedils and the Omarosians.

She had no interest in the former and no stomach for the latter, but a promise was a promise, especially when it was given to the Ard Rhys.

So as she flew *Wend-A-Way* into the Elven home city, preparing to set about the business that had brought her back, she was already thinking of how she would fulfill those promises while limiting the amount of inconvenience and discomfort each would entail. On landing, she took her travel bag and walked from the airfield to the cottage she shared with her sister to ask her thoughts. But Arlingfant was not at home, so she dropped her bag and set off for the Gardens of Life to find her.

Her walk through the city took her past many of the familiar landmarks of her childhood, conjuring up memories of other times, many of them connected to her family and friends, all of them building blocks for the life she now led as a Druid. She had always been different, a stubborn rebellious child who insisted on knowing when others chose to leave well enough alone, a talented magic wielder in training who even at a very young age could already sense things hidden from her sister and friends. She didn't know how she could do this, why she was born this way, but she knew it set her apart and it would shape the way she grew. What it did was teach her early on about the importance of self-sufficiency and resolve when loneliness was the consequence of being different.

She had never minded being what she was, even in the worst of times. It was hard when she was forced to endure Arlingfant's occasional resentment and envy while they were children, but both vanished when her sister was made a Chosen and given special recognition of her own. And Arlingfant had never refused her the way their mother had, not early on when the differences first began to emerge or later when she had gone to Paranor. The competitiveness that had marked much of their childhood never interfered with the trust they felt for each other. Whatever happened in their lives, their commitment to each other remained the same—a foundation for a relationship grounded in love and admiration.

So she never considered speaking about her purpose in coming back with anyone other than her sister—although she knew Ellich, who was more a father to her than an uncle, would have given her good advice and much-needed support.

But there was no one as close to her as Arlingfant.

Not even Bombax, whom she loved so much.

And especially not her mother.

She found her sister engaged in planting fresh roses not far from where the Ellcrys shimmered red and silver in the afternoon sunlight, majestic and serene, the centerpiece of the garden. Created by a powerful conjuring of ancient Elven magic and sustained through a sacrifice of Elven lives over the centuries, the tree was a talisman upholding the impenetrable wall of the Forbidding behind which creatures of dark magic had been banished during the last wars of Faerie. The Ellcrys kept the Elves safe from their most ancient enemies; their lives had always been and would forever be directly tied to the life of the tree. Ancient history now, centuries in the past, the story had taken on the trappings of fable. Yet the tree was living proof of the fable's validity. Not all that long ago, its magic had failed and the wall of the Forbidding had begun to erode and its creatures to escape, and the truth behind the legend had been brought home in the most dramatic of ways.

She gave the Ellcrys a long look, admiring its radiance, overwhelmed just by being in its presence. Her own magic connected her to that of the tree, a shared origin, a link to something profound and not entirely dissimilar. She knew the story of the tree's history, especially of its death and rebirth during the reign of the great Elven King Eventine Elessedil. She knew of the sacrifice made by his granddaughter, and no one who knew that could help but feel awed by the power of the magic with which the talisman was imbued. That such a wonder existed—a tree with such power—was overwhelming and magnificent. The Elves might have lost their magic through the centuries, but as long as the Ellcrys existed they would continue to be reminded how impressive and vital such magic could be.

All of which made it difficult to understand how they could endure their loss with such indifference, with such pointless stoicism, a dedicated refusal to try to change things when the magic was so clearly a part of who they were. She would never understand, if she lived another hundred years, how they could be so willing to let go of what had once been the foundation of their lives and done so much to shape their history.

She walked over to Arlingfant, tapped her sister on

her shoulder, and embraced her when she leapt to her feet in surprise, as happy as she was that they were together again.

"Oh, I missed you, Aphen! Even for the few days you were gone! I'm so glad you're back!" Arling was effusive, flushed with pleasure. "Tell me everything that's happened. Come, sit over here with me where we can talk!"

She walked them over to a quiet spot away from the other Chosen and sat them down, her expression revealing her eagerness. "Will you stay now? Will you return to your work searching the archives?"

Aphenglow smiled and shook her head. "I am only back a short time before I return to Paranor."

She could not tell Arling the truth, could not mention the diary at all, and must be careful that she said nothing that would reveal what the Druids were about. She could justify evasiveness but not lying openly and so could not say anything that would result in the latter.

"How long, Aphen?" Her sister's disappointment was clear.

"A few days. I need your help. I was allowed to return under two conditions. First, I must find someone to act as my bodyguard. I told the Ard Rhys of the attacks on me, and she is worried that I am in danger. So she insisted I secure a protector. Do you know of someone who might accept the job? I know so few people now."

Her sister hesitated. "Let me think about it. What was the second condition?"

"That I speak with Mother."

"What do you intend to say? Why does the Ard Rhys insist you speak with her?"

Aphenglow shrugged. "She dislikes it that we are so at odds. She wants me to try to close the breach I created by choosing to become a Druid. She wants the damage repaired."

All of which was true. Arlingfant shook her head. "It isn't you who created the problem. So don't say that. Mother is the one who is being unreasonable, refusing even to speak with you. She is the one who should take the first step."

"But she won't, so it is up to me. I have to try, at least. I will go to her as soon as I leave you. The Ard Rhys is right. No family should be split as we are."

Her sister reached over and touched her shoulder. "I will go with you. It might help if I am there."

But Aphenglow shook her head. She couldn't allow that. Not if she wanted to speak openly to her mother about the connection between the Elessedils and the Omarosians. "I need to do this alone, Arling. It will be enough if you help me with finding a protector."

Arling grinned. "It's hard for me to imagine anyone protecting you. It is easier to see it the other way around. Besides, won't you be leaving again right away?"

"Not necessarily. There are a few other things I must do."

How much should she tell Arlingfant? Certainly not about the diary or the Omarosians or the missing Elfstones. But what about the request she must make of her grandfather that she be allowed to borrow the blue Elfstones to take them to Paranor and the Druids? Arling would hear about it quickly enough in any case. She would not be able to ask her grandfather privately. He was King before he was her grandfather, and the request she would make must be made both to him and the Elven High Council. Such audiences did not long remain a secret from the general population.

She got to her feet. "I had better go to Mother while I am still feeling brave. Can we meet and talk later, after you have finished your work here?"

Arlingfant quickly agreed, rising with her, giving her another hug, telling her she loved her and wished her

well on her meeting with their mother. Aphenglow
hugged her back and turned away.

It took her only a few minutes to walk from the Gardens of Life to their mother's home—her own home
once, but that seemed so long ago. When she was close
enough to see it through the trees, she stopped in the
shadows and watched it for a time, gathering her
thoughts and her courage. Standing outside the house
like this, waiting to speak with her mother, made her
feel like a little girl again. It reminded her of how she
had felt when she had done something wrong and been
forced to confess it—ashamed, guilty, regretful, and a
bit frightened of the consequences.

Yet she had done nothing wrong here and had no reason to feel any guilt. Nor was she a little girl required to
answer to her mother for her life's choices.

But still.

She walked to the door and knocked softly. No one
came at first, but then she could hear a stirring on the
other side of the door and sense a presence. Still, nothing happened. She waited patiently, tightening her resolve for what she must do.

When the door opened, she was shocked at how old
her mother looked. Once a woman of great beauty, she
now appeared haggard and worn, her soft radiance diminished and her familiar smile absent. Instead her expression was empty of life.

"Mother, please listen to me," she said quickly, suddenly desperate to hear her mother's voice, to do what
the Ard Rhys had asked of her and repair the relationship. "I don't want us to . . ."

Her mother straightened, lifting one hand quickly to
silence her. "Are you still a Druid?" she asked, her voice
sounding as if it belonged to someone else.

Aphenglow hesitated. "Yes, but . . ."

"Come back when you're not."

And she closed the door in her daughter's face, locking it behind her.

Aphenglow left in something of a daze, head down, stunned by what had just happened even though it wasn't entirely a surprise. She felt tears come to her eyes and streak her cheeks, and she wiped them away hurriedly.

This was so unfair, she thought. This was so wrong. Why was her mother being this way? After so long, why wasn't she willing to talk to her own daughter?

She couldn't bear to think on it, couldn't stand the pain of having to do so, and she chose instead to go visit with her uncle. She found him working in his garden behind the home he shared with Jera, down on his knees, weeding and planting, this big man handling the fragile little plants with such care and affection.

"Aphen!" he exclaimed on seeing her, and got to his feet with a smile. He saw her face and stopped. "Why so sad, child?"

"I've come from seeing Mother." The tears came anew. "Once again, she would not speak to me."

Ellich took her in his arms. "She cannot get past your decision to become a Druid. She cannot bring herself to accept it. But she is otherwise unhappy, too. She speaks to almost no one these days. Not even to me."

"Why will she not speak to you? You were once as close to her as I am now to you."

Ellich released her with a shrug, stepping back with a smile. "I have done something to displease her. Does that sound familiar?"

Jera appeared, coming out of the house and down the veranda stairs to give Aphen a hug and a kiss. The three sat down together in the sun at a small garden table and drank cold ale while Aphen pushed aside the residual pain of having tried and failed to speak with her mother and instead spoke of how things were at Paranor and what she was doing back again so soon. She deflected most of their questions with harmless answers, just as she had done with Arling, saying only that matters went well with the Druids and she was back to do a little more with her research.

Finally, she got to a place where she was ready to tell Ellich the real reason for her coming.

"The Ard Rhys has determined to undertake a quest that ultimately will benefit all of the Races, Uncle." She was speaking now directly to him because he was the one who would have to help her. It didn't matter that Jera was present, though; Aphen knew that her uncle kept no secrets from his wife, and in this case there was no reason to do so anyway. "It requires use of the Elfstones if the journey is to be made easier, and I would like an opportunity to ask my grandfather to borrow them. How do you think I should go about it?"

Ellich shook his head and pursed his lips. "He will listen to you, even if you go to him directly and speak to him in private. He loves you that much. But he will not act on such a request unless it is made before the High Council. And with Phaedon present. My nephew will be King soon, perhaps yet this year. My brother grows weary of ruling and may choose to step down. Phaedon senses this and makes it a point to be a part of everything that happens in court." He gave her a rueful grin. "Do I sound bitter?"

Aphenglow shook her head. "You sound pragmatic."

"Thank you. I don't resent my nephew's eagerness to be King. But I do question his ability to govern well. He is ambitious and headstrong. Worse, he sees his own vision as singular and does not listen to others. A bad combination. It worries me."

Jera made a shushing sound, and her husband nodded his agreement. "Enough of that. I would suggest you let me arrange an audience with the King and High Council where you can make your plea. If you come before them both, you will not risk embarrassing your grandfather by appearing to try to take advantage of your special relationship. There will be debate, and some—perhaps all—will resist your request because ultimately it is a Druid request. May I ask exactly what it is you need the Elfstones for?"

She hesitated. "They might show us what it is that we are seeking. They might show us where it is hidden."

"Which would be what?"

"I am forbidden to tell you that, Uncle. I am sorry, but the Ard Rhys feels it should be kept secret. I can only say that it will be of immense benefit to the Elves if it is found."

Ellich nodded. "Well, I am content not to know. But evasiveness will not sit well with either your grandfather or the High Council. At least you are being direct about it; maybe that will help. I will arrange things. Tell me, have you given any further thought to my suggestion that it might be time to think about coming home for good? Your mother misses you."

"Does she?" The words were out before she could stop herself from speaking them. She recovered with a smile. "This isn't the right time to pursue that particular discussion, Uncle."

He studied her a moment and nodded. "No, I suppose not. Can you stay for dinner? Jera and I would like that very much."

She begged off, having already decided to spend the evening with Arlingfant. But she agreed to come the following day and have dinner with them then.

She remained awhile longer, speaking of other things, particularly of the King's health and the demands of his office. Her grandfather was not particularly old, but he had not been well for the past two years, afflicted with a variety of illnesses and injuries, laid up or slowed by one thing after the other to the point that he had begun to ponder openly the possibility of stepping aside in favor of Phaedon. Indeed, the possibility had become a probability. It was only a question of time.

Finally, the day wearing on and the conversation dwindling to long pauses, Aphenglow made her excuses and departed for home. She always enjoyed her time with Ellich and Jera. She supposed they had become her surrogate parents, the ones she missed and still needed, substitutes of the best kind. It made her sad to know she was closer to them than to her mother, but there seemed to be no help for it. She no longer had any hope of being able to change their relationship unless she gave up her Druid robes, which she would never do.

She had almost reached her little cottage, walking down the familiar path that led to her doorstep, when she saw someone sitting on the steps of her porch. She slowed, trying unsuccessfully to make out who it was. She had almost decided to turn back, to circle around and come in from behind. But the figure on the porch— with eyes as keen as her own—had already seen her, risen, and was waiting. She had no choice but to continue on the path if she did not want to look foolish or frightened, and so she did.

As she approached, she took a quick inventory of her visitor, whose features she could better discern now. A young man, close to her own age. Tall and lean beneath loose-fitting forest clothing, sporting a shock of unruly hair cut short and so blond it was almost white. No visible weapons save a long knife strapped to his waist. Skin burned brown by long hours in the sun, brilliant blue eyes that didn't look as if they missed much. The promise of a nice smile revealed in a faint twisting at the corners of his mouth.

She had never seen him before and had no idea who he was. But she found herself intrigued.

"Hello, Aphen," he greeted. "I'm told you need a bodyguard. I would like you to consider me."

She stopped right in front of him. "Who are you?"

"You don't remember?" His smile faded a bit. "We trained together as Trackers. I'm Cymrian."

A faint memory came to her. He had been two years older than she but a few younger in terms of maturity. They had been barely more than children when they started their instruction together.

"Arlingfant asked me to speak with you. Coming here and waiting was her suggestion." He paused. "Just so you know, it was because she asked. Not because . . . of anything else."

"Then she must have faith in you."

"My sister is a Chosen, too. They work together in the gardens, know each other pretty well. Will you consider me?"

She gave him a measured look. "Why would you want to do this?"

He shifted his feet to reset his stance. "I'm looking for something to do. This seemed like a good fit for me."

"Do you have any experience?"

"As a Tracker. I'm good at that. But I have other skills. I can protect you."

She almost laughed out loud. He was a far cry from what the Ard Rhys wanted for her, but closer to what she wanted for herself. She didn't much care if he could protect her or not as long as he was able to keep out of her way. A Tracker could do that. A Tracker could disappear right in front of you. But was he capable?

She glanced down at the long knife. "Are you any good with that?"

He shrugged. "I'm good with any weapon."

"Can you put it in that tree over there?" She pointed to a slender alder situated about twenty yards away.

"Where would you like it?"

That stopped her. "In that bole about halfway up the trunk. Do you see it?"

He moved so fast that she had barely finished asking the question before the knife was out of its sheath and in his hand. His arm swept up in an underhand throw and the long knife struck the center of the bole with a dull thump.

She nodded slowly. "All right. The job is yours. Just stay out of my way and do what I ask. For now, that means shadowing me wherever I go without letting me see you. Keep me safe from whatever you decide threatens. Can you do that?"

He nodded silently. She extended her hand, and he took it. "I'm sorry I didn't remember you."

He smiled faintly, took back his hand, and walked over to the tree to retrieve his knife. Once he had it, he kept going until he disappeared into the trees.

There was something about him, she thought. She sensed it, but couldn't give it a name.

She was still standing there staring off into space when Arlingfant came out of the house. "Did you give him the job?"

Aphen nodded. "He was your choice?"

"Don't you think it was a good one? Did you remember him?"

"Not sure yet about the first, no to the second."

They walked into the house and sat at the table off the small kitchen. Arlingfant looked amused. "He didn't think you would. I thought of him after you left me. He's changed since you knew him. He killed a man not too long ago. An Elf. He was in training to join the Home Guard—a natural, given his skill level. But he got on another trainee's bad side, and when the instructor wasn't looking the trainee tried to cripple him during an exercise. Cymrian reacted instinctively and killed him. His sister told me. But, you know. Once you've killed another Elf, you can't be in the Home Guard."

Aphenglow understood. There were certain prohibitions that could not be violated. Killing another Elf in service to the King was one.

"But why does he want to work for me?" she asked.

Her sister grinned. "Don't you know?"

Aphen gave her a perplexed look. "No, I don't know."

The grin broadened. "Well, you'll figure it out." Arlingfant rose. "Let's fix ourselves something to eat and then we can talk some more. How does a vegetable stew sound?"

It sounded wonderful. Aphenglow followed her into the kitchen, and for the time being pushed thoughts of Cymrian from her mind.

13

APHENGLOW SPENT THE BALANCE OF THE FOLLOW-
ing day working in the underground storerooms that
housed the Elven histories and related archives, continuing her search for information on the missing Elfstones. In particular, she was hunting for more
information on Aleia and the rest of the Omarosian
family and the connection between the two. She wanted
to be certain she hadn't missed anything here before
turning her attention to the Chosen histories.

She found exactly nothing she didn't already know.
Except for one thing.

While searching the writings peripheral to the Elven
histories, she found herself sidetracked by references to
various maps of the times in which the writings were
recorded. Wondering how much of the Faerie world
might have been mapped in the earliest of times—
particularly the time of Aleia Omarosian—she left her
place among the writing archives and moved over to
where the maps were stored. She searched them
front-to-back without success, but then found a further
reference to an ancient file that seemed to be missing.
This, in turn, led her to another room entirely, where
piles of old maps were bundled in stacks, and she spent
the next three hours scouring these.

In the end, she found something unexpected.

Something that might prove even more useful than the diary.

It was a map, crudely rendered and enigmatically labeled, of the world as it existed in the period during which Aleia Omarosian and her immediate family had lived. Aphenglow was able to identify the time period for three reasons. First, the Elven home city of Arborlon was clearly labeled, although it was located in a different place than where it was now; second, the city of Parsoprey—on the other side of the Dragon's Teeth Mountains—to which Aleia had gone to visit her grandparents, was also identified.

But third and most important, Rajancroft—the home city of the Darkling boy who had stolen the Elfstones after being rejected by Aleia—was labeled, as well.

Even though two of the cities were gone completely and the third moved to a new location, it should be possible to determine approximately where each had once been on the present-day map by using the mountains as a measuring stick.

Which meant it might be possible to find the ruins of Rajancroft and perhaps even the location of the missing Elfstones.

That effort would be aided immeasurably if she could persuade her grandfather and the High Council to allow the Druids to use the seeking-Stones.

She sat quietly for a time after that, speculating on how she might make this happen. She must be strong, but not too aggressive, in presenting her cause. She could afford to press, but not antagonize. There was bound to be resistance, but she had to find a way to overcome it. She had to turn that resistance into support, however grudgingly given. All sorts of approaches suggested themselves, but none of them seemed quite right.

And admittedly, it was still a gamble. As she had speculated before, surely someone over the centuries had tried to use the blue Elfstones to find their mates and failed. There was no reason to think that she and her fellow Druids would be any more successful.

The most difficult part of this business was not being able to be candid about what she was doing or why. Elves in general did not like obfuscation and deceit, and by keeping from them the whole of what she knew of the Druid mission she was perilously close to crossing that line. But she had been told her parameters when she'd suggested this, so she couldn't very well complain about it now.

She left the palace shortly after, deciding to go early for her dinner with Jera and Ellich. Perhaps getting out of the storerooms for a bit would help clear her mind. As she left the palace and started down the road leading to her aunt and uncle's home, Cymrian appeared from nowhere and fell in beside her.

"Any problems?" he said, his eyes shifting here and there as he walked next to her.

"Where have you been?" she asked, a bit disgruntled that she hadn't seen him before this.

"Close by."

"All day? I never saw you once."

"That's the point, isn't it? If you could see me, so could someone else. I couldn't come inside the palace, but I figured you were safe enough there."

"I'm safe enough anywhere."

"Are you?"

She gave him a look, but said nothing.

"Where will you go now?"

She hesitated before telling him, finally deciding there was no reason not to. "To my aunt and uncle's for dinner. Jera and Ellich."

He nodded. "Good people. Say hello for me."

Then he drifted away, peeling off into the woods and disappearing in the same way he had the day before. She stopped to watch him go, intrigued in spite of herself. She found him inexplicably interesting and couldn't provide a reason for it.

She enjoyed the remainder of the afternoon in the company of her aunt and uncle, and when Arlingfant arrived later on, the four shared the evening meal and several hours of reminiscence and laughter. It was the most relaxed she had felt in days, and when she arrived home that night she went straight to bed and fell immediately asleep.

The following morning, she appeared before the King and the High Council to make her request.

She rose early, but not early enough to catch Arlingfant, who had already gone off to the Gardens of Life to celebrate the sunrise with the Ellcrys and the other Chosen. Ellich had told her the night before—taking her aside for a moment's private conversation—that arrangements had been made for her to appear in the Council chambers at midmorning. She had been calm about it when told, but felt nervous now that the audience was almost at hand. She gave more thought to what she would say, knowing even as she did so that the direction the appeal would take would ultimately depend on the reaction of the King and members of the High Council to the idea of allowing the Druids to use the Elfstones.

When she walked out the door on her way to the Council chambers, she found Cymrian waiting. She realized she had never mentioned him to her aunt and uncle, even after promising herself she would do so. Her unhappiness at having let that slide kept her from saying anything rude. Instead, she smiled disarmingly.

"Keeping close watch over me?"

"Keeping you in sight."

"I have to appear before the High Council."

"I know. I'll be with you."

"They won't let you in. The audience is closed."

He nodded. "Maybe. Maybe not."

They walked on as she pondered this equivocation, wondering what he meant. Surely they wouldn't allow him into a closed Council session. Not with his violent history. In point of fact, she didn't want him there anyway. What she had to say wasn't meant for his ears. The fewer people who knew about her plans for the Elfstones, the better.

"Well, I don't need you to accompany me," she said finally. "There's no need for it. I'll be safe enough."

"Will you?"

She looked over at him to see if he was joking. He didn't appear to be. "In the presence of the members of the High Council and my grandfather? Who would dare to harm me?" she demanded, suddenly angry.

He shrugged. "The same people who would dare to try to kill you in your own house?"

She stopped short. "How did you know . . . ?"

"Your sister told me. Did you think I would be doing this if I didn't believe the threat was real? She had to tell me why you needed a protector or what was the point of asking for one? You should be a little more forthcoming with me. I'm your friend. You should act like you trust me."

She immediately bristled. "I trust you! I just don't think you need to be a part of everything I do!"

"Or perhaps part of anything. If you want me to be of any use, you have to think of me as your shadow. I have to be there all the time, not just when you think it is convenient." He paused speculatively. "Or would you like me to go?"

She almost told him she would like exactly that. But then she would be back to looking for another bodyguard if she were to keep her promise to the Ard Rhys. So she bit back the first words that came to mind and simply shook her head.

"I apologize. I admit I am not comfortable with this. I am used to looking after myself. It feels awkward having someone do it for me."

He looked off for a minute. "We both went through the same training when we were schooling to be Trackers, and I remember how much better you were than I was at almost everything. You probably think you still are." He looked back again. "But you're not. You have the use of Druid magic, which I don't. But when it comes to hand-to-hand combat, I am more experienced. I want you to trust me on this and let me do my very best to keep you safe. Will you agree to that and let me do my job?"

They faced each other wordlessly for a minute, and then Aphenglow nodded. "Do what you think is necessary. I won't argue with you anymore unless I find what you are doing personally invasive."

He stared at her. "I'm not sure what that means, but I think I can accept it as a condition. May I accompany you to your audience with the King?"

She gave him a small nod. "You may."

They continued on, not saying anything now, just walking together. Aphenglow wasn't sure she had resolved how she felt about having Cymrian as her shadow, but was satisfied that she had backed him off sufficiently that he would be careful about how far he encroached on her personal life. She would have a talk with Arlingfant later on about the quality of her choice.

They reached the Council Hall and were met by Home Guards at the entry doors. They identified themselves, and to Aphenglow's surprise they were both admitted. She had been certain the guards would turn Cymrian away, but they hadn't even tried. Inside, standing in the hallway that encircled the chamber, he turned to her again.

"I won't go any farther than this," he told her. "I know you want privacy in this matter, and I can do my job from out here. I just wanted to be close enough to reach you if you should need me. I will be waiting right outside the chamber doors."

She left him there, moving over to where the Captain of the Home Guard, a man she didn't know personally but could identify from his insignia, was waiting.

"Will you tell the King I am here?"

"Sian Aresh," he introduced himself, bowing slightly. "The King already knows. Come with me."

He turned around, knocked once loudly, released the heavy latches, and pushed the doors open. When he stepped through, she took a deep, steadying breath and followed him in.

It had been a long time since she had been in the chambers of the Elven High Council. Years. She had been a little girl then, trotting after her grandfather as he led her to this sanctuary where no one could enter uninvited. He had made it a special treat, a journey into a room where all the major decisions governing the Elven people were made, where laws were debated and passed, where honor was bestowed on those who had earned it and punishment visited on those who had transgressed. There had been such a mystery to it, and at the time it had seemed a huge, forbidding place. There had been no one but the two of them, and her grandfather, still fit and spry at eighty, had played leap-frog with her before the King's throne.

She had been so happy that day. It had been such fun.

It didn't feel as if anything of that time remained as she stood just inside the doors and looked down the Council table past the stern faces of the members of the High Council to the careworn face of her aged grandfather. Emperowen Elessedil had been King a long time. He had come to the throne in his twenties, well before the time he was expected to rule, made King by fate when his parents had died in an accident. He had been King now for the better part of eighty years, and his age was catching up with him. He no longer played games with granddaughters and grandsons, no longer even smiled. In the twilight years when peace and contentment were expected, he was struggling with illness and the pressing demands of a transfer of power in which he no longer had faith.

His heir apparent sat next to him. Phaedon Elessedil, his only son and Afrengill Elessedil's older brother, was a moody, passionate man whose character and disposition were ill suited to what was expected of a ruler of the Elven people. He was not well liked and certainly not loved, and those who supported him did so out of fear or ambition. He was a poor choice to lead his people, but by chance of birth and rule of law the issue was settled. The best his father could do at this point in his life was to prolong the inevitable, although he probably continued to have hope things would somehow work out.

Aphenglow knew most of this from talks with her sister and the few visits she had paid to her grandfather in the time she had served with the Druid order. Because of her diminished status, she could say little about her grandfather's decision to allow Phaedon to succeed him on the throne. But she knew it was a mistake the Elves would live to regret, even though the mistake was not of their doing.

Phaedon looked bored and indifferent. He was studying something off to his right, but unless it was one of the members of the High Council there was nothing there to study. She shifted her gaze to the King's left and the more welcoming countenance of Ellich Elessedil, who gave her a small nod and a smile.

The other members of the Council offered a variety of looks, but none of them seemed particularly encouraging.

She felt very out of place and very much the intruder in the black Druid robes of her order. She should have worn something less confrontational, she chided herself, and immediately regretted it. She was the representative of her order and should not appear otherwise.

"Welcome, Aphenglow," her grandfather greeted her, his voice civil but very weak. "Do you wish to speak to this Council?"

She took a step forward. "I do, High Lord. I have come to make a request, one that you might initially be inclined to reject out of hand, but if you hear me out I believe you will be persuaded to support it. I am here on behalf of the Druid order and its Ard Rhys, but it is our people who will be affected most directly by your response to what I am seeking."

"Our people," Phaedon repeated, not bothering to look up from the handful of papers he was shuffling. "By which you mean the Elves, I gather?"

His rudeness surprised her. "I do," she replied.

"Yet you wear Druid robes?"

"Phaedon, let her speak, please," the King said quietly.

"I only seek clarity," his son replied, again without looking up.

There was a long silence, as if everyone was waiting on a further exchange.

"You said you have a request?" Ellich asked Aphenglow finally, breaking the silence.

"I do." She gathered her thoughts. "The Druids have discovered an Elven magic from the Old World, one long thought lost. It is not certain that this magic can be found, or even that it still exists. To determine both, the Druids will go in search of it. But the way is unclear. There are no explicit directions that would aid us. It would help immeasurably if we were to be given temporary use of the blue Elfstones."

She didn't miss the hurried exchange of looks among the members of the High Council. Only the King, his son, and Ellich showed nothing.

"I dare to ask this of you, High Lord, because we feel we can rely on you to honor the agreement that was made between your grandmother, when she was Elven Queen, and our Ard Rhys when she was at the beginning of her service to the order. At that time, Khyber Elessedil returned the blue Elfstones to the Elven people with the understanding that should it become necessary at some later time the Druids would be allowed to borrow these Stones for limited usage. We submit that such a time is at hand. If the need were not so great, we would never ask this of you. That I have come to you with this request should indicate how important we think it is that you agree."

"This matter will need serious discussion," offered one member of the Council. She didn't know him, as she didn't know any of them save those in her family and the First Minister, an older woman who at one time had been friends with her mother.

"I am at your service," Aphenglow said.

"If you were really at our service, you would not be here making this request," Phaedon declared, his head lifting suddenly, his eyes fastening on her. "If you were really at our service, you would still be living in Arborlon and helping us instead of helping the Druid order."

"It is possible to help both, Phaedon," she replied quickly. "It is not necessary that I choose."

"But history has taught us otherwise," Phaedon pressed. "The Druids have deceived us time and again.

They used us and then took from us. We have expended lives in our efforts to serve them, and they have done little for us in return. Consider the outcome of the war on the Prekkendorran and the onslaught of the Federation heathens. Our King was killed along with his sons. Our Elven Hunters were all but obliterated. The magic wielded by the Druids did almost nothing to help us. Your own Ard Rhys abandoned her people, stole the Elfstones, and went off with her uncle to resolve a private concern. If not for a considerable amount of luck, we might have lost everything."

Aphenglow shook her head. "I don't agree. I think the Druids were the ones who saved us all. If not for the leadership of the Ard Rhys—if not for Khyber Elessedil borrowing, not stealing, the Elfstones—the efforts of the Federation to overrun and occupy our homeland might well have succeeded."

"But if Grianne Ohmsford hadn't so foolishly allowed herself to be duped by those serving in her own order and gotten herself imprisoned inside the Forbidding, the threat from the Federation would never have materialized. Why am I even arguing the matter? This is all a waste of time. Why should we do anything you ask? You are no different than Khyber Elessedil; you have betrayed us by making the Druids your new family. And now you crawl back because you need our magic? Why shouldn't we tell you to use your own instead of asking to use ours? Isn't it apparent that you are no longer one of us? You have disappointed your grandfather and your mother. You have turned your back on all of us. Go back to where you came from!"

The ensuing uproar drowned out her retort. The members of the High Council were on their feet instantly, some yelling in support, some in denigration. Even Ellich was shouting at Phaedon, who calmly ignored him, keeping his eyes on Aphenglow. Only the King sat quietly, looking down at his hands.

"Enough!" he said finally, raising his hands in a gesture for order. The room slowly quieted, and the members of the Council took their seats. "We are in session," he continued. "We will act accordingly. Personal attacks are of no help."

"Duly noted." Phaedon gave a dismissive wave. "What magic is it you seek, Aphenglow?" he demanded. "Does it have a name?"

"Yes, what is it you hope to find?" another member of the High Council echoed.

"Enlighten us," Phaedon pressed. "If you really need the use of the blue Elfstones in this mysterious business of yours, then surely you have no objection to telling us what it is you seek. Surely we have a right to know what is so important."

She nodded in agreement. "You do have that right. Yet I cannot tell you. I have been sworn to silence on the matter."

"How very convenient!" Phaedon leaned back and shook his head in mock surprise. "So even though you will not tell us what it is you are searching for, you persist in asking us to provide you with the use of the Elfstones? And this is based on an agreement that I, for one, have never heard about? An agreement between our dead King and your half-dead Ard Rhys?"

"Phaedon!" The King's hand slammed down on the tabletop with such force that the blow echoed through the chamber. "You will not speak this way about Khyber Elessedil! She is a member of our household and entitled to your respect!"

Phaedon shrugged. "I meant no disrespect, Father," he said. "I speak of her as others do. She outlives us because of her magic, and some think she does not really live at all. Not as we define life. Some say she lives a kind of half life."

"I can assure you that she is fully alive and well aware of how matters stand," Aphenglow interjected quickly. "I was with her not three days ago. As for not being able to tell you what it is we seek, there are reasons for this. If word were to reach other ears, especially in the Federation, it would complicate matters immensely and place us all in fresh danger. The fewer who know, the better. The way to finding it will likely be treacherous enough as it is. The magic itself is not entirely understood. We do not ourselves know yet what it might do. We must act cautiously. Secrecy is important."

"Isn't it always important when it comes to the Druids?" Phaedon asked, shifting his eyes away from her for the first time, directing his question to the members of the High Council. "Isn't that always the excuse? Isn't everything you do at Paranor shrouded in secrecy?"

"Why do we not use the Elfstones ourselves to find the magic?" the First Minister asked suddenly. "Why give them over to you? If the search is so dangerous and the magic belongs to us anyway, shouldn't we be the ones to brave it? You said the recovery of this magic most affects the Elves, that it is a magic that was lost to us in earlier times. So why shouldn't we be the ones to undertake this quest?"

Aphenglow felt her heart sink. "With respect, First Minister, the Druids are better equipped to carry out a task of this magnitude. We have the necessary skills and experience. We have magic of our own to aid us. We are trained for this. Please let us prove it."

"I see no reason to agree to any of this," Phaedon said again. "The First Minister is right. The Elven people can employ the magic of the blue Elfstones better than any Druid can. Use of the Stones requires that the user be of Elven blood. Only three of the Druids now in service, you included, fit that description. We should send our Elven Hunters and Trackers on this quest and keep the Druids out of it."

There was a murmur of agreement. Aphenglow could feel her hold on things slipping away. She tried to think of a better argument, one that would sway the Council to her side. But the one she understood best was the one they would be least likely to respond to—that all magic belonged in the hands of the Druid order and not in the hands of the people of the individual Races because the Druids were less likely to be swayed by impassioned nationalism and self-serving politics.

"Besides, don't you already have possession of the Black Elfstone?" Phaedon snapped. "Why don't you try using that Elfstone instead of asking for the use of ours?"

Aphenglow barely managed to keep her temper in check this time, saying only, "You know the Black Elfstone won't help with this."

"Aphenglow."

Her grandfather's soft voice quieted the room. He had straightened in his seat, and because she knew him well from time spent in his company as a little girl, she could tell he had come to a decision.

"Grandfather."

He nodded. "Your grandfather first and last, but a King of the Elven people, as well. A way must be found to honor both. Tell me again. You require use of the Elfstones so that you can determine if what you seek still exists and then discover where it can be found?"

She nodded warily. This much had already been settled. There was no point in equivocating.

"Then here is what I will agree to. What I believe the members of this Council will agree to, as well. I grant your request. I will give you use of the Elfstones to accomplish your goals." He quickly held up one hand as

Phaedon and a few others started to object. "But you must use the Elfstones here in Arborlon. You may not take them out of the city. You may not take them back to Paranor. The agreement of which you speak says nothing about that. It only says that the Druids may have temporary use of the Elfstones when the need arises."

He leaned back in his seat again. "I know you believe this is such a time. Very well. Use the Elfstones and take what you have learned with you when you go. Remember your heritage when you do so. Remember who your real family is. Remember that we depend on you. Do not disappoint us. Do not betray the Elves."

He paused, waiting on her response. She had no choice. "I would never betray the Elves, Grandfather. Never." She exhaled sharply. "I accept your decision. I will do as you say."

Emperowen Elessedil, King of the Elves, nodded slowly. "I am satisfied. The matter is settled. This Council is adjourned."

14

"APHENGLOW!"

She hadn't quite reached the Council chamber doors when her uncle's voice brought her about. Ellich was coming toward her, beckoning for her to wait for him. The other members were filing out, moving past her without glancing over, their expressions grave.

When Phaedon walked by he gave her a smile that was neither pleasant nor encouraging. "Good luck, Aphenglow," he whispered.

Ellich hurried over. "Your grandfather wants to see you in his private chambers at the palace. I'm to take you to him." He glanced over at Phaedon's departing back. "My nephew. What a waste. Ignore him. Everyone else does."

She didn't believe it for a minute, but she appreciated his efforts at trying to cheer her up. She was still trying to come to terms with her grandfather's decision to let her use the Elfstones but only here in Arborlon. She had thought all along that she would either be given the Elfstones to take with her or refused altogether. Given this new wrinkle, she would have to readjust her thinking. She would get half of what she had asked for, and she would have to make the most of it.

"I'm fine," she told Ellich, giving him a reassuring smile.

"I doubt that. You were counting on your grandfather to do the right thing, and he allowed himself to be swayed. That can't be easy to swallow. But what just happened is typical. A request is made. A proposal offered. Phaedon inevitably objects to all or part of whatever is voiced. My brother then splits the difference in the best way he can devise. But he will not go up against his son. There is a part of him that knows he should—even that he must—but he can't seem to find his way to doing so."

They were outside the Council chamber now, walking down the exterior hallway. She caught sight of Cymrian slipping through a set of doors far down the hallway. He glanced her way, gave a quick nod, and was gone.

"How long have things been like this?" she asked.

Ellich shrugged. "What year is it?"

So it was that bad. She should consider herself lucky, she realized. It could have been much worse. Fatal to her efforts, if her request had been denied altogether. She supposed she had never really thought that would happen, but she had been foolish not to anticipate that it might. Phaedon's control over his father was much stronger than she had been led to believe.

At least she would get one chance to discover where the Elfstones could be found—one chance to look at where they might be hidden.

She would have to make good use of it.

They walked down the steps leading from the Council Hall to the roadway and started for the palace. All around them, Elves were going about their business, paying no attention to Aphenglow, oblivious to everything in which she was involved. No one greeted her; no one even seemed to know her. She felt like an intruder. She felt again how alone she was, how far removed from her home and her people. Maybe it was the Druid robes. Or maybe it was simply that Phaedon was right and she no longer belonged. It was a bitter admission, and she refused to make it.

"You made the best argument you could, Aphen," her uncle said quietly. "I can't think of anything else you could have said. The problem is not in your presentation or even the rightness of your cause. It lies with an innate distrust of the Druid order, a distrust that has been in place since Grianne Ohmsford's days as Ard Rhys."

She moved closer to him, keeping her voice down. "I can understand their distrust of Grianne. She gave everyone reason to distrust her. And to fear her, as well. But she has been gone a long time. Khyber Elessedil is one of us. She's done nothing to earn such distrust. If anything, the Elves should be supporting her. And the Druid order. We should be allies, not antagonists."

"You are entirely right. We should." Ellich kept his head bent, but his eyes shifted this way and that. "But we aren't and we won't be anytime soon. Once settled in place, distrust is hard to dislodge. Especially when the Druids keep themselves so isolated from the rest of us. They deliberately hold themselves apart. Oh, I know the reasons for it. But that doesn't change the impact it generates. It is the appearance of things that matters. It looks elitist. It fosters resentment and suspicion."

She knew it was so. But having lived these past ten years with a foot in both camps, she also knew how wrong such thinking was. If anything, the Druids wanted to be accepted as allies by all of the Races. But it must be all. Any display of favoritism compromised their credibility. Staying aloof from the everyday lives of the Races was one way to reinforce their determination to remain impartial. The problem was that no one saw it that way. It felt to the average citizen as if the Druids considered themselves superior and preferred their own company to that of ordinary people.

When they arrived at the palace, Ellich led Aphenglow around to the north side and down a narrow pathway through tall hedges and flowering vines tied onto a series of trellis frameworks. Weaving their way through the maze, they arrived at a small, windowless door that was completely hidden from any other approach. Ellich stopped and knocked twice, paused and knocked once more. She heard a stirring on the other side; then the door opened and her grandfather stepped forward to embrace her.

"Aphenglow," he whispered as he hugged her close. "Child of light."

It was the meaning of her Elven name, but only her grandfather called her that now. Her father had done so when he was alive and her mother until she departed to join the Druids, and she was surprised to discover how much she missed it.

"Grandfather," she replied. "Thank you so much for helping me."

He stepped away from her, shaking his head. "We both know I could have done more. But doing more would have risked a confrontation with Phaedon and the other members of the High Council over the purpose of your request. It was vague enough that I couldn't put it to a vote, but not so vague that I couldn't do what I did. One opportunity, one time. I hope you understand."

She smiled. "Of course I understand. It isn't much different with the Druids. We argue all the time about what we should be doing and how we should be going about it. Everything is maneuvering and compromise. Are you well?"

He shrugged. "Well enough."

He brought her inside the room, one hand clasped possessively about her arm, and led her over to a sofa where he sat them both down. Ellich followed, closing and locking the garden door behind them.

"I have missed you so much, Aphen," her grandfather said. "You can't imagine. I think often of those days when you were a little girl and I was still young enough to play leapfrog with you. Do you remember? Of course you do. You used to laugh so."

She smiled and nodded with him, delighted by this memory, a favorite of her own. "We both laughed, Grandfather."

He put his hands on her shoulders, and his face grew grave. "Now tell me, child. Is there nothing more you can reveal to me of this search you will undertake? Of the nature of the magic you are seeking to recover? Here, in the privacy of my chambers, with only you and I and Ellich to hear, couldn't you tell me something more? Only just a little? It would help so with what I might be able to do for you."

Tears flooded her eyes unbidden. "I am sworn to say nothing," she repeated. "I gave my word to Khyber. Otherwise I would." She saw the hope that had momentarily glinted in her grandfather's eyes disappear. "I can tell you this much," she said hurriedly, not wanting to leave him with nothing. "What we seek is powerful and has the potential for doing much good. But it is an unknown quantity, and therefore very dangerous. Until we find it and examine it—possibly until we use it—we cannot know for certain the consequences of employing its power. What we do know is that if word of this reaches the wrong ears, it will likely encourage unwanted interest in our efforts."

Her grandfather leaned close, as if anxious to make certain. "And are you convinced of this, Aphen?"

She nodded. "I am. Knowing what I do of the possible impact of this magic, I think the danger is very great."

"Then perhaps this magic should be left where it is."

It stopped her for a moment, the possibility that he was right. What if they simply left well enough alone? But they were committed to recovering all of the lost magic of Faerie, of gaining possession so that it could be protected from those who would abuse it. Yet this was Elven magic, and only Elves could use it. Wasn't she admitting that the danger they were seeking to avoid lay entirely with her own people?

"I think we ignore the potential for destructive uses of any kind of power at our peril," she said finally. "But especially here."

"She is right, Emperowen," Ellich broke in. "We have learned that lesson often enough in the past. Every time we thought that by stepping back or turning away things would work out on their own, they didn't. They just got worse. That has been our history as Elves."

The King gave his brother a look. "I sense a rebuke in those words, Ellich. As if, perhaps, you might be referring to something other than Aphen's search for this lost magic. Something closer to home, perhaps?"

Ellich shook his head slowly. "No, brother. You don't need me to rebuke you. You need me to support you. So that is what I do. That is what I will always do."

The King turned back to Aphen. "What will you do with this magic if you find it?"

"Keep it safe," she answered at once.

"With the Druids?"

She nodded.

"When it is an Elven magic you seek? When it belongs to us?"

"It was lost by Elves. By our ancestors. Or given up, Grandfather. That road was traveled long ago. Magic no longer belongs only to the Elves; it belongs to everyone. It isn't meant for only one people. It must be used for the good of the people of all the Races."

"But only Elves can use Elven magic."

"Then other Elves besides those few already in residence must come to Paranor to train with the Druid order. I have asked for this before, but it seems that to go to the Druids is to become an outcast."

Her grandfather shook his head. "I cannot change the feelings of the Elven people, Aphen. I cannot alter history. When the Druids give us reason to trust them again, perhaps things will change."

There was no point in pursuing this argument, and so she simply leaned forward and kissed him on the cheek. "At least we trust each other," she whispered in his ear. She glanced at Ellich. "At least, the three of us share that trust."

Her grandfather nodded, smiling. "We must make the best of things, mustn't we, child?" He gripped her shoulders anew, then released her and rose. "I will give you the Elfstones now. Freely and willingly, in the way required, so that you may use them once, here within the confines of Arborlon. One time only, Aphen. Are we agreed?"

She smiled back. "We are."

"Wait here."

He disappeared through the chamber door and down the hallway leading deeper into the palace interior. She watched him go, and then sat quietly with Ellich, waiting for his return.

"He is doing what he can," her uncle said finally.

"I know that."

"He loves you."

"I know that, too. I do not blame him for anything he does. I am grateful he does this much."

"Not exactly what you had hoped for, though."

"It will have to be enough."

They sat together in silence after that, listening to the muffled twitter of birdsong from the gardens and trees outside and the murmur of voices from somewhere deeper within the palace. Aphenglow stared out the chamber window at a fleet of passing clouds and wondered how she could best use the Elfstones. What strength would it require to summon the magic, what images should she attempt to conjure, what interpretation might she need to employ to understand what she was shown? She knew how the blue Elfstones were meant to work, but she had never seen them used or ever thought that she would be the one to use them.

It should be the Ard Rhys who summons their magic. It should be Khyber Elessedil doing this.

But that choice had not been given her. She was the one who would have to manage the summoning, and she was not at all sure she was equal to the task.

Her grandfather, when he returned, came through the door quickly and quietly, almost as if fearful that he had been followed. He locked the door behind him, sat down again beside her, and held out his hand. His fingers gripped the drawstrings of a small leather pouch.

"Promise me, Aphen," he said. His aging face was troubled. "Promise me that you will not betray the Elves. That you will do your best to protect our interests as well those of the Druid order. Can you do that? Can you make me that promise?"

She nodded, her eyes locked on his. "I promise. The best I can do, I will do."

He lowered the bag gently into her open palm. "Then take the Elfstones and make use of them. You have until sunset to do so. Then you must return them."

He released his grip on the drawstrings and leaned back, waiting for her response. Her fingers closed about the bag, gripping it tightly. She leaned forward and kissed him on his cheek once more. "I love you, Grandfather."

Then she rose and went out the garden door with Ellich following close behind.

* * *

They walked together for a short distance, neither of them speaking, lost in their separate thoughts, and then she turned to him. "I need to do this alone, Ellich. I'm sorry."

He smiled, nodded. "Don't be. I expected as much. But be careful, Aphen. You have been attacked twice already. Oh, don't look so surprised. Arlingfant told me. You knew she would. She worries for you. As do I. So, please be careful."

He left her then, turning away for his own home. She was surprised to realize that she had pushed any thoughts of the prior attacks so far back in her consciousness, she had all but forgotten them. It was easy for her to acknowledge her status as an outcast—if not so easy to accept it—but difficult to think of herself as threatened in the city in which she had been born and raised.

She started walking again, mulling over her uncle's words. Would she be attacked yet a third time? Was that at all likely? Would they dare to come at her in broad daylight, with other Elves all around? If so, would they try to stop her from using the Elfstones? Would they attempt to steal them?

Well, she thought darkly, she was ready if anyone tried.

"Is it your intention to make things easy for any possible attackers by daydreaming?" Cymrian asked her, appearing suddenly at her elbow.

She glowered at him. "Isn't it your job to keep me safe? Do I need to be worried that the effort required is beyond you?"

"I can protect you. But it would help if you were to offer a modicum of assistance."

She hated that he had surprised her like this. She hadn't heard him until he was right on top of her, and that shouldn't have been possible. She took a deep breath, exhaled, and nodded.

"You're right. I wasn't helping. I can't seem to get used to the idea that here, in my home city, among my own people, I am in danger."

He nodded wordlessly, keeping pace at her side, his lean face grave. "Well, you might want to start."

"Where have you been, anyway?"

"Shadowing you."

She decided not to ask *how* he had managed this, but simply to accept that he had. She looked over at him. "You followed me after I left the Council chambers?"

"Isn't that my job?"

"Did you hear what was said?"

He shrugged. "I don't need to eavesdrop to protect you."

"You can't come with me."

"You keep saying that."

"I have to do something, and I have to do it alone. No one else can be present."

He smiled, shrugged. "Where will you go to do this secret something?" He saw her hesitation. "Not so I can eavesdrop, but so I can make a reasonable effort to protect you. I need to be close enough to reach you if there's trouble."

She gave him a look. "I don't think anything is going to happen, Cymrian."

"It won't if I'm close enough to prevent it."

She almost told him what nonsense it was to insist on this, but it would have involved an argument she did not care to engage in. "Very well. I will go to the south end of the Carolan, where the big oaks grow and it is sheltered enough for me to have privacy. Fair enough?"

He bowed his head, pursed his lips, and nodded silently.

"So you can leave me now and let me go on alone. And do not let me catch you spying on me."

He moved away from her and disappeared soundlessly. She walked on, using her heightened senses to track him, to make sure he hadn't lied. It wasn't that she didn't trust him; it was that she understood how great the temptation would be to watch. He was good at moving unseen and unheard, but she would not allow it this time.

When she was certain she was alone she stepped off the path into the trees and crept away.

She did not go to the Carolan. She had never intended to go there in the first place, but it was best if he thought otherwise. She went instead to the north edge of the city where the wildness crept close to the bluff edge and the forest was dark and deep. She worked her way through the trees to the small clearing to which she had gone to be alone when she was a child. It had been years since she had visited her secret hiding place, but she remembered well enough how to find it. The years fell away as she threaded her way through deep undergrowth and ancient trees, finding familiar memories all along the way, some in the form of recognizable terrain, some in the ephemeral form of abandoned dreams and lost hopes.

Soon enough she had arrived, and she was back in her childhood for a few precious moments before taking out the pouch with the Elfstones and spilling them into her palm. She stood staring down at the perfectly formed gemstones, admiring the simplicity of their design, the stunning depth of their blue color, and the play of light through their smooth facets. She had never seen them, had only been able to imagine how they would look. Her imagination had not been equal to the task.

She took a deep breath. What should she do next?

Three stones—one each for the heart, mind, and

body of the user, representing a combination of personal strengths that must be brought to bear. The weight and intensity of those strengths would determine the success of her effort.

But she had no image she could bring to mind of what it was she sought. She knew nothing of the place in which the missing Elfstones might be hidden, or even what they looked like. Those who had lived at the time they'd been stolen were long dead.

On what could she focus that would reveal what she wanted to know? What image would it take?

For a moment, she felt overwhelmed. What she had been given to do was so important that even the thought of failure was debilitating. This was the only chance the Druids might have to find what they sought, the only opportunity that might be given to them. And the opportunity belonged to her. What she made of it might well influence everything that happened afterward. She could not afford to make a mistake.

But what must she do? What image must she attempt to summon?

She stood lost in thought for a long time, considering her choices, finding them weak or convoluted or simply useless. Why was she finding this so difficult?

Finally, she walked over to a fallen log and sat down to think. She knew she was distraught, confused, worried, and a dozen other things and all of these were working against her. She took a moment to distance herself from the present, recalling the times she had come here as a child. She looked out across the few segments of the Rill Song that were visible through the trees where the river snaked its way west, a silver thread amid the deep greens. She looked at the sky, streaked with wisps of clouds and washed with sunlight. The day was bright and clear and smelled of home.

She wondered suddenly if perhaps she did belong here

among her own people rather than at Paranor with the Druids.

Perhaps Ellich and the others were right.

Abruptly she was back on her feet, pushing the thought aside, burying it. Elfstones tightly clasped, she stretched out her arm, eyes closed, summoning an image of three blue Elfstones nestled among a collection of others, their colors varied and shifting, all of them backdropped by a wash of whiteness that caused everything else to disappear.

She focused her thoughts on the image, allowed her breathing to slow and her body to relax and disappear into herself.

Where are you?

She felt a slow, insistent heat begin to rise. The magic was awake, an unmistakable presence within her. It stirred sluggishly, troubling her like an itch, then began to spread, flowing from her hand into her outstretched arm, into her chest and through her body, filling her up until she was consumed. She felt no fear as this happened; she experienced no distress. If anything, it felt natural to her. It felt familiar in the way that something you have never seen but always known in your heart feels familiar.

Show me what I need to know.

The heat turned to a brilliant blue light that enveloped her fist, swallowing it. The light intensified, building strength. She watched it happen, fascinated. The light pulsated; its steady throbbing seemed to match the beating of her heart.

Then the light broke free and shot away into the afternoon light and took her with it.

Surrounded by the blue glow of Elven magic, she rides it across the landscape of the Elven Westland, a passenger aboard a swift bird in flight. She is frightened at first, but almost as fast as it appears the fear is gone. She senses she is in no danger; she can feel the rightness of what is happening to her. She has summoned the magic, communicated her wishes, and now she is to be shown what she has asked to see. She need only pay attention to the signposts along the way. She need only take note of the path that the Druids would soon be required to follow. She must remember everything to help them do so.

She is whisked across the Rill Song and into the broad valley of the Sarandanon, the bread basket of the Elven nation. Planted fields and orchards spread away in patchwork fashion, squares and rectangles. Men and women work those fields. Livestock graze them. Homes and barns and pens mark the beginning and end of territories claimed and cultivated. Sunlight bathes the landscape, and time slows.

Then she is past the farmland and heading for the stark wall of the Kensrowe Mountains, the light suddenly angling north of the passes at Halys Cut and Baen Draw, north of the broad flat surface of the Innisbore. She is being taken into territory she has never seen, farther north still toward the juncture of the Breakline and Hoare Flats. This is Troll country, wild and mostly unexplored. The light angles this way and that through the mountain peaks, dropping far enough that she can see clearly the features of the ground beneath her. She sees strange, remarkable formations. A trio of rock columns have the look of sentries. A deep depression in the earth is riven with gullies and splits. Marshland is cradled between huge mountains and given life by a microclimate peculiar to a piece of land that cannot consist in total of more than a dozen miles.

The light carries her farther still, deeper into the mountains, much closer to the earth than earlier. She is skimming the ground like a swimmer riding the crest of a wave. She feels heat and cold envelop her in sudden bursts, unaccounted for by anything she is seeing. The mountains surround her, vast and immutable. Ahead, beyond the Breakline and Hoare Flats, lie miles of bleak wilderness that eventually lead to the Blue Divide. Only Wing Riders venture this far into the mountains, able to fly safely overhead aboard their Rocs, and even they come only when it is necessary. This is dangerous country, a treacherous landscape filled with creatures and *strangeness that Elves have only heard about and no one she knows has ever seen.*

But this is where she has been taken, so this is where the Druids must come.

Then everything begins to happen very fast. The blue light seems to pick up speed and the landscape to blur. The mountains and their distinctive formations lose shape and sharpness, and everything flashes by so quickly that she loses her sense of direction entirely.

Ahead, something shimmers in the darkness.

A curtain of some kind. A waterfall, perhaps.

But it is dark and troubling.

The blue light spears directly toward the shimmering, carrying her in its grip, a suddenly unwilling passenger fearful of what is about to happen. She feels an unmistakable urgency and finds herself holding her breath.

Caught up in the Elfstone magic, she strikes the shimmering surface and passes through. She feels no impact on doing so, but senses an odd change in her makeup—as if she has lost some part of herself.

Things get even stranger after that.

The blue light carries her through forests and over mountains and plains and across rivers and lakes. None of them look familiar. There is a fresh sense of urgency to the light's movement. A fortress flashes past, dark and scarred and jagged, and then something else—something she cannot identify—vast and circular and menacing. Down she sweeps through an opening in the earth, down into depths so dark she can see almost nothing. A flash of stone steps startles her, what appears to be a passageway follows, then a cavern, and then something massive and alive that stirs in recognition of the magic's intrusion.

And finally she spies a small metal box on which is carved a crest of crossed blades athwart a field of wheat with a bird flying overhead.

An instant later the blue light fades, the magic dies away, and she is back in her forest sanctuary staring out at the sunlit sweep of the Elven Westland.

She stood where she was for a moment, still caught up in the swiftness of her journey, stunned by the abruptness of her return. She stared out across the plains west from her vantage point on the heights, knowing she must remember everything.

It was all a jumble of images, but she knew she had to sort those images out, had to place them in sequence and store them carefully.

She was attempting to do so when she sensed movement behind her.

She turned just as the five black-garbed figures came at her out of the trees. They carried iron bars and wooden cudgels, and there were too many of them. She would have been finished if she hadn't still been holding the Elfstones. Her fear and desperation triggered their magic instantly. A fireball of blue light exploded from her clenched fist and hammered into her attackers, stopping them before they reached her, tossing them aside as if they weighed nothing.

She hesitated only an instant before bolting for freedom.

It was an instant too long.

They lay scattered about her in various stages of semiconsciousness, and she had thought to get past them before they could recover their wits. She ran hard, dodging bodies and limbs, but she missed noticing the man who had been farthest away from the blow dealt to the others. He was on his knees, crouched and ready as she sped past him. She was well within reach of the iron bar he gripped, and he swung hard at her as she fled, the bar connecting with her left leg. She went down screaming in pain, her shinbone broken, and he was on her instantly.

Sitting astride her chest, pressing the bar down hard against her throat so that she could not breathe, he whispered. "Give me the Elfstones. Quick now, or I'll break your neck, too."

Her air cut off, her body pinned, black spots obscuring her vision, she opened her fingers.

In the next instant, the man disappeared, his weight gone as he tumbled away. She gave out a gasp of relief, able to breathe again, and tried to see what was happening. A battle was being fought between her attackers and someone else. But there were bodies flying everywhere, and forest shadows were mixed with black-clad attackers. She could hear grunts and cries, the sounds of metal on metal and the sharp hiss of life suddenly cut short. Several of her attackers went sprawling anew, and this time they did not get up. Two—she thought them the last—fought in silent desperation against a newcomer. No one spoke. The battle was swift and brutal and final.

In seconds all of those who had sought to hurt her lay still, and Cymrian was kneeling next to her.

"You test my patience, Aphen."

She struggled to rise, but he pushed her down. "Don't do that. Your leg is broken and needs to be set."

She nodded and lay back obediently. "Thanks for coming," she whispered.

"I would have come sooner if I had known where you were."

She nodded again. "I know. It was foolish not to tell you the truth. I'm sorry."

"Just promise me you won't lie to me again."

"I promise." She met his gaze and held it. "I do."

He reached down and handed her the Elfstones. "I think it would be best if you kept these."

She took the Stones from him, fumbled them into her pocket, and watched in silence as he began the work of splinting her leg.

15

THE TALL THIN MAN WITH THE FLAT-BLACK ROBES
and eyes to match strode through the halls of the Federation Council chambers at midday like a wraith through a graveyard. His passage was soundless, but it drew immediate attention. Men and women stepped aside for him, offering fawning words and submissive gestures. He gave them nods of recognition, small acknowledgments with a lifting of his hand and a ruffling of his sleeve, meaningless gestures, his face dispassionate, his expression unrevealing. He kept his body still as he walked so that it appeared as if he were gliding. He kept his head bowed so that it seemed as if he were in some sense as deferential to them as they were to him.

But he was nothing of what he appeared, neither deferential nor dispassionate. He saw those he passed not as colleagues or equals, certainly not as friends or fellow citizens. They were of little importance to him, there to serve his purposes, whatever those purposes might be, there to fulfill whatever wishes might need fulfilling.

Though he would never let them see this. How he used them and how they responded were acts seemingly unrelated, in which everything was achieved as if in the natural course of things, as predestined and inevitable as the rising and setting of the sun.

It had taken him a while to reach a point where he was able to accomplish this. He had toiled as a mere functionary in the beginning, quiet and obsequious, always in the background, always letting others claim credit for the successes he had fostered. Years passed before he was able to elevate himself to a Minister's position, still a shadow among substantial men and women, still helping others without asking for their consideration, toiling in the warrens and hallways of the Council chambers and offices, one among many, but never one they noticed.

Until by the time they did, it was too late.

Though what would they do even if they knew the full extent of his duplicity? Demand he step down from the pinnacle of success he had achieved? Ask for an accounting? Seek his elimination?

All of these and more, he imagined. But they couldn't quite see him the way he was, and he never gave them reason to think of him as anything but a safe compromise in a maelstrom of warring factions that constantly sought to devour one another. Each of them believed in all seriousness that he was the lesser evil.

They would learn eventually, perhaps, if they survived long enough.

Drust Chazhul would teach them.

Really, he had been teaching them all along. They just hadn't been paying attention, save for a handful, and most of those were gone.

Ten days ago the former Prime Minister, a man neither old nor weak, had succumbed to an illness of such virulent purpose that it killed him within twenty-four hours. Its origins were a mystery to everyone but his eventual successor and his accomplice, and the intense struggle over his succession distracted those who might have looked into the matter more closely.

Everything had gone according to plans conceived well in advance of the need for them. Drust Chazhul made a show of refusing the nomination when his name was finally put forth to break the deadlock between the two candidates who were openly campaigning for the job. Satisfactory neither to each other nor to each other's followers, the two found themselves bypassed in favor of a man who barely colored in enough space in the political landscape to merit recognition and who, upon being nominated, insisted repeatedly that others were better qualified and more experienced.

In spite of heated objections from both real candidates, the non-candidate was elected and the new Prime Minister sworn in.

It had taken some doing to get the job done, to be sure. He had lobbied long and hard for the votes it required, all without seeming to do anything but offer advice and consolation to those who were openly hungry for the position, all without seeming to have any interest in the post. Some believed him an acceptable alternative to choices they could not tolerate. Some believed him ineffectual enough that they could manipulate him into serving their own purposes. Both were misguided.

What remained for Drust Chazhul was to solidify his hold on the position without seeming to do so. What would go furthest toward accomplishing this was the elimination of any serious competition.

It had been easy enough with the old Prime Minister, who suspected nothing. It might prove harder with the two who had lost the position they coveted and were more likely to want to change that.

But there were other fish to fry, so to speak, and his attention at the moment was occupied with something completely unrelated to threats from defeated rivals. They would not be too quick to want to act; neither of them yet suspected the role he had played in eliminating the old Prime Minister and in helping to discredit them. They would find out once they dug deep enough into the web of his machinations, but that would not happen overnight. By the time they knew enough to be worried, it would be too late.

Down the corridors he passed, lost in his private thoughts, to all outward appearances a man beset by the weight of his new responsibilities and given over to addressing the work that must be done. He was on his way to his private chambers—formerly those of the old Prime Minister—his work completed for the day, a good night's rest the reward that waited.

"Sleep well, Prime Minister," one fellow member of the Council called to him in passing.

"Well done, today," said another.

He nodded in response, giving nothing away, no reply offered. He turned down the west wing of the building, a private space now reserved for him alone. Guards flanked the entry and, farther ahead, the doors to his sleeping chamber. They straightened and came to attention as he passed, a response he secretly enjoyed. Puppets pulled erect by invisible strings that he alone wielded. Such fun.

Yet he understood, too, that his power had been bestowed with the sure and comforting knowledge that as a compromise choice for Prime Minister he could be easily removed. The history for such abrupt changes in Federation leadership was lengthy and colorful. No one much worried about it happening again. No one was immune to change, after all.

And so he was already planning how to avoid what had claimed so many before him, intent on being the exception.

He opened the doors to his private chambers and went inside, pausing in the entryway to see if Stoon had arrived yet. He had. Sitting in a chair well back in the shadows by the curtained windows, Stoon's sharp eyes glittered in the faint light cast by the candles on the fireplace. Drust closed the doors behind him and locked them.

"Been waiting long for me?"

The assassin shrugged. "I don't mind waiting. I do a lot of it."

Drust walked over to the windows and peeked through the curtains at the courtyard and surrounding buildings, checking lighted windows and darkened doorways. It was a habit he had never been able to quit, the need to reassure himself of his own safety as automatic to him as breathing.

Satisfied, he sat down in the chair across from the assassin and poured a glass of wine from the decanter. Stoon had already helped himself.

"To our success," he toasted. They drank, a sip only. Neither man used spirits for anything more than token pleasure. "What have you found out about the Druids?"

Stoon considered. "Not as much as I would like. Our spies cannot get close to Paranor's walls, let alone think about getting inside. They watch from the air in flits and from more distant stationary points. What we know for certain comes mostly from Arborlon. The Druid granddaughter of the King was there for more than a year searching the Elven histories for references to missing magic. She found something, and arrangements were made to determine what it was. They failed. Spectacularly. She proved more capable than the man I chose. When I pressed the matter with more than two, an Elven Hunter who had signed on as her protector intervened. He was even more capable. We lost everyone and gained nothing. Except that in this last attack, the young woman's leg was broken."

Drust Chazhul found himself growing impatient. "Are we getting to the good parts of this narrative anytime soon?"

"Patience, Prime Minister. I am merely setting the stage." Stoon was calm, unruffled by the rebuke. He knew Drust too well to be offended or troubled by anything the other said.

"When the King's granddaughter returned to Paranor with news of her discovery," he continued, "the Ard Rhys apparently woke from the Druid Sleep to determine what should be done about it. After sending the King's granddaughter back to Arborlon, she and the other Druids went out from Paranor to various places in the Four Lands in search of certain men and women. We don't know why. Whatever their purpose, it appears to be of no small importance; presumably, it has something to do with what was found in the Elven histories."

"But we don't know what that purpose is or who these people are?"

"Not yet."

"You can find this out?"

"I am in the process of doing so. But it will take time. No one must suspect our interest in this, the Druids especially."

Drust nodded. There would be no mistakes, no unplanned surprises, and no inconvenient witnesses to anything Stoon was planning. There never had been, not from day one of their unusual relationship, and he didn't expect that to change now.

Drust had met Stoon when the former was still a clerk serving a junior Minister. He was a man with few prospects but possessed of a sharp mind and a deceptively innocent appearance. In those early days, Drust used to frequent the taverns and alehouses in the seedier parts of Arishaig, expanding the number and variety of his relationships in an effort to find allies who might help him gain a foothold on the slippery ladder of advancement. Most of his co-workers in the ministries would never have gone to the places he went, and what few did went for the more obvious reasons and not to make friends. But Drust knew that advancement did not happen in politics if you simply sat back and waited for your luck to change. You made your own luck in this business, and sometimes it required you to associate with people who possessed skills and experience that you lacked.

Among those he met in the course of his nighttime outings was Stoon. A mutual acquaintance introduced them, although he had already heard Stoon's name mentioned and knew of his reputation as an assassin of extraordinary talent. Few knew much else about him. He preferred to keep a low profile and never speak of what he did, finding and choosing assignments that pleased him through word of mouth. Drust, understanding the rules of this relationship from the beginning, never asked Stoon about his work. He spoke instead about his own ambitions and plans, passionate and determined, demonstrating that his friendship might be worth something.

All the while, Stoon listened, sometimes smiled, seldom spoke, and never volunteered anything.

Eventually, Drust managed to gain an appointment as a junior Minister. His office—military debts and accounting—was so obscure and his duties so nebulous that he was left to run things as he chose. He made the most of this by befriending various officers in the Federation Army and Airship Command, and in the end won the support of a handful of important allies and an appointment to a ministry with a higher profile. His reputation within the Coalition Council as a man who lacked ambition but could get things done grew accordingly, and suddenly he was being sought out by other Ministers and asked for his opinions. His support became worth something and he gave it judiciously, never asking for anything in return.

Shortly after Drust was appointed as Minister of the Treasury, Stoon suggested they celebrate by meeting for a drink. As they sat in a quiet corner of a tavern he favored, the assassin said something completely unexpected.

"I've been thinking I might like to secure a permanent position rather than continue to freelance." He gazed around the tavern as if searching for prospects. "If you were to offer me such a position, I believe I would accept it."

Drust hesitated, not at all sure where this was going. Such an arrangement had never been mentioned before. "A permanent position? Why would you suddenly want that?"

Stoon shrugged. "We're just talking here. But if you were to offer, I would probably accept."

Drust shook his head. "I don't know that I'm ready for that just yet. One day soon, I think I will be. But for now, I am still trying to find secure footing with the Council."

"A worthy goal. One I am sure you will attain." He paused. "Unless someone more powerful than you decides you are becoming a nuisance that needs to be removed."

Drust felt a chill run up his spine, and it took everything he had to keep from showing it. "What are you suggesting? Whom are we talking about?"

Stoon shrugged. "As I said, we're just talking here. But you might want to reconsider my offer. Things happen. What if you don't hire me now and someone else does? All things considered, I would prefer to work for

you. You should think on that. But not for too long."
He paused again. "Failure to act in a timely manner can
be fatal."

Drust Chazhul saw at once what he was getting at
and hired Stoon that very night. Within a week, another Minister, one who was rumored to be coveting
the position of Minister of the Treasury, met with an
unexpected accident that claimed his life.

Since then, Drust and Stoon had cemented their partnership, working together behind the scenes to advance
the former's career to the point that he was now Prime
Minister and the most important person in the Federation government. It was Stoon who arranged for the position to become available when everyone else expected
the serving Prime Minister to hold office for many more
years. It was Stoon who found ways to eliminate any
obstacles that Drust encountered, smoothing the way,
opening the path, always being granted a voice in the
decision making and a substantial share in the rewards.
Stoon would never become a Minister of the Coalition
Council himself; allying himself with Drust was the
next best thing. What he lacked in prestige he made up
for in coin and comfort.

And Drust was very careful to make certain that
Stoon understood how highly he was valued. He supplied the assassin whatever he wanted in the way of possessions. He provided him access to his private chambers
through secret passageways that had been shared by
Ministers and their favorites in other times. As long as
he did so without being seen, Stoon was allowed to
come and go as he pleased. He was little more than a
shadow to those with whom Drust worked, and that
was the way they both preferred it.

"How do things stand with the Council members?"
Stoon asked, moving the subject away from the Druids.
"Have Arodian and Edinja come to terms with your

unexpected elevation to Prime Minister? Do they suspect anything?"

"They're confused still." Drust sipped at his wine absently, thinking about his rivals. "But I might want to do something about them before that changes."

"But not just yet. It will look suspicious if something happens to them so soon after the death of the old Prime Minister. It might be better to let a little time pass."

Stoon was right, of course. But he was missing the point. Drust shook his head. "I don't intend to eliminate *them*. I intend to eliminate any *threat* they might pose."

Stoon looked at him with interest. "How do you plan to do that?"

"I'm working on it."

"Are you? Well, you'd better watch your back with those two. They're every bit as clever as you."

Drust gave him a sharp look. "Then why have I been able to outmaneuver them so far? Why am I Prime Minister and not either of them?"

Stoon said nothing. He just stared at the other man, waiting.

Finally, Drust shrugged and said, "I take your point. I won't get overconfident. I know what has to happen, but I realize I shouldn't expect it to happen too quickly. In any case, I am more interested at the moment in my plans for the Druids than in worrying about Arodian and Edinja."

Eliminating the Druids and reducing Paranor to rubble was Drust Chazhul's primary goal as Prime Minister of the Federation. He had spoken out for years on the subject, riding the wave of resentment that infused every public discourse surrounding the Federation's stinging defeat on the Prekkendorran—a disaster that might be a hundred years past but felt as recent to most as yesterday. It was a defeat almost everyone attributed to the interference of the Druids on behalf of the Free-born allies. The Federation had been humiliated and its power sharply curtailed by the subsequent peace agreement. And although none of the current generation of Federation men and women had fought in that war, their hatred of the Druids was an inheritance passed down to them by their parents and grandparents—an inbred antipathy that politicians and military zealots continued to nurture.

Drust Chazhul used that hatred for the leverage it provided him politically. As Prime Minister and a career politician with boundless ambition, he understood that as long as the Druids existed the Federation's efforts at domination of the lesser Races and their lands would be curtailed. Which, in turn, meant that Drust's plan to grow his personal power base in tandem with Federation expansion faced an insurmountable roadblock.

He believed, as well, that the use of magic was an abomination that had somehow gained the upper hand over the far safer and more productive science that had determined the course of the Old World. He knew the stories of how failure to adequately and safely control science had led to the destruction of that Old World, but that didn't change the fact that magic was an elitist power that only a few possessed or even understood. Mostly, these few were Druids. That they should wield such power—power denied to others (especially himself)—was unacceptable. He did not believe the Druids were any better equipped than he was to determine what was and wasn't to be allowed in shaping the future of the human condition, and he resented strongly their insistence that only they understood the ramifications of magic's use well enough to possess and employ it.

Others did not agree, of course. Edinja was one of them. But that was to be expected; members of her family had been practitioners of magic for centuries and were not about to support someone who claimed they should now give it up.

Things were changing in the world of the Four Lands. The Federation had been the first to develop diapson crystals as a mean of achieving progress, usage that relied on a burgeoning new form of science that could be calculated and controlled and did not rely on chance and inheritance and talismans. Military use of the crystals was forbidden, of course. But no one in his right mind believed that the Federation had ceased experimentation and development of the weapons that had very nearly placed victory in their grasp until the Druids had snatched it away.

No, the Druids were an anachronism that needed to be eliminated, and Drust Chazhul believed he was the one who could do that.

"What plans are these?" Stoon asked suddenly, regaining his attention.

He furrowed his brow, thinking of something Stoon had said earlier. "What did you say about the Ard Rhys sending the King's granddaughter back to Arborlon?"

Stoon shrugged. "Our source in Arborlon tells us she asked the old King for permission to take the Elfstones to Paranor to help search for some magic she found reference to in the Elven histories. The King denied her, and that was the end of it."

"A quest, then? The Druids thought to search for this missing magic? They intended to leave Paranor?"

"Still do. The decision is made, Elfstones or no." Stoon was watching him closely. "What are you thinking?"

"That such a search will take time and effort. That while it is being conducted, Paranor will be left mostly unguarded."

Stoon shook his head. "I wouldn't bet on that, Drust."

But Drust Chazhul was on his feet, pacing the room, suddenly animated. "All we need to do is to find an excuse to visit while the bulk of the Druids are away, one that won't seem overtly aggressive. A diplomatically acceptable excuse. A visit to the Ard Rhys by the new Prime Minister of the Federation, perhaps. A courtesy call."

He wheeled back, facing Stoon. "Can Paranor's defenses be breached? Is there a way to get past them?"

The assassin smiled. "There is always a way. The trick is in finding it."

"I want you to work on that. While you do, I will lay the groundwork for my 'diplomatic visit.' Because of what I plan to do, I will need to take a sizable force with me to overcome whatever resistance I encounter."

"The Coalition Council will never agree to let you take a fighting force into Druid territory. They'll slap you down in a minute. Arodian and Edinja will see to it."

"Perhaps not." He felt excited, energized. "In fact, I might be able to make use of them." He grinned. "Don't underestimate me, Stoon. I know how to get things done that others wouldn't even dare to consider. You concentrate on your job, and I'll do the same with mine. Tell our spies to keep you advised on any preparations for an expedition made at Paranor. I'll want reports from Arborlon, as well. Anything at all about what's been found in the Elven histories or what's intended to be accomplished by this search. If there's a way to discover their destination or the specifics of its purpose or who might be helping them . . . anything at all."

Stoon nodded. "This is risky, Drust. If you overstep, your enemies will be on you like wolves on a lamb."

Drust Chazhul gave him a wicked smile. "Then they'd best watch themselves. This lamb might turn out to be a wolf in sheep's clothing. This lamb might devour them instead."

He drank the last of his wine. "Let's go our ways. Come to me tomorrow night. We'll see how things stand then."

He turned to collect his coat and hat. When he turned back again, Stoon was gone.

16

At Paranor, Aphenglow Elessedil sat propped up in her sleeping chamber bed, rereading the notes she had written regarding her use of the blue Elfstones three days earlier in Arborlon. She had made her report to the Ard Rhys and her fellow Druids that morning, but she felt compelled to make certain that she had left nothing out. Her broken leg, splinted and bound, lay stretched out before her, a sour reminder of how badly things had gone awry.

Even as she was being carted back to her cottage, after the attack by the black-clad assailants and her rescue by Cymrian, her leg throbbing with pain and her mind awash with the consequences of her disability, she was recounting in her mind the details of what the Elfstones had shown her. She was afraid she would forget something if she didn't, aware of the quixotic tricks memory could play if one failed to revisit its first impressions quickly. Later, aboard *Wend-A-Way,* she had taken the time to write it all down. The more she went back over it, the better her chances of not forgetting anything.

She was close to the end of her current perusal when she realized that all she was doing was finding a way to occupy her time. Confined to her bed, unable to participate in the preparations for the journey that would take the bulk of the Druid order in quest of the missing Elfstones, she was frustrated and bored and very much afraid that she might be the one who was left behind. No one had said so as yet, but the implications had been apparent after she gave her report. Condolences on the damage to her leg, regret that she would be bedridden for a week and splinted for two more, pitying looks. She was an adept at using her magic to heal, but there was only so much you could do with a break this bad. Cymrian had set it, her sister had wrapped it carefully, but she was disabled nevertheless.

Knowing she should not broach publicly the question of whether she would be allowed to go with the others, she had kept her peace. The time to ask would be later, in private. The one to ask—the only one who mattered—was the Ard Rhys.

She could hardly bear the waiting.

Arlingfant and Cymrian had accompanied her back to Paranor, taking charge of her safety and transportation in the wake of this latest attack on her person. She had tried to dissuade Arling from coming, insisting her duties as a Chosen came before caring for her sister—an assertion that was quickly brushed aside. Arling would not be missed for the time it took to see Aphenglow safely placed under the care of her fellow Druids.

Leaving Arborlon at once had not been a point of debate. Cymrian insisted she was no longer safe in her home city, the attack absolute proof that her purpose in coming back had somehow been compromised. There was no one aside from her family and himself she could trust and nothing further to be accomplished by remaining where she was. Better she be returned to the Druids, and Cymrian and Arlingfant were the right ones to see this was done. Cymrian could fly an airship and Arlingfant could see to the needs of her sister.

Aphenglow had not argued the point. Her only regret was that her need to leave now prevented her from accessing and searching through the Chosen histories for information on Aleia Omarossian as she had planned. But that could wait for another day. For now, she must go to a safer place and impart what she had learned through the use of the blue Elfstones to the Ard Rhys.

Any doubts she had harbored about Cymrian had been erased in the aftermath of his rescue efforts. After finding her in spite of her efforts to lose him, he had stood alone against five trained, experienced assassins, men bearing the distinctive eagle mark of a well-known Federation-connected league—who should have been able to overcome a single defender with little difficulty. He had killed all five. Not intentionally; he had hoped to take one alive to question. But in a struggle of this sort, it was difficult to hold back—a point brought home graphically to Aphenglow when she had taken the life of her last assailant and discovered how quickly you needed to react and how little time you were allowed to measure the force required to save yourself.

In both instances, she was lucky to be alive. She was grateful to Cymrian, and she had told him so.

Even so, there was still something about him that troubled her. She had resolved to find out what it was.

Arlingfant seemed to have no similar reservations. She and Cymrian had formed a fast friendship that had grown stronger since they had embarked on the *Wend-A-Way* back to Paranor. Joking, laughing, and very much at ease with each other, they had bonded quickly—so much so that Aphenglow felt a twinge of jealously in spite of herself at not being an equal partner in this friendship.

Mostly, though, she just felt disgruntled and troubled by the circumstances of her own situation.

And, she admitted, staring out the window into the

gray of the late-afternoon sky, rain clouds forming up to the west, she was worried about Bombax, the only member of the order who had gone out and not yet returned.

This was not all that unusual. Bombax was headstrong, independent, and had a long history of coming and going on his own terms and according to his own timetable. Because he was so experienced, the other Druids did not worry for him as they might have for one another. In fact, they barely gave it a thought. But they were not in love with him as Aphenglow was; they had not chosen him as a life partner.

They did not sense when something was wrong as strongly as Aphenglow did.

But there was no help for it. All anyone knew was that he had set out for the cities of the Borderlands, intent on finding aid for their quest. They had no way to track him, no way to seek him out, and no particular desire to do so. If anything, he would resent the intrusion. Aphenglow knew this. What frustrated her was that even though she knew not to go looking for him, she could not have done so even if she wanted to. She resented her inability to act; she was angered by her incapacitation.

She hated that all she could do was sit in this bed and wait.

She was mulling over her unfortunate state when Khyber Elessedil appeared suddenly and unexpectedly in the doorway.

"May I speak with you, Aphen?"

Right away Aphenglow knew something was wrong. When the Ard Rhys bothered to ask if she could talk to you, you could be certain she had something unpleasant to say.

"Is it Bombax?" Aphenglow replied at once. "Has something happened to him?"

"This doesn't concern Bombax." The Ard Rhys walked over to the bed and sat down beside her. "How are you feeling?"

She grimaced. "Bored. Frustrated. Anxious to be doing something."

"You are doing something. You are mending. Are you using your skills to speed the healing?"

"Three times a day, no exceptions. I think I can begin walking in a day or so."

The Ard Rhys smiled. "Let's not rush things, Aphen. You can only do so much."

"I want to go with you," Aphenglow blurted out, unable to contain herself any longer. "You have to let me! You need me! Without me, you can't be sure of where you're going. I'm the one who saw the vision. I will recognize landmarks you might miss. Please! Let me go!"

Khyber Elessedil shook her head. "You are so eager. What if this turns out to be something other than what you expect? What if it leads to nothing? What if it is all a trick of some sort? Magic can betray even us."

"I don't care. I want to be there. I'm the one who found the diary. I deserve to go!"

"You do deserve to go. Not only did you find the diary and bring it to the rest of us, but you recognized its value right away. You found the connection between Aleia Omarosian and the Elessedils. You opened so many doors, even when doing so endangered you. I do not in any way underestimate your contributions."

She sighed. "That said, I want you to remain here. Wait, hear me out. I need someone to keep watch over Paranor, a Druid with wits enough to know what to do if anything threatens in my absence. That would be Bombax, if he were here."

"But you need Bombax!" Aphenglow was insistent, desperate to change the other's mind. "I'm not as skilled with magic. If you wait for him, perhaps I will be well enough for you to reconsider your decision to leave me."

"We have no idea when he'll return. Even use of the scrye has failed to reveal any trace of his whereabouts. We cannot wait longer for him. Our expedition will leave tomorrow. Someone either knows or suspects what we are about. If they dare to attack you in your own city—in your own home—then there is reason to believe they will come after us. The quicker we act, the more difficult we make it for whoever hunts us."

"But, Mistress, a few more days . . ."

"No, Aphen. The matter is settled. I want you here. You are incapacitated through no fault of your own, but incapacitated nevertheless. You lack mobility and strength. If we are threatened or even attacked, you become a liability that risks the lives of others because you cannot defend yourself as you need to. You know this. I regret you have suffered this setback, but disappointment is a part of all our lives."

Aphenglow fought back her tears. *I will not cry!* "How will you manage without me to guide you? What will you do when you come to a place you don't recognize and cannot ask me what I saw in my vision? My notes are thorough, but there is no substitute for having seen firsthand what it is we seek. You cannot know what difficulties you might encounter later. I have to be there!"

"Not if I perform a skiving of those memories so they become my own." The Ard Rhys paused. "Will you agree to that?"

A skiving. Aphen flinched. An excising of layers of images forming certain memories in one person's mind and transplanting them into another's. Few Druids— few magic wielders of any sort—had the skill to accomplish this. Khyber Elessedil was one.

But it was an intrusion into the mind, a trespass into

space that was the sole property of the owner. It had never been done to Aphenglow, and she had thought it never would.

"I don't want anyone in my mind," she said quietly, firmly. "I cannot endure it."

Khyber nodded. "I don't blame you. I would not ask it of you if there were a reasonable alternative. I promise not even to glance at anything but the Elfstone vision. A quick excision and then I am gone. If you experience pain or fear, I give you leave to banish me."

"I don't know."

The Ard Rhys reached over and took Aphenglow's hands in her own. "Yes, you do. You know."

Aphenglow nodded. She did know. She was a Druid first and always, and she would do what her Ard Rhys asked of her because that was the commitment she had given.

Khyber readjusted their hands so that Aphenglow's were open, palms up, and her own were resting lightly on top of them, palms down. "Look at me, Aphenglow. Look into my eyes and do not look away."

"I hate this," Aphen said in response.

"Keep looking at me. Think about the vision. Any part of the vision. Don't think of anything else but that. Let your mind relax and drift from one image to another. Keep remembering. Look at me. Look at me."

Aphen obeyed, feeling the first twinges of the expected invasion, a sort of tingling that began in her hands and slowly worked its way up her arms, through her neck, and finally into her head. She forced herself not to move, not to react, just enduring it, letting the skiving happen. The presence of the Ard Rhys was unmistakable, the feel of her moving around in her mind, touching here and there, prowling. Aphenglow wanted to scream, to throw her out, to stop what was happen-

ing and erase its memory as the tide might erase all
traces of passage on a sandy beach.

But she could not do that. She had given her word.

She must hold fast.

Then, without warning, it ended. The presence of the
Ard Rhys vanished, the invasion was over, and her mind
and body were hers again. She felt Khyber's hands withdraw, moving up to grip her shoulders.

"That was very brave of you," the Ard Rhys whispered and kissed her on the cheek.

Aphenglow closed her eyes and shook her head slowly.
"Just don't ever ask me to do that again."

There was no response. When she opened her eyes,
Khyber Elessedil was gone.

Shadows everywhere. Darkness all around.

Drust Chazhul worked his way cautiously down the
deep gloom of the hallway leading to Edinja Orle's
chambers, already questioning the wisdom of his decision to visit her in this manner. He had wanted to speak
to her somewhere private, somewhere their conversation wouldn't be overheard. He knew he had no hope of
persuading her to come to his own chambers, so he had
decided on the bold approach of asking to come to hers.
Surprisingly, she had agreed without a moment's hesitation.

But she wanted him there after dark when he would
not be seen and she could be certain of his intentions.

She could never be certain of that, he had thought at
the time, but he admired that she believed she could.
But then he, too, was risking something by coming
alone to her, when he would be most vulnerable to
whatever harm she might choose to inflict on him. So
when he had agreed to her terms, he had mentioned
casually that he would tell Stoon and his other retainers
that they would not need to accompany him—just to

advise her that someone would know where he was going, lessening the chances of her attempting anything unpleasant.

And he was not entirely without protections of his own. He was never without those.

But this darkness was annoying and made it difficult for him to maneuver, and he wondered how she could manage to do so herself. He groped his way along the wall, recalling the distance from the entry to the first door, keeping one hand stretched out in front of him to let him know when he reached it.

Even so, he came up against its rough surface less ready than he had expected to be, banging his hand and scraping his knuckles against the iron hinges. Cursing softly, he felt around for the handle, grasped hold, and twisted clockwise, half expecting that it would be locked.

But the latch released and the door opened smoothly. Beyond, a large entry was lit with a single smokeless torch of the sort favored by those who commanded magic. Edinja's talent was legendary; she far outstripped anyone else in Arishaig. She might have been marginalized on the political spectrum because of it, given that tolerance for any use of magic was severely limited in the Federation these days, save that her family was old and established and greatly feared. No one with any sense—which included himself—wanted to risk incurring the enmity of the Orle family. So until recently he had ignored her attraction to magic and been careful to stay on civil terms with her.

That state of affairs had lasted until he secured the position of Prime Minister. Now he was not at all certain how she felt or what she intended to do about him.

He crossed the entry to the door beyond, this one smaller and less forbidding. Perhaps it was the light that made it so. He paused and knocked softly.

"Come," he heard her say from within.

He opened the door and found himself in a room draped with silks and layered with carpets and throws and pillows. It looked to be less a reception chamber than a bordello, but he brushed that thought aside quickly. Candles burned everywhere, and the sweet scent of incense filled the air. He tried not to breathe it in but could not avoid doing so.

Edinja reclined on a couch at the back of the room. She was robed and hooded, though her fine, soft features were visible in the candlelight. She wore silken slippers on her tiny feet, ribbons flowing from her long silver hair. The rings that adorned her fingers glinted softly, small flashes of silver and gold. There was an unmistakable glow about her dusky skin that suggested an inner light. She was beautiful in a sharp, angular way, though he had never looked at her himself like that, only acknowledged what others said and thought. She lived alone, unmarried and unpartnered. It was said she took lovers now and then, but no one seemed clear on who or even what they were. Not that it mattered in the least to him.

Her only true companion lay stretched out a few yards away against the back wall. Cinla, sleek and sinewy, was a moor cat of average size, but striking design. Her strange reddish gold color was an exquisite rarity. Like all moor cats, she had the ability to appear and disappear at will, sometimes without even seeming to move. She accompanied her mistress outside her chambers every now and then, even on occasion into the Coalition Council chambers, but mostly she remained hidden from view. Drust himself had seen the big cat only once.

There were rumors about the relationship that existed between Edinja and Cinla, but they were of the sort that most often originated from malicious gossip and lacked any basis in truth. Still, there was a troubling intelligence in the moor cat's green eyes as she studied Drust. He held her gaze only a moment before looking away.

"Good evening, Prime Minister," Edinja greeted, indicating a chair close to where she rested.

"Good evening to you, Minister Orle," Drust returned. He moved over to the chair indicated and sat down. "I appreciate your giving me this opportunity to speak with you alone."

"And I that you were willing to come to me in my chambers so that this meeting could be conducted discreetly."

He smiled. "I am flattered to be allowed into such a private place."

"It must be difficult finding time for meetings such as this these days," she responded, dismissing his compliment with a small wave of one tiny hand. "Given the demands of your new office."

He decided not to let that pass. "Let me say something right up front. I am fully aware that you wanted the position of Prime Minister and that you are less than happy that I now own it. I didn't seek it out and perhaps I should have refused when it was offered. But it seemed wrong to do so when you and Commander Arodian were at such odds. I took it as a means of avoiding further conflict, not to satisfy any need of my own. You may not believe me, but this is so. I am aware that you are better qualified to be Prime Minister than I am. So is Arodian, for that matter. I have said so publicly. I am here for that very reason. I cannot do this without your help."

"Is that so?" She said it as if it were hard for her to believe. "You think yourself inadequate? You believe you require my poor skills to help you navigate treacherous waters?"

"An overly dismissive way of phrasing the level of

your skills and experience, Edinja. But however you see yourself, the time has come for us to work together. I am approaching you first. I have not spoken to Arodian. I will tell you something quite frankly. I neither like nor trust him. He is too ambitious and too arrogant for me to believe he will lift a finger on my behalf. You, I think, are more farsighted."

"Or at least more pragmatic." She gave him a shrug. "I don't see the purpose in waging war with you, Drust. I haven't the time or energy for it. My turn as Prime Minister will come soon enough. Oh, not that way. In the orderly course of events, the position will find its way to me. But for now, I would consider acting as your adviser and confidante, if that is what you are seeking from me?"

"It is exactly what I seek."

She rose suddenly and walked across the room. "Something to drink? A little wine?"

"A little only."

She made a point of letting him see her pour the wine into both glasses from the same decanter. Then she carried it across the room to him, tasting it herself from her own glass before handing him his, letting him know it was safe to drink.

"I don't think you would poison me in your own chambers," he said, taking a substantial drink. He glanced down at the wine and nodded. "Very nice."

She laughed softly. "You would be surprised what I would dare to do. But poisoning you is not high on that list. Something else is, however. Before I agree to work with you, we need to reach an understanding about my use of magic. You are on record as opposing its use. You wish to see all practice of it abolished. That presents a problem for someone like myself."

"I can see that it would. But I am firm about this. Magic is unpredictable and dangerous. It is a tool of the elite. Only a few have it, and the rest of us can only look in through the window and wonder at its attractive glitter. Worse, most of it is controlled by the Druids, and the Druids are the Federation's enemy."

She nodded, shrugged. "I care nothing for the Druids. I dislike them as much as you do. But I cannot give up using magic simply to satisfy your obsession with furthering the use of science. We need a better approach to solving this problem."

He watched her drink a little more wine from her glass. "Do you have a suggestion?"

"I do. Wage your campaign against magic, but confine it for now to the Druids. Their order is far and away the most obvious and unattractive congregation of magic users. No one likes or respects them, and any attacks on them will be met with widespread indifference. Perhaps somewhere down the road, a few years from now, after the Druids are destroyed and your own position secured, you can find a way to make an exception for me and those who act for me."

Drust Chazhul frowned. He didn't much care for making her any promises. "Perhaps," he allowed.

She frowned. "You patronize me, Drust. I can hear it in your voice and see it in your eyes. You say what you think will keep me compliant, but you have no real intention—"

She stopped suddenly, a startled look on her face. Her hand went to her throat and her mouth opened as she gasped for air. Drust Chazhul stared at her in a mix of confusion and shock.

"What have you done?" she hissed at him.

He shook his head quickly. "Nothing! I . . . don't . . . What's wrong? What's happening?"

"The wine!" She was on her feet, throwing away her glass, clutching now at her chest. "You've poisoned it!"

"No! I've done nothing!" He reached out to catch her

as she lurched toward him, but she pushed him away. "Edinja, this wasn't my doing!"

"Liar! Pretending . . . friendship, and all . . . the while . . ."

Cinla was sitting up straighter, watching it all, but not doing anything. Not yet. Drust looked in the moor cat's eyes and began to back away, edging toward the door. What was happening here? Edinja had dropped to her knees and was bent over, retching violently. Drust knew he should do something, but he couldn't think what it was. If it was poison, one needed to know what kind in order to provide an antidote. Her symptoms suggested something of every poison he knew.

"Treachery!" Edinja shrieked.

Then she toppled over and lay still.

Dead. Drust knew it at once. Her eyes fixed, her skin turned blue, her inner glow gone dark, her voice silenced. A white froth leaked from between her lips, pooling onto the floor.

Drust kept backing away, aware that Cinla was on her feet now and moving over to where her mistress lay. It would only be seconds before the moor cat turned her attention back to him. He had to get out of there before that happened. None of this was his doing, but if he were found in her chambers like this he would be blamed anyway. No amount of explaining would save him.

His eyes still on the moor cat as it sniffed Edinja's motionless body, he backed into the chamber door, fumbled for the handle, released the latch, and was on the other side almost before he knew it. Making sure the latch was set, he rushed across the entry to the larger door, wrenched it open, and fled into the blackness beyond.

17

Khyber Elessedil stood at the stern railing of the *Walker Boh* as she sailed west out of Paranor and watched the Druid's Keep slowly disappear into the eastern horizon. She could see it for a long time as the airship proceeded at a slow, steady pace toward the western wall of the Dragon's Teeth, its dark peaks ominous even in the bright sunlight of midday, spears extended toward the blue bowl of the sky. She had thought she might see Aphenglow come out to witness their departure, but the young Elven woman did not appear.

What she had not told Aphen, but what the other might have guessed, was that she had returned directly to Paranor from Patch Run precisely because she knew the young Druid's memory of the path the expedition needed to take was essential and must be skived if Aphen was to be left behind—a decision she had already made. She had chosen this effort over chasing after the Ohmsford twins, knowing Bakrabru was on the way to their Westland destination in any case and convinced that she could persuade the boys to join her once she had plumbed Aphen's memories and collected the other members of the company.

None of which relieved her feelings of guilt over how she had used Aphen and then discarded her.

The Ard Rhys shook her head, tamping down a pang of disappointment. She knew how bitter Aphen was about being left behind and wished she could have done more. But she imagined that in the end no one could help Aphen but Aphen herself. It might take time, but as her leg healed her heart would mend, too. She would come to accept that Khyber's choice not to take her was the right one. Bombax would return, and she would find other things to occupy her time.

Besides, they might all be reunited sooner than anyone thought. She hadn't been trying to placate Aphenglow when she had suggested as much. She wasn't at all sure that this present effort would lead to anything conclusive. It might well lead to nothing. Or it might turn out to be only the first step on a much longer journey. Tracking down something that was thousands of years missing, lost in a time that no longer existed by a Race that had been reduced to a fraction of its former size, would likely be much more complicated than anyone believed.

Anyone but herself, she amended—someone who had lived long enough to know better, who had experienced the rebel Shadea a'Ru's attempt to gain control of the order and survived the struggle it had taken to prevent that from happening.

So long ago now. So far in the past.

She watched the last vestiges of the fortress fade into the distance and experienced a strange feeling of regret at leaving, something she hadn't felt in a very long time.

"She will be fine, Mistress," Garroneck said at her elbow. "She is a strong young woman."

Khyber gave him a smile. "I know that. I just wish we could have found a way to include her."

The big Troll shrugged. "Perhaps she wasn't meant to be included. There might be something else that requires her talents."

"A nice thought." She nodded slowly. "I hope you are right. Mostly, I hope she will be able to do what is needed at Paranor in our absence. Leaving her with only her younger sister, her Elven protector, and a handful of your Trolls worries me. I hope Bombax comes back soon."

"You know he will. He always does. And don't underrate the capabilities of my Trolls, Mistress. They are more than a match for anything that might threaten Aphenglow or the Keep."

She nodded absently, redirecting her attention to the forward decks on the big warship. "What do you think of those three?"

She was referring to the two men and one woman that her Druids had brought back with them from their forays into different parts of the Four Lands in compliance with the urgings of the Shade of Allanon.

"An odd bunch," Garroneck declared.

An apt description, she thought. Each very different from the others, all very different from the Druids.

Skint was a Gnome Tracker recruited by Carrick—small, dark-faced, and decidedly uncommunicative. The Druid had found him in a small village at the foot of the Wolfsktaag Mountains in the Anar. He had known Skint from his childhood in the Eastland, where Carrick's father had managed a mining business. His father had used Skint as a hunter and trapper to feed his workers and protect his operation, which was a long way from anything approximating civilization. Skint's value, Carrick had explained to Khyber, was that he was exceedingly adept at finding his way through places he had never seen before, at reading signs, and at ferreting out dangers. As a boy, he had spent time with Skint—though his father had never found out about it—so he had witnessed firsthand how clever the Gnome could be. Skint wasn't a pleasant fellow, but he was very good at what he did. If you were with him and in danger, he was your best chance at finding your way to safety.

Seersha had brought back a Dwarf Chieftain. His name was Crace Coram, and he was something of a legend. He was the son and grandson of former Chieftains of their people, the Quare Rek, and he had inherited wars with Gnome tribes that went back several centuries. His father was killed in battle by members of one of those tribes, the Zek'ke, when Crace was just twenty, and he had been named leader by his people immediately. Only days later the Zek'ke had attacked again, knowing his father was dead and expecting to find the Quare Rek in disarray. At first, they were, fleeing in all directions. But Crace Coram rallied them in midflight, sought out the Gnome leader responsible for the death of his father, and single-handedly killed him and three others who were trying to protect him. Then, with fewer than thirty men, he drove the Zek'ke from his village and pursued them for three days through the mountains, the Dwarves under his command killing the fleeing Gnomes one by one.

When he finally caught up to the survivors, the Gnomes threw down their arms and begged for their lives. Crace Coram granted their wish, extracting a promise that none of them or any of their families or friends or members of their community would ever participate in another attack on the Quare Rek. The Gnomes not only agreed, they kept their word.

But the Dwarf legend was no longer Chieftain of his people. He had passed on that responsibility to his oldest son. Seersha had come from a neighboring village and had known Crace Coram all her life. When she had found him and explained her purpose, he had agreed at once to come back with her. His respect for Seersha and for the Druids was enormous, and if he could be of help to them he was more than willing to do so.

Besides, he had added with a smile, he had nothing better to do with his time.

Of the third choice, the strange young woman brought along by Pleysia, the Ard Rhys knew nothing at all beyond her name.

Oriantha.

She was sitting now at the bow of the vessel, deep in conversation with her friend and mentor. Pleysia was gesturing as she talked to the young woman, insistent and determined. Whatever the subject matter of their discussion, Pleysia was passionate about it. At times, it seemed to the Ard Rhys, almost angry.

"I think I need to learn something more about Pleysia's choice," she said to Garroneck.

She left him at the stern of the vessel, walked past the pilot box, went down the three steps to the mid-deck, and continued forward. Pleysia and Oriantha sensed her coming and ceased their conversation immediately, turning to watch her approach.

She knelt down next to them so that she was on eye level and cocked an eyebrow. "Are you settled in?" she asked Oriantha.

The young woman nodded, but said nothing. In fact, she hadn't said ten words since being introduced. She seemed pleasant enough, if odd looking. There was nothing Elven about her; if anything her strong features were almost feral. Her face lacked softness of any kind, and her lithe young body was hard and lean and layered with muscle. There was nothing special about her otherwise, nothing to suggest what it was she could do to help them. When asked why she had been chosen, she had deferred to Pleysia, who had refused to say. They would find out when it was time, the latter had advised obstinately, but not before.

Khyber Elessedil glanced from one woman to the other. "It might be a good idea if we talked now about what Oriantha can do for this expedition, Pleysia. I don't mind if we keep it among the three of us, but I think I have to insist that you tell me. I've trusted you this far, but I don't want to be caught by surprise later."

She waited. Pleysia glanced at her companion and shook her head. "It must wait awhile longer, Mistress."

The Ard Rhys felt a rush of irritation, but she kept her expression neutral. "How much longer, Pleysia?"

"We sail for the Westland to find the Ohmsford twins. Isn't that so? A journey of not more than two days?"

Khyber nodded. "That is so."

"I ask your forbearance until then. When we reach our destination, I will tell you why Oriantha is so important to this expedition. You have my word on it."

Khyber thought about asking why two more days made any difference, but then thought better of it. By asking, she would be opening herself up to another argument. Better to just let things alone.

She smiled. "Very well. We'll wait. Please remember your promise."

She rose and walked away, vaguely dissatisfied.

Aphenglow watched the *Walker Boh* depart from the window of her bedchamber, still propped up by pillows, her splinted leg stretched out in front of her. She did not witness the liftoff and the long, slow swing west, but could see the airship through her window as it flew away from the castle and disappeared into the horizon. It took a long time to disappear completely, and by the time it did she was in tears.

She was alone for the moment. Arling was exploring the Keep with Cymrian in the company of Krolling, the Troll who had been given command of the guard contingent left to watch over the Keep. She sat thinking for a time, pondering this and that, letting her mind skip from one subject to the next, trying not to direct her thoughts but letting them wander where they chose.

"I hate this!" she whispered finally, her anger breaking through.

She thought suddenly of Bombax, still not returned, and she threw off her lethargy and growing sense of helplessness and swung her legs off her bed and stood. She was surprised and vaguely irritated at how strong her leg felt. She had been employing her healing talents regularly, but hadn't tested the results before now. Had she known she could bear her weight this well, she might have fought harder to be included in the expedition.

She took a step away from her bed and almost instantly felt her leg give way. She barely managed to keep herself from falling.

She sat down again and stayed there for long moments, gathering her resolve. She would not even consider quitting. Hoisting herself off her bed a second time, she hobbled carefully to the far corner of her chamber. Her walking staff was leaning against the wall, and she took it in hand. Better supported now, she made her way to the door and out of the room.

Her destination was a hundred feet down a hall and three floors up to the highest room in the highest tower of Paranor. It took all her energy to get there, and she suffered a good deal of pain in the process. When she had climbed all sixty steps, she limped across the entry chamber to the ironbound wooden door that led into the cold room.

Even though the Ard Rhys had not found any trace of Bombax by using the scrye waters, Aphenglow thought she might have better luck. She was much closer to him than Khyber, more deeply invested. She might see things that others would miss or simply overlook. Reading the scrye waters was an art, and sometimes success was achieved for intangible reasons. It was a better use of her time trying to discover if that were true rather than sitting around. Doing anything was better than doing nothing.

She released the latch and pushed open the heavy door to the cold room. The drop in temperature as she entered was immediately noticeable; on the walls condensation had turned to smears of ice, and she could see her breath when she exhaled. The chamber occupied the whole of the top floor of the tower, a surface area forty feet in diameter and fifteen feet high. It was empty save for a platform constructed of massive blocks of bluestone on which a broad basin rested. The shallow bowl of the basin was filled with greenish waters that looked to have the consistency of a thicker liquid, something approaching oil. The waters swirled in a clockwise motion, the movement barely discernible.

Aphenglow approached and looked down into the basin. Layered across its bottom were geographic features and strange symbols that represented the whole of the Four Lands and some places beyond. Anyone unfamiliar with Druid lore would not have been able to recognize what they were looking at; only a Druid could read the scrye waters. Grianne Ohmsford had built it that way using her considerable magic, back in the infancy of her rule as Ard Rhys, when she had been beset by enemies and disbelievers on every side and had felt keenly the need to monitor their uses of magic from afar.

If Bombax had used his magic at any time over the past few days, the scrye waters should reveal when and where and measure the potency of the use.

The scrye shimmered slightly as she passed her hands across its surface. She was careful not to touch the waters, allowing herself instead to trace their swirling patterns in the air above. There were no discernible disturbances. She took her time, reading them carefully, focusing first on the Borderlands and then allowing her search to radiate outward to the other lands, one after the other. She felt herself merge with the movement of the waters, traveling as they did, cutting across the lines of power that encircled the world, tracking each to places near and far.

Only once did she sense something. Far out in the wasteland beyond the wall of the Breakline, in country where almost nothing lived, she encountered a disturbance unlike anything she had come across before. She lingered on it a moment, but it was brief and gone almost as quickly as it had come. She was able to tell that it had happened before but could not determine if it had produced any consequences.

In any case, it had nothing to do with Bombax.

She lifted her hands away and stood looking at the scrye waters in what amounted to an admission of defeat. There was no sign of Bombax; she had found no hint of where he was or what had happened to him.

She stepped away from the basin. Apparently her life mate had not found a need to use his magic since leaving Paranor, which was a good sign. If he were threatened, he would have done so. She had to accept that wherever he was and whatever he was doing, he was not in any particular danger.

That was what she told herself, but not what she believed in her heart.

Her damaged leg aching steadily now, she limped out of the room and made her way back down the stairs to her bedchamber. By the time Arlingfant and Cymrian returned from the tour of the Keep, she was back in bed and there was nothing to say that she had ever left.

* * *

In Arishaig, Drust Chazhul paused just inside the entry to his quarters and stared down at the piece of folded white paper lying on the floor.

Another one.

He felt a twinge of fear and uncertainty as he reached down to pick it up, knowing right away what it was. Shielding his movements from the guards who stood at watch to either side of the doorway behind him, believing they would never dare to look, but cautious anyhow, he unfolded the paper and read the words printed on it.

I KNOW WHAT YOU DID

He was filled with helpless rage. Who was sending him these notes? Who could possibly have known what had happened in Edinja's chambers two nights before? No one had seen him come or go; no one but Edinja and her cat had been present. Yet this was the third of these notes in less than two days and still not a clue as to who was sending them.

Or why.

It was this question that bothered him most. Why were these notes being sent? What purpose did they serve? If someone wanted something from him because of what they believed he had done to Edinja, why didn't that someone tell him what it was?

He turned back to the guards. "Did anyone come to see me while I was gone?" he demanded. "This morning, while I was in Council?"

The guards exchanged a hurried look. "No one, Prime Minister," one answered.

"You're quite sure of that?"

"Very sure. We were here all morning, both of us. No one even approached your chambers."

He turned away and went into his rooms, closing the

door behind him. Just like the other times. The notes appeared inside his rooms, but with no evidence of how they had gotten there. If he had not trusted Stoon so completely or had been able to conceive of any advantage the other might gain by doing this, he would have suspected him. After all, Stoon was the only one who had access to his quarters, the only one who could come and go without being seen.

There were the chambermaids, of course, but they had to pass the guards to get in to do their work. Besides, he had questioned them already, a thorough and not entirely pleasant examination that had yielded nothing. The women were dull and frightened, and he could detect no hint of duplicity in their responses.

No, this was someone else—someone with talent of the sort that Edinja had possessed.

But Edinja was dead, and he still had no idea who had killed her or why. Whoever thought he was responsible and hiding it was mistaken. But there was no way he could relay that information to his persecutor without knowing who it was.

Of course, once he found out, he wouldn't waste five seconds trying to explain anything. He would simply have Stoon remove the source of the problem.

Speaking of which, he was waiting now for his confederate to return with news of Edinja's death. No one had reported it yet, not even after two days of her absence at the Council meetings. Surely retainers of some sort must have found the body. Why were they hiding it? Were they somehow involved with whoever was sending him the notes?

He felt his paranoia spiraling out of control and quickly tamped it down. He poured himself a glass of wine from the decanter, started to drink it to calm himself, and stopped. He studied the wine and then set it down again. He wasn't ready to drink wine again quite yet.

Which made him wonder anew why the poison had affected Edinja and not him. Had it already been in her glass when she poured the wine? How could the killer have known which glass she would use?

He went over to the couch and lay down to nap. He felt on edge and irritable from everything that had happened since his meeting with Edinja, as if his life had somehow taken a wrong turn. He wished he had never asked for the meeting. He wished he had never gone.

He even found himself wishing she were still alive. He had wanted her dead, but not this quickly and not in a way that was out of his control.

He fell into an uneasy sleep, but woke instantly when he heard the panel in the wall slide back and Stoon appeared through the opening. He sat up at once, rubbing the sleep from his eyes.

"What did you find out? Tell me."

The assassin hesitated. "Edinja has disappeared."

Drust stared at him. "What does that mean? She's dead. How can she disappear? You mean someone took the body?"

"There isn't any body. According to the retainers I spoke with there isn't even any sign of a struggle."

"No body? What about the cat?"

'Sitting there where she usually sits, I gather. I didn't get inside for a look. This all comes from Edinja's servants. They don't know where she is, but apparently she isn't there. Maybe she isn't even dead."

"No, she's dead. I watched her die." Drust rose and walked over to the table, picked up the glass of wine he had poured himself and handed it to Stoon. "Smell this."

The assassin did and shrugged. "You believe it might have been poisoned?"

Drust snatched back the glass and set it on the table. He handed Stoon the note. "This came while I was in Council."

Stoon glanced at it. "Same as the others. Did the guards see anything?"

"No. I have to find out what is happening, who is doing this. I have to put a stop to it. You didn't learn anything? Anything at all?"

"Nothing. But that's only because no one knows anything. Except for whoever is doing this."

"I don't understand it. What can anyone gain by this? Tormenting me for something I didn't do? Suggesting that I am responsible and implying that I should be held accountable because of it? It's madness!"

Stoon nodded. "It feels to me as if tormenting you is the whole point. Who would want to do that?"

Drust shook his head. "The line goes out the door and down the hall since I became Prime Minister. It's the nature of the job. But no one has threatened me like this before. No one has deliberately made themselves my enemy. Not even Edinja did that. Nor Arodian."

Stoon walked over to the table with the wine and sat down in one of the high-backed chairs. "Well, you should be pleased that with Edinja dead and gone, you only have one troublemaker left to dispose of. What shall we do about Arodian?"

Drust shook his head. "I have to think about it. Is there news about what's happening at Paranor?"

"It's the reason I'm here. The *Walker Boh* departed earlier today with what looks to be nearly a full complement of Druids and Troll guards. Our spies tell us the Ard Rhys herself is aboard. The airship flies west, but the destination is unknown."

"West? Surely not to the Elves again?" Drust thought about it. "I'm guessing the King's granddaughter remains. Her leg was broken in the attack at Arborlon. But maybe the rest have left."

He paused, looking pointedly at Stoon. "This might be the opportunity we seek. If we act quickly, we might be able to rid ourselves of both the Druids and Paranor. But how . . . ?"

He looked away a moment, and then back again. "We need to get inside Paranor. It would be better if we didn't have to force our way in. Is it possible to arrange for someone inside to open the gates for us?"

Stoon, tall and lean, bent forward like a vulture eyeing prey. "Anything is possible, Prime Minister. Anything."

18

APHENGLOW ELESSEDIL'S instincts about what might have happened to delay Bombax's return to Paranor were not misguided. Far from it. His efforts to find help for the Druids in their quest for the missing Elfstones had not gone well. Rather, they had gone spectacularly awry.

He had flown south to the Borderland City of Varfleet, thinking to seek out someone with magic the likes of which the Druids did not possess. After all, if the Shade of Allanon felt the members of the order lacked sufficient talent to accomplish what was needed, it stood to reason they needed to find someone who possessed magic of a different sort. So that was what Bombax, never short of confidence and determination, meant to do.

In the course of his travels, he had heard of a man who could make himself disappear. He had heard of one who could shape-shift. He had been told of a woman who could transport herself instantaneously from one place to another. The sources of the stories were reliable, and the stories themselves had been repeated often enough that he had reason to believe at least one of them might be true. Finding even one such talented magic user would be invaluable in getting into heavily guarded or magic-warded places that the Druids might come across in their search. He would have preferred someone who could sense the presence of dormant magic—that would have been extraordinary—but he had never heard of anyone who possessed such a talent.

Still, you never knew.

So he had gone to Varfleet, where most of the stories had originated, with certain preconceptions about the sort of people he was looking for.

Men and women gifted with powerful magic tended to be solitary and nomadic. They did not seek out lives involving families, friends, homes, spouses, and children. They were rootless by choice, keeping apart, hiding their talents, and living their lives behind walls of secrecy. They did so in order to protect themselves but also because they saw themselves as outsiders. When people close to you discovered you possessed extraordinary talent, it changed both their behavior toward and expectations of you. Druids avoided the fallout of this reaction by living in a community of magic users. Men and women came to the Druid order with raw, undeveloped talent and hopes for what they might achieve with training. They joined with an understanding that magic was to be used to help others and never for selfish reasons. They became one another's friends and family.

But men and women like the ones he was looking for kept apart because they had no interest in sharing their talent with the larger world or even one another. Instead they hired out for money or simply took what they wanted because they could. Too much magic, too much talent, too little regard for others—it was a dangerous combination. This was fine with Bombax. He wasn't looking for new recruits to the Druid order. He was looking for mercenaries who could be hired to perform a specific task and then dismissed to go back to their previous lives. There would be fewer complications that way when the quest for the missing Elfstones ended. Nothing would remain between employers and employees save memories. He left Paranor convinced that keeping a reasonable distance between the Druids and the people they sought would be the better choice.

Aphenglow would have disagreed, but she was of a different character than he was and possessed a different worldview.

He wondered sometimes what had drawn them together. She was young and naïve and possessed of a strong sense of commitment. He was worldly, experienced well beyond anything he had revealed to her, and believed that in order to survive the damage visited on you by the world's pitfalls and heartaches you had to distance yourself from its needs. It was fine to share yourself when and where you could, but you had to accept that there were limits to the sacrifices you could make.

Aphenglow did not believe such limits existed.

They loved each other in different ways. She loved him for his tough-mindedness and self-confidence and an unexpected tenderness of heart that manifested just often enough to sweep aside her doubts about his brash and impetuous behavior. He loved her for her calming presence and for an inner strength of character that never seemed to waver. The combination was enough, he supposed, to sustain the relationship. But he was not naïve about such things, and he could already sense the ways in which the ties that bound them might fray and eventually break. He would be sad when it happened, but he would survive. She would be devastated.

He was thinking of her on his first night in Varfleet as he roamed from tavern to pleasure house to gambling den, looking for familiar faces and interesting conversation, seeking sources of information that would lead him to one of the magic wielders he sought. Perhaps if he hadn't, things might have turned out differently, although even afterward Bombax could not bring himself to believe so.

Shed of his Druid clothes and trappings, dressed instead in the trader's garb by which he was commonly known in Varfleet, he sat in a tavern with three hardened men who made their living hunting and trapping when easier choices didn't present themselves. Not hunting and trapping animals, of course, but people. Slaves for the mines and the factories, for the fields and the quarries—men, women, and children alike, all in demand for work done in secret, distant places where there was little chance of rescue and no chance at all for escape. He knew two of them casually and while passing by their table had heard one of those he knew mention a man who could shape-shift. It caused him to pause long enough to say hello and offer to buy all three a glass of ale.

It had taken him almost ten hours of rambling around from place to place to stumble on even this small scrap of information. All of his usual sources had dried up, and no one he had talked to could tell him anything he didn't already know. But the men he was sitting with seemed to have a concrete idea of where at least one of those he was looking for could be found. Even so, the information was provided slowly and only after an initial exchange of coin and some ruminations about the difficulties of life in Varfleet, which led to a further exchange.

But in the end Bombax had what he wanted and was on his way out the door when the roof caved in.

He had been drinking steadily, but only small amounts, not so foolish or inattentive as to allow himself to become intoxicated. Nothing seemed unusual to him until he stood up and started for the door. Even then, for the first dozen steps, he experienced only a mild sense of imbalance, one that caused him to blink and try harder to focus his movements as he neared the door.

But he had only just taken the first step outside when all his strength simply melted away and he collapsed into a deep pool of blackness.

When he awoke, he was lashed to a wooden framework that rested against the wall of a cavernous warehouse empty of almost everything but himself. His mouth was similarly wrapped, the whole of him trussed in such a way that he could neither move nor speak. Someone, he thought right away, knew who and what he was and what it took to stop him from using magic to free himself. Unable to gesture or speak, he had no means of summoning the magic that would free him. His second thought was for the three men in the tavern who had drugged him and given him up to this fate. Although, he corrected himself quickly, he could not jump to conclusions about who had done this to him. The drink had been drugged, but someone besides the three could have done it. He had no clear way of knowing.

What he did know was that he was a captive, and that it almost certainly had to do with his being a Druid.

He glanced at his surroundings. The warehouse was old and dilapidated, and parts of it were missing or falling apart before his eyes. Whole sections of the roof were gone, and pieces of the walls high up near the joists, some thirty feet off the floor, were splintered or broken. Debris littered the floor in mounds.

But the heavy doors at either end were solid enough, and he was willing to bet they were locked, as well. There were no windows, and besides the doors and the holes in the roof no other visible ways in or out. He tested the ropes that bound him and found them too tight to loosen or to wiggle out of. No surprise. He watched rats scurry about in the gloom, eyes shining with reflected light from a sun only just visible through a gap in the far wall.

Sunrise or sunset? He couldn't be sure.

He waited a long time afterward for someone to come. When someone finally did, it was dark, the light gone, the world beyond his prison lit only by stars and a thin wash of torchlight thrown off by the city. He might not even have known anyone was there if not for the slow hissing of breath in the darkness.

"Doesss you know thisss plassse, Druid?"

A Mwellret. The sound of its voice was unmistakable. Lizard creatures, they made their homes in the far Eastland, mostly in the swamps below and caverns within the Ravenshorn Mountains. Seldom did they get this far west. Bombax could count on the fingers of one hand the number of times he had even heard of Mwellrets being sighted in Varfleet.

"Catsss gotsss your tonguesss?" the voice hissed at him, sly and insinuating, a teasing that made Bombax want to tear the speaker's head off.

Instead he kept still and waited. His chance would come.

"Thirsssty?" the voice persisted.

Bombax heard movement—a rustle of clothing—as the speaker approached. Then cold water was poured down his face and into the gag. He sucked at it eagerly, drawing it from the cloth into his parched mouth. It had a slightly bitter taste, but he didn't care; he drank it anyway. The water trickled down his throat, easing his thirst. He kept his eyes closed as he drank, feeling the Mwellret's breath on his face, knowing he must not look in the creature's eyes, that if he did those eyes could take control of him and make him a slave. The

Mwellret was testing him, seeing if he would let his guard down.

"Prisonersss are troublesss for usss," the voice continued, the shadow of the speaker backing away again. "Essspecially Druidsss."

A pause. Bombax waited, searching the darkness for the Mwellret's face. *Tell me who did this? Who is responsible?*

"Stayss with usss only another day. Then leavesss for visssit to thossse who pay usss to take you prisssoner."

Who? A name!

But the Mwellret was already moving away, and in seconds it was gone.

He was alone again for a long time. Eventually, he fell asleep. He hung from the rack like a side of meat, pinned fast, but sagging where the ropes failed to hold him up. When he woke, the sunlight piercing the openings in the failing walls of the warehouse like spears, he was aching and sore. Where the ropes bound him, the skin was bruised and rubbed raw. He worked his limbs and body to encourage circulation of his blood, flexing his hands and feet, chasing away the numbness and residual tingling.

At some point they would have to cut him down, and when they did he would be ready for them.

But he worried that his strength would be depleted and his reflexes slowed by his bondage. He might have the will to act, but lack the means.

He hated himself for letting this happen.

Then, unexpectedly, he heard voices outside, the words unclear but unmistakably human. He listened as they came closer, trying to make out what they were saying, to decide how many there were. He heard them move down the wall behind him toward the far end of the building, and then cease suddenly. He waited. He tried calling out, but the gag was tied too tightly in place for him to do more than emit a muffled grunt. He strained at the ropes, banging his body against the wooden frame he was lashed against, trying to create any sort of sound that might attract attention. But he couldn't manage even that.

The voices went away, and he was left anew in silence and gloom. His one chance, gone. He felt a wave of despair wash through him, but quickly forced it away again. He would not give up on himself. One way or another, he would get out of this.

Long minutes passed before he heard a scrabbling at the far door, metal on metal, and the sharp click of a latch releasing. He peered through the gloom, his hopes renewed. A crack appeared in the darkness as the door opened and a slim figure slid through. But then the door closed again, and the silence returned.

He waited for a sound—any sound—to break that silence. But nothing did.

"Thought I saw something back here," a voice announced suddenly, startling Bombax so that he jerked against the ropes in surprise. "Earlier, when my mates and I were peeking through cracks in the boards, that was you I was seeing."

A figure stepped into the light. It was a boy, older rather than younger, somewhere close to manhood, his body tall and slim, his face narrow and sharp-featured, his expression cocky.

"So what's your story, I wonder?" He peered at Bombax. "You must have become a serious irritation in somebody's backside to end up like this. I should set you free, I guess. But maybe that's not the right thing to do, given the likely nature of those who brought you here."

Bombax kept staring at him, waiting. He couldn't do much besides hope that the boy's instincts persuaded him to make the right decision.

The boy hesitated, and then shrugged. "Well, least I can do is hear you out, listen to what you have to say. Better make it a good story, though, or you're back on your own."

He reached around Bombax's neck and began working on the knots securing the gag. "Those boys knew what they were doing. Can't get these knots loose." He stepped back, reached down, and brought out a slim, wicked-looking knife. "Let's try this. Hold real still now. Else I might cut your throat by mistake."

It took him two quick swipes with the knife and the gag fell away. Bombax opened his mouth and breathed in great gulps of fresh air. But when he tried to thank the boy, he couldn't make the words come out as anything other than an unintelligible grunt.

"What's wrong?" the boy asked, watching him struggle. "They didn't cut out your tongue, did they?"

Bombax shook his head. He mimed swallowing. Whatever liquid the Mwellret had let him drink had paralyzed his vocal cords.

"Oh, some sort of poison?" The boy shook his head in sympathy. "Makes it kind of hard for you to tell me what's wrong, doesn't it? I'm sorry, but I might have to leave you here. Like I said, I can't chance letting you go if it's the wrong thing for me to do."

Bombax shook his head quickly, sighed and nodded. He understood. He tried again to speak, but nothing intelligible came out.

"You're in a fix," the boy said.

Bombax nodded.

The boy studied him some more. "Well, I can't see leaving you, whatever the reason you're here. No one deserves this. If you'd done something really bad, whoever's responsible for this would have just killed you and been done with it. This looks to me to be something else."

He stepped forward again, took out the knife a second time, and began cutting the ropes that bound Bombax to the frame. When the ropes fell away, the Druid fell with them, his body so numb and aching he couldn't stand. The boy tried to catch him, but Bombax was too big and heavy for him to hold, and the best the boy could do was break his fall.

"Guess you were strapped up there awhile." The boy held him up in a sitting position, bracing him in place while Bombax tried to work the circulation back into his arms and legs. "You want some water?"

Bombax nodded. The boy helped him move over to a wall where he could prop himself up before disappearing back into the gloom. Bombax kept working at his limbs, thinking that he probably couldn't even manage to get back on his feet and out of there if the Mwellret returned. Because he couldn't speak and couldn't work his hands properly, he couldn't work his magic, either. He might be free, but he was virtually helpless.

The boy returned after a time carrying a ladle filled with water. "The water's okay to drink," he told Bombax. "It's clean."

Bombax drank, easing the dryness, opening his throat so he could breathe better. He grunted in thanks and handed the ladle back.

"Look, I'd do something more for you if I knew what it was you wanted me to do," the boy said.

Bombax nodded. He made writing motions with his hands.

The boy shook his head. "I don't have anything for that. Here, use the floor. Write in the dust. Start with your name."

Bombax did so, using his finger.

"Bombax," the boy repeated. "I'm Deek Trink. Now tell me what you want me to do."

Bombax thought about it for a moment, trying to think how to explain it. Then he wrote a single word:

PARANOR

"Paranor?" the boy exclaimed in surprise. He looked at Bombax with fresh eyes. "Is that where you're from?"

Bombax nodded.

"You're a Druid?"

He nodded again.

"You want to go back there?"

Another nod. Bombax wrote a second word in the dust:

AIRSHIP

The boy frowned. "You want me to find you an airship?"

Bombax shook his head. He was getting frustrated with being unable to talk. He pointed at himself.

"Oh, you've got an airship and you want me to get you to it?"

Bombax nodded.

The boy, who had been kneeling next to him, stood up. He used his boot to rub out the words that Bombax had scrawled in the dust. "Can you get on your feet and walk?"

Bombax nodded. He struggled up, but then stood in place swaying unsteadily. His legs didn't seem to want to move and his head was spinning.

The boy laughed. "Well, you can't walk far, that's sure! You better let me help you. Here, put your arm around me."

The boy moved next to him and helped him loop his arm across his shoulders. The boy adjusted himself, put an arm around the Druid's waist, and started walking him one step at a time. Slowly, they crossed the warehouse floor toward the door at the far end, an endless, torturous process that quickly sapped what little strength Bombax could muster. They made it to the door and back outside. The day was gray and cloudy, and the air was filled with the smells of fish and kelp. Out in the bay that opened off the Runne, fishermen were working their nets and stringing lines. The boy stopped long enough to take a cautious look around the docks before starting up again.

They continued this way back along the dockside, following the wall of the warehouse to where another warehouse began. Beyond that, several more warehouses were visible, dark and looming and dilapidated. Solid ground looked to be a long, long way off.

"Don't worry, we don't have to go far now." He could hear the boy huffing as he spoke. "But we can't stop. Not out in the open like this. Should have asked you who did this so I would know who to look for. That's it. Keep moving. Down over here. See those steps?"

They reached a set of rickety wooden stairs that led down to the water and a small platform to which a skiff was tied. Together they maneuvered down the steps to the platform and climbed into the boat, where an exhausted Bombax sat down heavily, shoulders hunched, head hanging between his legs as he gasped for air.

Deek Trink knelt next to him, the tiny boat wobbling with the shifting of his weight. "You get down on the floor between the seats and I'll cover you with a canvas. Can't risk you being seen until we're away from here. I'll row us out from this dock and back to shore where I can hide you until I get your airship close by. I don't think you're going to get to it on your own. Or even with me to help carry you. Can you tell me how to find it? Tell me where it's moored? I can fly it, if it's not too big."

Bombax nodded. He was so dizzy and sapped of strength that it was all he could do to focus on the boy's words. He had never felt like this. It made him wonder what sort of drug the Mwellret had fed him.

"Good enough. Save it for later, though. We need to get out of here first. Lie down, now. Let me cover you up."

Bombax did as he was told. He lay still as the boy covered him and then felt him shift his weight onto one of the two wooden seats and heard him set the oars in their locks.

When they began to move, the sound of the oars pulling against the water and the rocking of the skiff quickly put Bombax to sleep.

19

EARLIER THAT SAME MORNING, MANY MILES TO the south, the Federation Flagship *Arishaig* lifted away from the city for which she was named and started north toward Paranor. She was followed by a fleet of four other airships—two warships like herself, ships-of-the-line; one huge transport; and a scouting vessel built for speed and maneuverability. Almost a thousand men were aboard the five vessels counting crews, Federation soldiers, and Drust Chazhul. Of those, most had no clear idea where they were going, and only the Prime Minister and Stoon were aware of the real purpose of the journey.

Even Lehan Arodian, newly appointed commander of the *Arishaig* and Minister of Defense of the Coalition Council, whose considerable power matched that of Drust, did not know the whole truth.

It had taken some doing to bring all this about. Theoretically, Federation Prime Ministers were expected to visit other heads of state throughout the Four Lands. But in practice those who held the office rarely ventured outside the Southland, confining their visits to undisputed parts of the Federation. Only now and then, when it was necessary, would a Prime Minister go out into the other three lands or surrounding territories, and then only because such a visit would in some concrete way further Federation interests. That Drust Chazhul should choose to go to Paranor raised more than a few eyebrows, given the tensions existing between the Federation and the Druids. But he deflected criticism and doubts voiced by members of the Coalition Council by pointing out that establishing some sort of relationship with Paranor early on in his term of office would be the first step toward finding a way to change their attitude. Ignoring the Druids, as they had done for many years, had failed to work; it was time to try something more creative.

It was only a short step from there to convincing them that a sizable force was needed for the journey. If the Druids were to be persuaded, they needed to be reminded of the considerable power the Federation commanded. They needed to be shown an example of what they would be up against if they made the Federation their enemy. The arrival of a fleet of warships bearing the Prime Minister would go a long way toward accomplishing that.

They were further convinced when it was suggested that Lehan Arodian, one of their most capable and trusted soldiers and a member of the Council's Inner Circle, be given command of the expedition. That had been Stoon's idea. Make him a part of the supposed delegation. Name him commander of the fleet. Then drop him overboard somewhere on the way. An accident, of course. Accidents were known to happen aboard airships.

It was a gamble on Drust's part, to be sure. But big rewards usually required big risks. Drust Chazhul was ready to take one here.

Standing on the bridge of the *Arishaig*, watching the towers and walls of the Federation capital city begin to diminish as the fleet eased into formation in preparation for sailing north, he paused a moment in his thinking to study the man who was now the chief obstacle to his efforts at holding on to his office.

Like Edinja Orle, Lehan Arodian came from a powerful family of politicians and army commanders dating back three centuries. He was a soldier first and foremost, but after years of service he had gone on to become a member of the Coalition Council. A dual role of this sort was allowed under Federation law, and he was a logical choice to act as Minister of Defense. Because of his family history and oratorical skills and because he was respected and liked by the soldiers he commanded, he had risen fast in political circles to become the obvious choice as successor to the old Prime Minister. He would have been so named if not for the campaign mounted by Edinja and the secretive efforts of Drust to position himself as an acceptable compromise to either.

Failure to gain the position of Prime Minister had done little to diminish Arodian's ambitions; of that, Drust Chazhul was certain. In fact, there was every reason to think that Arodian himself had been responsible for Edinja Orle's death. With Edinja out of the way, any real threat to his ambition to be appointed Prime Minister was eliminated. It would not take much for him to persuade the Coalition Council to reconsider their choice; and if that happened, Drust was out of a job. After all, he had been a compromise choice in the first place, and there was no longer any reason for compromise. Thus the decision to name Arodian commander of this expedition. It gave the Minister of Defense the impression that Drust was deferring to him, and at the same time it took him outside the city walls, away from the comparative safety of his family, and put him in a place where he could be disposed of. Lehan Arodian might be going out on this expedition, but he was most definitely not coming back.

Drust walked over to the commander and stood next to him. "Fine day for flying, isn't it?" he offered.

"Not as fine as you might think." Arodian didn't look at him, his eyes directed forward. "Clouds to the west? Storm coming on, maybe two, three hours off. We won't be past the Prekkendorran by then. Be right out in the open when she strikes us." He glanced over, smiling. "Hope you remember to lean over the side if you get queasy, Drust. This is new stuff for an office dweller like yourself."

Drust smiled back, ignoring the other man's failure to address him as Prime Minister. "I'll do my best not to disappoint you."

The other nodded. "We're flying a lot of canvas for a simple visit. This feels more like the buildup to an engagement."

"Does it?"

"Three ships-of-the-line? A transport crammed with soldiers? Yes, it most certainly does. I know you sold the Council on this being a simple courtesy call, but I think you might have something more in mind. Maybe you know something the rest of us don't about the state of the Druid defenses?"

Drust shook his head. "I just think a show of force doesn't hurt when dealing with people who don't much like you. They might come around quicker if they see what they could be calling down on themselves."

"Especially if you find a reason to use that force. Don't be too quick to go up against the Druids, friend Drust. They've got magic that puts our scientific developments to shame. Including all our diapson-crystal-powered weapons. If you want to subdue them, you need to use cunning."

Just what I was thinking, Drust mused silently. "If you say so."

He walked away before Arodian could say anything

more. He had an uneasy feeling about the way the other was so bold in challenging his intentions, as if somehow he already knew what they were. Well, he might have guessed, of course. Arodian was no fool. But whatever he was, it wouldn't matter after tonight.

After tonight, he would be dead.

Aphenglow Elessedil was working in the garden, her walking staff close at hand, damaged leg wrapped in a lightweight splint and carefully stretched out in front of her where she could avoid doing anything that might injure it further. Her healing was progressing rapidly, the exercises and uses of her magic producing notice-able results. She needed the splint now only for protec-tion; she no longer required it in order to move about. Leaning on her staff and taking slow, cautious steps were protection enough. At night, she slept without the splint. And she could get to her feet by herself and wash and dress herself without assistance.

She was well enough, in fact, that she was eager to do something more active. But Arlingfant was insistent that she not rush things, making it a point to monitor her sister's activities to make sure she didn't.

Right now, Arling was off fetching lunch and cold drinks for a picnic. But she would be back soon enough, and Aphen was feeling lazy enough in the sun's warmth, her hands buried in the dirt as she planted flowers and pulled weeds, that she did not feel like arguing the mat-ter.

Across from her, Cymrian sat on a stone bench con-structing a bow. He had gone out of the Keep into the surrounding forest—something Krolling had advised against—searching for the right piece of wood from which to fashion the bow. He'd come back with an eight-foot length of ash and been working on cutting it down and shaping it to form for the past two days. He was always somewhere close at hand, even now when they were safe behind Paranor's walls. He was as much her shadow as Arlingfant, and sometimes it felt as if she was never alone. She had repeatedly suggested that he could go back to Arborlon; she would be fine where she was. In fact, he could take her sister with him so she could return to her duties as a Chosen.

That suggestion had been firmly rebuffed by both. They would leave when she was healed and when they felt she could be safely left alone. That time had not yet arrived.

Nor had Bombax, she thought suddenly.

It was getting harder and harder as the days passed not to obsess over his absence. She had been back to the cold room twice since that first time and used the scrye waters to try to detect some sign of his magic. But nothing had revealed itself, and she was stuck with wondering and worrying and waiting some more.

Which was what she was doing once again when Arlingfant came running down the pathway shouting, "He's back!"

Aphenglow didn't need to ask whom she meant. She scrambled to her feet, trying to be careful of her damaged leg. Her sister came charging up to her. "He's hurt, Aphen. Some boy had to bring him back. They're down in the healing ward."

As quickly as Aphenglow's injured leg would let her, she hurried to reach him. Forgotten were the warmth of the day and the enjoyment of gardening. All Aphenglow could think about was how badly Bombax might be hurt. She quizzed her sister, but Arling couldn't give her any answers. Bombax, it seemed, had lost his voice and much of his muscular control.

"He seems delirious! I don't think he even knows where he is!"

It wasn't an exaggeration. They found him lying on a

bed, strapped in place by the Troll guards who had carried him in from his airship. He was thrashing and crying out and looked to be in the throes of a form of madness. Aphenglow hurried to him, bent close, and called his name repeatedly. But he looked right through her, as if he didn't know who she was and didn't care.

"What will you do?" her sister asked, hands on Aphen's shoulders to steady her as she backed away from the bed and its wild-eyed occupant.

For a moment, Aphenglow panicked. She didn't recognize the illness from the symptoms she was seeing. This was something new. Her panic was exacerbated by how much she loved him and how desperate she was to do something to help him.

Then she shook off her uncertainty and went to work. She fed him teaspoons of althenin, a nightshade derivative that acted as a relaxant and calming agent. She had Arling bring her cold cloths to bathe his face and cool him down; when she felt his forehead, he was burning up. She dismissed everyone except her sister—including the boy who had apparently returned him to Paranor, flying him home in Bombax's own airship—wanting to empty the room of everyone who wasn't necessary to what needed to be done. Arling had worked with her before in Arborlon and knew how to behave. Besides, Aphen couldn't move about as easily as Arling and needed her sister's superior mobility to fetch and carry.

When the althenin had taken effect and Bombax had stopped thrashing and was lying in a semi-stupor, she examined his mouth to be certain his tongue hadn't been damaged and then called up the magic that she hoped would heal him.

She placed her hands on his face, closed her eyes, and slowly, carefully began to probe his damaged body. Using a magic that allowed her to discover the source of the sickness attacking him, she found the residue of a liquid he had apparently swallowed that had robbed him of both his voice and his muscle control. A dangerous side effect, it appeared, was that it was rendering him increasingly delirious and psychotic. She searched for the places where the poison was doing the most damage and slowly worked it out of his body, withdrawing it through his pores and turning it into a fine mist that evaporated in the open air.

She worked on him for a long time, a tedious and thorough cleansing of every part of his body. Arlingfant kept watch over them both, standing close at hand, bringing cold cloths to lay on Bombax's forehead and feeding him additional althenin when he started to wake and move about. Keeping Bombax still while she worked was crucial to her efforts, Aphenglow explained, and her sister saw to it that he remained immobile.

When she finally finished her ministrations, night was coming on. She sent Arling off to find them food and drink and sat alone beside her life mate while he slept. The poison was extracted now, the thrashing ended, the worst of it past. But she would not leave him until he woke and she was certain he was well again.

She sat with him all night.

Aphenglow slept on and off during her long hours of keeping watch, making sure at regular intervals that Bombax was sleeping comfortably. But when she woke at sunrise she found him awake and staring at her from the bed. When he gave her that familiar smile—the one she loved so much—she leaned down and kissed him passionately.

"I was worried for you," she whispered.

"I was worried, too."

"You can talk again?"

"So it seems. I didn't even think about it. I just did it."

"How do you feel?"

"Good. Much better. Whatever was in me is gone. Was that your doing?"

She nodded. He reached up and stroked her face, and they kissed again.

Then he told her everything that had happened to him after he had reached Varfleet. She listened intently, a mix of emotions surfacing as she did so: shock, relief, and anger. She was surprised at their intensity and even more surprised when anger overwhelmed everything else.

"What in the world were you thinking?" she demanded when he had finished. "Going into the worst part of Varfleet to find someone to help us? Mixing with people who would cut your throat for your shoes? Don't you see what you did? You put yourself in danger for no good reason!"

His rough, handsome face tightened. "It seemed a good enough reason to me. A little risk was necessary. We needed magic of the sort that couldn't be found by staying in the better neighborhoods."

"That's very funny. But it almost cost you your life. Or maybe something worse. Who knows what the Mwellrets had planned for you? It appears you were to be turned over to someone else. What do you think that might have led to?"

"I don't know. It doesn't matter now." He gave her a look.

"Not this time it doesn't, but what about the next? You think you are invulnerable! It's maddening! No one else takes the chances you do. Do you ever stop to think about that?"

He looked suddenly hurt. "Why are you so mad at me?"

"Because I love you, and I don't want to lose you! I think more of you than you do of yourself! You put yourself in these dangerous situations and you expect me not to mind?"

He sighed. "I expect you to understand."

"Well, I don't! I don't understand! Not any of it!"

"What if I promise not to do it again?"

"Now you are being condescending." She was furious. "You tell me what you think I want to hear and everything will be all right. Is that it? Keep me happy until you do it again? Because you will! You can't help yourself!"

He looked exasperated. "What am I supposed to do, Aphen? What can I do that will please you? It seems nothing will, listening to all this."

She stood up, limped across the room, and turned back to him. "I can't answer that right now. I'm exhausted. I'm relieved to have you back and terrified you might go away and do this to me all over again. Remember that time you went to Arishaig and posed as a courier so that you could get inside the chambers of the Coalition Council? Remember when you penetrated the quarters of the Red Guards and had to fight your way out? Alone? In the middle of Federation country?"

He stared at her. "What happened to your leg? What have I missed while I was away?"

She smoldered. "Nothing. I don't want to talk about it. At least you noticed. Finally." She glared at him. "Go back to sleep. That's what I'm going to do."

She stomped out of the room without looking back.

Aboard the *Arishaig*, the decks were mostly empty of life. A helmsman steered the vessel north, a lookout slouched in the crow's nest atop the mainmast, and a pair of soldiers stood watch across from each other, port and starboard amidship. The night was dark and moonless, the cloud cover heavy over the Prekkendorran, a shroud of mist rising off the lowlands of Clete some miles ahead to drift south toward the advancing Federation fleet. Except for the creaking of the rigging and the snores of sleeping men, the warship was quiet.

Drust Chazhul came on deck and moved toward the aft railing, breathing in the night air, steadying himself for what would happen in the next few minutes. Stoon would be in place by now—although Drust did not have any idea at all where that would be—ready to spring out when needed. They had gone over the plan a dozen times. Arodian's personal attendant had mentioned to Stoon, when the assassin had engaged him in conversation down in the servants' quarters and plied him with considerable alcohol, that the commander liked to watch the sunrise each morning from the fantail, the launching deck for the handful of flits the airship carried. The fantail was positioned aft below the command deck and the pilot box, hidden from view from the men who would be on watch. The plan was for Drust to confront him there and hold his attention long enough for Stoon to get in position, and then the assassin would grab the commander and throw him over the side of the airship.

They were flying at somewhere around two thousand feet. No one could survive a fall from that height.

Drust was confident. There would be no witnesses. Arodian would not suspect an attack; he knew himself to be physically superior. It would all be over quickly.

Drust Chazhul could feel the flutter of expectation in the pit of his stomach. Edinja was dead and gone and, after tonight, Arodian would be on his way to join her. There would be no one to threaten him after that.

He thought momentarily of the mysterious notes he had received suggesting he was responsible for Edinja's death, wondering again at their source. Could it possibly be Arodian? He couldn't fathom how the man had managed it, but he didn't dismiss the possibility outright. If the notes stopped coming after tonight, he would know.

He paused momentarily at the steps leading down to the fantail, fidgeting and edgy as he searched for and found a solitary figure standing at the aft railing. Lehan Arodian, watching the first silvery rays of sunlight creep above the horizon.

Taking a deep breath, he started down the steps to the fantail, eyes fixed on the other man.

"What's this?" The sound of Arodian's voice startled Drust, and he stopped where he was, still six feet away. Arodian didn't bother to turn around. "You don't have any bad intentions, do you, Drust? Sneaking up on me like this?"

Drust recovered his composure. "Of course not. I noticed you from the command deck and came down to say good morning. Beautiful sunrise, isn't it?"

Arodian shook his head as he turned to face Drust. "The truth isn't in you, is it? You knew you would find me here. Why not admit it?"

Drust feigned surprise. "You misjudge me. I am not that sort of person."

Arodian came forward a few steps, away from the railing. "You are exactly that sort of person. Otherwise we wouldn't be here."

Drust felt a twinge of uneasiness. "I don't see how you can make such wild statements . . ."

Abruptly, he was seized from behind, wrapped in an iron grip. A callused hand fastened on his throat, silencing the shout he was trying to make. He was lifted off the deck, his feet left dangling as he struggled in disbelief and terror to free himself.

Lehan Arodian walked over to stand right in front of him. "Little man," he hissed. "You should have been content to warm the Prime Minister's seat until I was ready to take it back from you. Did you think you could make it your own at my expense? Did you, little worm?"

Drust stared at him, wide-eyed. He thrashed harder, desperate now to escape. But the hand about his throat only tightened further.

"You should have paid better attention to what was going on right under your nose, Drust. You were so concerned about Edinja and me that you missed it entirely. Throw him over."

Drust Chazhul was carried to the railing of the fantail, still kicking and trying unsuccessfully to scream, fear the only emotion left to him.

This can't be happening!

"Help me hold him!" he heard a familiar voice say. "He's breaking free!"

Stoon! No!

Arodian hurried over, reaching out to seize hold of him as well, and now four hands were gripping him, hauling him right up against the railing, lifting him . . .

Then suddenly Stoon shifted his powerful hands to Arodian's neck, cutting off his air and with it the cry he tried too late to give. Off balance and caught completely by surprise, Arodian went over the railing with a wild thrashing of arms and legs and disappeared into the darkness.

Stoon helped a shaken Drust Chazhul to his feet, straightened him up, and patted him on the back. "Are you all right?"

Drust shook his head, feeling anything but. "I thought you'd betrayed me!" he hissed in fury. "I thought you were really going to do it! Why didn't you tell me what you were planning?"

He was so angry he was shaking. But Stoon only shrugged. "If it didn't appear you believed I was betraying you, I wouldn't have been able to get him to the railing without cutting his throat. His body might be found. We want this to appear to be an accident, don't we?"

The Prime Minister rubbed his throat gingerly. "What was wrong with my plan? Just get his attention long enough for you to push him over! What was wrong with that?"

"It was weak. Transparent. A chance meeting at dawn on the fantail with no one else around and you come upon him without bad intentions? He would have seen through it right away. I had to convince him beforehand that he was in danger and that I, wishing to free myself of an indentured bargain, would willingly do to you what you expected me to do to him. He had to believe that his money and a promise of freedom would buy my services. He needed to think that with my help he could turn the tables on you, could make you the victim. It appealed to his sense of irony. He liked the idea."

"I thought I was a dead man."

Stoon laughed, infuriating Drust further. "You were never in any real danger. What would I gain by betraying you? You and I are built the same way, come from the same place. Don't you see, Drust?"

He wasn't at all sure he did. And he couldn't stop thinking about how it had made him feel, to believe he was about to be killed by his supposed confidant and ally.

It would be a while, if ever, before he would put himself in another situation where his life depended on the assassin's loyalty, he promised himself.

Then, his anger beginning to fade sufficiently that he could relish Arodian's demise, he stood with Stoon by the fantail railing, composing himself as he stared east to watch the sunrise.

20

"THERE'S AN AIRSHIP COMING IN FROM THE EAST," Mirai advised, pointing back toward the Bakrabru airfield from which she had just come. She brushed strands of her blond hair from her face, glancing over her shoulder. "I think it's flying a Druid flag."

Redden and Railing leapt to their feet, but Farshaun Req was a little slower to rise. Age played a part in this—he was more than seventy, after all—but mostly it was demonstrative of the way he reacted to almost everything. Slow and measured, no need to hurry, everything in good time. Once on his feet, the other three waiting on him impatiently, he took a moment to stretch limbs cramped from sitting.

For the last two hours he had been engaged in conversation with the twins about ways they might modify their skimmers to make them go faster. No one knew more about building and flying airships than Farshaun. One of the chief reasons the twins had been so eager to accompany Mirai to Bakrabru was the prospect of talking with the old man about their latest project and finding out how he thought they might improve the design.

It was Farshaun, after all, who had taught them to fly airships back when they were just becoming interested in learning but lacked the necessary guidance and skills.

Their mother was against their flying anything following the death of their father, but she had relented when it became clear that if she wanted to maintain even a modicum of control over her wild sons she was going to have to toss them a bone now and then. Better that they learn to fly safely before they just threw all caution to the winds and went off on their own. So she had agreed to let them go to the village of their cousins, the Alt Mers and Meridians, to study under the man who was recognized almost everywhere as the premier authority of his time.

"A Druid airship?" he asked Mirai speculatively. "What would a Druid airship be doing all the way over here? Are you sure of what you saw?"

Mirai, who was always sure about everything and didn't like to be questioned, shrugged. "I could be mistaken."

She said it in a way that suggested she most certainly wasn't.

Farshaun smiled. He liked Mirai Leah. She was competent, prepared, cool, and calm in the hottest of situations. He had never seen her ruffled. It didn't hurt in her business dealings that she was beautiful, too. Certainly Redden and Railing thought so. He wondered suddenly how that intriguing triangle was going to resolve itself—which someday soon, he suspected, it must.

"You are not often mistaken, Mirai," he offered by way of conceding the point. "Shall we find out what it's doing in our backyard?"

They departed the shade of the grove of maple trees where the boys and he had been conversing and walked back toward the village and the airfield. Bakrabru wasn't large, but it did sprawl. Much of this was due to the terrain: a centrally located flat where the airships were built, housed, and launched, and the surrounding hills where the residents of the village—most of whom were engaged in airship construction, maintenance, and usage—made their homes. This mix of trades and lifestyles had marked the history of the village for more than a century. There was some debate over which of the Four Lands produced the finest craftsmen and fliers, but none when it came to naming the Rovers of Bakrabru among the top three. They had constructed airships for the Free-born during the wars on the Prekkendorran, and some among them had even fought in those wars. The Ohmsford brothers could point to several of their own family members whose names were almost legendary, including their great-uncle Redden Alt Mer, for whom Redden was named, and his sister Rue Meridian, their grandfather's mother and the wife of Bek Ohmsford.

But they were all gone, and it was Farshaun Req who schooled the Ohmsfords of this generation. Schooled Mirai Leah, as well, for that matter. All three of them had been coming to Bakrabru to learn from him for the better part of the last ten years. They were good students and quick studies, sharing an intensity and determination that had enabled them to advance quickly to the front ranks of the best and most able he had ever taught.

The twins were a bit reckless, of course, but even that could be a positive when you were engaged in racing Sprints. He gave them a momentary glance, thinking again how closely they mirrored each other—so closely he couldn't tell them apart. So far as he knew, no one could, not even Sarys. Only Mirai could make an instant distinction, and no explanation as to why that was so had ever been given, although speculation ran rampant in some quarters.

They crested a rise and caught sight of the shingled roofs of the buildings that marked the westernmost boundary of the village. Bakrabru was one of the first permanent Rover villages, the beginning of a substantial change in a nomadic way of life that before had defined the Rovers as a people. The village was situated inland from the Blue Divide and set close to the western shores of the Myrian. Its location allowed for testing the aircraft assembled by the shipbuilding families both in the air and on water. It was ideally suited for both construction and experimentation, providing the villagers with the flats necessary for situating the sprawling complex of warehouses and hangars used for building and storage, as well as proximity to the lake for docking finished aircraft and the surrounding hill country for protection and escape from raiders.

The need for the latter had never been put to the test because no one in the history of the village could remember anyone ever attacking Bakrabru. No one would want to. The Rovers were engaged in building some of the most deadly airships in the Four Lands, some of which were always kept armed and ready for use. It made better sense to engage them in commerce than war.

"Don't the Druids ever come here?" Railing asked suddenly.

Farshaun pursed his lips thoughtfully. "Not in the last few years. They don't often leave Paranor these days. Not unless they are tracking down rumors of lost magic. That's become their whole purpose in life."

"So this visit must be important," Mirai said.

"Must be. Maybe they need a new ship built. We've given them good ships over the years. Given them the best." The old Rover glanced over at her. "Don't let that get back to the Federation, though. We do business with them, too. Got to keep everyone happy."

They passed through several clusters of cottages and outbuildings that had been walled away to form compounds built to withstand attack. Most looked a bit unready for such an event, the brick and adobe walls starting to show cracks and the metal hinges on the gates rusted. Farshaun wondered suddenly if they were taking things too much for granted at Bakrabru. Just because no one had ever attacked didn't mean they couldn't do so now. All it took was a change of mind, and that was the sort of thing that could happen on a whim.

They were still not within sight of the airfield when the black hull of the Druid airship hove into view, still several hundred feet off the ground as she maneuvered into position for a landing. She was long and sleek, built for speed and maneuverability. Her light sheaths had been trimmed to about half of what she could call on when at full sail and flying for speed. But even the reduced amount of canvas was impressive, and all of them stopped to watch as she came about and gave them full-on views of her elegant lines.

"That's a beautiful ship," Redden whispered.

"She should be," Farshaun declared, giving him a look. "I built her."

They started walking again, the younger three moving closer to the old man. "For the Druids?" Railing pressed.

"For the Ard Rhys herself. For Khyber Elessedil. She came to me looking for a flagship, one that would stand up to anything the Federation might be flying. Something that would outfly and outperform any other airship, but something, too, that looked so impressive you couldn't help stopping in your tracks just to admire her."

"Like we did," Mirai said, smiling.

"Like you did. Like everyone does when they see her for the first time. She's the *Walker Boh*. A warship disguised as something less threatening, but clearly the better craft no matter what she goes up against. The

Ard Rhys says she reminds her of the stories of the Druid she's named for. Can't say if she's right or not about that. Building her was my last big effort as a shipwright—the last where I had a hand in everything. After she was done, I let others take the lead and just offered advice when it was needed. I'd done my part. I just wanted to teach."

"Just to teach, huh?" Redden repeated sarcastically. "Good thing there's something you can still do."

Farshaun smiled. "Can do it better than you, too."

They watched the black hull of the *Walker Boh* settle earthward and disappear from view. They hurried a bit now, wanting to see who was on board.

When they finally crested the last of the hills in the chain separating them from the airfield, they saw that the *Walker Boh* had anchored perhaps a dozen feet off the ground, mooring ropes attached to rings screwed into posts that had been buried deep in the earth. A handful of Trolls were bringing down the last of the light sheaths and detaching the radian draws while rope ladders were being lowered over the gunwales. Black-clad Druids were climbing down along with an assortment of others while a clutch of airfield workers gathered around to watch.

Already on the ground and looking around was a striking-looking older woman with Elven features and long, gray-streaked dark hair. She wore the familiar black robes, but unlike the others she bore a silver patch sewn into the left front panel.

When she saw them approaching, her gaze steadied and she started toward them.

"Well, well," Farshaun said softly. "The Ard Rhys herself." He raised his hand in greeting. "Something's afoot."

With his three young charges in tow, he walked down the hillside to find out what it was.

"Well met, Farshaun Req," she greeted the old man, extending her hand as she came up to him. She was not as tall or physically imposing as she had seemed from a distance, but she exuded an inner strength and determination that was arresting. She carried herself as if she knew there wasn't anything she couldn't manage, and he wasn't sure at all that it wasn't so.

"Mistress," he replied as he took her hand in his own and bowed in deference. It was an odd gesture, one he knew neither the twins nor Mirai had ever seen him make before because it was reserved only for her.

"Are you well?" she asked him, looking into his eyes as if to discern the answer for herself.

He shrugged. "I'm old. But, even so, well enough. And you? I heard you were using the Druid Sleep. Has something happened to wake you?"

"It is the reason I am here."

"You've come to ask for help? A new airship, perhaps?"

"I've come to ask for help, yes. But not from you. From these boys." She turned to Redden and Railing. "These boys who are no longer boys. I haven't seen them since they were children. Now they've grown big enough to be called young men. Can we go somewhere to talk?"

She announced she must speak with Redden and Railing alone, so Mirai and Farshaun would have to go somewhere else until she was finished. Both twins insisted that whatever she had to say to them she could say in front of the other two since they did not keep secrets from one another. But when Khyber suggested she was the one who was keeping all the secrets, and it might be better if things stayed that way, Farshaun beckoned Mirai away with him without arguing, leaving Redden and Railing alone with her.

"I apologize for that," she said to the twins, "but when you hear what I have to say you might think better of me for keeping this just among the three of us. There is some danger involved just in knowing what I am about to tell you. There is likely to be a great deal more if you decide to accept the offer I intend to make."

An argument could be made that the word *danger* was a lure that drew the twins like bees to flowers. They were young and wild and eager for an adventure, and no one had offered them one for a long time. They were instantly intrigued.

She led them up the hillside to a copse of fir and sat them down in a grassy space where they could look out over the airfield and the activity taking place as the *Walker Boh*, already stripped of her sails and securely moored, now had her radian draws lashed in place. On the ground, her crew of Trolls had begun setting up a staging area for collecting and loading the supplies they required to continue the ship's journey.

"I went to Patch Run before coming here and spoke with your mother," the Ard Rhys said. "She didn't like it that I was looking for you and didn't want me to involve you in Druid business. She refused at first to tell me where you were. I was straightforward with her about what I was proposing, and because she loves you and worries for you she told me to go away. In the end, I made it clear that finding you was too important for me to do what she was asking. If she wouldn't help me, I would find you anyway. She relented and told me where you were."

She paused. "I am telling you this so when you hear it all later from your mother you won't think I was hiding anything."

"Mother hates airships," Redden said quietly. "Because of Father. He was killed in one. She blames the Druids."

The Ard Rhys nodded. "I know this. There is risk here, as well. When you fly airships, there are always risks. Your mother knows this, but cannot accept it. She blames the Druids for something that was not their fault. It was no one's fault. You can weigh that along with everything else after you hear what I have to say. Be patient until then. Let me say everything before you speak again."

She went on to tell of the discovery of Aleia Omarosian's diary, written in the days of Faerie and lost or misplaced ever since, and of the possibility that the missing Elfstones might at last be found. But they could not allow them to be found by just anyone, she added. The Druid order must recover them because management and proper usage of magic were the order's responsibility and principal purpose. The reason she was in Bakrabru to speak with them was because of her visit to the Hadeshorn and her summoning of the spirits of the dead in the hope they would give her information that might help in her search.

"It was Allanon himself who appeared—something that I believe indicates the importance of this matter. His shade gave me little enough with which to work, but did make it clear this was an undertaking of great importance. His shade also advised that the Druids alone would not be enough to accomplish what was needed. Others must go with us on this expedition. Specifically, he mentioned you."

"Railing and me?" Redden exchanged a quick look with his brother.

She nodded, smiling in a way that made her look tired and worried both. "I would not be here if the shade had not been so insistent about it. A reminder was given that every important quest involving magic since the time of Shea Ohmsford and the Warlock Lord has involved members of your family. The shade insisted it must be so this time, as well."

"But isn't it true shades aren't always reliable?" Redden asked carefully.

"It is. They dissemble and prevaricate and offer half-truths to questions asked. But I did not sense that here. The insistence on your involvement was not in response to a question. It was volunteered in a way that made it seem to be mandatory."

Railing shoved his brother. "What's wrong with you? We get to fly airships with Druids and go searching for lost magic and you aren't sure you want to go?"

Redden shoved him back. "I'm just asking a question. I'm not saying I don't want to go."

"Well, what are we arguing about? You want to go. I want to go. When do we leave?" Railing looked back at the Ard Rhys. "Isn't that what the invitation you mentioned earlier is about?"

The Ard Rhys nodded. "It is. I want you to come with us. No, that isn't putting it strongly enough. I *need* you to come with us. Allanon's shade made that clear. Without you, we diminish the chances of success. But I don't want you to make a decision blindly or in haste. I want you to think about it carefully. I want you to talk it over between yourselves and perhaps Farshaun and then sleep on it afterward before you make a final decision."

She paused. "There's one other thing I haven't told you. Allanon's shade also said it sensed this expedition would be very dangerous. Not all of us, it said, would come back alive. I believe that is probably true. Hunting for something as powerful as the Elfstones will attract dangerous enemies. The young woman who discovered the diary has already been attacked three times in her home city of Arborlon. Aphenglow Elessedil is my cousin, a member of the royal family, and a skilled magic user. Even these weren't enough to protect her.

Someone else already knows what we seek or guesses at its importance. It won't stop with Aphenglow. We can expect to have to fight for our lives and for the success of our quest at other times and places along the way. There's no use pretending otherwise. That isn't something you should ignore. The Druids accepted that risk when they chose to join the order. This isn't so in your case. You have no obligation to put yourselves in danger."

Redden exchanged another glance with Railing. "We aren't afraid. We can take care of ourselves."

"We've been taking care of ourselves since Father died," Railing added quickly. "Farshaun could tell you."

"I imagine so." She got to her feet. "Why don't you go talk to him now about what I've told you. If you are willing to come with us, then we want you. The invitation has been extended."

"Will Farshaun be coming?" Redden asked impulsively. "Wouldn't he be someone who could help with the airship if there was trouble?"

"What about Mirai?" Railing was quick to add. "She could help, too. She's been flying airships since she was ten years old. She's better at it than we are. We know Sprints and racing, but Mirai knows all about the big airships."

"She's a Leah, you know," Redden cut back in. "There's always been a Leah, too, on those quests you mentioned. On most of them, anyway. She should go if we do."

Khyber Elessedil shook her head slowly. The lines around her eyes and at the corners of her mouth deepened, suggesting for the first time that even the Druid Sleep could do only so much to keep aging at bay. "Maybe you have looked after yourselves since your father's death and can protect yourselves if the need arises. But can you protect Mirai, as well? You have the power of the wishsong to call upon. Mirai Leah does not. You should consider what that means."

The twins watched her walk back down toward the airfield, waiting for her to reach the flats before climbing to their feet.

"She's right, you know," Redden said quietly. "About Mirai."

Railing didn't answer.

They found her at Farshaun's house, a small cottage nestled in the southern fringes of the village, set alone in a grove of old-growth hardwoods canopied overhead by a vast umbrella of branches and leaves that left the cottage dappled with shadows and sunlight. She was sitting on Farshaun's tiny porch, watching him braid a lanyard that he intended to use as a sling for his conch shell, a summoning horn used by Rover airmen to alert one another to danger or to call for help in times of trouble. The Rovers had begun using them only recently and had found them a better tool than shouts or message birds when a swift response was necessary.

The twins walked up and sat down with the girl and the old man, and Mirai looked at them and immediately said, "What's wrong?"

"Nothing," said Railing.

"Everything," said Redden.

Then they recounted what the Ard Rhys had told them—the purpose for her coming to find them, the nature of the quest she was proposing, the extent of the danger it presented, their mother's efforts to keep them from going and Khyber Elessedil's efforts to persuade them to come anyway. Because even if she was telling them to consider things carefully, to think it all over before deciding, she clearly believed it was necessary for them to make the journey.

"The missing Elfstones," Farshaun mused when the twins had finished. "That would be something, if they could be found. I think everyone decided a long time ago they were lost forever and wouldn't be seen again."

"What do they do?" Railing asked.

He shrugged. "I don't think anyone knows. That's what I mean. Find the Elfstones and you find the answer to one of the greatest secrets of all time. Of course, maybe you open a can of worms instead. Finding magic of that sort could be the most dangerous thing ever to happen."

"But less dangerous for the Druids to find them than some others," Redden said.

"Maybe so. But we won't know until it happens. Things like this have a way of coming back to bite you. I'm just saying what you already know, all three of you. What seems like a good idea at the time can turn out to be a bad one looking back at it later."

"What will you do?" Mirai asked.

Redden shook his head. "We're supposed to think it over and make a decision. Railing's already made up his mind. He wants to go. I guess maybe I do, too. But maybe Farshaun has a point. This feels like one of those things we might decide later on was a mistake."

"Except this time making the wrong decision could kill you," she said quietly. "Your mother might be right about not wanting you to go."

"You always take her side," Railing griped. "If we did everything Mother told us to do we'd never do anything. We'd never go anywhere or see anything or fly airships or . . ."

"I get the point," she interrupted. "But we're not talking about the way you live the rest of your life. We're talking about *if* you live it. Pay attention to what's on the table."

"She's right," Redden agreed.

Railing gave him a look, then turned to Farshaun. "What do you think?"

The old man shrugged. "I'm not about to tell you what to do in this business. I can see the argument for both sides. You're big boys; you can decide for yourselves. You don't need any help from me or Mirai."

Mirai made a face. "I wonder."

"If it were you, Farshaun, would you go?" Railing pressed.

Farshaun laughed. "I don't know. What does it matter? No one has asked me to go. This has to do with you, not me."

"But what if you were asked?"

"I'd think about it, like you're supposed to do, and I wouldn't spend my time trying to find out what someone else would do! Especially an old man whose best years are behind him. Now get out of here, the two of you. Go!"

He chased them from his cottage and stood watching until they were out of sight.

"Cranky old toad," Railing muttered.

"He just doesn't want to make the decision for us. He doesn't want to have to live with the responsibility."

"I notice he kept Mirai with him."

"He doesn't want her to have to live with it, either."

"So what are you going to do?"

"What are you going to do?"

They walked on, undecided.

They went to bed that night with the matter unresolved. They were sleeping on Farshaun's back porch in hammocks, the air warm and sweet, the night sounds soft and distant. They had gone over the pros and cons of staying and going until they couldn't stand to think about it anymore, all without reaching a decision. Mirai had quit talking to them. Farshaun had ordered them to leave any further discussion outside his front door. Redden and Railing had grown weary talking about it and getting nowhere. Dinner that evening had been a desultory experience, and in the end they had eaten almost nothing.

There had been no further sign of the Ard Rhys. She had not come to them again. She had not asked them to visit the airship to look around, which they would have dearly loved to do. She had not sent any of the other Druids to talk to them. The entire ship's company had gone back aboard and stayed there.

Redden lay cocooned in his hammock, wrapped up and motionless. Railing was sitting on the porch steps, his blanket draped carelessly over one shoulder, staring out at the night. Inside the cottage, Farshaun was snoring.

"Can't sleep?" Redden asked from his hammock.

Railing glanced over his shoulder. "Not a wink. You?"

"Not much."

They were silent for a few minutes, the snores inside changing pitch and cadence.

"I'm going," Railing said suddenly. "I have to. If I don't, I'll wonder about it for the rest of my life." He paused. "But I don't want to do this without you."

"Don't worry. You won't have to. I'm going, too." Redden raised himself up, causing the hammock to sway. "Because I think the Ard Rhys is right. Finding those Elfstones is important. If we can help, like she seems to think we can, then we have to do so."

They went quiet again for a bit. It was decided, Redden thought. Just like that. Both of them had come to the same conclusion. Amazing, but that's how they were.

"You're not going without me," Mirai said from the doorway.

The twins looked around in surprise as she stepped out of the shadows and into the moonlight, her long hair unbound, her blanket wrapped around her.

"How long have you been there?" Redden asked.

"Hours. Sitting just inside the doorway, watching you, thinking. I don't know if you should do this, but I do know that you shouldn't do it without me."

"We'll have to send someone to tell Mother," Railing pointed out.

Redden cleared his throat. "I'm glad it won't be me."

21

On the following day, carrying a total of forty men and women as crew and passengers, the *Walker Boh* sailed west. The day was bright and sunny, the skies clear and blue, and the weather conditions favorable. There was palpable excitement as she lifted off, a sense of possibility that tamped down doubts and misgivings and left everyone aboard feeling ready and eager to be under way.

"Forty," Redden mused. "Do you think that's a lucky number?"

Railing shrugged. "I don't know. What do you think, Farshaun?"

The old man did not look up from the maps he was studying. "Doesn't matter how many you set out with. Only how many you bring back."

Railing looked at Redden and rolled his eyes.

They had announced their decision to go with the Druids that morning, and the Ard Rhys had wasted no time making preparations to leave. Little was needed. The few additional supplies that were required had been loaded the previous day; everything else was already aboard. Farshaun was asked to come because of his vast experience with airships and had agreed because of his friendship with Khyber Elessedil. He brought with him eight of his Rover kin to help sail the warship. While not directly denigrating the capabilities of the Trolls, he had nevertheless gently suggested that his people were better trained and more experienced than members of the Druid Guard, an assertion that neither the Ard Rhys nor the Trolls tried to contradict. Once the eight were chosen there was nothing to delay their departure, and by midday they were under way.

Farshaun was along for another reason, as well. While discussing with the Ard Rhys the details of where they were going and how they were going to get there, the latter had described the vision she had skived from Aphenglow's memory. It was clear enough that their journey would take them into the wilderness of the Breakline and the surrounding mountain chains, but that was about all either of them could tell. Even Farshaun, who had traveled that country extensively during his time flying airships along the coastal regions of the Blue Divide, did not recognize any of the places the vision had revealed.

But he knew someone who might.

Among the Rovers, there were those who chose to lead lives more resembling an earlier time, when established communities did not exist. Frequently, these throwbacks were traders and scavengers and made their way through the world in a solitary fashion and without any particular goals or plans. One among them—the one Farshaun believed might be helpful to the Druids— lived out along the far western borders of the Breakline in country so bleak and unforgiving that it seemed impossible anyone could survive it. Yet he had done so for more than twenty years, subsisting off the land, a hermit and a recluse. Now and then he would drift back within the boundaries of civilization to gather things he could not find in his own country, though he seldom bothered with human contact and never stayed for long.

Except that sometimes he would come to see Farshaun. The old man had known him before he went into the wilderness, and they had formed a friendship. It wasn't a friendship in the normal sense of the word. There were few expectations involved on either side; there was only conversation and often little of that. Mostly, it was the other man's strange ramblings and digressions.

But in some of those ramblings and digressions, he would tell of things he had dreamed would happen.

And then they would.

That strange ability to foresee the future, coupled with the fact that he knew the Breakline country like the back of his hand because he had spent so many years exploring it, made him someone Farshaun Req believed they should seek out before they undertook their search for the missing Elfstones.

Khyber, who knew something of seers and those possessed of prescient abilities—and who believed in their value—had agreed.

"This foreteller of the future you're taking us to see, the one who has the dreams?" Redden asked Farshaun suddenly. "Why is he called the Speakman?"

The old man paused in his study of the maps. "It's a name Rovers give to those who speak of a future that others can't see. In this case, it stuck. His real name was forgotten by most long ago and never used in the time he's lived in the Breakline. Now, he's just 'the Speakman' to everyone."

"But you knew him? You knew his real name?"

Farshaun nodded. "I don't use it, though. I don't say it aloud."

"What was he like before he went into the wilderness?" Railing asked. "Was he normal? Was he a boy like us?"

Farshaun gave him a look suggesting that the word

normal might not apply to them. "He was damaged. Now leave me alone."

The twins moved off to one side, closer to where Mirai stood in the pilot box working the controls that flew the *Walker Boh* westward. She glanced over and smiled, evidence of how much she enjoyed flying the big airship.

"I like watching her better than talking with Farshaun," Railing observed. "What an old crab."

"That's an understatement," Redden said.

He could have watched Mirai do anything or nothing all day long. How lucky they were that she had been allowed to join them. Even after she had announced to them that she was coming, it wasn't settled that she would be permitted to join the expedition. But the Ohmsford twins wouldn't have been comfortable going without her, and perhaps Khyber Elessedil had sensed as much, suggesting it might help their mother come to terms with their going if Mirai were there, too.

But Mirai didn't feel as strongly as the twins did about the advisability of undertaking this quest. She reminded them later she had decided to come mostly because she agreed with the Ard Rhys that it might ease their mother's concerns.

"It will kill her if something happens to you," she'd told them. "If you don't believe that's true, you had better rethink it. You're all that matters to her, even though you're mostly ungrateful clods."

Which was true enough, Redden knew, although he didn't much like thinking of himself that way. Whatever the case, he was pleased she was there. Railing was probably pleased, too, but not as much as he was, he told himself.

"What does anyone know about these missing Elfstones?" he asked Railing as they watched Mirai work the controls.

His brother shrugged. "Farshaun says no one knows anything. All of them disappeared centuries ago. Except for the seeking-Stones, and you and I know as much about them as anyone because of our family history. These other Elfstones can do different things, but no one knows what."

"What if they don't do anything that helps anyone? What if they do bad things?"

"Then the Druids lock them away, I guess."

"Seems like everyone's taking a big risk without knowing why. Seems like maybe they should leave well enough alone."

"You heard the Ard Rhys. She says they can't leave it to chance. If someone else finds the Stones first, they might use them the wrong way."

"Maybe. But it would have to be an Elf for that to happen. Only Elves can use their own magic, remember?"

"I remember. What's your point?"

"That this whole thing is a mistake."

Railing gave him a look. "If that's what you think, why did you agree to come?"

Redden shrugged. "Same reason as you. It's an adventure."

They flew north for the remainder of the day, staying east of the Rock Spur until they reached the fringes of Drey Wood and Elven country and then turning a few degrees west toward the Sarandanon. By sunset, they reached the shores of the Innisbore and anchored for the night. By sunrise they were flying again, this time along the ragged edge of the Breakline. The weather was changing now, the skies darkening with storm clouds and the air turning damp and hot. The landscape was bleak and colorless beneath them, the last of the forests and grasslands disappearing. The winds had picked up, and a firm hand on the controls of the airship was more critical than ever. Mirai and Farshaun and now and again another of the Rovers who had come aboard with the old man took turns, each giving the others a chance to rest when weariness took hold. The Ard Rhys stayed close to the pilot box, scanning the terrain ahead, intense and troubled as she watched everything carefully.

Redden overheard snatches of discussion between Khyber and Farshaun regarding the whereabouts of the Speakman. He moved about and might be found in any of a dozen places, but he frequented certain of those places more often than others and Farshaun was playing the odds. The Ard Rhys would have preferred something more definite, but there was no help for it. With a nomad like the Speakman, you took your chances and hoped for the best.

Shortly after midday they reached the first of his shelters and after setting down and taking a close look around determined that he hadn't been there in months.

They continued on, turning west into even less hospitable country, the terrain rocky and crisscrossed by chasms and deep gullies and riddled with strange smooth patches that Farshaun said were sinkholes.

"Step into one of those," he told Redden when the boy asked about them, "you might as well be stepping into quicksand. Only you disappear a whole lot quicker. Poof! Gone in less than a minute. No one knows how far down you might sink. Maybe thousands of feet."

In the late afternoon a squall caught up to them, and for thirty minutes it poured rain, the drops so large and icy they actually stung when they struck exposed skin. Everyone wrapped up in cloaks and hoods and hunkered down until the storm had passed. Afterward, they found ice balls on the decks, though within minutes they had melted away.

It was nearing dusk when they reached another shelter the Speakman favored, this one a cliff face riddled with caves in which any number of creatures might dwell. Farshaun, working the controls, set the airship down on a flat close by the base of the cliffs. When she was anchored, he climbed down with the Ard Rhys, the big Troll Captain Garroneck, and the Gnome Tracker Skint. Skint prowled the flats for a time, working his way toward the cliff face, and then nodded to them. There were signs of a human presence, and they were very recent. They led upward toward the caves.

The Speakman, if he was the one who had left the signs, could probably be found there.

Even though it was almost dark by then, the Ard Rhys wanted to act on this information immediately. Waiting risked losing their quarry, and she didn't want to waste any more time hunting for him. So with Farshaun, Garroneck, and Skint in tow, she went looking.

Redden and Railing, standing at the bow of the *Walker Boh,* watched them set out across the flats to where a series of steep, narrow trails wound upward along the cliff face.

"Do you think he's up there?" Railing asked.

Redden shrugged. "I wish they'd let us go with them."

"I got the feeling the Ard Rhys didn't want us to hear whatever the Speakman had to say."

"I got that feeling, too."

"She's worried about us."

"She thinks we're young."

"We are young."

"You know what I mean. That we're boys, not men. Still growing up and maybe not as dependable as she might like. We're only here because Allanon's shade said we should be. No one, her included, knows the reason the shade told her that."

They watched silently as the little party reached the base of the cliffs and began to climb the trails leading up to the caves. The sun was far west, approaching the horizon, a screen of mist turning it a deep gold as the eastern sky darkened with night's approach.

Redden sensed a presence at his elbow and found one of the Druids standing next to him, watching the searchers climb. There had been little contact between the brothers and the other Druids since they had set out, the latter keeping apart from everyone but the Ard Rhys and two men and one woman they had brought with them. Redden searched his memory for the name of the man standing next to him.

"That Gnome might be the best Tracker alive," the Druid offered, nodding toward the cliffs. "If anyone can find this seer, he can."

Redden nodded, still trying to remember the man's name. Carrick, that was it.

"The Ard Rhys tells us you both have use of the wish-song." His narrow features gave him a predatory look. "Have you practiced with it much?"

Right away, Redden didn't like him. But he smiled anyway and nodded. "A fair amount."

"But not to defend yourselves or other people, I don't suppose?"

Railing was still looking out at the cliffs, as if none of this concerned him. But Redden could tell from his expression that he was irritated.

"No, nothing like that," he acknowledged. "I suppose you have to defend people all the time, though."

Carrick nodded. "Now and then. How old are you?"

Railing had had enough. "I don't see why you need to know that," he snapped. "Do you think age has anything to do with whether or not we should be here?"

"I do. You are young and inexperienced. This is dan-

gerous business. I don't think you realize how dangerous."

"Does anybody?" Redden asked mildly. "This is new
territory for everyone, isn't it? Even the Ard Rhys thinks
so."

Carrick shrugged. "Less new for us than for you. I
don't pretend to think that your coming on this expedition is a good idea. You don't seem seasoned enough. I
worry that you will endanger us all with your inexperi-
ence. So try not to put yourselves in a place where that
could happen. Do what you are told and stay out from
underfoot."

He turned and walked away.

Railing kept looking at the cliffs. "'Stay out from
underfoot'? I have some advice for him, too, but I know
enough to keep it to myself."

Redden nodded. "Maybe because you have better
sense than he does."

Railing gave him a look to see if he was kidding.

Khyber Elessedil climbed the steep pathway toward the
cluster of caves that tunneled back into the cliff face,
feeling the strain of the effort in her aching legs. The
Druid Sleep might arrest aging, she thought, but it did
nothing to help you stay fit and strong. She kept her silence as they advanced, following the Tracker Skint and
Farshaun, Garroneck bringing up the rear. Their expo-
sure on the open cliff face made her uneasy, but there
was no choice in the matter if they were to reach which-
ever cave sheltered the Speakman. She needed to hear
what this strange man had to say, to discover if he recognized any of the landmarks the dream had revealed.
She found herself wishing—not for the first time since
setting out—that she had possession of the seeking-
Stones, making all of this unnecessary. If the seeking-
Stones had worked for Aphenglow, even after all these

centuries of revealing nothing, there was no reason to think they shouldn't work for her.

But they didn't have them, and they were very fortunate even to have been shown a vision of where the missing Elfstones might be found. She must settle for that.

The climb wore on, and the light faded. Once the sun was down, it would be pitch-black on the cliffs and any sort of progress would become very dangerous. She might summon magic to light the path, but doing so would reveal them to anyone who might be looking. She felt her frustration growing. Perhaps she should have waited until morning after all.

They reached the first series of caves and began to wind their way along the twisting trail that led past them. Now and then, Skint would drop to his knees to study the ground or examine the rock. At several entrances he paused as if he were considering going inside. Each time, he moved on. Khyber glanced upward along the cliff face. There were more openings ahead, all still higher up.

"This one?" she said to the Gnome at one point, pausing at a broad, high entry that seemed a perfect hiding place.

Skint made a sour face. "You wouldn't like what you'd find in there, Ard Rhys. Be patient. Leave this to me."

They trudged on, working their way back and forth past dozens of cave entrances. Not once did Skint suggest they enter one, or ask for illumination. Overhead, the clouds remained thickly massed and impenetrable. West, the sun had dropped behind the horizon, leaving little more than a thin wash of golden color.

Finally the Tracker stopped at what appeared to Khyber to be just another cave entrance, knelt to study the ground, and then said, "Here."

"He's inside?" Farshaun asked.

Skint nodded. "Should be. Call out to him and see."

"Speakman!" Farshaun shouted into the cave entrance, standing close, leaning in. "Are you there? It's Farshaun Req!"

Silence. They waited a few minutes, and then Farshaun called out a second time. Still nothing. More time passed. It was nearly dark now, the last of the light faded away. Khyber was growing impatient.

Then from somewhere back in the cave's blackness, a voice whispered suddenly. "Farshaun?"

"It's me," the old man answered. "I've brought someone who wants to speak to you. Can she come in and do so? It's very important."

"I don't like speaking to other people." The voice was soft and whispery, the soft sound of clothing being unfolded, hardly more than that. "I won't speak to anyone but you."

"You can speak to me, but she has to hear you, too. She's a Druid and she's searching for something you might be able to help her find. She's had a vision."

"A vision?" Khyber caught a note of interest in the paper-thin voice.

"She needs you to interpret it for her. There's no danger in this. You know I wouldn't bring trouble to your doorstep. Now, talk to us. Just to her and me."

Another long silence. Then a light flared back in the darkness, its source a mystery. "Just you and her. No one else."

"I promise," Farshaun agreed at once.

He started inside, groping his way forward with Khyber Elessedil right on his heels, leaving Skint and Garroneck behind. The strange light held steady as they advanced on it, but when they got close enough they could see it was a flameless torch of the sort favored by the people of the Old World. Immediately, it began to recede into the gloom.

"Come this way," the voice called back to them.

They went deep into the cave, following a passageway that frequently branched in more than two directions. The cave was a honeycomb of tunnels, and Khyber knew that if she'd had to ferret out the Speakman on her own, it would likely have taken a very long while. If ever, she amended, because she was willing to bet there was more than a single entrance and exit, too.

Finally, they reached a place where the light stopped moving as they caught up with it. They were in a wide space empty of everything but themselves and the light. The flameless torch was wedged into the rocks on one wall, but Khyber had to search the blackness to find the Speakman. He was sitting off to one side, obscured by gloom and shadows. She could not see his features at all and could only barely make out that he was tall and skeletally thin, his hunched-over body with its long legs and arms and oddly elongated head giving him the look of a praying mantis.

"Sit," he whispered to her. "Tell me of your vision."

She did as he asked. Seated on the cave floor, wrapped in her black robes, she recounted everything she could recall of the memory she had skived from Aphenglow. She described it all, from the peculiar landmarks to the colors she had seen and sounds she had heard. She described it all carefully, trying hard not to leave anything out save the identity of what it was she was seeking. The insect in the dark shifted its long limbs now and again, but otherwise sat quietly and said nothing.

Even after she had finished, the Speakman remained silent. And when she started to ask him a question, Farshaun quickly held up his hand to silence her. *Wait,* he mouthed silently.

The seconds ticked away, becoming minutes. Not a sound broke the deep stillness.

And then suddenly the Speakman shifted just enough to bring his angular features into the light, his body swaying slightly as he spoke in ragged, jumbled sentence fragments.

"Dark ways ... dreams of death in death's own realm ... all swept away but one ... lost to the vision ..." He went still, then began to sway once more, his voice ephemeral and ghostly. *"Not strong enough to weather ... such deep places, all in shadow ... spikes and iron plates ... stairways ... that don't come out and ..."*

He shuddered, his head jerking up suddenly, and Khyber Elessedil could see that his eyes had gone entirely white, the iris in each having disappeared.

"These places exist. The landmarks you seek. All exist. I know them, can tell you where to find them, all but the last. The waterfall of light is neither here nor there but somewhere in between. You should not go there. You should not. I see a killing ground. I see dead bodies scattered everywhere. I see ... something so dark it dwarfs ..."

He groaned softly; she could feel the sound rumbling in her chest, could hear its frightened shiver.

"This is a bad place. Very bad, very far away, this place, this kiln that hammers out men's souls and leaves them to blacken in the sun, a pit that will allow neither entry nor exit and holds evil and breeds monsters and ..."

He trailed off and went silent. Khyber and Farshaun exchanged confused glances. Neither could decipher what the Speakman was saying. Perhaps even he didn't know, given that he appeared to be communicating while in a trance. For the moment, there was no way to find out. He was lost in a vision of his own, gone to a place where they could not reach him.

"One!" he hissed suddenly, causing both of them to jump. *"One will return! One only!"*

Then he gave a deep sigh, and his eyes regained color and focus. He shuddered as they did so, arms and legs unfolding to splay out like broken sticks.

"Farshaun?" he whispered, as if not certain the old man was still there.

Farshaun rose and moved over to him, sitting once more, but much closer now. "I'm here."

"Tell me what I said."

The old man repeated most of it, Khyber listening from across the way, ready to add anything that might be left out or misstated, but staying put, not wanting to do anything to frighten the seer. That he had seen things, perhaps heard them, too, was undeniable. But she also knew he might not remember any of it. He had been deep under a spell of his own making when he spoke. It was like that sometimes with seers. What mattered was whether he could make any sense of it now.

When Farshaun had finished, the Speakman nodded slowly, and then said, "I know the landmarks. I have seen them in my travels. Save for the waterfall, as I have already said. There is no waterfall in that country. No water of any kind. I can tell you how to get to where it might be. But it is very dangerous. Too dangerous."

"Can you take us there?" Khyber asked him suddenly. "Can you guide us through the worst of it?"

The Speakman looked at her for the first time. His features were drawn and haggard, everything stretched out of shape and pinched by weather and age. He looked to be neither young nor old, but from some indeterminate middle region. He shook his head. "I travel alone."

"This one time?" she asked. "Can you make an exception? We need your eyes to help us find the landmarks I described and avoid the dangers you know." She hesitated. "It is important."

"She speaks the truth," Farshaun added. "You need go only as far as you want. But anything would help."

The Speakman looked back at him. His eyes were bright and depthless and filled with secrets. He gave them a half smile, one that reflected an irony they did not understand.

"If I go with you," he answered, "I won't be coming back."

The old man and the Ard Rhys exchanged a quick glance. "Why would you say that?" she asked.

He climbed to his feet, his tall, bony form hunched over in the gloom, his shadow crooked and skeletal.

"Because none of us will."

22

APHENGLOW ELESSEDIL WAS WALKING THE UPPER hallways of the Druid's Keep, forcing herself to ignore the ache in her broken leg, summoning her magic to buttress her efforts. She used her staff to support herself, burdened by a pronounced limp and a frustration that led her to curse her infirmity in a variety of imaginative ways. The pain told her she was stretching herself farther than she probably should. Still, if she wanted to get stronger, that was what she needed to do. It was a fine line between going just far enough and too far, but she trusted her instincts to tell her when the first began to edge into the second. So far, she wasn't there yet.

She had just reached the end of the hallway and was turning around to go back again, grimly satisfied with her momentary progress if not with her overall situation, when Arlingfant hurtled through a doorway at the far end of the passageway and came running toward her.

It was easy enough to see that something was amiss, but Aphenglow stayed where she was and waited for her sister to reach her. Trying to do anything more physical would be a mistake.

"Aphen!" Arling stumbled to a halt in front of her, breathing hard. "Federation warships—a fleet of them!

They've just crested the Forbidden Forest and are sailing right for Paranor!"

A jumble of thoughts crowded into Aphenglow's mind, but she dismissed them all as foolish. The Federation would never dare to attack Paranor. Not only would such an effort fail; it would also risk substantial repercussions from the governments of other lands. The Druids were a neutral power. It was understood by all that they were to be left alone. This must be something else.

"Up these stairs," she directed her sister, limping into the stairwell to the observation tower on her right.

They climbed as swiftly as they could, winding their way up the ancient stone steps.

"Who spied them?" Aphen asked, the strain of the climb more than she had expected. She gritted her teeth and quickened her pace.

"One of the Trolls on watch. He didn't know who they were at first, not until he put the spyglass on them and saw the Federation flag." Arling moved a few steps closer. "Are you all right? We have plenty of time."

That remained to be determined, Aphen thought. "I need the exercise," she responded instead. "How many ships?"

"Two warships, a light cruiser, a transport, and one that's quite a bit smaller. A command vessel or a scout, I think."

Too many to have good intentions. What did they want with the Druids? There hadn't been any communications between Paranor and Arishaig in months. Why now? Had the men on these airships come to see the Ard Rhys on business?

Or, she wondered suddenly, had they come because they knew Khyber Elessedil and the other Druids were away and believed the Keep and its remaining occupants were vulnerable?

They reached the top of the stairs and stepped onto the floor of the observation tower. Windows opened in all four directions, a series of two-foot-wide openings spaced evenly all around the circular room. In the center, a large permanently affixed telescope rested in its iron cradle atop a platform. Levers, gears, and wheels attested to its maneuverability. With Arling's assistance, Aphen climbed onto the platform, unlocked the mechanism, and swung the scope into position facing south.

She found the Federation fleet right away, advancing through a wash of sunlight and late-morning haze directly toward the Keep. She took a minute to study each ship, trying to intuit as much as she could from the look and feel of it, counting mounted weapons and armored heads.

"I don't like the look of this," she muttered.

The tower's outer door burst open and Bombax appeared, wrapped in his robes and carrying his heavy staff. He was healed well enough by now that he had regained his normal healthy pallor and most of the weight he had lost during his captivity, and he moved swiftly and easily as he mounted the platform and came up to her. "What do you make of it?"

They had patched things up sufficiently between them over the past few days that they were back to talking like normal people. Aphenglow still wasn't happy with the lack of common sense that Bombax had demonstrated in letting himself be made a prisoner of the Mwellrets, but they were trying to work their way through their differences of opinion on the matter.

"Dozens of armed men on deck," she said. "I'd guess a lot more are hidden belowdecks in that transport. Lots of rail slings, fire launchers, and something else mounted forward on the starboard and port bows of both warships."

"Let me see," he said.

She stepped aside for him, letting him peer through the scope. He needed only a moment. "Flash rips," he announced.

Strictly forbidden everywhere—something everyone in the Four Lands knew. Her uneasiness increased. Flash rips were big, dangerous weapons—cannons equipped with specially crafted diapson crystals that could burn an entire airship and everyone aboard it to ash if they locked on their target from close enough. Showing weapons of this sort made it clear the Federation meant business. At the very least, it was attempting to intimidate the Druids with a show of firepower. At worst, it intended to put that firepower to use.

"The warship on the right is the *Arishaig*—the Federation fleet's flagship," Bombax added a moment later.

"Is this Drust Chazhul's doing, do you think?"

He shook his head. "It's possible."

She locked her fingers on his arm tightly. "They know the Ard Rhys and the others are gone. I can feel it. Are the defenses up?"

He turned to her, his smile broad and relaxed. "Always. We're safe enough if they've come to play games. But let's see what they want before jumping to conclusions."

He leaped down off the platform and headed for the outer door. Aphenglow and Arling followed on his heels, all of them moving out of the tower and onto the catwalk that led to the parapets. They navigated the walkways until they had reached Krolling and a gathering of other Trolls standing just above the south gates, watching the Federation fleet approach.

"Any signals from them yet?" Bombax asked, immediately assuming command.

Aphenglow might have resented this more if he hadn't been senior to her. As it was, she felt a hint of annoyance that he did not say anything to her first. But she recognized it as an irrational response born of her on-going irritation with his poor judgment in Varfleet, so she kept silent.

"No signal of any kind." Krolling was big and burly and had the size and look of an immovable boulder. Garroneck's second in command was steady and capable.

Druids and Trolls and Arlingfant stood in a cluster atop the south gate, waiting for the airships to reach them.

"You should get under cover," Aphen whispered to Arling.

But her sister shook her head. "You might need me to help you."

They stayed silent after that, although Aphen moved down the parapets so that she and Arling were standing apart from the others. It was an automatic response to the realization that they should not all stand in one place where there was at least the possibility of an attack.

The airships drew to within three hundred yards before slowing to a stop, with only the *Arishaig* advancing much closer. Big and black, it loomed over them as it pushed through Druid airspace, hovering just outside the walls of Paranor before it swung broadside to the gate and the watchers on the walls.

There was a long silence as each side took the measure of the other, and then a voice rang out in the near silence.

"Greetings from Drust Chazhul, Prime Minister of the Coalition Council and leader of the Southland Federation! This is a diplomatic mission dispatched for the purpose of forming a working partnership with the Fourth Druid Order! We seek admittance to Paranor and an audience with the Ard Rhys! May we advance the *Arishaig* to the Druid landing station and be received?"

They were using a voice enhancer to magnify the speaker's words and lend them additional weight and importance. Aphenglow tried to identify who was speaking, but the decks of the warship were crowded with men, and it was impossible to tell.

"Did you send notice of your coming to the Ard Rhys?" Bombax called back, using magic to enhance his own voice.

A long pause. "Notification was dispatched more than a week ago," the answer came back. "A response signed by the Ard Rhys invited us to fly to Paranor for a conference."

A lie. Khyber Elessedil would have mentioned it. Aphenglow exchanged a quick glance with Bombax, shaking her head.

"No message was received," Bombax said at once. "No arrangements were made for the Ard Rhys to receive a Federation delegation. She cannot do so at this time."

Another long pause. "We have come all the way from Arishaig for this meeting. It is important we speak with the Ard Rhys. Will you inform her we are here?"

Bombax turned angry and frustrated; Aphenglow could see it in his face. *Don't say it,* she thought.

But she was too late. "The Ard Rhys isn't here!" Bombax snapped, his voice louder still. "Turn your ships around!"

Stupid! In the stunned silence that followed, she hurried over to him. "Why did you tell them that?"

He looked at her in surprise. "They already knew. You said so."

"I said I *thought* so. Now you've confirmed what they might only have suspected. Let me speak to them."

Without waiting for his approval, she turned toward

the *Arishaig*. "We apologize, but we are in mandated lockdown and cannot receive visitors until the Ard Rhys returns. An emergency has taken her away and your request, regretfully, must have been set aside. Our deepest apologies to the Prime Minister and the Federation. Please let us give you another date for your requested meeting."

There was no immediate response. Bombax, embarrassed and now angry with her, moved over by Krolling. On the wall, the members of the Druid Guard shifted restlessly. Arling came over to stand with her sister. "Will they leave now?"

Aphenglow shook her head to indicate she wasn't sure.

"We would like to leave a written declaration of intent for the Ard Rhys to read," the speaker aboard the *Arishaig* said suddenly. "May we land a flit inside the compound to deliver it?"

Aphenglow felt the hairs on the back of her neck prickle in warning. "We are in lockdown," she repeated. "We cannot receive visitors. Can we meet you outside the gates to accept delivery?"

"Will you identify yourself, speaker?" A different voice now, one less practiced at disguising impatience.

Aphenglow looked over at Bombax for guidance, but he was deliberately looking away. "I am Aphenglow Elessedil," she answered.

"This is Drust Chazhul. I am familiar with lockdowns, and they do not include diplomatic missions. I regard this refusal as a deliberate rebuke and a rejection of my efforts to establish a fresh rapport between the Federation and your order. If I am correct in my reasoning, say so and we will leave without further discussion. If not, then remember your place and allow us to land."

She felt herself flush. "Prime Minister, I appreciate your disappointment. But a lockdown at Paranor makes no exceptions, not even for diplomatic missions. Moreover, I am not simply authorized, but required, to refuse your request. This is neither a rebuke to you personally nor a rejection of your efforts. If you wish, you can land outside the walls and wait for the Ard Rhys to return. But I cannot tell you how long the wait might be."

The silence this time was chilling. On the decks of the *Arishaig*, men were moving about, taking up stations as if they knew what was coming. Aphenglow had the unpleasant feeling that a prearranged plan of action was being carried out.

She walked over to Krolling and Bombax and whispered to the former. "Are we protected against them?"

"Fully," the big Troll answered. Bombax caught her eye and nodded in agreement.

From the deck of the *Arishaig*: "I think you mean us harm, Aphenglow Elessedil," Drust Chazhul called out suddenly. "I think this refusal has nothing to do with a lockdown and everything to do with seeking to gain an advantage over us. I am beginning to suspect you lured us here. The history of the Druids is one of duplicity and subterfuge. An invitation was extended and is now suddenly withdrawn for no discernible reason. Are you hiding something behind those walls that we are not intended to see? Are you engaged in activity harmful to the governments and peoples of the Four Lands? If not, let us come inside!"

"Get down off the walls," she said at once to everyone around her, giving particular attention to Arling, who had been joined by Cymrian. To his credit, Cymrian immediately guided her sister to the stairs in spite of her obvious reluctance.

Bombax was beside her instantly, and the Trolls were off the wall and behind protective battlements and ramparts, weapons drawn.

"Your accusations are offensive and baseless, Prime

Minister," she called back to the warship. "Move your vessel away from the walls at once. Our conversation is over."

To her disappointment and dismay, the *Arishaig* instead swung her bow back around toward the gate and began to inch forward. She was coming directly for the walls she had been told to move away from, weapons uncovered and soldiers in place. This was the prelude to the attack she had feared all along, and she could do nothing to stop it. The wards that protected Paranor would engage automatically once the airship crossed the vertical plane of the south wall. Since the time of their creation and placement soon after the end of the war on the Prekkendorran, no one had ever challenged them or witnessed what they could do. The Ard Rhys might know, but neither Aphenglow nor Bombax had the faintest idea.

They were about to find out.

Aphen took a deep breath and brought up her magic to form a protective shield. She was aware of Bombax doing the same.

Then, without any warning whatsoever, a rail sling positioned somewhere lower down on the weapons ports of the south wall fired a full load of metal shards into the hull of the *Arishaig*. The sound was startling in the near silence—like a momentary torrential downpour of hailstones on a tin roof—yet the damage to the warship's reinforced steel plating was insignificant. Aphenglow had only a second to wonder who was responsible—who would be foolish enough to do such a thing—before the *Arishaig* responded by surging directly toward the Keep, all of her forward weapons firing at the fortress walls and towers at once.

The resulting explosions deafened her as she dropped behind the battlements, and the combined impact of scrap from the rail slings and white fire generated by the diapson crystals housed in the fire launchers caused the walls to shudder and crack. She scrambled for a vantage point farther away, catching a glimpse of Bombax as he moved in the opposite direction. When the flash rips opened up, everything was engulfed in smoke and ash and flames. By then, she was fifty yards down the parapets, crouched at the corner of the south wall and the mid-south tower, fighting to hold herself steady in the wake of a booming roar.

How can this be happening?

Then the *Arishaig* crossed the invisible plane of the walls, and the wards that protected Paranor struck back. The magic did so as if it were an invisible giant blowing off an annoying insect, its breath slamming into the huge warship with enough force to send her spinning away. All of her crew and most of her weapons went flying across the decks in a jumble of wood and iron and bodies. Screams rent the air, spars and light sheaths snapped loose and went flying into space, and the *Arishaig* bobbed and yawed as if caught in a windstorm.

Shades, Aphenglow mouthed in awe and disbelief.

Then Cymrian was at her side, crouched next to her in the lee of the wall. "What happened?"

"Magic wards the Keep, and apparently it decided enough was enough," she answered, still watching the *Arishaig* as she bucked and swayed and fought to keep flying. The other Federation ships were clustered about her protectively, but none of them tried to approach when she was so clearly out of control. "Where's Arling?"

"Down below, safe. I told her if she came up here you would just worry and not be able to concentrate." He gave her a quick once-over. "You're not hurt, are you?"

She shook her head. Down the way, several hundred yards along the battlements, Bombax was looking at them. She waved to him, signaling that she was all right. When he pointedly looked away, she was angry with him all over again.

The *Arishaig* had righted herself, and her crew was scurrying about, trying to put the weapons and shields back in place, restringing the radian draws and tightening down the light sheaths. Apparently, the Federation wasn't finished yet. Aphenglow glanced down the walls to the defensive ports and found Krolling and his Troll guards.

"Everyone stay down!" she shouted. "No weapons! The wards will protect us!"

The Federation transport had backed off and was landing in a clearing some distance off. The scout vessel had joined her. But the three warships had lined up anew in front of Paranor's walls and were slowly turning broadside to employ the maximum number of weapons possible. Aphenglow felt helpless, crouched down and watching with no real way to stop what was happening.

Then all the Federation weapons began firing at once, one after the other—rail slings, fire launchers, and flash rips—a cacophonous roar of discharge and recoil, the rush of missiles released and the crash of targets struck. Stone blocks cracked and shattered, wooden beams collapsed, the front gates—oak fully two feet thick and reinforced with iron plating—shuddered and split, and dust and ash clogged the air with so much debris that it became impossible to see anything more than a dozen feet away. For long moments the sounds were so overwhelming that the Keep's defenders could do nothing but crouch behind the walls and wait for the roar to subside.

When it did, Aphenglow raised her head and saw the ships turning from port to bring their starboard weapons to bear.

"We should get off these walls!" Cymrian shouted, crouched close beside her. "We aren't doing any good here!"

But she was determined to see this through. The wards had defended them earlier; surely they would do so again. She glanced down the walls at the damage done by the Federation weapons. There were gaps and cracks in the stone, but the Keep was essentially intact.

She shook her head at him. She would stay.

Then, as the airships turned all the way to starboard and prepared to launch a fresh attack, the wards she had known were there—that she had prayed would act to save them—finally responded. The giant that had swatted the airships away once already now turned visible. A darkness rose out of the Keep—a huge swirling form that might have been smoke or brume, but was clearly something far more substantial—coalescing to form the Keep's protector, hanging in the air over Paranor's walls. The giant howled in fury, a whirlwind releasing the full force of its power, exploding from the Keep with an audible blast, catching up the airships like toys and sending them flying—this time for hundreds of yards. Spinning, whirling, and juddering on wind currents that tore light sheaths to shreds, snapped off spars, and even brought down entire masts, the airships were carried away. Aphenglow saw the cruiser simply fall apart, its occupants spilling out of its shattered container like discarded toys. The other two, stronger and more durable, survived, but only just.

It was over almost before it began. Their giant protector had formed out of nothing, struck out at the airships, and faded away, all in about a minute. The air over Paranor was clear again, the giant gone as if it had never existed. It was the most incredible display of power that Aphenglow had ever witnessed. Whatever wards had been set in place to protect the Druid's Keep, they were deadly beyond belief.

Beside her, Cymrian breathed out in a harsh whisper. When she glanced down the ramparts to find Bombax, she saw mirrored on his face the same look she knew he would find on hers.

The Federation warships that had survived limped away to join the transport, each managing with some difficulty to effect a landing. Tattered, broken, and mangled, they looked as if they were derelicts destined for the scrap heap. It would take days to make them right enough to fly. Surveying the damage, she felt an undeniable sense of satisfaction.

Drust Chazhul and the rest of his command would think twice before attacking Paranor again.

23

DRUST CHAZHUL WASN'T THINKING TWICE ABOUT anything, in spite of what Aphenglow believed. Sitting off to one side from where repairs were under way to his battered airships, still shaken by the fury of the response from the Keep to the Federation attack, he had nevertheless already made up his mind about what he would do next.

He would not, of course, give up and go home. Nor did he intend to launch any further air attacks on the Keep, having acknowledged by now how pointless that would be. Nor would he try using his Federation army, which was intact and unharmed, in an all-out ground assault against the fortress walls.

He would, however, get inside Paranor.

With Arodian missing and presumed dead by all aboard—all efforts at finding the commander having failed—Drust had been able to hand over command of the army to Tinnen March, Arodian's capable if unimaginative second in command, a man the Prime Minister could work with far more easily than his predecessor. There had been little outcry following the announcement of Arodian's disappearance. Perhaps not everyone believed that it was an accident, but those who didn't were too afraid to say so. Better to let these things be when you were a common soldier.

The day was winding down, the sun drifting west, the night coming on, and the air turning cool. A watch on the Keep had been deployed right after the attempt to penetrate Paranor's walls had failed, with sentries dispatched to surround the fortress. Flits and pilots were assigned to monitor any attempts at an air escape. Whatever else happened, Drust had instructed March, no one was to get in or out of the Keep. No word of what was happening here was to reach the ears of the other Races until he had settled with the Druids. He didn't explain how he intended to do this, and the newly appointed army commander was smart enough not to ask.

In truth, Drust didn't think for one moment that he had the means to stop an airship from leaving the Keep. His own warships were too battered to leave the ground, and his cruiser was destroyed. A transport, a scout ship, and two dozen flits could hardly be expected to stop anything. But he wanted Paranor's defenders to know he meant business; perhaps they would hold off on any escape attempts if they believed themselves better off staying inside the safety of the walls.

By the time they realized they had misjudged the situation, it would be too late.

Stoon came up to him and stood waiting to be acknowledged. By now, no one questioned the assassin's presence. He was a common sight, the Prime Minister's man, his personal assistant. Stoon played his part by doing nothing to suggest that he was anything else. He kept a low profile and stayed out of the way.

Stoon started to speak, but Drust cut him off. "Not here. We'll walk."

They set off along the perimeter of the Keep's walls, safely out of sight in the woods, trailed at some distance by the omnipresent guards assigned to protect the Prime Minister. There was activity all around them—the sounds of wounded men, of hammers pounding on wood and metal, of shouted orders and replies, and of timber being felled to fashion new masts and spars. The smells of dust and grime and blood wafted through the air, and the earth where the fleet had camped was already torn up and rutted. Drust tried to avoid looking at it or breathing any of it in. He tried to distance himself from the unpleasantness it caused him to feel. He had already done what was expected of him. He had made it a point to commend the airship commanders and their immediate subordinates on the courage they had displayed during the battle and had assured them they had not suffered a defeat, only a temporary setback. He had issued everyone a ration of ale and ordered a second to be served along with the evening meal.

Now he just wanted it all to go away. Or better yet, for their mission be over and done with.

"What were the final numbers?" he asked Stoon when they were safely out of hearing.

"Over five hundred dead—more than three hundred from the *Wistral* alone. She took everyone down with her. About twice that number injured. Some of those will die, too." He paused. "Not a good day."

Drust nodded. He could barely contain his rage. "You want desperately to tell me that you told me so, that you warned me an attack would fail, don't you?"

Stoon shrugged. "You've just said it for me."

"You think I accomplished nothing today?"

"Not knowing exactly what it was you wanted to accomplish, I can't say. On the surface of things, it doesn't appear much was achieved."

Drust sneered. "You are so careful with how you

word things. You should have considered a career as a politician; you have the skills for it."

"I'm happy just as I am, thank you."

"I'm a bit less happy with you than you are with yourself. You realize that, don't you? Letting me think I was about to be thrown over the side of my own airship! I haven't forgotten."

"I have explained all that. It was the only way to dispose of Arodian. Anyway, with Edinja gone, as well, you have no immediate threat from within the Coalition Council. It's what you wanted."

Drust grunted, knowing that the other man was right but not in the least bit mollified by it. He was still shaken by how easily their assault on Paranor had been repulsed. He could still see that black cloud rising up from the Keep's walls and swatting his airships aside.

But he would not let Stoon see this. "Today's efforts were not made with the expectation of achieving victory," he declared firmly, determined to put the best face possible on what had happened. "It would have been excellent if we could have seized the Keep in one day's time, but contrary to what you might think I did not believe that was how things would go. I understood what we were up against. You notice, however, that the plan we arranged worked well enough?"

Stoon nodded. "They fired first, giving you cause to respond. Yes, I saw. But I think you believed your fire launchers and flash rips would be enough to overcome their magic."

"I won't argue that. I expected more from our weapons. But the Druids have had years to arm Paranor, and whatever magic protects it wasn't conjured overnight.

"Anyway, we might have done some damage even if we didn't get inside. You saw the walls."

"I saw them. They didn't look particularly damaged to me."

Drust rubbed his forehead, further annoyed. "Do we have a way to get into the Keep yet?"

Stoon shook his head. "I'm waiting to hear." He paused. "I think it will happen. I just don't know when."

"Soon would be good." Drust gave him a look. "Very soon would be better. I need to end this quickly." He paused. "I've put a lot of faith in this plan of yours."

Stoon smiled. "You said yourself it's worked so far. Paranor apparently attacked us first, so we were given cause to retaliate. Our key to opening the gates and sacking the place waits just inside. He'll do what he's supposed to do. I've used him before. He's dependable. He likes this sort of thing. It makes him feel superior when he thinks he's smarter than everyone else."

"I'll say it again—this has to happen quickly. Once word of our attack gets out, others will almost certainly attempt to intervene. I want us inside the Keep and in control of its walls before that happens. I want the Druids either disposed of or imprisoned. If your man is so smart, he should be able to do what is needed to make that happen."

"Patience, Drust."

"I don't have any patience left. I don't have any wish to be patient. I want this matter settled, Stoon." He said it quietly, but with an edge to his voice that the other couldn't miss. "If this turns into the debacle we both knew it might, I will be the one to face the consequences. I am fairly certain I can predict what those consequences will be. And what happens to me happens to you. Find a way to get us in!"

He wheeled away and began walking back toward the encampment, the heat of his anger rising off him like steam. He glanced at the darkening sky and felt a measure of relief. At least this day was almost over. Perhaps tomorrow would prove more favorable.

"One thing more," he said when Stoon was back beside him again. "When you do find a way in, I want you to be one of the first to enter." He gave the other a sharp glance and caught the small nod of agreement that served as a reply. "Not to put you in danger," he added. "But for something else entirely."

"Which would be?" The assassin sounded genuinely interested.

"I want you to take that Elessedil girl alive. After I have personally removed her tongue and cut off her hands, I intend to give her to the soldiers."

He strode on in silence, the image of it burning with bright promise in his mind.

When the attack ended and the Federation withdrew, Aphenglow left the ramparts and went down to find Arling to make certain she was all right. Cymrian trailed after her, and she let him come without comment. She ignored Bombax.

After reuniting with her sister and giving her a hug and a few words of reassurance, she left her with Cymrian and went off to find the rail sling that had been used to attack the *Arishaig*. She found it easily enough, but there was no sign of who had used it. More telling was her examination of the angle available for attack using that particular weapon. Even under the best of circumstances, the rail sling couldn't have done much more than dent the iron-plated underside of a Federation warship.

The ramifications of that conclusion were disturbing.

She decided to talk to Woostra. She had questions about the magic warding the Keep, and with the Ard Rhys absent she believed her best chance at getting answers was from Khyber Elessedil's personal secretary.

She found him where she expected, ensconced in his office outside the Druid Library. His scarecrow body was hunched over his desk, eyes scanning the pages of a clutch of books and papers spread out before him. He didn't even look up when she entered, merely gesturing to a bench to one side.

"Sit, Aphenglow. I'll be done in a moment."

She lowered herself onto the bench and waited patiently for the several minutes it took him to complete whatever it was he was doing. When he finally looked up, she said, "How do you do that?"

He looked puzzled. "Do what?"

"Recognize me without looking."

"Oh, that." He gave her a small smile. "Your footsteps. I can recognize any of you just from hearing you approach. Assuming I am paying any sort of attention."

She smiled back. "Really?"

He shrugged. "What can I help you with? Something to do with that Federation attack?"

"You know about it?"

"Hard not to with all the noise."

"Did you go out for a look?"

"No need to. The magic that wards Paranor repels anything or anyone not invited in. Always has. Always will."

"So she protects us?"

He smiled anew. "Druids might choose to see it that way. But that's not really how it is. Grianne Ohmsford put the wards in place before she left the Keep for the final time. But the wards protect Paranor, not the Druids. The Druids are simply inadvertent beneficiaries. Along with anyone else who might be inside during an attack." He rubbed his long nose with his finger. "Easier to protect something that doesn't move around than something that does. Druids come and go. The Keep stays right where it is."

She thought about it a moment. "So if there were an enemy inside—say, someone who managed to get invited in one way or another—the magic wouldn't let the rest of us know."

He gave her a long look. "What are you saying, Aphenglow?"

She shook her head. "I'm just mulling something over. This attack was provoked by someone who fired one of our rail slings from inside the walls of the Keep. I didn't see who it was, and no one else I talked to saw, either. But I found the rail sling that was used, and it was clear from the angle of trajectory that using it served no purpose. The angle of attack was all wrong."

"Then why . . . ?"

"Bother? To provoke a response to an apparent attack from us. These were Federation warships, fully manned and armed, and although they claimed to have been invited by the Ard Rhys and came expecting to be received, there was no evidence any of this was so. What they seem to have come for was pretty much exactly what happened."

Woostra nodded slowly. "So you think it was all planned? That the firing of the rail sling was a deliberate subterfuge by someone who was in their employ?"

"I think it possible. I haven't found a better explanation."

"And you don't know who this someone is?"

"Not yet."

He nodded again, and then went back to reading the papers in front of him. "Better find out then. No point sitting around here talking to me." He looked up quickly. "But the magic that wards the Keep can't help you with this. It can shelter you from attacks without, but not ferret out enemies within. Good luck, Aphenglow."

She departed his office and went back out into Paranor's halls, wondering what to do next. As she walked, she began going over the list of those who were within the Keep. She could eliminate herself and Bombax and Woostra and Arling. That left Cymrian, the Troll guards, and the boy who had rescued Bombax from the Mwellrets. If she was right about what had happened, it had to be one of them.

She was mulling over which when Bombax caught up to her. She flinched inwardly as he did so, prepared for the worst. She kept her eyes averted and continued walking.

"Are you thinking the same thing I am about all this?" he asked quietly, surprising her. "That this attack was no accident?"

She nodded. "Someone in the Keep fired that rail sling to provoke it. The attack was planned ahead of time."

His big hands tightened on the staff he bore. "One of the Trolls?"

"Hard to believe. They're sworn to us. Most have been here a long time."

"That Elf you brought into the Keep with your sister? What do you know of him?"

She stopped where she was, fighting down a surge of new anger. "That boy you brought into the Keep when you came back from Varfleet? What do you know of him?"

"I know he rescued me. He saved my life."

"Well, Cymrian did the same for me. He killed five men doing it, too."

She turned and walked on, forcing him to come after her. All at once, she didn't want him there.

"Why are you so angry?" he asked, grabbing her arm.

She stopped again and carefully extracted herself. "I don't like how you're acting. It isn't who you are. I'm not sure you've recovered from what happened with the Mwellrets."

"There's nothing wrong with me." He stared at her a

moment, and she could see the confusion in his eyes. "I love you, Aphen. I don't like thinking that maybe you don't love me."

It caught her by surprise. "Why would you say that?"

"That Elf follows you around like a puppy. What am I supposed to think?"

She shook her head. "I haven't given you any reason to doubt me."

"Maybe you don't see it the way I do. Do you still love me? Can you say the words?"

Impulsively, she reached up and touched his cheek. "Of course I can say them. I love you. You are my life partner. I didn't make that choice without giving thought to it. It was not done lightly or with any intention of not honoring it."

"I want to believe that," he said.

She dropped her hand to his arm and gripped it. "Let's leave this discussion for later. Let's concentrate on what's at hand. I want to find out who fired that rail sling. I want you to help me. Let's be united on this."

He nodded slowly. "That's how I want it, too."

"United, then." She gave him a quick smile. "We should talk to everyone. Maybe there's something we can learn."

"One thing you want to keep in mind, Aphen," he said. "It might not be one of the Trolls or the Elf or the boy. It might be someone else entirely, someone who managed to get inside Paranor without any of us knowing."

It gave her pause. She hadn't thought of that.

Twilight, and most within the Keep were gathered in the dining hall.

Deek Trink worked his way down the corridors, halfway certain that this time he was going to get caught. Bombax might not suspect him, but the Elven woman had already made him her prime suspect in the rail sling incident simply by process of elimination. He had hoped there would be a sufficient number of other logical suspects, once he got inside the Keep, to shift suspicion away from him. But there were only the members of the Druid Guard, the two Druids, the old man in the library, the Elven woman's younger sister, and that really scary Elven Hunter Cymrian. Of all of them, he was the one Deek wanted least to be around.

Not that he hadn't fooled Cymrian just like he had all the others. More that he didn't like how being around Cymrian made him feel. Uncomfortable. Revealed. Those eyes seemed to look right into you and see everything. Being charming didn't impress Cymrian one bit. Deek was good at winning over people, at making them believe whatever he wanted them to believe. He was clever at deceiving others, at giving a false impression of what he was like. He had always been good at it.

But Cymrian was having none of it. Nor, did it appear, was the Elven Druid he protected like a moor cat its newborn.

Deek hurried on through the lower levels of the Keep, pausing at corners and doorways to listen, all the while trying to look casual about what he was doing so that if he were caught he might still be able to talk his way free. He knew he could do it if he had to. He had gotten out of tougher situations than this one.

Well, maybe not tougher. But the knowledge of how much danger he was in was what excited him enough to make him want to take the chance.

Bombax and the Elven woman had come to him earlier to talk about the rail sling incident, and he had worked hard trying to satisfy them that he knew nothing about it. He had been hiding down below like he was told he should, frightened the Federation forces would prove too much for the Druids and he would be discovered and sent back to the Mwellrets. There was no reason for him to be firing a rail sling at a Federation warship, was there?

Of course, there was every reason if you were working for someone like Stoon. But no one here knew anything about that. All anyone knew was he had found Bombax in that warehouse, trussed up like a side of beef, and decided to help him get free, all at great personal risk. It was Bombax who had brought him to Paranor, offering safe haven. No one realized it was Stoon who had hired the Mwellrets to drug and imprison Bombax so Deek could arrange a rescue and thereby gain entrance to the Druid's Keep. No one realized he was there for a single reason only—to open a door in the walls and let the Federation army inside.

How could they? He was just a boy.

He wondered how much longer he could parlay that into a career. Not much, given the way he was growing. His boyhood days were coming to an end, and he would have to find a new way of deceiving people. There was always a way to be found, of course. He had learned that much years ago living on the streets, even before he met Stoon.

He glanced over his shoulder, thinking he heard something, and peered into the shadows of the long hallway. He couldn't be certain who might be down here. The Elven woman had assigned one of the Trolls in the Druid Guard to "accompany" him wherever he went so that he would stay safe. He knew what that meant. She had kept the Elven Hunter with her, which he could tell Bombax didn't like—was there something between them?—but then Bombax hadn't offered to keep Deek, choosing to leave him with the Troll. Not that Deek minded. It was easier to get rid of the Troll than it would have been to get rid of Bombax. Persuading the Troll to share a few glasses of ale he had surreptitiously drugged was easy enough. Deek only needed enough time to descend to the lower levels of the Keep, relocate the small, ironclad door he had found earlier, and mark it to let the Federation know it was open.

If he were quick about it, as he intended to be, no one would see him and he would be back in the guards' common room with his Troll watchdog before the other realized he was missing, looking for all the world as if he, too, had fallen asleep after indulging in too much ale.

He reached the door he had found days earlier and released the heavy locks—three of them, the Druids weren't taking chances—so that the door cracked open. He took a moment to make certain that no one standing watch on the walls could see him, and then, using a red dye he carried in a pouch, he drew an X on the outside of the door, tossed the pouch into a path of weeds growing against the walls, and closed the door without re-locking it. Easy enough. Federation scouts would find his well-marked entrance into the Keep quickly enough and at dawn a special detachment of soldiers would sneak through and open the west gates.

By midday, Paranor would have fallen.

He turned away from the door and started back down the hall. He would have preferred to flee the Keep right away, but leaving was not an option. His absence would be noticed and would lead to discovery of the open door. Stoon had told him to stay put until the attack came and the Keep fell; if he did he would not be harmed. Deek believed him, if only because he knew Stoon would want to use him again one day.

He reached a set of stairs leading up and began to climb. By this time tomorrow, it would all be over and he would be on his way back to Varfleet. He just needed to be patient a little while longer.

Something he was good at.

24

WHEN APHENGLOW ELESSEDIL WOKE AT DAWN ON the following morning, Bombax was already up and gone. She lay where she was for a moment, reflecting on last night, and on how they had bridged the gap that had opened a few days earlier by recapturing a little of what had brought them together in the first place.

But soon she was out of bed, washing and dressing, wondering what was happening outside with the Federation army. She was aware as she pulled on her black robes and laced them to her body that it was unusually quiet, even for Paranor. There was an air of expectancy that was troubling. No birdsong, no kitchen sounds, no voices coming from the walls.

Where was Arlingfant?

She went next door to see and found her sister gone, as well.

Now she was moving quickly—or as quickly as she could manage on her damaged leg—passing down the hallways and out into the courtyard. She could see Arling standing on the walls with Cymrian and what looked to be the entire complement of the Druid Guard still in residence at the Keep. They were staring out toward the Federation encampment, watching something she couldn't see. They had their backs to her and

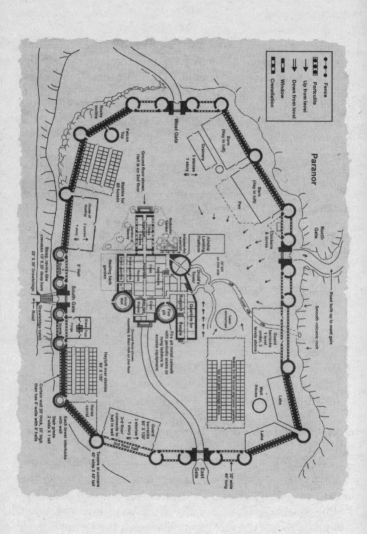

were so absorbed by whatever was out there, they didn't see her coming.

Aphen limped across the courtyard to the walls and climbed the stone steps to the ramparts, leaning heavily on the staff she had brought to support herself. She was much stronger by now, her broken leg mostly healed. It still ached, of course, but it was nothing compared with what she had experienced earlier, and she was good at ignoring pain. Everyone turned as she approached, and the looks on their faces were enough to tell her something was wrong. She slowed beside Arling, who pointed wordlessly out toward the Federation army camp.

Except that what she was pointing at was much closer. The entire Federation command was positioned right in front of Paranor's walls. Rank upon rank of armored men faced the Keep, their lines neat and straight amid a forest of spears, bowmen on the flanks and to the rear. They were standing silently, looking straight ahead, shields up, tense and ready as if awaiting a signal.

She was so shocked that for a moment she couldn't speak. "What are they doing?" she managed finally.

"That is the question, isn't it?" Bombax answered drily.

"They look as if they're getting ready to attack! But they can't intend to do that! It would be suicide!"

"So it would seem. But maybe they know something we don't."

Cymrian shook his head. "This looks like a feint. They can't scale these walls, so they're drawing our attention here while trying to get in some other way." He pushed off the wall. "I'm going to have a look around."

Swift and fluid, he jogged down the ramparts, heading toward the north wall. Aphen watched, envious of his agility and strength, anxious to regain her own.

She turned as Arling gripped her arm. "What do you think we should do?" her sister whispered.

Aphen gave her hand a squeeze. "Wait them out. They aren't doing anything yet. We have to be patient. Bombax, have you checked any of the approaches to the other walls?"

He shook his head. "You go. I want to stay with Krolling in case this isn't a trick and they actually do attempt an assault. They have ladders, so they might think they can scale the walls. Madness, if they try it. But who knows? Go on, Aphen. Take Arling with you."

She didn't particularly want to do that, but she guessed Arling was just as safe going with her as staying behind, and if they were together she could keep an eye on her sister. So together they set out for the west wall, descending the stairs from the ramparts to the courtyard, cutting across to the first of several walls that bisected the outer courtyards like spokes from a wheel, allowing them quick access through the Keep proper and the courtyards adjoining the west wall. Aphen was thinking that somehow things were getting away from them, that all their efforts to stay safe were on the verge of failing. It wasn't hard to pinpoint the source of this premonition; they still hadn't found out who fired the rail sling the previous day. If there was a traitor within the walls, they were very much at risk.

She had asked Cymrian the previous night for his impressions of the boy Deek Trink. "Too clever for his own good," Cymrian had responded. "Too ready to persuade you he's your friend when maybe he's not."

He didn't say aloud what was clearly in his mind—that he didn't like Deek Trink—but it was obvious enough. It made her think she should have locked the boy away in spite of Bombax. But that would have meant another confrontation, and she wasn't certain her suspicions were valid. It was easier just to have him watched.

Now she was wondering if she had made a mistake putting but a single guard on him.

"What do we do if they attack?" Arling asked suddenly. They were climbing the stairs to the west wall now, hurrying to have a look at what was happening outside. "Can we stop them? We're so few."

Aphen shook her head, unwilling to answer. In truth, she didn't know. Her only plan at this point was to rely on the wards of the Keep to protect them. If that failed, she didn't see how thirty could stand against what looked to be close to five or six hundred, even with Paranor's walls to protect them.

They reached the ramparts and peered over. The clear-cut area that separated the Keep from the forest lay empty below. No sign of anyone. But the walls had been built in a zigzag fashion to allow for defense from more than one angle, and from where they stood they could see only a portion of this one. So Aphen, wanting to be sure the others were safe, as well, began walking north with Arling trailing after in silence. Together they reached the end of that section of wall, rounded the watchtower, and turned down the next.

Instantly they saw the line of armed men slipping out of the trees and sprinting for the Keep, one after another, before disappearing inside through an open door.

Although Aphen had been looking for something like this and had been half expecting to find it, it was a shock nevertheless. She wheeled on Arling, backing them both away from the edge of the wall where they might be seen. "Run back for Bombax and Krolling. Tell them the walls are breached and the Federation is inside. Bring them here at once. Tell them to hurry!"

To her sister's credit, she raced away without arguing. Aphenglow continued ahead to the next watchtower, pulled open its heavy wooden door, and started down the winding stairs.

Federation soldiers were inside! The safety of the Keep was compromised and Paranor was at risk!

The words screamed in her mind, harsh and insistent, demanding she do something. She wondered how far inside the enemy had penetrated. She wondered what their orders were. At the very least they would try to open one of the four sets of main gates to let the others in. Her hands tightened on the walking staff as she limped from step to step, her senses attuned to the silence of the tower's dark interior. She heard sounds of movement, soft and furtive, from below. The soldiers were moving about in the hallways, settling themselves in place, waiting until all were inside before trying to reach the gates. How many would she have to face alone? How many would she have to stop?

Her leg began to ache, and she realized she was tense and stiff and forced herself to relax. She found herself wishing Bombax were there. Or Cymrian. Maybe Cymrian even more, so cool and collected and seemingly always prepared. But they were both elsewhere, and she couldn't depend on either of them.

She eased her way to the bottom of the winding stairway and stopped again in the lower entry. Passageways branched both left and right, but it was from the latter's dark interior that she heard the faint sound of movements. She realized that she was between the west gates and the soldiers—and they were advancing toward her, creeping through the shadows and hoping not to be discovered until it was too late.

She would have to stop them here.

She glanced around quickly. There were no interior doors on these passageways. Quick movement from one tower to the next was important, and so the corridors were kept open. The point was to stop an enemy before it got inside. Interior doors were more an obstacle to a defender than a help. Given that the Keep's walls had been breached only once before in its two-thousand-year history, it was hard to argue with the reasoning.

But now it had happened a second time, and Aphenglow wished she had at least one door she could put between herself and the invaders.

They were getting closer.

She tried to think what to do. She wanted to keep them contained in the narrow passageways of the Outer Wall where they couldn't spread out to the inner Keep. If they got into the courtyard, they would be all over the place.

The tower room was too confining to use the magic she would need to hold back the men pouring into the walls, but she had no choice. Going outside meant giving them a better chance to get behind her and reach the gates. She backed into the shadows of the next corridor, giving herself a clear view of the tower chamber and thereby a window of vision large enough to see the men she knew were coming.

Then she waited.

Drust Chazhul hunkered down in the forest just beyond the west wall, watching his soldiers cross the open space to where the tiny service door gaped open to admit them. Stoon was crouched at his side, the two of them counting heads as the soldiers disappeared inside.

"Good as his word," he observed softly.

"Always has been." Stoon was watching the top of the wall intently, scanning it end-to-end, searching for signs of the Druid Guard. "He's clever, that one."

Another two or three soldiers had made it inside. That made it more than thirty now. They had brought fifty, thinking that would be more than enough to force at least one of the main gates. They had left the rest of the army at the south gate as a diversion. A second force was hidden in the trees behind them waiting to enter when the west gate was opened by the advance party. It should happen quickly once all fifty were inside.

"Don't forget," Drust said. "I want the Elessedil girl alive."

Stoon shrugged. "Why bother? You'll just kill her anyway."

"Maybe not. After my soldiers have reminded her that insolence has a cost, I might still send her back to her grandfather."

The assassin gave him a look. "Kill her and be done with it. You don't want to play games in this business."

Drust turned away. "When are you going in?"

"In a little while. No need to rush things."

They went silent, watching as the last of the advance force disappeared through the doorway. On the walls above, nothing moved and no one appeared.

"I think I'll move over to the west gate and wait there." Drust was restless, impatient. "I want to be there when it opens." He rose, looked down at Stoon and smiled. "It's almost here. The end of the Druids and their precious Keep. The end of their magic. And I will have been the one who brought them down."

Stoon was tempted to suggest it was a little early to celebrate, but he managed to hold his tongue.

When the first of the Federation soldiers crept out of the corridor across from where she was hiding, Aphenglow was ready for them. Her magic summoned, she let the first three attackers get clear of the opening and then stepped into view. The soldiers reacted at once, bringing up their weapons and rushing at her. But the Druid magic slammed into them and threw them back against their fellows, clogging the passageway with screaming, cursing men.

She didn't wait for them to untangle themselves, but went after them immediately. Shielding herself with magic spun from one hand, she attacked with magic thrown from her other—a heavy, weighted blow that crashed into all the soldiers she could see and flattened them in their tracks. The corridor became a madhouse, the shock of what had happened stopping the advance completely, forcing those still able to retreat. Those at the forefront of the strike yelled to their comrades to fall back. There were more doors farther down, Aphen knew, but at least they were farther away from the west gate.

Fair enough.

She went out the tower door, stepping into the open courtyard beyond, searching for the help she expected to find.

No one was there.

She stood where she was for a moment, shocked and confused. Where were Paranor's defenders?

Then she heard shouts and cries from somewhere on the other side of the Keep, and realized that the real battle was being fought elsewhere. She wanted to rush over to find out what was happening, but that would mean abandoning her defense of the west gate, which she knew would be a big mistake.

She would stay where she was needed.

She was making her way down the interior of the wall toward the next tower when its door was flung open and the rest of the Federation advance force poured out into the courtyard.

She stopped where she was. She could tell at once that she was too far away to stop all of them and with her damaged leg could not move quickly enough to remedy that. Changing her plans, she began crossing the courtyard toward the Inner Wall of the Keep, flinging shards of magic at the men who were coming at her. She took down a few, but the rest came on. They were ignoring the west gate, intent on reaching her instead. She dropped into a crouch, summoned the broadest strike she could manage, and unwrapped it like a sheet of hammered steel across their path. They were blocked and for the moment could not get through. She spun out the magic then folded it over them, cutting off their air.

Struggling to break free, they began to choke and gasp.

She knew the magic would not last long, but it gave her the chance she needed to escape. She could not stand against so many without aid. She hastened as quickly as she could for the safety of the Inner Wall, and with her back turned she only just managed to catch sight of the lean, swift figure coming up behind her. She swung back around just as her attacker dropped to one knee and sighted down the length of a long blowgun.

Reacting solely on instinct, Aphenglow managed to throw up a protective shield. The blowgun darts disintegrated on contact, the brightness of their poison exploding in red bursts against her shield as they did so. Aphenglow had risen and begun running once more, limping noticeably, when her attacker used the blowgun a second time. Even though she was ready for the attack, she stumbled and went down, the darts skimming past her head, black missiles in the bright morning sunlight.

This time when she rose, she went after him.

But her attacker had anticipated her and was already running the other way. She sent an entangling magic after him and brought him down in a jumble of arms and legs, his blowgun flying away. She would have done more, but by now the magic that had confined the Federation soldiers had collapsed and they were coming toward her anew.

There's no time for this, she thought.

Using magic to slow them—a tripping incantation

that ensnared their feet—she began backing away once more, keeping an eye on both soldiers and the blowgun artist. But her efforts had drained her, and she was beginning to stumble badly. Holding back her attackers was sapping what remained of her strength, and she was still fifty feet from the safety of the Inner Wall.

They were almost on top of her when Bombax appeared.

He surged out of a haze of smoke and brume and flew across the ramparts with a roar, charging down the stone stairway and leaping into the courtyard, black robes flying out behind him. He was screaming at the attackers to draw their attention, challenging them to come for him. The Federation soldiers turned away from Aphenglow, caught sight of the black-clad apparition across from them, and fled at once. The blowgun artist was already gone.

Aphenglow called out to Bombax, and he raced toward her, his dark face intent, his eyes wild and dangerous. Fresh attackers were appearing all about them, coming through courtyard doors and down off the ramparts. They seemed to be everywhere. Somehow the Federation must have breached Paranor's defenses in more than one place. Aphen kept backing away toward the Inner Wall, still using her magic, rallying against this new threat, trying to protect Bombax as he was protecting her.

He reached her while still on the fly, swept her off her feet without slowing, and raced for the closest doorway. Using his magic as he ran, he released the locking devices so that the door sprang open. Spears and arrows flew all around them, and Federation soldiers, howling in rage, closed in from three sides.

But by then they were through the dark opening of the Inner Wall entry and the door had slammed shut and locked itself behind them.

* * *

Stoon, bruised and battered and furious with himself, stumbled back down the corridor tunneling through the Outer Wall to the door that had let him in and pushed his way back outside again, heading for the surrounding forest. Behind him the fighting was intense, raging all along the Outer Wall. He didn't look back to see what was happening, having lost interest in being involved in any way. He was lucky to be alive, and he knew it.

He was almost to the trees when Drust Chazhul rushed out to meet him.

"What are you doing? You were supposed to stay inside and bring out the girl!"

Stoon waited until the other was right in front of him, and then said, "You want the girl, Drust? You go in and get her. I've seen all of her I care to see. I didn't sign on for this."

Drust seemed to catch the look in his eyes and backed away. "All right. Someone else will bring her then. But I can't believe you let . . ."

Stoon was right in his face. "Don't say it! Don't even think it! You didn't see what happened in there, but I'll tell you this. If you get your hands on her, you better kill her fast."

He swung away dismissively, looking back toward Paranor's walls and the sounds of battle. "What's going on in there? Your men were everywhere! The advance force didn't have time to open the gates. How did the rest of them get in so fast?"

Drust handed him an aleskin and waited for him to drink from it. "Your man managed to give us a second way in. The Druids and their guards were so busy watching for us from the south and then rushing to stop us from the west that he managed to reach the east gate unnoticed. Once it was open, we rushed a contingent of men over from the south to hold them. The Trolls fought to retake them, but couldn't manage it. Now we're inside. It's only moments until the Keep is ours."

"Ours, is it?" Stoon sounded doubtful.

"What can they do to stop us? We're inside their main walls. We can find a way to breach the Keep. You didn't see any strange magic stop us from getting through the gates once they were opened from the inside, did you? No, we've got them! Our right to finish them off is clear enough. They attacked us first; they brought it on themselves. That's what we'll tell everyone. There are plenty of witnesses to corroborate the story."

He grabbed Stoon's arm. "Come with me. Let's find a place to watch it happen."

Atop the battlements of the Inner Wall, Aphenglow and Bombax stood watching the Federation soldiers scurry about the courtyards below, removing their dead and injured and readying themselves for a fresh assault. Ten of Krolling's Druid Guards were dead and another five too badly injured to fight. The fifteen or so who were still sound enough to do so had taken up positions on the Inner Wall battlements to await the expected attack. It was not entirely clear yet what direction it would come from, but it was clear that it was inevitable.

"We can't hold back so many," Bombax muttered, watching the soldiers as they began to form up their lines. "Not if they find a way to get inside the Inner Wall, too."

"It's not your fault they got this far," she answered quietly. "We were all fooled by that boy."

"I'm the one who brought him inside the Keep. I'm the one who trusted him when I should have known better." Bombax shook his head. "I should have seen the truth."

"You were drugged by whatever liquid the Mwellret

poured into your gag. You were unable to speak or move properly, and you couldn't reason things out." She glanced over. "None of us would have done any better."

Bombax looked unconvinced. "I just hope I live long enough to get my hands on him. Five seconds would do it."

"We'll settle with him one day." She scanned the courtyards and the Outer Wall. "What became of him after he opened the east gate?"

The Borderman grimaced. "He slipped out to join his friends. If he were still inside the Keep, we wouldn't be having this conversation."

They were silent for a few minutes, standing close, lost in separate thoughts focused on finding an answer to the same question: What would happen when the Federation attacked the Keep? Aphenglow thought she should go inside and say something to Woostra. But what was there to say? That they were under attack? That they were all in grave danger? Woostra would already know as much. They were all trapped, and advising the old man of what that meant was unnecessary.

"It would help if we hadn't lost the airships," Bombax murmured.

But they had, and there was no help for it. The landing platform and their airships lay between the Outer and Inner walls, and the Federation had seized possession of both almost immediately. It didn't give them access to the Keep, but it kept the Druids from being able to escape by air. If they wanted out, they would have to walk.

They could do that, of course. There were tunnels that ran from the depths of the Keep to the world outside. But escaping would mean abandoning Paranor to an enemy, and no Druid would ever consider doing that.

Surrendering the Keep to Drust Chazhul and his Federation minions was unthinkable.

Cymrian appeared, white-blond hair streaked with dirt, Elven features intense. Wherever he'd been while she had been fighting her way clear of the Federation advance force and the blowgun assailant hadn't been any less dangerous.

"Are you all right?" she asked, giving him a long look.

He nodded, shrugged. "I almost had him."

Bombax looked over. "The boy?"

"I spotted him when I was coming back around the north wall to the east side of the Keep. I knew right away what he was doing. He had already gotten the gate open most of the way, but the Federation soldiers hadn't reached it yet. I went after him, thinking I could get to him before he did any more damage. But he heard me or maybe just sensed me and fled through the gate, screaming for help. It came too quickly for me to close the gate again in time."

"At least you tried." Bombax held out his hand, and Cymrian gripped it tightly. "We'll get another chance at him."

"There he is now," Aphenglow said suddenly.

The men looked where she was pointing. Deek Trink stood atop the Outer Wall perhaps three hundred yards away from where they watched, part of a small group of men studying the Keep from afar. Aphenglow recognized the blowgun assailant as one of them.

"That's Drust Chazhul standing with him." Bombax hissed out the Federation Prime Minister's name as if it were poison on his tongue. "This must have been his plan all along. Get the boy inside the Keep to open the gates for his soldiers after faking an attack to justify doing so. It was the boy who fired on the *Arishaig*, a ruse for prompting a Federation response." He glanced over at Aphenglow. "Just as you said."

They watched as Deek Trink pointed this way and that, clearly describing the defenses of the Keep, revealing what he knew about its strengths and weaknesses, sharing information he had collected with their enemies. Aphenglow felt a red-hot flush surface, climbing from her neck into her cheeks.

"I'll be right back," Cymrian said suddenly.

He turned and raced away, whipping past an approaching Arlingfant without a word. Arling gave him a glance and then joined her sister and Bombax. "Is anything happening yet? Aphen, are you sure you're all right?"

Aphenglow nodded. "I'm fine," she lied.

Arling had helped clean her up after her escape with Bombax, washing her wounds and applying salves. But there were wounds on the inside that couldn't be treated so easily, even though Arling could always detect them.

Down below, the Federation soldiers had their lines in place and were waiting for the order to attack. Apparently, the Federation army commander had decided that coming at the Keep from the west wall was the best approach. It was the one Aphenglow would have chosen, as well, which worried her. It was here that the Keep was most vulnerable.

"Won't the Keep defend us like she did before?" Arling asked. "Won't it be just the same with the Inner Wall as it was with the Outer Wall since no one is going to let them in voluntarily?"

Aphenglow wasn't sure. She wanted to believe this was true, but she didn't know enough about the magic's conjuring to be confident that it would respond. Maybe breaching the Outer Wall had negated its effectiveness. Maybe it hadn't been designed to defend if attackers got this far inside.

As they watched, a formation of flits eased into view from above the trees and hovered just beyond the perimeter of the main wall. Apparently, the Federation airships were going to try again. They would test the magic that had stopped them earlier, and if it failed to respond the pilots would use the flits and maybe something larger to force an entry from the air as well as the ground.

"Rail slings might stop them," Bombax muttered. "Knock them right out of the air, those puny little things."

Cymrian was back, moving to an open space on the wall close by. He was carrying the bow Aphenglow had seen him fashioning some days earlier in the gardens. It was a formidable-looking weapon, fully five feet long, its ends curved and notched to allow maximum draw, its surface polished to a bright sheen. Cymrian must have been working on it a long time, Aphen thought.

And then she wondered why he had brought it up here.

Without a word to any of them, Cymrian fitted a black arrow to the bowstring, lifted the bow so that the arrow was angled upward, hesitated, and then lowered it again. He looked beyond Paranor's walls at the trees, reading their movements, looked up at the sky and watched the clouds drift, and then brought the bow back up again, sighting along the length of the arrow as he pointed it toward the group with Drust Chazhul. They were paying no attention to him, their interest focused elsewhere. Cymrian drew the arrow all the way back to its iron tip, held it there for a long moment, and then released the bowstring.

The black arrow arced skyward, sharply outlined against the blue of the sky as it flew across the space separating the Keep from the Outer Wall, its trajectory steady and sure, rising and then plummeting into the group that surrounded Drust Chazhul and piercing Deek Trink's narrow chest through and through. The boy staggered backward a step, eyes wide with shock, and then toppled over dead.

For an instant, no one standing close to Cymrian said a word. Then Bombax exhaled sharply. "Shades!"

"That was the greatest bow shot I've ever seen," Aphenglow breathed.

"It was the luckiest," Cymrian grumbled, lowering his bow. "I was just trying to scare him, not kill him."

"I think I like this result better," Bombax said.

Across the way, Drust Chazhul and his group had scattered in all directions and were now crouched behind anything that offered protection. The rows of Federation soldiers lined up below had turned to look and were milling about uneasily, breaking ranks and looking back at the Keep as if at any moment an arrow could strike each of them, too. Even the flits, which until now had been hovering impatiently at the perimeter of the Outer Wall, had backed off so far they were almost out of sight.

Deek Trink's body lay abandoned on the ramparts. No one seemed willing to retrieve it.

Bombax nodded to himself. "Much better."

For about thirty minutes it seemed as if the Federation would postpone any further action until the next day. But then Drust Chazhul and his commanders and sycophants rallied the attack from behind the series of protective barriers where they had sought shelter. The soldiers who had broken ranks and scattered were reassembled behind spears and shields and unit leaders, presumably with promises of what would happen if they fled a second time, and the flits eased back into position just outside Paranor's walls.

Aphenglow watched in silent desperation. Arling was

beside her. Both of them stood between Bombax and Cymrian. All of them were thinking the same thing. If the magic that had warded the Keep thus far did not repel this fresh assault, they were finished. Paranor would fall, and they would have no choice but to flee into the tunnels beneath and from there out into the countryside, fugitives from their own home. They might stand and fight, but even with their magic to aid them, they would be quickly overwhelmed and captured.

But so much worse was what would be lost to the Federation and to Drust Chazhul. All of their histories and records that had been so painstakingly compiled down through the centuries, all of their talismans and artifacts, the chambers that had never housed any but those who were Druids, the cold room and the scrye, the depthless, bottomless well at the tower's heart that housed the dangerous and sometimes malevolent spirit of the Keep, the earth's furnace that gave her heat and presence, the landing platform and the airships. And most damaging of all, the belief that Paranor was impenetrable and the Druids invincible in their own fortress would be shattered. It was a stomach-wrenching prospect, one that none of those who were Druids could accept and none who stood with them could conceive.

They had talked briefly about taking action to save what was threatened, about hiding those things that could be hidden, about adding wards and spells. But even Woostra had dismissed the idea. It was too late for that; the job was too overwhelming. The Druid Histories were already protected against intruders, and the talismans and artifacts were well concealed. Best to trust to what had kept them in one piece for this long. Best just to have a little faith.

But more than a little might be required, Aphenglow thought, standing with the others, the tension ramped up to where it was almost unbearable, her skin crawling with it.

She watched as the Federation lines steadied, men and airships both, and everything went unnaturally still.

Then the battle horn sounded and the Federation army attacked. Lines of armored soldiers and bowmen rushed the Inner Wall and threw up scaling ladders and grappling hooks. Flits shot forward to clear the Outer Wall in an airborne assault on the Inner. Shouts and cries and the clash of weapons rang through the afternoon air, and the combined strength of hundreds threw itself against Paranor and the handful of defenders who waited.

It was a disaster.

Once more the shadowy presence warding the Druid's Keep surfaced, just as Aphenglow had hoped it would, as ready to protect the Inner Wall as it had been the Outer. Its dark, amorphous presence coiled like a serpent—a venomous, hissing creature. In the blink of an eye, it swatted away the flits, sending them spinning out of control into the woods from which they had emerged, effortlessly shattering their attempt to penetrate the plane of the walls. Then it sank into the stonework of the Inner Wall and reemerged as a suffocating black cloud extending outward from the stonework's vertical plane to knock away the scaling ladders and the men hanging on them and blow the rest of the soldiers back across the courtyard with a giant's breath that sent men and equipment whirling and spinning like so many autumn leaves caught in a north wind.

Everyone broke and ran after that, soldiers and unit commanders alike, fleeing the battleground for the comparative safety of the Outer Wall, where they huddled in shock and terror.

From behind his shelter on the ramparts where he knelt beside Stoon, Drust Chazhul signaled for the attack to be broken off. He slumped back against the stone barrier, enraged. "We're being made fools of!" he hissed.

But his watchful companion had remembered something he had heard the unfortunate Deek Trink mention while he was still upright. "Maybe," he mused quietly, giving Drust a careful look, "there's another way."

25

THE BLEAK EXPANSE OF THE BREAKLINE STRETCHED
away in front of her as the *Walker Boh* emerged from
the peaks of the Kensrowe and turned west toward the
miles of unsettled wilderness that would eventually end
at the shores of the Blue Divide. They were removed
from anything resembling civilization, flying over country uninhabited save for the hardiest and most primal
denizens of the Four Lands. A thousand feet up and
well clear of what dwelled below, they had only the
landscape to suggest the savage existence of those creatures. Farshaun might know a little of them from his
travels, and the Speakman surely knew a good deal
more, but the rest of the expedition had heard only stories.

Still, just looking at the vast, rugged emptiness—the
blasted earth that seemed to have been torn up and
thrown back down again in clumps, the ragged, gaping
fissures that ran for thousands of yards, the upheaval of
rocks that had become razor-sharp and weather-
pitted, the smooth flat surfaces of sinkholes said to be
bottomless and burrows that tunneled beneath the ruined surface and were said to house giant insects—made
Khyber Elessedil wonder if perhaps the Speakman's

prediction that none of them would return from this expedition was an accurate foretelling.

But she had come this far and would not turn back no matter how forbidding the land appeared, no matter the nature of the dangers that waited there, no matter her personal reservations. The lure of the Elfstones was too strong, the chance to recover so great a treasure overriding any thoughts of abandoning her quest. The Druids were equal to the task. Their magic and their experience would protect them.

No one other than Farshaun and herself knew of the Speakman's prediction. She had forbidden the old man from saying anything about it to the others and had instructed him to tell the Speakman the same. The musings of a seer were not always to be trusted, and even if his prediction were to come true it might do so in a way that was different from what it seemed on the surface. What mattered were his skills and experience as a guide, not his abilities as a seer.

So she told herself.

They had departed at sunrise. Before doing so, she had taken herself away from the others and, using her magic, called up anew the vision skived from Aphenglow's memory, so she could be certain of the landmarks she had been shown. In a deep trance, she saw again the familiar pinnacles of the Kensrowe and the blasted emptiness of the Breakline stretching ahead, then saw the triad of rock columns and beyond that the giant fissure gape open like a mouth that would swallow them all.

By the time she had returned to the others, the Speakman had come down from his cave to join them. Communicating only through Farshaun, he had signaled his readiness to proceed. Khyber let Farshaun act as interpreter, let him ask the Speakman the necessary questions and convey whatever answers were given. What she wanted was to make certain he concentrated his efforts on searching for the landmarks in Aphenglow's Elfstone vision.

So now they were under way, and in truth, she felt as if they were already halfway to their goal. They had passed the rock formation she had come to think of as the three sentinels—the trio situated in an open stretch of flatland, towering over their surroundings like guards at watch.

Khyber assigned Farshaun and the Speakman the task of spying out the huge fissure that was the next recognizable landmark in their search. Then she decided to follow up on the promise Pleysia had made to her days ago: to reveal the reason why she had chosen the girl Oriantha to accompany them. Either it had slipped Pleysia's mind or she had chosen to ignore it, but in either case it was time the promise be kept.

She found Pleysia and the young woman sitting alone amidships next to a pile of stores, once again deep in conversation. It was exactly how she had found them several days earlier, so deeply engaged it was as if no one else existed. She paused for a moment before approaching them, trying to imagine the nature of the relationship. On failing to do so, she walked over, whereupon, as before, all conversation came to an immediate halt.

"Pleysia," she greeted the Druid, nodding wordlessly to Oriantha. "You promised you would explain to me the reason behind Oriantha's selection for this expedition. Now is the time."

Pleysia sighed heavily and nodded. "I don't suppose I can put it off any longer. I hope you won't be angry with me, Mistress. Oriantha is a powerful and accomplished shape-shifter. She was born of a shape-shifting father and a magic-wielding mother who fell in love just long enough to conceive her before parting. None of it was meant to happen, but happen it did. And while the father disappeared and has not been seen or heard from since, the mother stayed close and saw to it that Oriantha was raised as she should be—even though she wasn't able to do this herself. Over time, Oriantha's shape-shifting ability began to manifest itself, and it became clear that she was gifted with both shape-shifting skills and select uses of magic."

She paused. "I had hoped to bring her to the order to apply for admission sometime in the next few years—even though I fully expected you and the others to refuse her. The order has never embraced the practice of allowing members of one family to serve the Druid Order at the same time."

Khyber nodded slowly. "Because the presence of one puts too much strain on the other and endangers them both. You are her mother, aren't you, Pleysia?"

Pleysia nodded. "Yes, Mistress."

"How is it that I've never even known she existed?"

"I've never discussed her with anyone. I kept that part of my life private. When I came to the order, I left her with my mother. She was five years old then. My mother raised her. I barely saw her during that time. I didn't know when I came to Paranor that Oriantha would inherit both her father's talent and my own. I suspected she had some ability, but did not realize how gifted she was. I should have been there to train her, but by then I had committed myself to the order and could do little. Mostly, she trained herself."

Khyber regarded her in silence for a moment. "You have broken the rules by bringing her on this expedition, Pleysia. Why did you do that? You knew it would be dangerous for her. Why did you choose to bring her to us now when you could have waited for a better time?"

The Elven Druid shook her head. "Mistress, please. I don't want to tell you that."

"If you don't, I will send Oriantha home at once," Khyber declared. She glanced over at the girl, who hadn't said a single word, but simply sat there, listening. "Oriantha, have you nothing to say?"

The girl's strong features tightened with resolve. "I came because I wanted to be with my mother. It was necessary for me to come."

"Did you know it was a clear violation of our rules?"

"My mother needed me."

"Is that what she told you? That she needed you? Did you come because you were asked or because you chose on your own to come?"

"Mistress," Pleysia broke in. "Let her be. She came because of something I said." She hesitated. "Because I told her I am dying."

It stopped Khyber where she was. Oriantha, this strong young woman who seemed chiseled from stone, had begun crying. Pleysia wrapped her arms around her and whispered in her ear.

"Dying?" the Ard Rhys said softly.

"I found out months ago. A healer told me. I am diseased within and there is no cure, not even with healing magic. I thought to be dead and gone before you woke from the Druid Sleep. I believed I could bring Oriantha to the Keep and, because I was dying, the other Druids would keep her until you woke. Then you might agree to accept her into the order. But then the diary was found, and I ran out of time."

She looked stricken, as if speaking the words gave power to the thing killing her. That she might be lying never entered Khyber's mind; the truth was mirrored in the faces of mother and daughter.

Pleysia released Oriantha and faced the Ard Rhys. "I know this is a dangerous journey. I understood what that meant. I went to her and I told her I was dying and there was a good chance I would not be coming back from this expedition. I asked her to wait for me, but she insisted she was coming with me. She said it was probably our last chance to be together. She did not want to give that up. She is a more gifted magic user than I am, and she was quick to remind me of it. If she could not go, neither could I, she argued. So I agreed to bring her with me."

Khyber sighed. Pleysia should have told her Oriantha was her daughter, but she understood why the Elven woman had kept it secret, fearful that her request to include Oriantha would be denied and the girl sent home. Knowing she was dying, she would be desperate to keep her daughter with her. Khyber questioned the wisdom of including her when she would be placed at such risk, but maybe Oriantha was more capable and experienced than her age would suggest.

She rose from where she was crouched beside them. "I am sorry this is happening to you, Pleysia. But I am worried for Oriantha."

"I will watch over her," Pleysia said at once.

"And I will watch over my mother," Oriantha added quickly. She hesitated. "Mistress, I am much stronger and better trained than you know. I can take care of myself and will not be a burden on anyone."

Pleysia nodded quickly. "I have witnessed this. She speaks the truth."

The determination she heard in their voices was convincing. It was too late to send the girl back anyway. They were too far out in the wilderness, and it would be too disruptive at this point to try to separate them.

"Oriantha can stay," she said.

Pleysia's smile in response was both bitter and sweet. "Thank you, Mistress. Thank you so much."

Oriantha murmured her thanks as well, leaning over to give her mother a kiss on her cheek.

Khyber nodded without saying anything further and walked away.

The day wore on and the *Walker Boh* continued its flight west. The weather was a strange mix of contradictions. Twice, sandstorms blew up from out of nowhere, huge windswept monsters that engulfed the airship in grit and dust and forced all aboard to hunker down with their eyes shielded, trusting that the vessel would find her way through. Three times it rained, each time hard and fierce, drenching everyone in spite of weatherproof gear, passing in minutes and moving on. Periods of haze enveloped the travelers and left them virtually blind as they flew with only a compass to point them in the right direction. Frequently, the Speakman had them change directions because of what he saw of the landscape below, and each time Khyber nodded her agreement, trusting that he would know what none of the others could.

It was nearing midday when they found the fissure shown in the Elfstone vision.

To say it was massive didn't begin to describe it. It was as if the entire earth had split apart, forming a chasm that stretched for miles in both directions. The fissure was black and filled with mist, and it emitted a haunting wail that reached the passengers and crew of the airship even as high up as they were, working through them like a nightmare's memory. The sides of the chasm were jagged, and there was no visible bottom. Where it began and ended was anyone's guess.

"Fifty miles long," the Speakman whispered.

"I believe it," said Farshaun. "What's making that sound?"

"The spirits of the dead."

Farshaun looked at him. "How would you know that? Have you been to the bottom and seen them?"

The Speakman gave him a look. "I have seen them in my dreams."

Redden and Railing were standing close enough to hear them, and exchanged a quick look. They peered over the side of the airship once more, tracking the split from one horizon to the other without finding an end.

"I hope we don't have to go down into that," Railing whispered to his brother, trying to be careful not to let any of the others hear.

"If we did, we'd probably come out on the other side of the world," Redden whispered back.

Farshaun stepped close. "If you did, you would probably find the spirits of the dead waiting to receive you." He snorted derisively. "Now, keep quiet."

The old man turned to Khyber. "We're close to the Fangs. Once there, we have to go on foot."

"We can't continue to fly?" The Ard Rhys was taken aback. "It's much safer if we remain aloft."

"Doesn't matter. We still have to go on foot." Farshaun walked away.

They flew on for two more hours, the morning drifting into afternoon. The weather changed once more, this time the skies turning hazy and overcast, the sun fading to a dull glow and a heavy mix of clouds and mist wrapping so tightly about the *Walker Boh* that Farshaun had to take her down to within a hundred feet of the ground just to see where they were. Additionally, he had to slow her to a crawl, afraid they would run into a cliff face or rock formation. At a dead-slow speed, they crept ahead until they encountered a wall of spiraling rock formations that speared skyward much higher than the hundred feet at which the airship flew and clustered so thickly they were impossible to sail between.

"The Fangs," the Speakman whispered.

Khyber Elessedil was standing close enough to hear. "How far do they stretch?"

"Miles," Farshaun answered after listening to the Speakman's whispered response.

"Can we sail around them?" She checked her compass. "We're flying west still. Can we turn north or south to get past?"

This time the Speakman addressed her directly, his insect body folding in on itself as he crouched down in the pilot box close to Farshaun. "You have to land the airship and walk. The marshland you look for is here."

Redden and Railing, still standing close enough to listen in, turned as Mirai came up beside them. "Grim land down there," she said. "It has the feel of a place that doesn't like visitors."

"Don't say things like that," Railing grumbled.

The Ard Rhys directed Farshaun to follow the Speakman's orders and set the airship down at the edge of the Fangs. The twins and Mirai could feel the descent begin as the Rover crew leapt up to work the light sheaths and radian draws. The mist seemed to thicken further as they dropped, closing in about them, wet and cloying against their skin. Mirai made a rude sound and wiped at her face.

No one was feeling particularly good about landing here.

When the airship was anchored and the rope ladders thrown over the side of the vessel, Khyber assembled everyone but the Druid Guard and the Rover crewmen on the aft deck. There were muted exchanges of comments and responses from those gathered as the Ard Rhys waited for them to get settled. More than a few gave worried glances at the forest of rock spears and mist serpents that formed a gloomy, shadowy wall ahead.

"We go on afoot from here," Khyber announced. "We'll take everyone but Farshaun, Mirai, and the Rover crewmen, who will stay to keep the *Walker Boh* safe for our return. Garroneck will choose six of his Druid Guards to remain behind, as well—an added precaution. The rest of us will enter the Fangs to search for a marshland. Once we've found it, we will decide what to do next. Are there questions?"

"I'll have to go, as well," Farshaun spoke up at once. "The Speakman won't go without me. Mirai and my Rovers are perfectly capable of caring for the airship without me."

Redden, standing close to Mirai, expected the Rover girl to object to being left behind. Staying close to the twins was one of the reasons she had been allowed to come. But to his surprise, she didn't say a word.

"Very well, Farshaun," the Ard Rhys agreed. "You come, as well."

She dismissed them to gather their equipment and weapons and meet on the ground in thirty minutes.

Redden glanced at the overcast sky, noted the position of the sun, and decided they had less than four hours of light remaining. He glanced again at Mirai, who was looking away, and then at Railing.

His brother shrugged. "I don't like it, either. Should we say something to her?"

Redden shook his head.

Thirty minutes later, the search party set out. With the Speakman and Khyber Elessedil leading the way, they pushed ahead into the forest of stone columns and within minutes could no longer see the ship and its occupants. Right away Redden felt uncomfortable with the size of the search party. It was too large and too unwieldy, an opinion he shared with his brother but otherwise kept to himself. Presumably the Ard Rhys knew what she was doing, and if she thought they needed twenty-odd people it wasn't his place to start criticizing. What Redden didn't like was the way they were spread out, so far apart as they picked their way through the maze of rock formations that those on the opposite wings of the loose formation often could not see one another.

Reacting to his instincts, he moved Railing and himself into the center of the search.

The group slogged its collective way through the Fangs for more than two hours, wending slowly through clusters of rock spears and wispy trailers of mist. No one spoke in anything other than a whisper and then only infrequently. The Trolls, by duty and nature guardians and protectors, positioned themselves at the perimeters of the advance. With the Ard Rhys at the forefront, the other Druids split apart so that Seersha was on the right wing, Carrick on the left, and Pleysia trailing. Skint was in the forefront with Khyber, where he could put his tracking skills to use, and the warrior Dwarf Chieftain Crace Coram was only a few steps behind. Oriantha stayed close to Pleysia. Redden and Railing had been placed in the middle of the assemblage, surrounded by protectors. All eyes constantly scanned the haze; all ears were pricked for any sounds that warned of danger.

They were deep into the Fangs and beginning to feel numbed by the strain of watching and waiting for something to happen when the insects attacked them.

The swarm came out of nowhere. The buzzing of wings was the only warning anyone got, and then the creatures were on top of them, biting and stinging. The insects were the size of large birds and quick to avoid all attempts at swatting them away. The Druids threw up various forms of magic to drive them off, but with the company scattered it was impossible to protect everyone at once. Redden and Railing stood back-to-back defending themselves with the magic of the wishsong, turning leaves and twigs into flying shards of metal that twisted and cut at their attackers. They downed a few, but there were hundreds in the swarm, their numbers darkening what little sky was visible overhead. The air filled with their buzzing.

Then someone began screaming, and the confusion of the attack reached new levels. Over to the left of where they stood fighting off the insects, the twins heard earth and rocks grinding together. Redden caught a glimpse of one of the Trolls tumbling from sight into a hole that had opened in the ground. He saw Farshaun reach for him, grab hold of his arm, try to pull him back, and fail. The Troll tumbled away, thrashing. Then the hole closed over again with a terrible crunching sound, and the Troll was gone.

Other holes began to open all around them, jagged fissures running six to ten feet long. Redden yanked Railing away from one that yawned right next to them just as his brother lost his balance and began to teeter on the edge. The fissures were actually moving like the jaws of an animal, working their ragged mouths back and forth.

Skint surged through the middle of the struggling members of the company, leaping the hungry mouths, yelling as he went.

"Procks!" he screamed. "Get out of here!"

Members of the company were already falling back, moving out of the area of attack as swiftly as they could manage. Pleysia, the girl Oriantha, a couple of the Trolls, and Crace Coram led the way. Khyber Elessedil, still fighting off swarms of giant insects, backed away last. With the insects in pursuit, everyone began a ragged retreat, swatting at their winged attackers while trying to stay clear of the Procks.

Redden and Railing had heard about Procks from the Rovers. Found mostly in the mountains of the Eastland, they surfaced in communities hundreds strong. They were living rock, an impossibility given life through a magic long since lost and forgotten. They swallowed anything that came within reach, catching hold of the unwary and chewing their victims to pieces even as they struggled to free themselves.

The company kept fighting off the snapping mouths, struggling to reach safe ground while avoiding the lethal stings and bites of the insects. It took longer than it should have, and both twins were exhausted by the time they had gone far enough that they could consider themselves safe.

Farshaun plopped down beside them, winded and red-faced. His arms and face were swollen with stings and bites, and there was blood on his hands. "Did you see what happened to that Troll? His leg went down into a Prock's mouth, and that was it. Skint and I tried to pull him free, but it was no use. Once they've got you, there's no getting away."

"I didn't think there were any Procks in the Westland," Railing said, wiping sweat from his face and finding blood, as well. "I thought they were only in the Ravenshorn."

Farshaun gave him a look. "There's everything out here in the Breakline. Everything you don't want to find."

The other members of the company had worked their way free of the Prock community by now, and the flying insects had broken off their attack and flown back to wherever they had come from. Close by where the twins were huddled with Farshaun, Khyber Elessedil was confronting the Speakman.

"Why didn't you warn us?" she demanded of him. "Why didn't you say something?"

The Speakman, matchstick arms and legs collapsed against his scarecrow body, looked at her as if he had never seen her before. His voice was surprisingly soft. "How could I warn you? I never saw those things before. Any of them. Last time I was here, they weren't."

Farshaun came up and crouched beside him. "Speakman. Did you say they were new? But that isn't possible. Things don't change out here. You know that."

"I know. But they have."

Redden and Railing inched closer to listen in.

"How many did we lose?" Farshaun asked the Ard Rhys.

She shook her head in disgust, her brow furrowing. "Only the one you couldn't save. We were lucky it wasn't more. But we can't have this happen again. We need the Speakman to warn us. He lives out here! He has to sense these things or we'll be decimated before we find anything!"

She kept her voice low, but the force of her words was unmistakable. Farshaun looked over at the Speakman, who nodded silently. "He'll do the best he can," the old man assured her.

"Let's hope so," she said, her eyes fixed on his. "Because at dawn tomorrow we're going to try this again."

26

Khyber Elessedil did not speak to any of them again that day save for Farshaun. She knew she had become obsessed with finding the missing Elfstones and had reached a point where almost nothing else mattered. She hated seeing anyone die, but she had already accepted it as inevitable, given the nature of the dangers they faced. What she hated most was not being sufficiently prepared for the bad things they would encounter, so she had made up her mind that they would be ready on the morrow for anything.

How she would accomplish this was not entirely clear, but she knew to begin by speaking at length with Farshaun about making the Speakman look harder for what might be lying in wait.

Farshaun was obliging, but he insisted the Speakman was already doing all he could, and it was obvious something was happening in the Fangs that was as new to him as it was to the rest of them. If he had never encountered these dangers before—didn't even know they were there—Farshaun didn't think there was much the Speakman could do about searching them out now. Perhaps she would do well to put Skint and Seersha at the forefront to help him. Their tracking and wilderness skills were probably the equal of his own, and even if they didn't know the country they could use their instincts and experience to intuit dangers as well as he could.

Khyber agreed, although none of this gave her reason to feel confident about the Speakman. She was using him out of necessity, not because she thought he was up to what was being asked of him. He was clearly fragile emotionally, and his reclusive life did not suggest he would function well in this larger community, no matter the importance of his presence.

But she had no choice in the matter. She needed a guide, and he was the best she had.

She put aside her ponderings over the fitness of the Speakman long enough to wonder if she should ask the Ohmsford twins to use the magic of their wishsong to help to provide protection for the company, as well. But she was loath to put them at further risk. She was mindful of her promise to herself, as much as to Sarys, to do her best to protect the twins, and she intended to keep it.

Besides, after today, anyone on the expedition with magic skills would be using them without her having to tell them.

She had taken the search party all the way back to the *Walker Boh*, unwilling to risk having them spend the night in the open after today's encounter. Better to start fresh in the morning, even if it meant covering some of the same ground twice. She went to bed early, more tired than she had realized.

As she lay rolled up in her blanket on the decks of the airship, listening to the singing of the wind as it blew through the radian draws, an unpleasant feeling that something was very wrong began to creep over her. She couldn't put her finger on exactly what it was, only that it was there and seemed uncomfortably familiar. She pondered it until she fell asleep—a long, slow process—but was not able to pinpoint its source.

By morning, she had forgotten the matter, and with the same members of the expedition she had chosen for yesterday's search party—plus another of Garroneck's Trolls to replace the one they had lost—she set out again. She had decided they would choose a new starting point and find a different route in, hopefully avoiding the Procks and flying insects by doing so. To accomplish this, she had Farshaun fly the *Walker Boh* south for several miles to a place the Speakman claimed he knew well enough to anticipate any dangers—if, he was quick to add, nothing had changed. He relayed all this through Farshaun, no longer willing to speak to her directly. He was still traumatized by Khyber's reaction of the previous day and frightened that he might disappoint her again, Farshaun told her in confidence. He warned her again that the Speakman's emotional state was uncertain. If she wanted his help she would have to be gentle with him.

She didn't like Farshaun speaking to her in such a way, and now she was worried that the Speakman wasn't stable enough to be relied on. But she had few options in the matter, so she had to try to find a balance between caution and insistence.

When they left the airship this time, they found themselves in hill country. The Fangs still formed a deep wall in front of them, but now they were confronted with rolling terrain riven by deep gullies that looked to have once been riverbeds. This day, like the previous, was misty and clouded over, the sun and sky completely hidden, the air thick with brume. She kept the members of the company close together as they entered the Fangs, with the Druids interspersed throughout the line of march. She led the way with Farshaun and the Speakman and had Seersha and Crace Coram provide a rearguard.

Everyone was told to keep close watch.

Redden and Railing, once again placed in the middle, gave each other a knowing glance. The wishsong, while versatile, wasn't much good at detecting danger, and their experience with this sort of thing was pretty limited.

"Hope she's not counting on us," Redden murmured to his brother, who simply nodded in reply.

This day's trek through the Fangs was very similar to that of the day before, but more draining physically. Going up and down hills as they wound through the maze of stone formations required more effort, and even though they could see no sources of moisture, the air was oddly thick. The farther in they went, the heavier it got. No one was saying much, and when they did it was whispered and short. Even Redden and Railing, normally comfortable with sharing their thoughts and making wry comments, remained silent, concentrating on putting one foot in front of the other.

Twice in the next four hours Khyber allowed the company to take short rests. Each time she spoke to the Speakman through Farshaun, reassuring herself that everything was all right and nothing unusual was in evidence. The Speakman indicated through nods and gestures to Farshaun that this was so.

Nevertheless, she was uneasy. She had discovered about two hours into the Fangs that her compass had quit working. She believed they could find their way out if they needed to even without the Speakman's help, but she could not be certain in which direction they were going. There were few markers in this wilderness by which to track their forward progress and none to make their way back save those they made themselves. The perpetually haze-clouded sky would not let her read clearly the position of the sun during the day or the stars at night. Everything looked exactly the same. Even after hours of walking she couldn't be certain which was forward and which was back. She couldn't even be certain they weren't going in a circle.

The Speakman had reassured Farshaun they were maintaining a straight line and approaching the edges of the marshland she was seeking. But her confidence in the recluse's abilities, already badly eroded, had not improved. His disturbing behavior alone was sufficient to cause her doubts. He had begun to mutter to himself, nodding and shaking his head, gesturing with his hands and addressing the ground in front of him as he walked. He shambled as if his balance was off, and he hugged himself. Sometimes he cried. When she looked at Farshaun for an explanation, the Rover just shrugged. This was the way the Speakman was, he seemed to be saying.

Worse still was the hermit's insistence on saying things that suggested it didn't matter what they did because they were all doomed. He said them only to Farshaun, but she was frequently present when he did. It was unnerving at best. She didn't believe it, didn't think for a moment that he knew what was going to happen from one minute to the next. But the constant repetition of the prophecy was wearing on her, and she asked him to stop saying it.

But he couldn't seem to help himself, even after Farshaun spoke to him, so she let it go.

The slog through the Fangs wore on. By now they had been walking for the better part of six hours, and while nothing had attacked and no obvious dangers had threatened, time was slipping away and they still hadn't found the marshland they were searching for.

Then suddenly the smell and texture of the air changed; there was a fresh dampness to it and a fetid scent. She glanced down and saw that the hard rocky earth had muddied in places; hints of what had recently been standing water were visible. She caught up to Farshaun and touched his shoulder.

He turned, saw the questioning look on her face, and nodded. "We're close now, Mistress. The marshland should be just ahead."

They continued through a fresh cluster of rock formations, finding swamp grasses and trees strung with moss more gray than green filling the gaps between. The way forward became clogged with vegetation and required more effort to pass through. The edges of the marshland appeared in stagnant ponds and long fingers of weedy swamp that angled about like snakes. There were still no signs of life except for the steady hum and click of insects that only showed themselves in momentary bursts.

Everyone was on edge now. Before, they had seen nothing but blasted rock and rutted earth. Now there were plants and trees with hints of color in the foliage and grasses and dampness, and the tedium of their earlier trek gave way to heightened wariness. The improvement in the look of the terrain should have had a heartening effect, but the abruptness of the shift was unnerving.

Khyber called a halt and walked away from the others a few paces, again going into a deep trance to recall accurately the images skived from Aphenglow's mind. She settled herself, her breathing slowed, her magic surfaced in an enfolding haze that wrapped her close, and the vision replayed itself in slow motion behind her eyes.

There should be mountains, she remembered.

She opened her eyes, rose, and glanced all around. But the rock formations and heavy undergrowth blocked her view. She was down too low to see anything. She needed to get to a higher place. She needed to climb something.

She shook her head at the idea; she was older now, and had limitations.

"Skint!" she called to the Gnome Tracker, and the

others in the search party drifted over, as well. "Can you climb one of these rock formations? Or maybe one of these trees?"

"Not the trees," the Speakman blurted out at once. He cringed at the sound of his own voice, looking for Farshaun, moving over next to him. "No one should climb the trees," he whispered.

Skint was studying the nearby rock formations. "I don't know. There's not much in the way of handholds."

"I can do it." Railing Ohmsford stepped forward eagerly. "Redden and I both, if you want."

Redden appeared beside him, giving him a look. "You brought grippers?"

Railing nodded. "Do you want us to try?" he asked the Ard Rhys.

Khyber Elessedil managed to keep from grinning at his obvious eagerness. "One of you will do."

"Then I'll go. It was my idea." He dropped his backpack and began rummaging through it. "There's nothing to it, really. Redden and I do it at home all the time with tougher climbs than this one."

Moments later he produced a strange pair of gloves and boots that had the appearance of animal paws. He sat down and slipped them over his bare hands and feet, then flexed his fingers and toes and walked over to the closest formation.

"See you at the top," he declared, and began climbing the tower as if he were a squirrel going up a tree. His gloves gripped the rock face effortlessly, finding purchase even on the most vertical of surfaces. Using his booted feet for leverage and balance, he shimmied his way to the top—something close to a hundred feet—in a matter of minutes.

"Now what?" he called down to Khyber.

She shook her head in amusement. "Do you see any mountains?"

He took a moment to look around. "I don't see much of anything but clouds and mist and the tips of these rock pillars. There's a big body of water to our right—I can see bits and pieces of that."

He stopped talking, continuing to look. The other members of the expedition waited expectantly. Khyber was already thinking of which direction they should take if no mountains appeared.

"Wait!" Railing called out suddenly. "I see them. A cluster of big, narrow peaks, off to our left. The mist was hiding them. A few miles off, over there." He pointed.

The Ard Rhys took note. "Good work. You can come down now."

Railing engaged in a controlled slide that brought him back to the ground. He took off the boots and gloves and started to stuff them back into his pack, then noticed the way Skint was eyeing them and handed them over. "Here. You take them. Redden and I have another pair."

Skint accepted the grippers, nodded his thanks, and immediately began to examine them.

They set out again on a course for the mountains. Their march took them west and north along the fringes of the marsh over terrain sufficiently level that climbing hills was no longer required but dodging quicksand and sinkholes was. The mix of rock formations and heavy brush and trees continued to plague their progress, and Khyber was aware that the members of the expedition were again spreading out to find passage, getting farther away from one another. She called them in twice, but the problem persisted.

She was just about to call them in a third time when the party was attacked.

* * *

At first, Redden didn't see their attackers but only heard
them. Growls and snarls and something that approached
screaming shattered the quiet, and then the creatures
were charging the expedition from everywhere at once.
The Druids, positioned on the four sides of the company, struck back, fire lancing from fingers and staffs
and slamming into the attackers. They moved like
dancers as they shifted their attacks from one creature
to the next, never staying in one place for more than a
few seconds. The fire was resilient and sharp-edged,
and it both cut and shredded when it struck its targets.
But the creatures attacking were too many, and the
Druids could stop only a few. The rest got past them
and went for those at the center of the group.

Redden, standing back-to-back with his brother once
more, summoned the wishsong, singing the magic to
life, modulating his voice to shape it, creating out of
particles in the air hundreds of sharpened bits of metal
that whizzed about like tiny hornets and cut at the
attackers as they launched themselves at the pair, either
stopping them altogether or causing them to veer away.
Redden caught only brief glimpses of what they were up
against—small, hunched over versions of Spider
Gnomes covered in bristling hair. Hideous to look at,
faces twisted and misshapen, they darted in and away
again with terrifying ferocity, little more than swift and
agile blurs possessed of teeth and claws.

Brief images of the struggle flashed through his mind
as he fought to protect himself. He saw one of the Trolls
stagger and fall, the creatures all over him, teeth buried
in his thick hide. At the forefront of the advance, Khyber Elessedil and Garroneck fought to protect themselves, as well as Farshaun and the Speakman. Carrick
went down, the little monsters tearing and ripping at
his body. But blue fire exploded from the pile in a mas-

sive burst that threw the attackers off, and abruptly the Druid was on his feet again.

Then Redden caught sight of the girl Pleysia had brought with her, the one no one knew anything about. There was only just enough of her left to recognize: she had transformed into something else entirely. Grown suddenly larger and leaner, she ripped through the creatures that came at her like a huge moor cat, tearing them apart as they sought to bring her down. She flung them away with fingers suddenly become wicked claws, and her snarls were more dreadful than those of her attackers. The boy got only a quick look before he was back to fighting for his own life, but it was enough to tell him there was a great deal more to this girl than what had appeared on the surface.

Finally the creatures fell back, disappearing into the undergrowth as swiftly as they had come. The members of the company pulled themselves together, ripped and bloodied and exhausted. But everyone was still standing and ready to fight again, something that Redden was certain was going to be necessary.

The Ard Rhys pointed ahead. "There's an escarpment at the lower end of those peaks!" She was breathing hard, gasping out her words. "If we make it that far and find a way up, they won't be able to get at us so easily! Now run!"

The members of the company charged forward in a tangled knot, ignoring wounds and weariness, eyes fixed on their goal. It became visible in moments, a broad shelf stretching for several hundred yards. They saw, as well, a trail leading up. All they needed was five minutes.

They didn't get it. The creatures came at them again, hordes of them, intent on trying to drag down their quarry from behind. Trailing as rearguard and closest to the pursuit, Seersha wheeled back and used her magic to throw up a wall of fire between themselves and their pursuers, igniting everything from stone to water to bare earth with crackling flames. But the creatures shifted their angle of attack and began coming at them from the flanks. A running battle ensued, terrible and vicious. Another of the Trolls went down and disappeared, then another. Javelins and clubs flew into their midst as the attackers tried to cripple the defenders. Screams and howls rose from all around, omnipresent and pervasive. So quick and elusive were their assailants that Redden found himself experiencing the strange sensation of fighting against things that could appear and disappear at will.

They had almost reached the base of the escarpment and the narrow trail that wound to its top when a club thrown from the left caught Railing just below the knee and sent him sprawling with a scream of pain. Redden was next to him at once, standing over him protectively, using the wishsong to whisk stones from the rocky ground in a whirlwind that sent the deadly missiles flying out in all directions to ward off the claws and teeth that would tear both his brother and himself apart. His attackers kept coming at them anyway, but he would not leave Railing. No matter what, he would not leave his brother.

Panicked and overwhelmed by superior numbers, he could not manage to stop them all. He fought back with everything he could muster, but his strength was beginning to fail him. Abruptly the creatures were on him, knocking him backward, flattening him against the earth.

It would have been the end of him if not for Crace Coram. The burly Dwarf Chieftain appeared out of nowhere, flinging the creatures aside, swings of his huge mace breaking heads and shattering bones in a furious counterattack. The voracious creatures scattered in the face of such fury, and for a second the entire assault collapsed. Without pausing, Coram scooped up Railing, threw him over his shoulder as if he weighed nothing, and charged after the others, with Redden close on his heels.

The members of the company scrambled up the winding pathway, hunching their shoulders as darts, javelins, and clubs flew all around them. Some of their attackers gave pursuit, daring to follow them up the pathway, heedless of the withering Druid Fire launched by Khyber Elessedil and Carrick from the escarpment. But when the last members of the company were safely off the trail and onto the heights, the creatures quickly turned back, skittering down the slope and disappearing into the brush and grasses.

Crace Coram lowered Railing to the ground, knelt next to him, and began to examine his leg. The boy was grimacing in pain, doing his best not to cry out as the Dwarf's fingers moved carefully over his injury.

"Leg's fractured," the Dwarf declared after a moment. "Bone has to be reset." He looked over at Redden, who was kneeling across from him. "Hold his shoulders. Skint, grab his other leg."

Both did as they were asked. Redden, knowing what was coming, closed his eyes and gritted his teeth in anticipation. Coram placed his hands carefully on the boy's damaged leg and gave a quick, hard pull. Railing screamed once and fainted.

The Dwarf nodded to Redden and Skint to let go, and then he climbed to his feet. "He needs to have splints strapped to keep the bones in place. Find some lengths of wood."

Skint went off across the escarpment toward the cliffs and a scattering of trees backed up against the foothills. Redden felt his brother's forehead, and glanced up at Crace Coram. "Thanks."

The Dwarf nodded. "Keep him still until that leg is splinted and bound good and tight. Shouldn't be hard. He won't wake for a while."

Khyber Elessedil came over to make certain the Ohmsford twins were being attended to, giving Redden a wan smile and a touch of her hand on his shoulder. Redden glanced around at the company, all of whom were either on watch at the edge of the escarpment or binding one another's wounds. He counted heads and found two of the Druid Guard missing. Everyone else seemed to have made it clear.

Then he caught sight of the Speakman, who was hunched over, rocking back and forth and moaning softly. Farshaun knelt close, trying to soothe him and at the same time shield him from the others. He wasn't having much luck with either.

"There's no backbone in that one," the boy heard Pleysia mutter as she walked past him, stone-faced. Oriantha followed in her wake, head lowered. The girl had returned to normal, the lethal fury and bestial savagery gone. She caught Redden looking at her, and he turned away quickly.

The boy was still sitting beside his brother when Farshaun came over and knelt next to them. "How is he?"

"His leg's broken. Crace Coram rescued us both."

"The Dwarf's a warrior. We could use a few more like him." Farshaun glanced over at the Speakman, who was still whimpering, balled up in a knot to hide his face. "I think we've lost our guide. He's become completely unhinged by this."

"Can you help him?"

"Not if I keep him here, I can't. I have to take him back." He glanced down at Railing. "Your brother, too, I expect. He can't go any farther."

He got up and returned to the Speakman before Redden could ask him how they could possibly expect anyone to transport Railing back through such dangerous country. He would have to be carried out, and given what they had already experienced, that seemed impossible.

Skint had been gone a long time, long enough that Khyber Elessedil began to inquire after him, having not seen him since he departed in search of splints for Railing's leg. Gathering those should have taken no more than ten or fifteen minutes, and it was well past that when he reappeared, approaching at a fast trot. Coming over to Redden, he handed him the splints, breathing hard.

"Can you do this without me? The splints go here, here, and here." He pointed out each place and handed the boy some strips of cloth that he had stuffed in his carry bag. "Use these to bind him up."

Then he turned to Khyber, who had walked over to join them. "I've found something," he announced, eyes bright and eager. "Right back there, between those cliffs. I don't know what it is exactly, but I think you should see it for yourself."

The Ard Rhys frowned. "You don't know what it is? What does it look like?"

"A waterfall."

27

LEAVING SEVERAL OF THE TROLLS FROM THE DRUID
Guard to keep watch at the edge of the escarpment,
Khyber Elessedil gathered together the remaining members of the expedition. When she noticed Redden
Ohmsford still sitting by his brother, she called him
over, as well. She could detect the reluctance mirrored
on his face, but she had already made up her mind he
was needed.

She was energized by Skint's discovery while at the
same time reluctant to act on it immediately. She had
hoped she might be able to give her followers a little
more time to recover from the attack they had just
fought off before setting out again. Everyone was worn
down, and many were injured. They hadn't eaten or
drunk anything since that morning save what they had
managed during their abbreviated stops. Sunset was
only a few hours away, and a night's sleep would help
everyone.

On the other hand, they were at constant risk in this
country, and that wasn't going to change. Several of the
party were already dead, and unless they moved quickly
more might soon join them. They needed to get this
business over and done with. These attacks troubled
her. The creatures they were encountering were unfa-

miliar. She should have been able to identify them, but couldn't. Even the Speakman, who had been living in this country for many years, claimed not to have seen them before. If that was so, why were they seeing them now?

Something felt very wrong.

She made her decision. The enigmatic waterfall was just a short distance off. Delay in their advance meant risking another attack, and the best way to avoid that was to keep moving. If they could solve the mystery of the waterfall today, they would be able to start out fresh in the morning toward the completion of their search for the missing Elfstones.

They were close, she sensed. They needed to go on.

How much of this was sound reasoning and how much wishful thinking was difficult for her to determine. She understood that many of her decisions so far had been driven by her belief that finding the Stones was of overriding importance. It was a conviction that persisted even in the absence of concrete evidence—a certainty born of faith and instinct and a lifetime of experience dealing with magic.

"The waterfall is close," she told those assembled. "I want us to investigate it now, not tomorrow. I think we need to move as quickly as we can, given what's happened so far. We are at constant risk, and the more time we take to complete this search, the greater that risk becomes."

She looked from face to face. "So this is what we will do. Seersha will remain here with Railing Ohmsford, Farshaun Req, and the Speakman. Two of my Druid Guard will stay with them. The rest of us will continue to the waterfall. We will explore it before it gets dark and then either bring the others to join us or come back here. Tomorrow, we will decide who continues on this journey and who goes back."

No one voiced any objection, and no one offered a comment on her decision. She would have felt better about it if someone had. But not even Pleysia, usually so contentious, had anything to say.

She dismissed them for a short rest before setting out and went immediately after Redden Ohmsford, catching up to him before he could reach his brother.

"Walk with me," she asked him.

She moved him away from the others so they were alone. She noted the strain on his young face as she considered how much she should tell him now and how much she should keep for later.

"Your brother will have to be sent back," she said, deciding that it was best to be direct. "He can't keep up with the rest of us, and I can't risk injury to others by asking them to carry him. You understand this, don't you?"

He shook his head. "I don't want to leave him."

"I know. But I need you more than he does."

She saw the confusion mirrored in his eyes. "I have to stay with my brother. I have to look out for him."

"I can't let you do that. I need you to come with me. Remember what I told you when I came to Bakrabru? Allanon's shade insisted a member of the Ohmsford family must come on this expedition. That was what brought me looking for you in the first place. That requirement hasn't changed. I need one of you with me, Redden. Railing can't come any farther. It has to be you."

He started to object, but she silenced him by lifting her hand to his face. "I spoke privately with Mirai on that first day after I decided to leave her behind. I gave her one of two coins. If I require help, I need only break my coin in half; her coin will shatter, as well, and she will know to fly the *Walker Boh* to me. The coin will show her the way. She knows she can get word to me in the same way, by breaking her coin in half, should help be needed. As soon as we return from exploring the waterfall, I will summon Mirai and have Railing flown out along with Farshaun and the Speakman. He will be safe then. But the rest of us might not be if you don't agree to stay here with us."

She could tell he was unhappy with this, but again she had no choice. She couldn't risk losing both of them when she was so close to her goal. He must be made to understand this.

Apparently, he did. He nodded reluctantly. "I'll come. I just want to be sure Railing is safe."

"You have my word," she told him.

But she could tell from the look on his face he wasn't convinced.

Thirty minutes later the diminished expedition set out for the waterfall with Skint leading the way. Redden glanced back once at his brother, who was still unconscious. He hadn't tried to wake him, thinking it better not to. Perhaps he would be back before Railing woke. Farshaun had agreed to make sure his brother was kept safe. Knowing Railing was with Farshaun made all the difference. Redden didn't think he could have left his brother otherwise.

Even so, he felt uneasy about separating from him. First it was Mirai, now Railing. They had come on this journey as a team, friends and more, promising to watch out for one another. It was one thing to become separated from Mirai, but Railing? He found himself contemplating what it meant not to have his twin with him. Redden might be the one who was most likely to take the lead, but they were always together. He was going to have to work hard to remind himself that his brother wasn't there.

He wasn't sure how he would handle that.

I won't be gone that long, Redden promised himself. *This won't take more than an hour or two.*

The company reached the beginning of the woods and followed Skint into the trees. Now Redden had a clearer view of the cliffs and could see how the peaks were jammed together in a series of jagged spikes very likely formed by a cataclysmic upheaval in the distant past. The cliffs appeared to form an impassable wall, an impression that became more of a certainty as they exited the woods and found themselves at their base.

Skint pointed. "Over there. I wouldn't have seen it at all if I hadn't been searching for wood to make the boy's splints and caught a glimpse of its reflection."

Redden looked, but didn't see anything.

But Skint was already moving away with Khyber Elessedil right on his heels, leading the company around a cluster of boulders to where a narrow split opened into the rugged face of one of the larger cliffs, a shadowed opening that caught just enough of the misty light filtering down from the heavily overcast sky to illuminate a shimmering ribbon wedged within the rock. Redden squinted, trying to decide what he was looking at. The ribbon had the look of a waterfall, and yet it didn't seem as if that was what it was. Everyone studied it for a few minutes, but no one was able to decide.

Redden moved a few steps closer, up to where the Ard Rhys was standing with Skint and Garroneck.

"I still can't make out what that is," the Gnome was saying.

"Nor I," she answered him.

"I don't like this, Mistress," the big Troll rumbled. "It doesn't feel right."

Redden didn't like it, either. He glanced around at the others, and on most faces found a mix of uneasiness and uncertainty.

"Let's have a closer look," the Ard Rhys announced.

The members of the company moved forward with Pleysia and Oriantha bringing up the rear, watching over their shoulders for anything that might be coming up on them from behind. The advance was stealthy and cautious, and no one spoke as they neared the shimmer. Shadows closed about them, cast by the high walls of the split. A peculiar positioning of the shimmer within the wedge allowed sunlight to play over it even when it seemed to reach no other place within the gloom. Redden tried to fathom how this was possible but failed to find an answer.

Khyber walked right up to the glittering light with Skint and Garroneck close behind. It was clear by then, even to Redden who was near the back of those assembled, that the shimmer was not water but light that gave the appearance of water. The Ard Rhys motioned for everyone to stay back as she studied the light, then probed it with magic conjured through a series of intricate hand movements.

When she had finished her examination and was apparently satisfied with what she had discovered, she looked back at her followers and said, "Magic made this, but I can't identify its source. It doesn't appear to be harmful, but I will have to test it to be certain. Everyone will wait here while I do."

When Garroneck muttered what must have been an objection, she added. "Yes, that includes you."

Without hesitating, she stepped into the shimmer and disappeared.

The wait for her return went on for long minutes. Twice, Garroneck started for the light, and twice Carrick caught his arm and shook his head firmly. No one knew what the light would do to anyone entering. It might not even take those entering to the same place. Redden tried to see what lay on the other side, but he could only make out rock walls and clustered shadows.

The reappearance of the Ard Rhys was both sudden and startling. She emerged from the shimmer all at once, her black cloak wrapped close.

The members of the company immediately crowded close to hear what she had to say.

"The light opens into a tunnel," she told them. "The tunnel winds through rock walls I could not see, but could feel when I stretched out my arms. The tunnel ends at a second shimmer—like this one but much darker and more resistant when I passed through it. On the other side is country similar to what we have here— bleak and empty and gray. I took time to look around and see if anything dangerous waited, but nothing showed itself. Nothing threatened me while I was in the tunnel, either. I think we should go through now and have a look around and then decide if we want to make camp there rather than here. I've tagged the opening so that we can find our way back."

This time there was heated discussion. A handful of those in the company, chief among them Garroneck, thought it would be better to stay where they were until morning and then send a small party back through the tunnel for a closer look around. Most of the others wanted to continue now rather than wait.

Redden kept silent, even though he believed they should rethink the whole business. He didn't like what he was feeling, and his instincts were seldom wrong when it came to making choices like this one. He wondered if anyone else was feeling this way besides the handful who had already spoken. He glanced from face to face.

To his surprise, he found Oriantha watching him. She gave him a brief nod. She knew what he was looking for.

Before he could decide whether to approach her, Khyber Elessedil announced that they were going into the tunnel, all of them save for Skint, who would take Khyber's coin and return to let the others know what was happening. If they weren't back by nightfall, Seersha was to use the coin to summon Mirai and the *Walker Boh*. Railing, Farshaun, and the Speakman would be flown back out immediately, and Seersha and Skint would wait for the company's return. Skint objected heatedly to being chosen, pointing out that he was the one best equipped to act as guide for the company. But his arguments did not change Khyber's mind, so off he went, trudging back down the defile.

Khyber waited until he was gone and then turned to the others. "Stay close together. Don't let the darkness confuse you. Put a hand on the shoulder of the person in front of you if necessary. But I don't want lights of any kind, real or magic. We don't know what that might draw, and I don't want to find out the hard way. It takes about five minutes to go through. We can do it in the dark."

"You stay in front of me, boy," Crace Coram said quietly, leaning close to Redden. "I'll watch your back."

They went through the bright shimmer and into the darkness beyond in a long line. Redden felt the Dwarf Chieftain's hand resting on his shoulder and kept his own on the back of the Troll who was walking just in front of him. It was impossible to see anything; the tunnel's gloom was impenetrable. Navigating the blackness of the passageway seemed to take forever, but nothing happened to them as they moved through.

They reached the second shimmer, this one considerably darker and more resistant to their approach. It was as if it had a thicker substance; they could feel it pressing against them as they attempted to breach it.

"Keep going!" Khyber shouted back to them. "Push ahead!"

They did so, heads lowered against the membrane of gloom resisting them.

They emerged from the tunnel's darkness through an opening in a huge mound of boulders, blinking against a heavy wash of gray light, and found themselves in country that replicated what they had just left behind. Redden glanced over his shoulder—past Crace Coram, Pleysia, Oriantha, and another Troll—but he found no sign of the peaks they had passed through. There were peaks, but they were far in the distance and huge, spread out across the horizon behind him in a massive wall. He looked up at a sky shrouded in mist and gloom and could find no trace of the sun. He tried to orient himself from what he remembered of the Westland wilderness they had flown over. But he knew so little of this part of the world that it proved impossible. His best guess was that what he was seeing were the mountains of the Breakline.

The rest of the company was looking around, as well. None of its members seemed able to orient. Redden was reminded that the Ard Rhys had brought no one with them who had any personal knowledge of the country. Both Farshaun and the Speakman had been left behind.

"We won't want to go much farther than this without someone who knows what they are doing."

Oriantha was standing right next to him, bending close, her voice too soft for anyone else to hear.

"That's what I think, too," he replied.

She nodded. "I know. I saw it in your face. Your instincts are as sharp as mine." She glanced around. "I don't think anyone else sees things like we do. Not even my mother."

Then she was gone, drifting back to where Pleysia was engaged in a discussion with Carrick, the two of them arguing quietly, but vehemently. Redden wondered about her again. *Not even my mother,* she had said. Had he heard correctly? Had she just told him that Pleysia was her mother?

The Trolls had all clustered to one side, where Garroneck was speaking to them privately. Carrick and Pleysia were still arguing, with Oriantha looking on. Crace Coram had walked up to the Ard Rhys. Redden was standing alone now, studying his bleak surroundings, when the dark shimmer through which they had just passed—along with the cluster of huge boulders that framed the opening from which it hung suspended—disappeared.

For a second, Redden just kept staring at the space the shimmer and rocks had occupied, waiting for it to reappear, certain it would, convinced it must. When it didn't, he felt a hot surge of panic sweep through him.

In the next instant, the dragon attacked.

It dropped out of the sky without a sound and no warning save for the enveloping black shadow of its descent. It was easily the biggest creature Redden had ever seen, and while he had never come face-to-face with a dragon he knew what it was. Studded with horns and ridged with spines, its body was covered in black scales encrusted with patches of moss and lichen. Redden smelled it before he saw it, its fecund scent instantly recalling damp earth and rotting deadwood. Its wingspan was fully thirty feet, and its tail even longer than that. It was impossible that such a massive creature could manage to get airborne, let alone fly.

"Dragon!" he managed to scream before diving for safety.

Oriantha was already moving, hurtling into her mother, sweeping them both to one side and out of harm's way.

But the rest had only enough time to glance up before it was on top of them.

The Trolls took the brunt of the attack, clustered together and thus easily the biggest target for the dragon. Garroneck and two others were killed instantly, the dragon's massive claws crushing their bodies, its teeth tearing at their unprotected heads. One minute they were there and the next they were reduced to body parts scattered about the ground amid splashes of bright red blood. Redden heard Khyber Elessedil cry out as the dragon's tail whipped about, catching her across the back and sending her flying.

Crace Coram, standing right next to the Ard Rhys, was quicker. Avoiding the tail as it swept past him, he rushed the dragon from behind and scaled its backside. Barely slowing as he reached the spikes that ran the length of its spine, the Dwarf clawed his way forward. The dragon reached back for him, jaws opening wide, but Carrick and Pleysia both attacked it from the front, Druid magic striking at the creature in fiery bursts that slammed into its head and neck and drew its attention away from the Dwarf.

Oriantha was down on the ground on all fours, becoming the beast Redden had seen earlier, all feral and wolfish as she crouched next to her mother. Redden scrambled up and started forward to help, but then stopped in his tracks.

What did he think he was doing?

Frozen with indecision, he hesitated.

Crace Coram was all the way up the dragon's back and onto its neck by now. The dragon twisted its head in an effort to avoid the Druid Fire being thrown at it by Carrick and Pleysia while at the same time trying to shake loose the man clinging to its neck. The remaining Trolls had joined the battle, darting at the dragon, jabbing at it with swords and spears. One of them got too close, and the dragon snatched him up and ground him into the earth. Oriantha, turning ever more bestial, was circling the creature, looking for an opening.

Only Redden was hanging back, unable to do anything but watch.

Then, abruptly, the dragon took to the air, spreading its wings and lifting away. The Druids and the Trolls tried to stop it, but the dragon shrugged off their efforts, too big and burly to contain. Crace Coram had climbed all the way up to its head and was hammering at it with his iron mace. But even that didn't slow it.

At the last minute Oriantha made a sudden rush, caught hold of a leg, and scrambled onto the dragon's back. Pleysia screamed in rage and disbelief and tried to follow her daughter, but the dragon had already risen too high. Together, she and Carrick continued to strike at the beast as it rose, fought to bring it down again and failed.

The dragon soared into the sky, its two riders clinging to it, the Dwarf hammering it with his mace, the beast girl tearing at it with teeth and claws.

In seconds it was only a dot on the horizon.

Railing Ohmsford came awake with a start, eyes blinking rapidly, and wondered where he was.

"There, now," someone said, pressing down gently but firmly on his shoulders. "Easy does it."

He looked up into Farshaun Req's face, remembering. "Where's Redden?" he asked.

The old man explained everything, not wasting words, trying his best to reassure the boy. But Railing, though he understood the reasons for it, was distressed that Redden had gone on without him. He couldn't help himself; he didn't like being separated from his twin for any reason. The two were always together, and he especially didn't like it when one of them might be in danger.

"How bad is my leg?" he asked.

"It's broken in two places." Farshaun pointed to the splints. "You'll have to go back to the ship, boy."

"Not without Redden, I won't." He raised himself up on one elbow, wincing as a jolt of pain ratcheted through his injured leg. "How long have they been gone now?"

"Several hours." Farshaun looked skyward. "Getting dark. They should be back soon."

The boy looked around at the Trolls, standing over by the edge of the escarpment with Seersha and Skint. The latter glanced around, saw that Railing was awake, and wandered over.

"Feeling better? Leg all right? I set those splints myself."

Railing nodded. "Farshaun says you found the waterfall and the company went into it, my brother with them."

Skint nodded. "Wasn't actually a waterfall. It was some sort of light. The Ard Rhys sent me back to tell the rest of you what happened. She said they would be back after they took a look around."

Railing started to push himself to his feet. "I can't wait for that. I have to find my brother now."

"Here, here!" Farshaun pushed him down again. "You can't walk on that leg without support. You'll make it worse if you try."

Skint was staring off toward the cliffs. "Maybe I should have a look around while we're waiting. Just to see if anything's happened."

He wandered back toward the trees and disappeared. Railing and Farshaun watched him go. The boy glanced at the darkening sky and felt the first twinges of uneasiness begin to settle in.

Then Seersha hurried over to them and knelt, her blunt features troubled. "There's movement in the rocks below the bluff. I think those little monsters are getting ready to mount another attack."

She gave them a look. "If they come at us after dark, I don't think we can stop them. We have to get out of here right now."

Khyber Elessedil regained consciousness. She saw Pleysia on her knees wailing in despair as the dragon disappeared. Carrick and the Trolls were staring after it, stunned looks on their faces. She called to Redden Ohmsford who, having regained a small measure of his composure, hurried over.

"Help me up," she ordered.

She said it in a way that did not allow for any argument, and he did as he was asked, lifting her back to her feet. She was surprised at how easily he lifted her, as if her age had sapped her of substance and left her little more than skin and hollow bones. She took a moment to find her balance and then stepped away from him. "Are you all right?" she asked.

He nodded. "But the dragon took Crace Coram and Oriantha."

She glanced at Pleysia, still kneeling on the ground, keening softly. She knew Garroneck and several other Trolls were lost, as well; she had seen it happen. She took in the huddle of Trolls who remained; only four of them were left. Her entire Druid Guard, decimated. She saw Carrick staring at her accusingly.

Then Redden said, "The way back is gone."

She turned, not sure she had heard right. "What?"

"The shimmer we passed through to get here. It's disappeared."

She looked in the direction he was indicating and found no sign of it. She took a moment to scan the entire area carefully. Nothing. What was happening?

Something tweaked her memory, something she had learned long ago when Grianne Ohmsford was Ard Rhys and the Druid order was in shambles. Grianne had spoken of what had been done to her, of what she had endured to survive inside . . .

She couldn't finish the sentence, couldn't bear the weight of it. Because suddenly she understood everything. Giant insects. Packs of creatures that in the time of Faerie would have been recognized instantly as Goblins.

And now a dragon, she whispered to herself.

A dracha.

All things that Elven magic had locked away centuries ago, imprisoned ever since by the magic of the Ellcrys.

She exhaled sharply. *Shades!* They weren't in the Four Lands anymore. They were somewhere else entirely. They were in a place they weren't supposed to be able to reach, a place held inviolate by ancient wards that had somehow begun to erode.

They were inside the Forbidding.

28

FOR THE REMAINDER OF THAT DAY AND ALL OF THE next, Drust Chazhul and his Federation army did not attempt any further assaults against Paranor. They held on to the Outer Wall and the landing platform and its airships, and stationed sentries on the walls and towers and on the perimeter of the surrounding forest so that no one could come or go without being seen. They built watch fires in the courtyards to keep the Inner Wall and towers illuminated, and whenever the Druids used magic to put the fires out they quickly reignited them. No attempt was made to communicate with the defenders, and it was soon clear any communication would have to come from those trapped within the Keep.

From behind the Inner Wall, Aphenglow and her companions listened to the sounds of construction. Attempts were made to catch a glimpse of what was being built, but even from the highest vantage points in the Keep's many towers they could see nothing.

"Siege machines," Bombax declared, dismissing the matter.

But Aphenglow wasn't so sure. Drust Chazhul had to realize by now that direct attacks against the Keep were doomed to failure. Siege machines were just more of the same, so why would the Prime Minister and his army of commanders bother? Something else was happening, but she couldn't decide what it was. Even Cymrian, who was usually so quick to decipher such puzzles, could not come up with an answer.

They considered again further attempts to protect the most valuable talismans and artifacts hidden within the Keep, including the Black Elfstone, but again decided against it. They bandied about the idea of attempting to get word to one of the Border Cities or to Arborlon in an effort to summon help. But a journey of that sort would have to be made on foot, and it would require a three-day slog just to get clear of the Dragon's Teeth. From there, it would be another two days either to Tyrsis or Arborlon unless they could borrow or steal an airship or a horse. With so many sentries and patrols, the chances of being seen were good, and that would generate a pursuit. Worst of all, even if someone managed the journey successfully, there was nothing to say that help of any kind would be given.

If word could be gotten to the Ard Rhys and the other Druids, help was assured. But no one knew exactly where the members of the expedition were or how to reach them.

So in the end, the defenders decided to outlast their attackers and trust to the strength of the wards. No one wanted to abandon the Keep, in any case; not even the Trolls were in favor of leaving. Better to stand their ground and fight, Bombax repeatedly insisted, than flee and show their backsides to the likes of Drust Chazhul.

Again, Aphenglow wasn't so sure.

On the second morning of the siege, she went into the depths of the Keep to find Woostra. She had gone to see him right after the initial assault had failed to inform him of what had happened. He had greeted the news with his usual calm indifference, declaring he was unsurprised and uninterested in anything involving the

Federation. The Keep would protect herself and by doing so, protect them. He had more important matters to occupy his time.

Aphenglow, wondering what could be more important than an army of soldiers trying to break down Paranor's gates, nevertheless had departed without further discussion.

But now she found herself increasingly uneasy about what might be happening outside the walls. They were seemingly safe and had proclaimed themselves so— well, Bombax had, at any rate, always so confident and self-assured. But everyone was edgy and disgruntled at being trapped in their own fortress and troubled by the size and determination of the enemy that had penned them in.

Aphen felt the need to explore the matter further.

In large part, this was because the Keep was speaking to her again.

It had begun to do so almost immediately after the last Federation assault had been broken. The voice spoke in whispers and sighs, in fragments of sentences and odd words, the language archaic and barely recognizable. Aphen, who knew at least parts of all the old Elven languages, nevertheless struggled with this one. The voice was plaintive and hushed, and in its tone she discovered more than what she could decipher from its words. Worry, a sense of urgency that lacked a source but was clearly important, and a harsh demand for action all came through clearly. It was a summons, and she understood in a way she could not explain that it was directed to her and her alone.

So she went back to Woostra, hoping he could explain what was happening, that his vast knowledge of the Keep and its secrets might give her the answers.

She found him in almost exactly the same place and

position as he had been two days earlier, bent over his books, scribbling furiously.

"Aphenglow," he greeted without looking up.

"Can you give me a moment?" she asked, seating herself at one end of a bench otherwise crammed with books and papers.

He lay down the pen and faced her. "I was wondering how long it would take you. You're here about the voice, aren't you?"

She stared. "Can you hear it, too? Do you hear it the same way you hear our footsteps and know whose it is?"

The wrinkles of his aged face deepened when he smiled. "It belongs to the Keep. I hear it, but I had to learn to listen for it. It doesn't speak to me, as it does to you. But then you have always had a special connection to the Keep, haven't you?"

She nodded.

"Can you understand what it says to you?"

She hesitated. "Sometimes. Not the words so much as the tone. I can feel it in my heart. Like now. It wants me to do something. It seems anxious, even desperate, for me to understand what that something is."

The old man shook his head. "I don't know that this has ever happened before, Aphen. The Keep sometimes responds to our needs, but I have been reading the Druid Histories and cannot find mention of it speaking to a Druid."

"Then why is it doing so now?"

"I don't know. I've been hearing the voice for years; I knew it was there. But it was only very recently I understood to whom it was speaking. I thought at first it was the Ard Rhys. But after she was in the Druid Sleep, it still whispered. Then, when you went to Arborlon, the voice stopped and I realized it must have been speaking to you. When you returned and it started up again, I was certain."

"There's no record of this ever happening before? Not even to Allanon or Grianne Ohmsford?"

"None. I have been reading through the Histories these past few days trying to discover if anything's been written down about this. It struck me that this most recent effort to communicate is a warning. Something crucial is happening. I am speculating now, but I think the Keep is trying to tell you what that something is."

She leaned forward eagerly. "Why would it do that?"

He hesitated, cocking an eyebrow at her. "I think it feels threatened in some way. I think it's trying to protect itself. I think it wants you to help."

She cocked an eyebrow back at him. "It seems to me the Keep's done a pretty fair job of protecting itself."

"Appearances can be deceiving. What has protected the Keep so far is magic conjured up and set in place by Grianne Ohmsford before Khyber Elessedil succeeded her as Ard Rhys. The magic Grianne created was powerful and effective, but it was not an original part of the Keep. Do you see where I'm going with this?"

She shook her head.

"There is a second, older magic that wards Paranor, one that dwells beneath the Keep's main tower, deep underground. This magic was created when Paranor was brought into the world to serve as a home for the Druids, and its purpose is much darker. Do you know of it?"

"I've heard rumors," Aphenglow said. "Tell me more. What does it do?"

"It can do a couple of things. It can be used to ward the Keep against intruders, even in the absence of its Druids. Walker Boh used it that way when he flew the *Jerle Shannara* to Parkasia. Once set in place, the magic will protect Paranor until any of the resident Druids return to release it from its task and reopen the Keep. Simple enough."

He paused. "It can also serve a much darker purpose. It can be used to destroy every living thing it finds within Paranor's walls and then to seal the Keep and hide it away. Poof! Everyone dead and the Keep disappeared. That has happened only once, when Allanon knew his life was ending and no Druids would be left to succeed him. Mord Wraiths had occupied the Keep and were destroying it, so he summoned the old magic. When it had finished with the Mord Wraiths, Paranor disappeared from the world of men."

Aphenglow stared at him, appalled. "What are you saying? That you think the Druids are going to be wiped out a second time? That the Keep is asking to be closed away again?"

Woostra sighed wearily. "Pay attention, Aphenglow. The reason for the Keep's insistence on communicating with you—in my opinion, mind you—is that it feels it is in danger. Perhaps Grianne Ohmsford's wards are not sufficient to protect it. Perhaps it feels threatened by the Federation; perhaps something else is going on. Whatever the case, there are choices to be made, and I have just told you what they are. But I can't tell you what you need to do. To find that out, you must go down inside the well that houses the old magic."

"I don't understand," she insisted. "Why would going there help me?"

"Because you need to get close enough . . ." He trailed off sharply. "You really don't know, do you? I thought you did. Don't you understand? The voice comes from there."

She shook her head. "What are you talking about? I thought it came from the Keep."

"If you had listened more closely and tracked it to its

source, you would have realized by now it doesn't come from the Keep—it comes from within the pit!"

He held up one hand to stop her from interrupting. "Don't ask me if I am sure of this because I most assuredly am. I discovered it for myself just the other day—the closer you get to the pit, the easier it is to understand the voice. Although I still can't understand it the way you can. It is the old magic speaking, but you are the one it speaks to. If Paranor and the Druids are doomed, you are the one who needs to find out. If it's simply a matter of setting the old wards in place, you need to find that out, too. But nothing can be determined without going to the source and hoping that proximity will provide you with the answers you require."

He turned back to his books. "There, I've said everything I have to say on the matter. It's up to you now. Maybe my speculations are entirely wrong. But I don't think so."

Aphenglow looked down at her hands where they rested in her lap. "But why has it chosen me?"

"Good question." Woostra did not bother to look up. "You should ask it when you get close enough to do so."

For long moments, Aphenglow sat there debating what the old man had told her. Then she stood and went out the door.

She really had no choice. If she wanted to test Woostra's theory, she needed to enter the Keep's main tower and descend from its lower levels into the huge pit that opened all the way down into the black center of the earth. She didn't want to do this, didn't want to be there even for the barest few seconds. She had gone into the pit only once, when she was newly come to Paranor and still exploring its boundaries, and she still regretted having done so. The cold and dark had a visceral feel, and she could sense the presence of something old and dangerous and inhuman. *Magic,* she had thought even then, dark and cunning, but she could not put a name to it.

When she had asked the Ard Rhys, Khyber had told her she was not to go down there again. What lived there was ancient and immutable and should be left to slumber undisturbed until the end of time.

She had not pressed the matter further, just happy to know she needn't go back. Now she wished she had insisted on knowing more. Perhaps some of what was happening now might have been avoided.

The main tower was a huge structure settled at the north end of the Keep, thick and massive in its look, but deceptive, as well. Nowhere was it evident that it tunneled into the earth much farther than it rose above it, and nowhere did the Outer Walls reveal the nature of the unpleasantness trapped within.

Only when she opened the huge ironbound door that led into the depths of the tower and began her descent was she reminded of what was concealed from the world outside. Stone stairs wound downward into endless darkness amid smells and tastes so unpleasant and sounds so insidious they made her cringe. She shuddered in spite of herself, trying in vain to close off the assault on her senses, to push back against the physically intimidating presence the tower's walls exuded. Her entire being screamed at her to turn and flee back from where she had come, to warn her that to continue meant an encounter so terrible she could not expect to survive it.

Yet she did not turn back. Driven by her fear of what was at stake, compelled by the knowledge that only she could discover the truth behind the Keep's insistent whispering, she kept going. The descent was not easily made, but her Druid training and her strong sense of responsibility buttressed her efforts. She had not told anyone what she was going to do. Woostra would know, of course, but if anything happened to her it was difficult to tell how much time might pass before he noticed she was missing.

She heard the whisper of the voice almost immediately—the familiar susurration of words and phrases that almost made sense and to which she could almost put meaning. In her heart, she knew she had done the right thing by coming. The voice reflected a sense of relief; she was expected and she had not disappointed. She was where she should be, the voice was saying. She was where she was needed.

Dampness formed on her exposed skin, cloying and chill. The air was stale and thick with age and closeness. Nothing born of the pit, nothing that resided within its stone vault, ever saw anything of the outside world. Here, things did not change. What was so a thousand years ago was still so today. Imprisoned by stone and time, this tunnel into the earth's center was an encapsulated environment, its components immutable.

She hated everything about it, but did not reveal her feelings by voice or gesture, believing it wiser—however irrational—to keep her distaste hidden.

The voice was growing clearer, the words beginning to form images that wormed their way through her subconscious to where she could glimpse them in her mind's eye. Even so, she wasn't sure at first what she was seeing. The images were in a context she did not recognize. She slowed her descent and then stopped altogether on one of the tiny platforms that marked her downward progression, pressing back against the stone of the tower wall and closing her eyes tightly.

Something creeps and climbs . . .

Something green and lacking in substance but filled with dark intent and raw hunger . . .

Something skitters through the darkness, figures hunched over and crawling like rats . . .

Something feral waits . . .

Something huge and violent bursts from darkness into light amid splashes of red and screaming so terrible and futile and endless . . .

She blinked rapidly in shock, reopening her eyes and staring out into the gloom of the tower and then into the deeper darkness of the pit. She could hear a wicked hissing, and she knew there was something alive down there. And just as she had known six years earlier, she knew at once what it was.

The magic that lived in the pit.

The magic that had dwelled there since Paranor was constructed.

The magic she had come to find.

What was she to do? She wanted to turn and run. But she began to descend once more, moving to the next platform, deeper into the gloom. She was almost completely wrapped in darkness now, but she was afraid to use her magic to provide additional light, afraid it might attract the thing below. Afraid it might rise to seek her out. She never once doubted it was possible. She would listen to its voice and study the images the voice conjured, but she could not stand her ground if it came for her.

She knew she could not do that.

Aphenglow.

She heard her name spoken clearly and distinctly, but nothing more. It was so unexpected that for a moment she thought she was mistaken. She waited. The whispering began again, slow and insidious and menacing, solitary words spoken out of context, fragments of sentences stripped of relevance, and with them came the attendant images, newly formed and decidedly different, but every bit as terrible. She tried again to make sense of them, and failed.

She reached the next platform and halted once more, again leaning back against the tower wall, closing her eyes. Understanding would come to her, she felt. Some small knowledge, some recognition. The voice was trying to communicate but hadn't found a way yet. Ancient language was all it knew. Images formed of words that didn't quite connect or reveal were all it could manage.

Tell me, she whispered in her mind. *Try.*

The voice continued to whisper, scary hisses that suggested angry snakes, but its meaning remained obscure. She listened carefully, but she could not decipher it.

Tell me what you want.

She went down another level, tried again to understand, failed, and went down still another level. Now she was so deep she could hear the voice breathing and see the strange greenish glow of the resident magic. She was so frightened her hands were shaking. She could sense its power, and she felt dwarfed by it. She must not wake it. She must not. Its voice came to her from out of dreams and sleep, from a subconscious that transcended both. She did not know what this meant, but understood it should be left alone.

Yet she couldn't do that. She needed it to speak to her. She needed to know what was happening.

Leave, Aphenglow.

The words stopped her where she was. She waited for the voice to say something further, but it stayed silent.

She turned toward the wall of the pit and placed her hands flat against its cold, damp surface, absorbing its rough feel, reaching for something more. What did the magic intend to do if she left? Which choice would it make for Paranor?

Don't seal the Keep. She spoke to it in her mind, begging it to heed her. *Please, don't. This is our home.*

The voice responded in rapid bursts, a flood of words, garbled and raw sounding:

. . . tunnels . . . boring machines . . . walls . . . compromised . . . matter . . . of time . . . cleansing . . .

Then, a shriek:

Get out! All of you! Now! Leave them to me!

The words exploded inside her mind, disjointed and wild, and she jerked away from the wall in response to their blackness and rage, averting her face, cringing in fear.

In the pit beneath her, the greenish mist heaved upward as if trying to break free, and the hissing it emitted was slow and fierce and penetrated to her core.

But she understood now what the voice was trying to tell her. She knew what was going to happen.

Take them! she screamed in response, the words white-hot coals in her mind. *But spare the Keep!*

In spite of her damaged leg, heedless of the pain it caused her, she flew up the stone stairs, back out of the darkness and into the light.

29

By the time she regained the ground floor of the main tower, safely out of the black pit that housed the ancient magic she had gone to find, Aphenglow Elessedil was a mess. Her clothes were disheveled and stained with damp and sweat, her face and hair were smudged with dirt, and her leg ached so badly she could barely walk on it. She limped from the tower to the adjoining courtyard and crossed to the steps leading up to the ramparts of the Inner Wall, searching for anyone at all. She was scared and frantic and desperate to impart what she knew.

She had so little time, she kept thinking. So very little.

She was close to collapse when she encountered Krolling descending the stone stairway she was coming up.

"Aphenglow?" he questioned in shock.

Everything was spinning. She toppled over and he caught hold of her. "Call the others," she gasped. "I have something . . . I have to tell . . ."

Without a word, he picked her up like a child and carried her back up the stairs and along the ramparts. On the way, they found Bombax and several more of the Druid Guard, who fell into line behind them. Krolling took her all the way to the tower where her sleeping chambers were located and then into her bedroom, where he placed her carefully on her bed. By then, Arlingfant and Cymrian had appeared as well. Her sister ran out of the room in tears, but quickly returned with warm water and cloths and set about cleaning her up.

"What happened?" Bombax demanded, looking as if he wanted to inflict serious pain on someone. "Who did this to you?"

She shook her head. "No one. Find Woostra. I need . . . him here, too."

She lay back again, closed her eyes, and gave herself over to Arlingfant's tender hands, soothed by the feel of the damp cloth on her face, catching stray drops of water on her tongue and feeding them into her parched mouth. She couldn't remember how she had gotten to this state, couldn't imagine she had missed it happening. What she could remember was the descent into the pit, following the whispering of the voice, the lure of its beckoning, as she tried to discover what it wanted. What she could recall were the darkness and damp and the presence of the terrible thing that lived within them. She kept hearing its voice in her mind—the one that had spoken so clearly at the end—shrieking at her. She kept hearing it repeat the same words over and over.

Get out! Now!

Woostra came through the doorway, and they were all present save for the Trolls still on watch atop the Inner Wall. She forced herself to sit up, gently moving Arlingfant away. "Later," she told her sister, silencing her protests.

"We're compromised," she told them, keeping her voice calm and steady. "The Federation is tunneling under Paranor's walls out where we can't see what they're doing. They aren't building siege machines; they're burrowing into the Keep. They've discovered the magic that wards us doesn't extend below the walls. We have to get out of here right away. I don't know how much time we have, but I don't think it's a lot."

"Aphen, wait a minute!" Bombax interjected. "How do you know all this?"

"The Keep told me." She saw the mix of confusion and disbelief in his eyes. "Don't doubt me on this, Bombax. Paranor has always spoken to me. The voice was always there. It was Woostra who suggested I might be hearing the old magic that dwells in the pit beneath the main tower. He told me it might be trying to tell me something and was doing so because Grianne's wards were failing."

She turned to face Woostra. "You were right. When I went into the tower, the voice began to whisper to me right away. At first, I couldn't understand what it was saying. I went down into the pit. I went so far down I couldn't see where I'd come from. The farther down I went, the clearer the whispering became. I began to understand words and then phrases. I could tell the voice was coming from the thing that lived in the pit, from the old magic conjured when Paranor was built. I could feel it stirring; I could see it moving . . ."

Bombax reached for her arm. "Aphen, calm down. Maybe you just thought . . ."

"Don't patronize me, Bombax!" she shrieked at him in fury. "Just listen! I heard it! I saw it! It was real! And the last thing I heard was so terrifying I ran back up those stairs . . ."

She caught her breath, shook her head. "It wants to come out of there, whatever it is, whatever it intends, and it's telling us we don't want to be here when it does."

Bombax nodded slowly, chastened. "All right, calm down. I believe you. I do. Don't be angry with me. I just needed to be sure you believed yourself. You're asking us to leave Paranor, Aphen. To abandon her to the Federation."

"It isn't exactly what she's asking," Woostra said, pursing his lips thoughtfully, giving the big Druid a long look.

Bombax hesitated. "You think the old magic won't let that happen, that it will stop the Federation?"

"I think it will do whatever it needs to do to protect itself. I think it wanted Aphenglow to grant it permission to come out of the pit and put a stop to what's being done to it. And it is warning us not to be here when that happens."

"But we can't allow that! Not without the Ard Rhys giving permission for it! Not without her even knowing!"

"We have no idea where she is," Aphenglow pointed out. "And we don't have time to find her."

"She's beyond helping us," Woostra added. "Beyond even advising us. We have to make this decision on our own."

There was a long silence as those gathered looked from face to face. "The first thing we have to do," Aphenglow said finally, "is figure out how we're going to get out of the Keep without getting killed."

"We can use the tunnels," Cymrian offered.

She shook her head quickly. "Not without chancing an encounter with the Federation. They're inside already—or if not, close to being so. We don't know which of the tunnels they are in. Probably, they are in more than one. Maybe, they are in all of them. Some of us might make it. But we have wounded and injured to consider. If we go, no one gets left behind."

"If we split up, we might have a better chance of avoiding them," Cymrian pressed.

"If we split up, we reduce our strength." Bombax shook his head. "Then we risk being cut apart piecemeal. Besides, how will we ever find one another again once we're outside?"

"If we get out, we still have to cross through the forest on foot to reach the Dragon's Teeth," Krolling added. "We'll be hunted down by Federation flits."

"Not if we're careful enough to—" began Cymrian.

"But maybe the Federation will be too busy worrying about what's coming after them in the—" interrupted Bombax.

"Wait, wait, wait!" Aphenglow exclaimed impatiently, cutting through the jumble of voices and silencing them. "We've forgotten something. What about the Druid Histories? Can they be protected?"

"Of course!" Woostra sounded almost indignant. "The Histories are protected by a magic that cannot be breached by anyone who isn't a Druid. They've survived attacks on Paranor before. They'll survive this one, too."

"So how do we escape before this happens?" Bombax asked, looking at Aphenglow for an answer.

She pushed herself into a sitting position. "I don't know. You and Cymrian figure it out. Arling, help me up."

"But, Aphen—" her sister started to object.

"Help me up!" Aphen snapped.

She had spoken more harshly than she had intended but it was too late to take it back. Arling looked stricken, but moved to help her rise.

"I'm sorry," Aphen whispered as her sister put her arms around her and lifted.

"It's all right," Arling whispered back.

Leaning on her sister, Aphen moved toward the sleeping chamber door. "I won't be long," she called back to the others. "Start packing whatever you think we might need to take with us. We leave as soon as I get back—one way or the other."

She had gone all the way down the length of the hall and was turning up the stairs that led to the cold chamber and scrye waters when she realized she could have had Krolling carry her and been there in half the time. But she didn't want anyone carrying her, didn't want to be reminded of her weakness, and liked being close again to Arling, so she let it be.

They climbed two levels of stairs and turned down the passageway that led to the cold room. It was hard going because Aphen was still exhausted from her encounter in the pit, and her leg ached from the hard use to which she had put it. But she pushed ahead wordlessly, letting Arlingfant provide support and encouragement, thinking as she did so how much she loved her. She hated herself for snapping at her sister; even those few words were too many. She would not do that again, she told herself. No matter how angry or upset she got, she would not take it out on Arling.

They reached the cold room, and she turned to her sister. "I have to do this alone. No one who isn't a Druid is allowed in the cold room. Will you wait for me here? I shouldn't be long." She paused, seeing the look on her sister's face. "Don't worry. I'll be all right."

Arlingfant gave her a hug and stepped away. "I'll be waiting."

Aphen slipped inside and closed the door behind her. The room was draped in shadows that resisted the intrusion of even the small amount of light filtering through the windows high up on the only exterior wall. The air in the room was chilly and damp, and Aphen shivered involuntarily.

She moved as quickly as she could to the stone basin set at the center of the room, climbing onto the platform that supported it so she could read its strange greenish waters. She had not used the scrye since she had sought to find traces of Bombax when he had failed to return to the Keep, but now she would attempt to determine the whereabouts of the Ard Rhys and the expedition she led. If the Druids must abandon Paranor—no matter the cause—the others must be told. She and Bombax must find them and give them warning. To do that, she must read the waters and determine from traces of magic expended approximately where they were.

She stood over the basin and stared down into the scrye, watching as the greenish waters stirred sluggishly in their familiar clockwise manner around the walls of the stone container. The basin was shallow, and she could see the extended map of the Four Lands and surrounding territories etched in its base. Extending her arms so that her hands were poised just above the surface of the waters, she began her search, reading the lines of power that stretched across the earth, probing for any disturbance. Concentrating on the Westland, where the Ard Rhys would ultimately have gone, she quickly found what she was looking for. Traces of expended magic could be traced across miles of unsettled country far west of the Breakline.

Attacks of some sort, Aphenglow concluded. Some of the traces were older than others, so the attacks most likely had taken place on separate occasions over a series of two or three days. She marked in her memory where the last of them ended. That would be the starting point for those fleeing Paranor.

Then she cleared her efforts with a wave of her hand, and the waters of the scrye returned to their former state, their movement slow and steady and placid once more.

When she departed the cold room, closing its door one final time, she knew she might be closing it on a part of her life, as well. It was almost more than she could bear.

*   *   *

Night had fallen, the sunset an hour gone.

"If we can't walk out of here, we'll have to fly," Bombax announced.

Aphenglow had returned from the cold room and the company of defenders had gathered once more in her sleeping chamber. It seemed odd to her that her private space had become their war room, but by unspoken mutual consent that was what it was.

"How do we do that without an airship?" she asked. "Ours are all in the hands of the Federation."

"We steal one back," Cymrian answered. "Bombax and I have been talking it over. We think we can manage it. Especially now that it's dark, we won't be so easy to spot. If we can get out onto the landing platform we can take control of at least one airship before they have a chance to stop us."

"The Federation still guards the platform and our ships, but they aren't putting much into the effort," Bombax continued, leaning forward, his expression eager. "They've got maybe a dozen guards up there, and they've blocked off the ramp leading out of the Keep. They think that's enough to keep us off the landing platform, but they're wrong. There's a metal catwalk attached to the underside of the ramp, and if Cymrian and I can sneak across it we can come up on them from behind."

"You and Cymrian," she repeated.

The Elf nodded. "Bombax and I are best suited for the job. Everyone else will be needed to help the injured Trolls onto the ship once we've seized it. We'll have to move quickly. Once they see us—"

"I know," she interrupted. "But it's not the Federation we have to worry about."

"The thing in the pit," the other guessed.

"It won't take long for it to reach the Keep proper once it starts to come out."

"When will that happen?" Bombax asked.

Aphen shook her head. "I don't know. It might be happening already. Woostra? What do the Histories tell us?"

The keeper of the records shrugged. "Not much. It takes a summoning to release the ancient magic, and you've already provided that."

"Surely it won't do anything until we're safely out of here," she said. "It made a point of warning us to go. Won't it wait until we do?"

Woostra fixed her with a baleful eye. "Would you like to risk finding out? Delay long enough, and you might."

They moved quickly after that, gathering everyone together at the north end of the Keep just inside the doors that opened onto the ramp leading to the airships. They pulled the last of the able Druid Guards off the walls and brought the injured ones up from the sickroom. Since the Druid airships were kept well supplied, they took nothing with them but their weapons, personal possessions, and the clothes on their backs.

"I cannot believe we are doing this," Aphenglow said to Bombax at one point, standing close to him in the midst of the chaos surrounding their efforts to prepare for departure. There were tears in her eyes and her face was stricken. "How did we let this happen?"

The big man put his hands on her shoulders. "No one *let* this happen."

"I think maybe I did. I think maybe I caused it when I brought that diary back."

"You've had a rough time of it, Aphen. You've been forced to take on a lot. Don't be so hard on yourself."

She hugged him to her, feeling his arms enfold her as she did. "You've been through a lot, too."

"We're Druids," he said. "And these are extraordinary times."

She shook her head. "No, these are terrible times."

They were close again, at the beginning of a fresh start in their too-often strained relationship. Her life partner, her love; she wanted his support. She needed him to be with her when they were forced from their home and had everything they knew taken away from them.

That it was necessary to leave was difficult enough. That she should have to endure it without him would have been unbearable.

"We've been given no choice," he told her. "If there had been another way, you would have been the first to recognize it."

"There is no other way. I know that."

"You didn't want to be the one to do this," he added.

"I didn't want any part of it."

His arms tightened about her. "Nor I. But here we are. And we can't change things, no matter how much we might wish we could. Which reminds me."

He picked her up without a word, hushing her when she started to object, and carried her down the hallway, cradling her in his arms. Knowing he had his mind made up about whatever it was he intended, she pressed her head into his shoulder and let him go.

When they reached her sleeping chamber, he set her on her feet and disappeared into her room. When he came out again, he was holding Aleia Omarosian's diary. "You almost left this behind," he said, handing it to her.

In truth, she had. In the rush to make preparations for leaving, she had forgotten it completely. She leaned forward and kissed him hard. "Thank you so much."

He shrugged. "I don't think we're quite done with it. Do you?"

She smiled and hugged him. "Not quite." She leaned away so she could look at him. "But you didn't need to carry me all the way back here to retrieve it. You could have just brought it to me."

"And missed having you all to myself, even if just for a few minutes? Do you think I'm crazy?"

Then he picked her up again and carried her back down the hallway to where the others were waiting.

30

EVERYTHING HAPPENED QUICKLY AFTER THAT.
Bombax and Cymrian, the former stripped of encumbering clothing and weapons and the latter armed with a dozen blades strapped to his arms and legs and torso like body armor, left the other defenders at the doors leading out to the airship landing platform and went down through a utility hatch into the crawl space that led to the catwalk.

"Wait until you know the barricades are down and the way to the airship is clear before you open these," Bombax instructed Krolling, pointing to the huge iron-bound doors with their massive slide bars and multiple bolt locks. "Don't open them otherwise. Not to try to help us out, not for anything. If we don't make it to the airships, take as many as you can and go into the tunnels and do your best to find a way out."

Aphenglow, standing close, listened and felt something clench in her stomach. That Bombax and Cymrian would fail, that they should be killed, was unthinkable. Even in the abstract, she rejected it out of hand. "We'll be ready when you are," she assured him, looking him in the eye in a way that left no doubt as to how she expected this to go.

Bombax smiled. "You should be the one going instead of me, as fierce as you are."

She blushed, leaned in, and kissed him hard on the mouth. "I'll come after you if I have to." She glanced at Cymrian, who was looking away. "You, too. I need my protectors."

"You don't need anyone," Cymrian declared, giving her a momentary glance before looking away again.

They moved into an adjacent hallway, to where the hatch cover stood ajar, slipped through the opening, and were gone.

"Come on, Arling," Aphenglow said at once, taking her sister's hand, telling Woostra and the Trolls she would be right back.

She had been thinking about this since she knew what the Borderman and the Elf intended to do, wondering how she could put herself in a place where she could watch over them even if going out onto the catwalk was not possible. Even if she couldn't go with them, she reasoned, perhaps she could find another way to help.

At the very least, she would be able to see what happened.

She took Arling up to the next floor, fueled by a rush of adrenaline that masked the pain in her leg and the weariness that flooded through her body. At the bottom of the stairs, she led her sister into a small anteroom adjacent to the Outer Wall and from there through a doorway that opened onto a raised ledge warded by a half wall. She motioned for her sister to crouch down, and together they climbed four steps to what was no more than a ten-foot-long observation balcony that overlooked the landing platform and the airships.

From this vantage point, they might be able to see what happened once Bombax and Cymrian traversed the catwalk and came up behind the barricade.

Aphen put a finger to her lips. No talking. There were

slits cut into the stone blocks of the half wall, and the sisters peered through these at what lay below. The Druid airships moored to a series of locking rings numbered six, and while none of them was the size of the *Walker Boh*, midsize vessels like *Arrow* and *Wend-A-Way* were large enough to carry all of the defenders in the Keep. Two airships would have been better than one, but they could make do with one if they got away quickly enough to put some distance between themselves and their pursuers. Flits were fast enough to catch up to them no matter what, but flits lacked sufficient firepower to bring down ships the size of *Arrow* and *Wend-A-Way*—and Federation airmen lacked the flying skills of Gnome raiders in any event.

That's what she told herself, even though she had her doubts and could not entirely banish them.

The barricade constructed by the Federation to block the rampway was a makeshift affair of logs and crates and hunks of metal plating. A pair of rail slings and a fire launcher had been mounted on portable swivel stands and faced toward the Keep. Torches wedged in crevices and set in iron stanchions burned in bright patches in the darkness. Perhaps twenty soldiers loitered about, a few of them watching the Keep, most visiting with one another and throwing dice. There were no guards at all back where the airships were moored. The soldiers did not look as if they expected anything to happen soon and certainly not where they had been stationed.

Aphen smiled grimly. It would be a very unpleasant surprise indeed when Bombax and Cymrian appeared.

Farther away, out on the battlements of the Outer Wall, a handful of Federation guards were hiding behind half walls and bulkheads where they undoubtedly hoped they were at least marginally protected from the uncanny bowman who had killed Deek Trink.

Aphenglow scooted along the stone-block wall to where she had a slightly better vantage point. Arling came right behind her. From where they were situated above the rampway, they could see nothing of the cat-walk or the progress of the Druid and the Elf who by now were navigating it. It was supremely frustrating.

The sisters waited, huddled together behind the wall, eyes on each other, listening to the voices of the Federation soldiers clustered below.

Then Aphenglow heard the sound of radian draws being snapped in place and diapson crystals powering up. She had just enough time to peer through the slits in the half wall before *Arrow* had shed her mooring lines and lifted off. Bombax had chosen to take back his own airship, as she had suspected he would—familiar with its weaponry and operation, comfortable behind its controls. She could see him situated in the pilot box, already swinging the airship around so that its starboard rail slings were turned toward the barricades where the Federation soldiers were scrambling in every direction. Cymrian had cocked all of the slings, and now he was racing back the way he had come from one sling to the next, releasing their triggers.

Shards of metal flew everywhere, tearing into the barricades, shredding them. The Federation soldiers not caught in the firestorm and dispatched had flattened themselves against the decking to either side, finding cover wherever they could.

Then abruptly Cymrian disappeared.

Aphenglow searched the decks of *Arrow* for him without success. Bombax had turned his airship so that her bow was facing toward the barricade, assuming a course that would take her either through or over its center and to the doors leading into the Inner Wall of the Keep.

Cymrian was still nowhere to be found.

Then she saw him. His white-blond head flashed across the landing platform, darting through the shadows between airships until suddenly he reappeared aboard *Wend-A-Way*. Apparently the Elf and Bombax had decided to steal both ships to rescue their companions, thinking the chance to do so too good to pass up. In seconds Cymrian had the light sheaths raised, the radian draws locked down, and the thrusters engaged. *Wend-A-Way* lifted off, swinging around to join *Arrow*.

Behind the barricade, the Federation soldiers still standing had recovered enough to try to stop them. A handful had converged on the only weapon still available to them in the wake of the initial raking of the wall, a rail sling situated on the far left of the barricade. Bombax, focused on his efforts to surmount the barricade, nevertheless saw them. Without leaving the pilot box, he summoned the Druid Fire and sent it hurtling into the soldiers and their weapon. Both vanished in a cloud of debris and smoke.

But with his attention momentarily diverted, he missed seeing the Federation soldiers atop the Outer Wall who were now alerted to his presence and scrambling to ready a fire launcher on the battlements directly across from him. As *Arrow* sailed over the top of the makeshift barricade, the men manning the fire launcher fired it point-blank at *Arrow*. An explosion of fire flew right where Bombax was standing at the controls and the pilot box simply disintegrated.

Aphen screamed and surged to her feet, Arling clinging tenaciously to one arm, trying to pull her back down again.

For a second the air was so clouded and thick with debris and smoke that it was impossible to tell anything. Aboard *Wend-A-Way,* Cymrian had abandoned the pilot box to man her starboard rail slings, turning them on the Federation soldiers at the fire launcher on the battlements of the Outer Wall. It only took a single shot to smash them both. Then he was back in the pilot box, easing *Wend-A-Way* forward to where he, too, disappeared into the roiling cloud left by the hit *Arrow* had taken.

As Aphenglow struggled in Arling's grip, *Arrow* surged back into view, a stricken wreck with her controls gone and her mainsail shredded. At first she couldn't find any trace of Bombax, but then Arling screamed out his name and pointed. The Druid was clinging to what was left of the mainmast, bloodied and dazed, holding himself upright by what appeared to be sheer determination. *Arrow* dropped toward the rampway, listing and on fire, struck hard enough to shatter the keel, and slid forward toward the barred doors to the Keep and the defenders hiding behind them.

Aphenglow and Arlingfant abandoned their observation post, rushing back inside, out into the hallway and down the stairs as fast as they could manage. When they reached the lower hallway where they had left Woostra and the Trolls, they found everything in chaos. The doors leading in from the landing platform ramp had been smashed in; *Arrow*'s bow jutted through the opening, charred and still smoking. *Wend-A-Way* was parked midair to the ruined vessel's port side, using *Arrow* as a shield to protect it from the masses of Federation soldiers gathering on the battlements of the Outer Wall while the Keep's defenders loaded the wounded and then scrambled aboard themselves. Rail slings and fire launchers were being turned on *Wend-A-Way* and her passengers, but none of them had been mounted where they could do much damage and there was no time to move them. Clouds of smoke from *Arrow*'s burning wreck made it more difficult still to see clearly what was happening.

Aphenglow searched frantically for Bombax, unable

to find him. But then Cymrian appeared beside her, caught her arm, and shouted that Krolling had carried the big Druid off *Arrow* and put him aboard *Wend-A-Way* and she must board, as well. Right now.

Minutes later the entire company of defenders had gained the decks of *Wend-A-Way,* and the airship was lifting off and turning north for the safety of night's concealing darkness.

Drust Chazhul had ordered Federation army commander Tinnen March to dispatch every soldier under his newly designated command to the landing platform in an attempt to stop the Druid escape, but the effort had failed. Flits had given pursuit, but with night settled in there wasn't much reason to hope they could do anything. The Federation ships still weren't able to fly and fight, so there was nothing to do but let the Keep's defenders go their way.

At least, he told himself, somehow managing to keep his burgeoning rage and frustration in check, he had control of Paranor and whatever treasures it hid.

Stoon, standing at his side, warned him that it would be wise not to go in himself until his soldiers had been able to make certain it was safe. There was nothing to say the Druids hadn't left traps for the foolish and unwary.

Reluctantly, Drust had agreed. He would have his chance soon enough. He would loot the fortress of her treasures, of talismans and artifacts, of histories and records, of all things Druid, and then he would tear it down. It might take some time, but he would use every soldier available to him and when he was finished there would be nothing left for those who had escaped him to come back to. He would raze the Druid's Keep down to its foundations and obliterate all traces of the Druid order.

He would put an end to magic's greatest stronghold and then begin the task of cleaning up whatever remnants might have been left behind.

"Once Paranor is destroyed, there will be time enough to hunt down the rest of the Druids and put an end to them for good. Then all the other magic users, as well." Drust gave his companion a smile. "I'll be appointed Prime Minister for life after that."

They stood together in the darkness on the Outer Wall ramparts and watched as Federation soldiers poured into the Keep through the smashed doors off the airfield ramp. *Arrow* was no longer burning, her blackened hull crumbling and still.

Drust was about to comment on his plans for the remaining Druid airships when he saw a strange greenish glow seeping through cracks and crevices in the doors and windows of the lower levels of the Keep.

"What do you think that is?" he muttered.

Stoon shook his head, watching silently.

The glow began to climb upward, infiltrating the Keep floor by floor. Within the tower walls, men began to scream in terror. Those not yet inside hesitated and then quickly fell back. The light had begun to pulse, as if it were reacting to the screams.

"Get those men out of there," Stoon told Drust.

But Drust was unable to do anything except stand and watch, fascinated by what was happening. The greenish light was flooding the rooms and passageways of the Keep, and the screams of the men inside were intensifying. Men appeared on the ramparts and balconies and at windows, thrashing and flailing as clouds of mist enveloped them. Some, driven into a frenzy, began throwing themselves off. They fought and clawed and shrieked as the mist attacked them. Those who tried to escape their fate failed to do so. Those who tried to push past simply disappeared. The green mist filled the

Keep from basement to tower pinnacles, and everything in between was consumed.

Those Federation soldiers still outside were fleeing for the gates of the Outer Wall, not even bothering to listen to the orders shouted at them by their superiors to stand their ground or make a disciplined retreat. Tendrils of the mist snaked along the ground in pursuit, snatching the fleeing men off their feet and dragging them back inside the Keep.

Not too far from where he stood, Drust watched as Tinnen March scrambled down the stairs of the wall and ran with them.

"We have to get out of here," Stoon declared, grabbing Drust Chazhul's arm and dragging him away.

They clambered down the steps to the courtyard and ducked inside a hallway leading to one of the smaller exit doors. Drust was so badly shaken it didn't even occur to him to argue. He let himself be led like a child down the corridor and back outside, then across the barren stretch of clear-cut and into the trees beyond.

When they had reached the shelter of the woods, they turned back to watch what was happening. The greenish light had enveloped the whole of the Druid's Keep. It was climbing the walls like a live thing. It was hunting. A kind of odd vapor rose off the ancient stones as it slithered across them, like steam cooling, and the screams emanating from inside began dying away, turning into gasps and groans and finally going silent.

"It looks as if your plans for looting the Keep might have to wait," Stoon observed drily.

"Only until morning," Drust declared, evincing a confidence he didn't feel. He was never going back in there, that much he knew. "We'll send our men back in then."

"Don't bother asking for volunteers."

Drust felt a weariness sweep through him as he

watched the glow pulse softly against the darkness. "I wonder how many died in there?"

Stoon shook his head. "Do you really want to know?"

"Most must have made it out."

Stoon did not respond.

"Well, it's not our problem."

Drust turned abruptly and started walking back through the trees toward the Federation encampment, already mulling over what he would have to do to minimize the damage. He couldn't go back and face the Coalition Council without having accomplished more than this. He might have driven the Druids out of Paranor, but the fortress was still mostly intact and not in Federation hands. Hundreds of Southland soldiers were dead and many more wounded. His time as Prime Minister would be over if that was all he had to show for this expedition.

"We'll go back in tomorrow," he repeated firmly. "When it's light again. We'll loot her and begin tearing down the walls. That greenish stuff won't still be there by then. You'll see."

"Will I?" Stoon asked mildly. "Maybe. But I'm not sure you will."

"What are you talking about?" Drust snapped, irritated with the other's intractability.

"I'm just saying I don't think you're going to be here tomorrow."

Drust wheeled on him furiously. "Of course I'm going to be here tomorrow! Where else would I—"

A white-hot fire exploded in his chest, bringing a gasp that Stoon's rough hand over his mouth only partly managed to muffle. He was suddenly aware of the knife protruding from his body as Stoon's free hand grasped the hilt and twisted.

Stoon shoved the knife in deeper. "I've put up with you long enough, Drust," he whispered. "I don't have to do that anymore." The knife slid out and then back in again, bringing new pain and shock. "You were never even half as smart as you thought."

He released the Federation Prime Minister and let him fall. Drust Chazhul was dead before he struck the ground.

Aboard *Wend-A-Way*, Aphenglow Elessedil was crouched beside Bombax where he lay stretched out on a bed in a forward compartment, stripped of his clothing and covered with a sheet. Ointment had been spread over his entire body, providing some small relief for his burns. He had broken both legs and one arm and several ribs, and his internal injuries were so severe there was no reasonable chance of treating them. His breathing was shallow and labored, and his gaze distant and empty.

"Everything hurts," he murmured.

She had given him medicines to help with the pain, but they weren't doing much. She held one hand loosely, letting him know that she was there.

"I'm dying, Aphen."

"Shhhh, shhhh," she whispered. "Don't talk."

Arling, kneeling next to her, rose and cleared everyone out of the room. "I'll be just outside," she said before leaving.

Her sister knew. She was giving Aphen these last minutes alone. There was nothing she could do. There was nothing more any of them could do. Tears spilled down Aphenglow's cheeks and fell on the sheet draping her life partner.

"I shouldn't have let you go without me," she told him, bending close. "I should have been with you."

He sighed. "Think how much worse . . . I would feel . . . if you had done that."

"I love you so much. I can't lose you."

"The choice . . . isn't yours . . . or mine."

"Stay with me. Try to stay."

The faintest hint of a smile twisted his burned lips. "I'm right . . . here."

Then he exhaled slowly and was gone.

"Brave Bombax," she whispered, and released his hand.

31

THEY FLEW *WEND-A-WAY* ALL NIGHT NORTH INTO
Troll country to the village Garroneck, Krolling, and
their companions called home, and left the injured
Trolls to be cared for by family and friends before turning west. After that, they flew to Arborlon. The airship's passengers caught snatches of sleep when they
could, talked with one another now and then, and spent
long periods of time looking out over the countryside as
Wend-A-Way crossed the Streleheim Plains to the Valley of Rhenn and on into the Elven home city.

Leaving Woostra and the Trolls aboard *Wend-A-Way*
at their own request—but only after arranging for food
and water and fresh bedding to be supplied to them—
Aphenglow, Arlingfant, and Cymrian wrapped Bombax in a sheet and carried his body from the airfield
into the Ashenell through the fading afternoon light
until they had reached a plot of ground close by that
was designated for the Elessedils. Together they dug his
grave, lowered him into it, and stood looking down at
him in silence until Aphen began speaking. She spoke of
his character and determination and of his contributions to the Druid order. She didn't speak about them as
a couple. She would have said something of that, of
what he had meant to her personally, of what they had

meant to each other—Bombax and she, lovers and life partners—but she could not manage to do so. It was too personal and hurt too much, and speaking of it would have been more than she could bear. She had been saying the words to herself ever since he had died. Better that she leave it there, she decided. What he had meant to her belonged to her, cradled in her memories, safely tucked away. One day she might speak of it to someone else, but this was not that day.

They walked back together afterward to the gates of the burial grounds and stood looking out at the city. No one said anything. It had already been decided that on the morrow Aphenglow and the Trolls would fly into the Westland wilderness in search of the Ard Rhys and the rest of the Druids. Woostra would wait in Arborlon for their return. Arlingfant, in spite of her objections, would remain behind as well, resuming her duties as one of the Chosen.

Cymrian, to Aphenglow's surprise and confusion, insisted he was coming with her to find the other Druids. She told him it wasn't necessary; he told her it was. She told him he had done what was required of him; he told her she couldn't be certain of that.

"You still don't know who was responsible for sending those men to steal the diary and perhaps try to kill you. You don't know another attempt won't be made, even if you aren't in Arborlon. I took the job as your protector, and I don't think it's time for me to give it up yet. Unless, of course, you are dismissing me."

"No, no, I wouldn't do that." She felt frustrated, trapped by her sense of obligation to him. "It's just that you've done so much already, and I don't want you to feel you have to do anything more."

He smiled enigmatically. "What else do I have to do that matters? I've done exactly what I wanted to do by becoming your protector. All I'm asking is to be allowed to continue."

It was impossible to argue with him, so she let it go.

"I'll feel better knowing he's with you," Arling told her later as they walked back together to their cottage. Cymrian had gone, having obtained Aphen's agreement that he could go with her. "If I can't go, at least he can."

Aphen nodded noncommittally. "I suppose." She thought about it for a minute. "I guess I just don't understand why he's so insistent about this. You would think he would be glad not to have to put himself at risk for me any more than he already has."

Her sister laughed out loud. "You still don't understand, do you?"

Aphen frowned. "Understand what?"

Arling shook her head. "I can't tell you. I promised."

"Tell me what?"

Her sister shook her head. "I can't talk about it. In fact, I refuse to talk about it. You'll just have to figure it out on your own."

They walked the rest of the way in silence.

Aphenglow was awake before sunrise the following morning. She dressed, slipped out of the house, and sat on the veranda steps to wait for Arling to join her. She had promised to walk her down to the Gardens of Life, where Arling would participate in the ritual greeting of the new day in the presence of the Ellcrys. By then, the sun would have risen and the day would have arrived; Aphen would be airborne and winging her way west.

In her head, she had already departed.

It was only a few minutes later before Arling was beside her, dressed and ready. "Sleep well?" her sister asked.

"I dreamed of him," she answered.

Arling knew who she meant. "I'm sorry. I know it's hard."

Aphen shook her head. "That's what's so strange. It isn't all that hard anymore. It hasn't been since he died. I can't explain it. In the dream, he was still there, alive and well, but I couldn't touch him. He was smiling, laughing, enjoying himself, but I wasn't with him." She hesitated. "I think I've been losing him for a long time. I think subconsciously I might have known."

"You've been letting go."

She nodded. "It feels like it. I still hurt thinking of him. I still want him back with me. But . . ."

She shook her head, unable to finish. Then she added. "It makes me feel disloyal to think like this."

Arling took her hand and squeezed it. "You're grieving, Aphen. You're entitled to do that in the best way you can. There isn't any right or wrong to how you do it."

Aphenglow supposed that was so, but it didn't make her feel any better. Overall, nothing that had happened since she had found Aleia Omarosian's diary had worked out for the better. Bombax was dead, Paranor was abandoned and lost, the members of the Fourth Druid Order were scattered to the four corners of the earth, and the Federation was hunting for them—all because she had thought it a good idea to find the missing Elfstones. She was beginning to question her judgment about almost everything in her life.

"I want you to be careful," she told her sister suddenly.

Arling looked at her in surprise and then grinned. "Why would I need to do that? No one is interested in me."

"I just want you to watch out for yourself. Just promise me. You said you'd feel better knowing Cymrian was watching over me. Fair enough. But I'll feel better knowing you are watching out for yourself."

She was serious enough that the smile dropped away from her sister's face. "All right, Aphen. I'll be careful."

When they reached the gardens, they embraced and kissed. None of the other Chosen had arrived yet; Arling was early for the ritual greeting. Dawn was still half an hour away. They stood together for a moment, holding each other.

"Will you come back for me after you've found the Ard Rhys?" Arling asked.

"I'll come back as soon as I can. I promise."

"Even if it's only to tell me you are safe."

"Even if it's only for that."

They smiled at each other, cried a little, and parted.

Arling watched Aphenglow walk into the trees, a hundred thoughts tumbling through her head, most of them having to do with going after her sister. But Aphen wouldn't want that, having already made it clear that Arling would not be allowed to go with her. Further insistence would achieve nothing. It would only make Aphen feel worse. Arling had tried her best to convince her sister to take her along and failed. Because she loved her sister more than anyone in the world, Arling knew when to leave well enough alone—even though it cost her something to do so.

Instead she walked down into the Gardens of Life and sat beneath the Ellcrys, trying to calm herself. Gazing at the tree helped. The brilliant red and silver mix of leaves and bark, the grand sweep of her boughs, the shimmer of her canopy in the starlight, and the calm that seemed to envelop her like a protective mantle were a balm that soothed and comforted. Arlingfant always felt better when she was close to the Ellcrys, and that feeling infused her now, reminding her why she had sought to become one of the Chosen and why her selection had left her feeling so fulfilled.

Her thoughts drifted and she closed her eyes.

"Come back safe, Aphen," she said softly.

She was still listening to the echo of her words in the ensuing silence when she felt a gentle touch on her shoulder.

Then, as if borne on the momentary breath of wind that blew ever so softly across her face, a voice whispered.

–Child, I have need of you–

HERE ENDS BOOK ONE OF
The DARK LEGACY OF SHANNARA

THE STORY CONTINUES IN BOOK TWO,
BLOODFIRE QUEST

Read on for an excerpt from
Bloodfire Quest

Book Two of
The Dark Legacy of Shannara

by
Terry Brooks

*A remarkable stand-alone series set
a hundred years after the High Druid of Shannara*

◆

In the hostile and blasted country of the Forbidding, the survivors of the search party for the missing Elfstones stared at the Ard Rhys in disbelief.

"What did you say?" Carrick was the first to break the silence, his stance aggressive. He glared at the Ard Rhys. "Tell me I misheard you."

Khyber faced him squarely. She was not in the least intimidated, Redden thought as he stood off to one side, watching the confrontation unfold.

"We are inside the Forbidding," she answered. "Just as Grianne Ohmsford was a hundred years ago. Trapped."

Carrick shook his head. "That isn't possible."

"I'm afraid it is. The shimmer of light we passed through was a breach in the wall that had been deliberately altered to suggest it was something other than what it really is. Even my magic failed to detect it. As did your own, Carrick."

"But you can't be sure of this! How do you know?"

"The look of the land. The creatures that attacked us on our way in—things not of our world but very much of this one. Giant insects, Goblins. The dragon that at-

tacked us and then took away Oriantha and Crace
Coram—when there aren't any Drachas left in the Four
Lands. The way the opening was there one minute and
gone the next. There's no mistaking what we saw. Any-
one who knows the history of the Four Lands and its
Races would know the truth of it. We are inside the
Forbidding."

There was a stunned silence.

Then Pleysia, still on her knees, began to laugh hys-
terically. "How much worse can this get? We've lost
half our number. A dragon has carried away my daughter and the Dwarf. We found our way in and can't find
our way out." Her laughter died away into sobs. "All of
us are caught out on the wrong side of a door we can't
even find, let along open! Caught among creatures that
will tear us to bits once they discover we're here. It's
madness!"

Carrick whipped around to say something, and then
stopped short. "Your daughter? That odd girl is your
daughter? Why didn't you tell us?"

Pleysia hauled herself to her feet, her eyes dark as they
fixed on him. "Would it have made any difference to
you? What do you care about me and mine, anyway?"

The Trolls were pressing forward as well, talking
among themselves, lapsing into their own guttural language as they gestured at the bodies of Garroneck and
the other dead. Redden took a step back in spite of himself, even though he wasn't the one being threatened. If
anything, he was being ignored. It was Khyber Elessedil
who was bearing the brunt of everyone's rage and fear.

"Stay calm," she ordered, raising her voice only a little.

"Stay calm?" Carrick looked wild and dangerous.
"We have to get out of here, Mistress. Right now!"

"I'm not leaving my daughter!" Pleysia screamed at
him. "We don't go anywhere until we find her!"

Redden looked around uneasily. They were standing out in the open, and the sound of their voices would carry a long way. If there was anything else out there hunting, anything as dangerous as that dragon, it would find them with no trouble.

"Come close," the Ard Rhys ordered them, indicating both Druids and Trolls. She did not look at Redden, but he stepped toward her anyway. "Now listen to me," she said, looking from face to face. "We can't go back the way we came. The way we came is gone. Or if not gone, lost to us. But before we give up completely on finding it, we should use our magic to see if it can be revealed. Carrick? Pleysia? We should at least try."

So they did, each one of them separately, conjuring Druid magic and sending it abroad, sweeping the countryside for a hint of where the door might be concealed. But even though they kept at it for long minutes, it showed them nothing.

I could try using the wishsong, Redden thought. But then something else occurred to him.

"Maybe we shouldn't be doing this," he said suddenly. All heads turned. "Doesn't the use of magic attract other magic? Especially here, where there is so much of it?"

"He is right," Khyber Elessedil said.

"But we can't stand here and do nothing!" Carrick insisted. "What does it matter if we use our magic or not? The things that hunt us in this monstrous land will find us sooner or later anyway. Our only chance to escape them is to discover a way out and take it!"

The Ard Rhys shook her head. "Maybe nothing is hunting us. Except for the dragon, the creatures that inhabit the Forbidding might not even know we are here. Not yet, anyway. Remember how we got here. The blue Elfstones showed Aphenglow that this was the way to the missing Stones. Her vision was clear enough to get us this far, and everything we have done has followed that vision exactly. Even the shimmer of light was a part of what she was shown. We were not lured here. We came of our own free will at the direction of the seeking-Stones. Whoever created this trap didn't know that we would be the ones to fall into it."

"What difference does that make?" Carrick demanded. "We don't have the blue Elfstones now. We can't use them to find a way out."

"No one is suggesting we can. But we shouldn't make the mistake of thinking we're trapped by something that hunts us. We may yet find a way out. We mustn't panic. We must stay calm and remain together. If we are judicious about it, we can still use our magic to find another doorway. If the Forbidding has eroded in one place, it has probably eroded in another."

Redden wondered about that, but since he knew nothing specific about the way in which the Forbidding worked, he kept still about his doubts.

"Redden," the Ard Rhys called to him, and he glanced over quickly. "Just to be certain that we overlook no possibility, will you try using the wishsong?"

He nodded and summoned the magic to seek out the shimmer of light through which they had passed, picturing it in his mind. Quickly enough the blue light flashed to a place perhaps a hundred feet away from where they stood, flaring out in a broad swath. But open countryside was all they saw. Nothing else was revealed.

Nevertheless, acting on the wishsong's response, the three Druids went at once to the place where the magic had spun out, searching for anything that would suggest a doorway back through the Forbidding. But their efforts were in vain. No opening appeared, no sign of a way through the invisible wall that imprisoned them.

"I've had enough of this!" Pleysia snapped. "I'm

going after my daughter. Those who want to come with me can. Otherwise, I'll go alone."

She stalked away from them, suddenly looking much stronger and more determined. Redden and the others watched her for long minutes before Carrick muttered, "We shouldn't let her go off without us. Besides, there's nothing for us here."

Khyber Elessedil nodded. "Let's stay with her, then. We can keep searching for a way out as we go."

Which meant she had no better idea to offer and perhaps recognized that their situation was much more hopeless than she wanted to admit aloud.

They set off—the three Druids, the four Trolls, and Redden—heading in the direction that the dragon had flown. It felt futile to Redden, who would have preferred staying where they were. Maybe Seersha, who had been left behind with Railing and the others, would come looking for them and be able to guide them back again. Maybe the opening would reappear after a while.

But the decision wasn't his to make, and he could feel the despondency and loss of hope that appeared to infect the others working its way through him, as well. He wished he had never agreed to come with the Ard Rhys but instead had remained behind with Railing. He wondered how Railing was. At least his brother wasn't inside the Forbidding like he was, but matters might not be going so well on the other side of the wall, either. After all, those Goblins would still be hunting them, and possibly other things by now, as well. They were still deep in the interior of the Fangs, and if Seersha didn't get word to Mirai to come rescue them, it would be a long and dangerous trek back out again.

And Railing couldn't walk with his broken leg. He would have to be carried. Helpless.

Redden walked in silence for a long time, watching Pleysia lead them—almost as if she knew where she was going. He tried to imagine Oriantha as the Elf Druid's daughter and failed. They seemed nothing alike. Yet there was a clear connection between them, one that went beyond friendship. He shifted his gaze to Carrick and watched the tall Druid for a time, his aspect somber and detached. Then he glanced over at the Trolls, muttering among themselves as they lumbered along.

Finally he moved up alongside the Ard Rhys.

"Do you think one of the others might come looking for us?" he asked her quietly, "Maybe Seersha or Skint?"

"Maybe. If they do, the tag I left on the opening will alert me. If it's Seersha, she will recognize it and know it for a warning to stay back until I return for her." She glanced over. "Is that what you were wondering? If I made a mistake in deciding to leave and come along with Pleysia?"

He flushed. "It had crossed my mind."

She smiled, the wrinkles in her face smoothing in a way that made her seem decidedly younger. "I thought so. I considered staying where we were. But we would have had to come looking for Oriantha and Crace Coram eventually. We couldn't leave either of them behind." She paused. "You have your wits about you, Redden Ohmsford. You'll be fine."

He nodded, not so sure about that. "So you think the Elfstones are really in here somewhere? Like you were shown by the vision?"

She nodded. "It would explain why they couldn't be found for so long. Aleia Omarossian's Darkling boy must have had the missing Elfstones in his possession when the Forbidding went up. The magic took all the dark creatures and whatever possessions they had on them and locked them away. Others trying to find the Stones after that wouldn't have been looking in the right place—not even in the right world. And the seeking-Stones wouldn't have been able to penetrate the wall of the Forbidding until now, when it's begun to fail. The blue Stones found a chink in the armor. Too bad we didn't recognize it for what it was."

"But at least now we know where they are, and we have a chance of finding them."

"Maybe we know. Maybe we have a chance. But finding the missing Elfstones isn't necessarily what we need to do at this point. Even if we found them, we couldn't be sure they would help us get out of this mess. With the Forbidding crumbling, our priorities have changed. If the wall goes down, everyone in the Four Lands is at risk. We need to escape and give warning of the danger. We need to find out why this is happening."

She shook her head, as if to emphasize the dilemma. "I would like nothing better than to complete our search. But to find the Stones now, we would need time to search them out—and that's time we don't have. Even then, I wonder if it would be worth it. I wonder if any of this has been worth it."

There was more than a hint of discouragement and frustration in her voice. He walked on with her for a few minutes more and then dropped away, leaving her to her own thoughts, thinking how hard it must be for her to know she had been seduced and deceived by the vision. Lives had been lost because of it, and more still might be lost before this was over.

His own among them.

The trek continued through the remainder of the day, but there was no sign of the dragon or their missing companions. They came down from the mountains to the plains of the south, moving in the general direction the dragon had taken. The terrain was barren and empty, a mixture of rutted earth dotted with scrub and rock, and forests in which leaves and grasses had turned gray and the trees had a skeletal look. There was no sign of water. There was no movement on the ground or in the air. The land looked dead and broken.

Every so often, the Ard Rhys or one of the other Druids would use magic to search the countryside ahead, but each time the effort failed. Once, they caught sight of something huge in the distance, a massive creature lumbering across the plains toward the mountains beyond. The Ard Rhys had them stop and hold their positions until it was safely past before allowing them to continue on. More than once, they came across piles of bones, sometimes acres of them. It was hard even to guess at their identity from what remained, and they skirted these killing grounds warily.

By nightfall, they were confronted by an impassable wilderness of swamp and saw grasses, and they were forced to turn west to seek a way around. After walking awhile longer, the Druids agreed they should make camp before it got too dark to see. The Ard Rhys chose a patch of desiccated spruce that offered cover and at least marginal protection from the things that might be hunting them. No one felt comfortable spending the night in such an exposed position, but there was nothing better anywhere close at hand. The Ard Rhys strung a warding chain around their sleeping ground that would sound an audible alert should anything try to attack. The company agreed to set a watch that would work through the night in two-hour shifts.

They arranged themselves in a circle so that the ravaged spruce trees provided a wall around them. The trees were almost completely stripped of needles, and their twisted limbs cast crosshatched shadows over the little party like a cage. Redden was so uncomfortable and on edge that he offered to sit the first watch, hoping that by the time it ended he might be tired enough to sleep.

They ate their meal cold, aware that their supplies

were meager and would not last more than another day or so. They might be able to replenish their food, but water would become a problem quickly. How could they know what was safe to drink in this world? Sitting together and talking quietly, aware of the darkness deepening as night closed in about them, they tried not to talk about it.

We don't belong here, Redden kept repeating.

He was dirty and hot, and his skin itched. He found a pool of stagnant water while it was still light and took a quick look at his reflection. Same red hair, blue eyes, and sunburned face that he remembered, but all three looked leached of color and the rest of him resembled a scarecrow set free of its pole. He brushed at himself for a moment and then gave up. Nothing he did would make any difference.

When the others went to sleep, Redden kept the first watch in the company of one of the Trolls, sitting back to back with him at the edge of the circle of sleepers. Time dragged like an anchor, and to ease its weight he summoned his best memories of Railing and himself flying Sprints through the tangle of the Shredder and out over the flat blue surface of Rainbow Lake. It was as good a way as any to distract himself, replaying the twists and turns of the courses they had flown, remembering the rough spots and the wild dips and leaps, and even letting himself recall what he had felt like on seeing Railing crash on their last flight before leaving for Bakrabru and the start of this journey.

Eyes sifting through the layered shadows in the darkness, ears sorting out sounds that he recognized from those that were new, he kept himself alert and wide awake. But when his watch was finished and he rolled himself into his blanket and closed his eyes, he was asleep in moments.

And then awake again faster still.

Something was wrong.

He forced himself to remain perfectly still while he scanned the darkness, trying to determine what had woken him. It took him only a moment.

Carrick and another of the Trolls had taken the second watch. Redden saw the body of the latter sprawled on the ground close to where he had been sitting when the boy fell asleep. It was clear from the twisted position of his limbs and the way his head was thrown back that he was dead and had died hard.

There was no sign of Carrick.

Redden sat up slowly, looking around in all directions, finding nothing but the still forms of the other sleepers and the dead Troll.

Then he looked up.

Carrick was hanging head-down about twenty feet above him, firmly grasped in the jaws of something that resembled a giant insect. His eyes were open and rolling wildly, but he hung limp and unmoving as he was hauled upward through the skeletal branches. His eyes found Redden's and his mouth worked in silent anguish.

Then a second of the insect creatures appeared from out of the trees to seize the body of the Troll and begin to lift it away.

In the shadows, just visible as bits of movement in the gloom, more of the creatures were advancing.

Redden threw off his blanket, scrambled to his feet, and summoned the wishsong. He reacted instinctively—not out of bravery or daring, but out of fear. The magic surfaced in an explosion of brightness that lit up the whole sleeping area, brought all of the sleepers awake instantly, and caused the insects to hesitate. Fighting to keep it under control, Redden concentrated the magic in the cradle of his hands and turned it on the creature that had hold of Carrick. The wishsong flared upward in a burst of power that exploded into the monster with such force that it was cut in half. Down came the beast and Carrick both, the severed pieces of the former thrashing as if still alive, the latter a limp rag doll unable to do anything to help himself.

Redden threw himself aside as the head of the insect slammed into the ground only feet from where he was standing, mandibles snapping wildly.

By now Khyber Elessedil and Pleysia were striking out at the other insect creatures, using their Druid magic to drive their attackers away from the camp. The Trolls were clustered next to them, weapons extended in a circle of sharp steel. But the insects kept attacking, trying to find a way past the fire and sharp blades. One or two would hang back while the others tried to distract the defenders and then rush in suddenly, hoping to catch someone unprepared.

But Redden had regained control of the wishsong and quickly joined the battle, sending a wall of sound from his magic into the largest cluster of the giant insects, throwing them back, slamming them into trees and rocks. Overmatched, the advantage of surprise lost, the insects wheeled about and skittered back into the darkness and were gone.

Redden was suddenly drained. He slumped to one knee and was surprised to find Pleysia next to him, holding him. "Are you all right, boy?" she asked, leaning close. He nodded. "Good. I don't think we can afford to lose you. That was quick thinking."

A few feet away, the Ard Rhys had gone to Carrick, carefully turned him over, and laid him on the ground with his head cradled in her lap. The Druid's eyes had stopped rolling and his gaze had steadied, but he was bleeding from his nose and ears, and his face was as white as chalk. Khyber was working murmuring quietly, her hands making small gestures as she fought to hold back the death that was already claiming him.

"They came right over the top of my wards," she muttered to herself.

"They knew they were there!" Pleysia snapped. "The wards drew them!"

"Steady, Carrick," Khyber soothed. She leaned close so that he could see her. "Don't give up."

His eyes shifted to find her. "So quick . . . no chance . . . to do . . ."

He shuddered and went still, dead in her arms.

Pleysia released her hold on Redden and stood next to him. "We're all going that way before this is done," she whispered. "All of us."

Then she turned her back on them and walked off.